NEW CREATIONS

Praise for New Creations

Here's a story that will lift your spirits and, for those of us over a certain age, take you down memory lane. *New Creations* celebrates family in all its messy grit and glory. You will alternately laugh, cry, and maybe cringe as you read about Floyd's many adventures—and probably see in him, Susan, or Emira one of your relatives. He'll tug on your heart with his desire to be a better person, which is truly what we all want to achieve in life.

> —Susan Pope Sloan, author of the Rescued Hearts of the Civil War series (award winning Rescuing Rose, Loving Lydia, and Managing Millie)

New Creations is a heartwarming, sentimental exploration of love, legacy, and the unexpected ways our lives intertwine. Sarah Hanks is a skilled storyteller, expertly mining the rich emotional territory of the story's dual protagonists: regretful family patriarch, Floyd Douglas, and his granddaughter, Emira. A must-read for anyone who appreciates an emotionally resonant story that reminds us how much a single person matters.

> —Shaen Mael, author of Carol finalist, *To Heal a Heart*

From laugh-out-loud funny to somber and poignant, *New Creations* is a tribute to what the world considers an average life but God makes abundant and meaningful. Hanks celebrates the beauty of those small actions we don't realize God is using—a fun read about the true purpose in every believer's life.

> —Pamela Baker, writer and book reviewer

The author weaves a poignant tale of self-discovery and enduring family bonds. Through braided timelines, we follow a man's journey to uncover the true worth of his life, juxtaposed with the unwavering support of his granddaughter, who knew his value all along. This novel will resonate with anyone who has ever questioned their place in the world and is a heartwarming reminder of God's relentless love.

—Kristine Delano, Tyndale author

With seamless transitions, *New Creations* effortlessly moves between past and present, immersing readers in nostalgia and displaying Hanks' adeptness at crafting authentic characters. New Creations is so inspiring, I'll keep it in my re-read pile!

—N. Y. Dunlap, author of The Misadventures of Itchy Izzy

Edited by Joanne Biscoff

ISBN 979-8-9854789-6-9

Dedication

To Papa

The best man to ever cut someone's ear off

In loving memory of Nana

Acknowledgments

This novel is a bit different than my others and was a labor of love in every way. I couldn't have done it without the help of my family. My Papa supplied many hours of stories of his past, as did my mom and uncle. Many thanks to them for supplying the needed material for Floyd's adventures. Thanks to my husband and children for dealing graciously with this crazy writer.

Thanks also to Shaen Mehl, Rebekah Weum, and Kristine Delano for their gracious assistance in wrangling the rough draft of this manuscript into something far more worthy of your readership. And to the Scribes critique group for polishing her up. I appreciate everyone who took time to make this story better.

I am beyond grateful for my late aunt Kathy (Karen in the novel) who prayed our family into the Kingdom. Here's to all the praying moms, grandmas, aunts, sisters, etc. (and men too) who stand their ground and don't give up. May you see the fruit of your prayers.

Prologue

1954

Floyd Douglas ducked as a fist sailed toward his head. Focusing on Sammy Shuholder's freckled face in front of him, he delivered a hook with his left arm, followed by a blow with his right to the boy's gut. Sammy doubled over and toppled to his knees. Floyd grinned so wide the orange slice he'd used as a mouthguard nearly fell out.

Sweat beaded between his shoulder blades, and his chest heaved. He waited as his brother Rich counted. The elation that coursed through him as Rich lifted his hand in the air and declared him the winner of the neighborhood boxing match was nearly more than his twelve-year-old body could handle. He could float on air.

Cheers erupted, followed by a chant. "Flo-oyd. Flo-oyd. Flo-oyd." He raised both arms and spit his mouth guard in the dirt. The commotion drew the attention of the Barrington girls. They'd walked over from their house down the street. Pretty dames. From the edge of the crowd, they offered shy waves while batting long lashes at him. He flashed them his famous lopsided grin and flexed some more.

"Look this way, Floyd." His sister Karen pointed her box camera toward him.

He puffed out his chest. This would make the front page of the neighborhood newspaper the kids put together each week.

Yeah, his future was crystal clear. Floyd Douglas. Professional Boxer. All this, but on a grander scale.

Crowds would shout his name. As a middle child in a family of six children, attention was hard to come by. But he'd make a name for himself.

Just as the group of ragged boys converged to lift Floyd in the air, Pop's car motored down the street and careened into the driveway. The rowdy voices quieted. Floyd's friends backed away. Sammy scrambled to his feet and scampered off, hand covering his bloody nose. What was Pop doing home so early?

Pop spilled out of the car and nearly tumbled onto the concrete. Beer sloshed out of the can he held as he opened his arms wide, surveying the scene around him. Karen and Floyd's other sister, Veronica, scuttled inside. The crowd dispersed until only the sons were left.

"Rich. Danny. Mark." Pop nodded to each of Floyd's brothers or at least nodded somewhat in their directions. His aim was off.

Pop bumbled toward Floyd, who stiffened. Floyd's jaw clenched, the sweet remnants of orange juice in his mouth now souring. Pop slung his arm around Floyd's shoulder and teetered to one side. Floyd grabbed the back of Pop's shirt to hold him steady.

"Floyd, my boy. Were you boxing?"

"Yes, sir." He ground the words out. If only Pop hadn't shown up to ruin everything.

"Ah." He tapped his son on the chest with a shaky hand. "Like father, like son."

Floyd bristled. "What do you mean?"

Pop attempted to straighten. In doing so, he stumbled backward. Once again, Floyd steadied him. "I used to want to be a boxer. Was pretty good too." The old man slurred his words.

Floyd spit out a humorless laugh. "You?"

"Yeah, me," Pop shot back, his bleary eyes focusing on Floyd. "I was good. The best." He took a few faltering steps, exchanging punches with imaginary targets, swinging both arms at ghosts. Beer leaped out of his can with each movement as if begging to escape the embarrassing scene.

Floyd's brothers hung their heads and kicked at the dirt.

Danny ventured a glance at the haunted man. "What happened?"

Pop stopped swinging and took a long gulp. "I met your mother." He dropped the can and crushed it under his heel.

Anger swarmed Floyd's belly like a horde of wasps at the contempt in Pop's tone. He couldn't mean that. Couldn't blame it all on Mom. It was the booze talking. Always had been. Mom was the best thing that had ever happened to his dad and far more than he deserved.

He wouldn't be anything like this man.

"I don't want to box anymore." He hardened his gaze at his father.

The drunk shrugged as if he couldn't care less what Floyd did or didn't do with his life. It might be true. Floyd might as well be invisible to the man. The wasps buzzed louder, swarmed harder, their wings beating against his rib cage as thoughts converged in his head.

Who would care for Mom? Who would treat her right? Make her proud?

He clenched his jaw. He would. "I'm going to make something outa myself."

"What are ya gonna do if you don't use your fists? Use that puny brain of yours?" His father's guffaw blended in with his brothers' snickers.

Floyd bristled again. He wasn't stupid. He got decent marks in school and knew more about current events from reading the newspaper than most kids his age. It was just like Pop to put him down. So what? Floyd had given up on trying to impress his old man long ago. But Mom? What would make his devout Catholic mother beam with pride?

What if … what if he became a priest? His chest warmed at the thought. Yeah, that was the ticket. A priest was that farthest thing from his pop and Mom would be tickled pink. He could picture himself in a vestment.

"I'm going to be a priest." He tilted up his chin at the announcement.

His brothers' snickers rolled into all-out laughter.

Was it that hard to believe? He already went to mass every day. Would it be that hard to keep going for … life?

He ignored their cynicism and tilted up his chin. "I will. Just watch me."

Chapter One

2010

Emira's mouth unhinged when she turned into the parking lot of her grandparents' salon. She paused midsentence in the phone conversation with her husband, Kade. When had the place gone from pristine to dingy? The floor-to-ceiling windows, striped barber pole, and hand-painted sign on top were the same as always, as familiar as her own face in the mirror, but something had changed. What was it?

She parked in front and frowned at the empty waiting area. The sign on the window boasted that the shop was indeed open, but the only evidence of life inside was a half inch of Papa's white hair peeking over his booth. At least he had one customer. But at eleven in the morning on a Saturday? This was normally his busiest time.

As she scanned the other storefronts in the strip mall, her gaze zeroed in on the health food store adjacent to her grandparents' shop. A fresh coat of paint complimented the new signage in the windows, complete with social media handles. The sleek, modern update made the salon look like a broken-down dump in comparison.

Kade's voice interrupted her musings. "Emira? You still there?"

"Sorry, yeah. But I'm at the shop now. Gotta run. Don't forget the baby needs to eat in an hour." She made a kissing noise and hung up before her three-year-old could jump back into the conversation and regale her with random facts about *Velociraptors*. Praise the Lord for a hubby who gave her a break from the children from time to time. She'd missed alone time with Nana and Papa. When was the last time she'd visited without the littles in tow?

The bell jingled as she opened the door. The sound of clippers buzzing was the backdrop to the soft cadence of Papa's familiar voice.

He peeked through the doorway of his booth. "Hiya, Princess. Didn't know you were stopping by today." His gaze shifted over her shoulder. "You came alone? Where's my Teddy Bear and Doodlebug?"

"Hi, Papa. Yep, it's just me." She dropped her purse behind the desk and then meandered to the back of the shop. "Have you seen Teddy's lovie? I think he left it here the other day." Nana's booth was empty. A quick glance at the back dryers showed no customers and no grandma. Emira returned to Papa's booth and leaned her hip against his doorway. "Where's Nana?"

Papa motioned to the older gentleman sitting in the chair. "Hey, Ralph, this is my granddaughter, Emira."

"Hello," Ralph called from inside the booth.

"Good morning." She gave him a smile. Ah, yes, she remembered. The customer always came first. Sometimes endearing, but today, she tempered her annoyance. Papa hadn't answered her question. "How are you today?"

"Fine. Yourself?"

"Good, thanks." Okay, now that the small talk was out of the way, she gave Papa a pointed look.

"The blue rabbit? Haven't seen it."

Well, that was one of her questions. It had faded into the background next to the other. "Where's Nana?" she asked again.

"At home."

"On a Saturday?"

He made a noncommittal sound and kept his gaze zeroed on the customer's head. Was business *that* slow? Or was something else going on?

"Hmm." She'd have to swing by the house to visit. How strange to see her grandpa there alone. The two of them had always been a team, intertwined in every memory she had of this place.

She stepped to the back and swiped a handful of peanuts from the gigantic can next to Papa's faded green recliner. Popping a few nuts into her mouth, she peeked behind it. It leaned slightly to one side, indented where his body had carved a place for itself over the years. No lovie. She checked around and even inside the garish yellow minifridge that had to be from the eighties. Humming like a backup singer with a smoker's cough, it held salami, cheese, and mustard, but no lovie.

The brown salon chairs were empty of blue fabric. She trailed a hand across the back of a chair. They still proved functional, but the cracks in the leather and ashtrays on their arms proved trends had long since passed them by. No wonder business was slow. Their target market lived in nursing homes.

She shook her head and strolled to the front, searching under each seat. When nothing turned up, she straightened the magazines on the rack out of habit. She'd always found immense satisfaction in organizing them, no matter that the customers would scramble them up again in no time. She shuffled *People* to the left, *Time* right beside it, and *Good Housekeeping* on the right. She'd loosened up over the years and didn't bother with alphabetical order, but she did stack the most recent editions in front. She cringed. Was 2005 the most recent edition? And why did they still have magazines from the nineties?

What this place needed was some updates. Ideas swirled. New flooring and chairs, fresh paint and lighting. Maybe Papa could even hire a marketing and social media manager. It was beyond time he had an online presence. Virtual booking would bring in more customers.

"How does that look?" Relief swept over her at her grandpa's familiar question. He was almost finished. Once Ralph left, she could ask about Nana. She wasn't sick, was she?

"Great job as always, Floyd. I'm really going to miss this place."

Her hand stilled on the magazine rack. Miss the place? Was Ralph moving away?

"Me too, but it's time. Past time, really."

Papa's voice echoed in her ears. *It's time. Past time.* Time for what? Dread expanded like a balloon in her chest. No. He wasn't saying …

The two men exited Papa's booth and stepped toward the cash register. Ralph handed Papa a twenty-dollar bill. "Enjoy retirement. Think of me when you're playing a relaxing game of golf."

Retirement? *Time* magazine fell from her now sweaty grasp and sprawled onto the forest-green carpeting. As she bent to retrieve it, her head swam. Retire. Papa was going to retire? Why hadn't he told her? What would happen to the shop? She scooted onto a chair instead of attempting to stand upright on shaky knees.

The men continued their conversation, oblivious to the fact they'd sent her reeling. Papa chuckled. He pressed the brass buttons, and the cash drawer sprung open. "Relaxing and golf are two words that have never gone together for me. It's the most frustrating game on the planet." He handed Ralph four dollars.

Ralph laughed and waved him off. "Keep the change."

Papa nodded his appreciation. "Thank you kindly."

"Goodbye, Emira," Ralph said before shuffling out the door.

As soon as the door clicked behind him, Emira's questions tumbled out. "What's going on? You're retiring? When?"

With a heavy sigh, Papa came over and settled into the seat across from her. "I've been cutting hair for a long time. Fifty years, Princess. Most of my life." He rubbed his stubbled jawline. "I'm tired."

Her eyes stung. She sucked in a breath and blinked rapidly. She shouldn't be overly sentimental. He was seventy years old. He deserved to retire if he wanted to. "What will happen to the shop?"

The ancient wooden desk with the antique cash register. Nana and Papa's side-by-side padded booths with thick rubber mats under their barber chairs. And those ancient hair dryers. She could still picture a line of old ladies sitting in their curlers under those dryers. What was the song they had enjoyed hearing her sing the most when she was a child? Was it "Let Me Entertain You" or "Somewhere Over the Rainbow"?

Oh, she loved this place, despite the cigarette smoke that clung to her clothes upon entering and the hair that always seemed to attach itself to her hem by the time she left.

"A lady came in this morning and offered to buy it."

"What lady?"

What kind of person came door to door making such offers? A developer? Maybe the woman wanted to tear down the strip mall and build duplexes. Or … hadn't the manager of the health food place next door mentioned something about wanting to expand?

Papa shrugged off her question. "We're signing papers this evening."

She catapulted forward. "That quick? She offered this morning, and you've already accepted?"

He shrugged. "I've thought about it before, on and off, but yes. She came in, made an offer, and I'm taking her up on it."

"Today?" If only Emira had come in earlier.

He nodded.

"Isn't that a bit … impulsive? This is a life-altering decision. Don't you think you should take a week to think about it?"

He ran his hands over the chair arms. "Nah. I know what I want."

"But you could change your mind. What if you wake up next month and miss it?"

"I won't."

"What does Nana think?"

"She said to do what I want."

Emira arched a brow at him. "Really?" What tone did her grandma say that in? A straightforward one or one with subtext? A challenge, a dare. She couldn't imagine Nana not having an opinion about this.

"We're getting old. This job isn't easy anymore. We want to relax. I know you love this place, but we can't hang on to it forever."

She blew out a breath. Of course, this had to come eventually, but she couldn't fathom not having New Creations in her life. She patted his knee. "I'm happy for you." She blinked to drive away the threat of tears. Papa did not need her sentimentality right now. He needed her support. "I hope you got a good price for it."

His shoulders relaxed. "I did."

Papa stared out the window, a pensive look on his face. As if a thousand thoughts shuffled through his mind. Maybe he was in financial trouble. Obviously, business was slow. Perhaps he felt he needed to sell before it went under. Yes. Now that she studied the stoop to his shoulders and lines marring his forehead, it made sense. No wonder he'd made a quick decision. Guilt prickled that she'd been too distracted with the kids to notice how stress had been weighing him down.

"That's great. Use that for a comfortable retirement, then." At least, with his house paid for, the proceeds from this sale would provide for him and Nana as they enjoyed the rest of their days in peace. This was good and right. And still hard. Was it possible he'd change his mind?

He sighed long and hard, then focused his gaze on her. "Why are you *really* here? You need some money?"

"What? No!" She waved him off. No way would she take a thing from him. "If you sell, you'd better keep all the money for your future. Don't give it away."

Though he pretended not to hear her, the side of his mouth twitched upward. He rubbed the wooden arms of the chair again. She focused on the spot where the stain had worn off in the center to avoid his knowing gaze.

"You normally come around here alone when something's eating at you. If it's not financial trouble, what is it?"

Shoot. Why'd he have to know her so well? She stood, plucked a sucker from the wooden lollipop stand, unwrapped it, and stuck it in her mouth. She came here to forget about everything else, and his announcement had been an effective distraction.

"I need to find Teddy's lovie."

He gave her a pointed look.

Fine. "My dad called."

Papa's brows lifted. "And?"

Her stomach wobbled at the uncertainty. "He wants to come for a visit." There went that hot lump in her throat again.

"How long?"

"Three weeks."

"What'd you say?"

She bit off the end of the sucker and tossed the stick into the wastebasket. "I told him I had to talk to Kade, and I'd call him back." She settled in the chair across from him again. "Kade's okay with whatever I want to do. I need your advice. You've been a father figure in my life, a stable one." Everything she knew about what it meant for a man to be there for his family, she'd learned from him.

"What are you afraid of?"

At his question, hiccups clawed up her throat. Soon hot tears spilled down her cheeks. She answered between panting breaths. "That he'll sweep into our lives, make us fall in love with him, then leave … again." She swiped at her face with her sleeve. "He's never even met his granddaughter. He's only met Teddy once. They're going to love him, and then their hearts are going to break like mine did … does." The last word caught in her throat like a shard of glass.

She catapulted to her feet. She was being ridiculous. With two doting grandparents and a loving, though overworked, mother, she'd had a good childhood. So what if her dad went MIA? It was greedy for her to long for unwavering love from him too.

She needed to move, to *do* something. She found the can of cleaner and accompanying rag in the back and proceeded to remove products from the glass shelves behind the desk. "Obviously, I can't let him break the kids' hearts. I have to tell him he can't come. He can't blow in and out of our lives like the wind. It's better if he's not a part of our lives at all."

Papa's gentle voice massaged a knot of tension from her shoulders. "I didn't have a great father myself. But I do know the best thing I ever did was to forgive mine."

Emira turned, rubbing the soft fabric of the rag between her thumb and forefinger. "How?"

He shrugged. "It took an act of God. He changed my heart."

"Forgiveness is a choice." At least that's what everyone said.

"Yes, but He still has to heal your heart for it to take root."

She wiped the shelf, removing a thick layer of dust. "Well, mine still hurts." And when her emotions throbbed, she yearned for something familiar. The sound of clippers and smell of perms. This shop. Where would she turn now?

She cast a longing glance toward the back where she used to sweep and mop and perform for customers. "This was the best job I ever had."

He chuckled. "Those were good days. You took all my tips."

"Earned them fair and square." She couldn't quite manage a smile. This shop had been her anchor throughout her entire life. The one stable, unchanging presence. How could she weather three weeks with her father without it? But how could she turn away the one person she'd longed for most of her life?

She needed solid advice. Something more than wait for an act of God. Slinging her purse over her shoulder, she strode to Papa and kissed him on the cheek. "Love you. I'm going to see Nana."

Emira walked into her grandparents' one-story ranch without knocking, as usual. "It's me," she called out as she hung her purse on the coat-tree by the front door.

"Princess?" Nana rounded the corner wearing fuzzy socks, sweatpants, and a baggy sweatshirt. No matter that it was eighty degrees outside, Nana was always cold. An indent pressed the left side of her short, curly brown hair flat, evidence that she'd taken a nap. "What are you doing here?"

Emira drew Nana close for a hug and peck on the cheek. Cigarette smoke emanated from her clothing. "Came for a visit. Missed you."

"Missed you too. You hungry? I'm not sure what I have, but I'll find something."

Emira settled on the couch. "No, not hungry. Come sit with me."

She patted the cushion next to her, even though experience proved it futile. Nana wouldn't sit down for more than a minute at a time. If ADD would have been a diagnosis back in her day, Nana would have fought against medication for it.

Instead of joining her, her grandma disappeared into the kitchen. Drawers slid open and closed. Banging and clattering ensued from inside cabinets and the fridge. "I've got cookies in the freezer. Or what about those chips that come in a can you like? What are they called?"

"Pringles."

"Yes, Pringles. I know I have some around here somewhere."

"I don't need anything to eat. I just want to talk to you."

Another clank and soft thud. What was she doing in there? A moment later, she emerged with a bowl in hand. "Ice cream. You never turn down ice cream."

Emira accepted the offering, but once again patted the spot beside her.

"Just a second. I need to put this away, and I spilled a little. I have to clean it up."

Emira sighed and dug into her bowl of rocky road. At least some things would never change. Ice cream upon every visit. It was a small comfort.

Her grandma hummed "When the Saints Go Marching In" as she bustled around the kitchen, and though Emira couldn't see her from the living room, she could picture her just the same. Always either cooking or cleaning. See? Her world wasn't as catawampus as she'd feared.

But when she'd scraped the very last drop of chocolate goodness from her bowl and Nana had quieted but still hadn't emerged, an unsettled feeling gripped her. She stood to take her bowl to the sink.

When Emira entered the kitchen, Nana turned from wiping down the sink and gasped. She clasped her chest. "Emira! What are you doing here?"

"What do you mean? You knew I was here."

Nana's eyes clouded. "Yes, yes, of course. Are you hungry? I think we have ice cream."

Emira's stomach dropped as if she had plunged down a steep hill on a roller coaster. "Nana?" She held out her bowl. "You already gave me ice cream."

Her grandmother squinted, then blinked, and clarity dawned in her expression again. "Oh, of course. Sorry. I'm getting old. Let me take that." She grabbed the bowl and set it in the sink. "You wanted to talk, right? What about?"

Dread sank claws into her heart. Nana had forgotten she was there? Surely, she wasn't … Could she be …? No. She was merely getting older. Having a forgetful spell here and there wasn't cause for alarm. It happened to everyone when they reached her grandmother's age. Heck, half the time, Emira couldn't remember where she'd put her phone. That didn't mean *she* had dementia, did it?

No. Nana knew exactly who Emira was and why she was there. Her mind had wandered for a moment was all. No use allowing worries to spin out of control.

Emira cleared her throat. "Papa's selling the shop. Did you know that?"

Nana nodded and turned the sink on, sloshing water into the bowl. "Yeah, I know."

"How do you feel about it?"

She chuckled. "That man is going to do what he wants to do."

"But it's your shop too. What are you going to do with yourself without New Creations?"

"You think I want to cut hair?"

Emira blinked back at her. "You don't?"

"No! Never did. I only went into it because Floyd needed someone to work on the ladies. It's not like it was a lifelong dream of mine, and it certainly wasn't his dream."

Wait, what? Her head spun. Branded into her memory was Nana standing behind her barber chair, eyes twinkling, laugh spilling over onto her white-haired customers. It was as if she'd been born to be a hairstylist. Emira couldn't imagine her doing anything else. And … what had she said about Papa? "What are you talking about? Papa loves being a barber. He's always wanted to be one."

"No, honey. It's been a fine career that provided for the family, but he kind of got roped into it. He's put in his time. Now he can do what he wants."

She needed to sit down. It was all too much to take in. She backed up until her calves bumped against a dining room chair. Lowering into it, she rubbed her temples. Papa had spent his entire life working at a job he didn't even care for? *Let the man do what he wants.* What in the world *did* he want? "He said he's going to relax." She spit out a laugh. "We both know what a joke that is."

"Yeah, that'll last a couple of days."

"He'll go crazy sitting around the house." She pictured him lounging in his favorite recliner for the evening. But all day every day? "It'll kill him."

She winced at her pronouncement. She hadn't meant it literally, but as she stared at his brown leather recliner now, she wondered if her statement might hold a shred of truth. Papa's mind and wit were as sharp as ever. If he hibernated at home, surely they would wither. The decline he'd kept at bay would creep up on him with a vengeance.

Nana placed a glass of water in front of her on the table before retreating toward the kitchen sink, just out of view. She tossed reassurance over her shoulder. "I'm sure he'll find something to do."

Yeah, but what? What would he do? Emira nearly downed the entire glass, gulping greedily. This was ridiculous. It was none of her business. Her grandparents had the right to live their own lives without her meddling. She had enough to worry about. Nana was right. Papa would find something to fill his time. He'd be fine. They all would.

She hadn't come here to badger Nana about Papa's future plans, anyway. She'd wanted to ask her advice about Dad. Nana never held back opinions, and Emira needed a dose of tell-it-like-it-is right now.

Question in mind, she straightened her shoulders and reentered the kitchen where Nana stood smoking a cigarette, staring vacantly out the window over the sink. "Hey, Nana, I was—"

Her grandmother's yelp interrupted her. She jumped, then fought to catch her breath.

Nana braced a hand on the counter. "Emira! You scared me half to death."

Chapter Two

1954

Floyd Douglas walked alongside the River des Peres with his brothers Danny and Mark, as well as some of the neighborhood boys. He wrinkled his nose at the stench that wafted with a breeze. The River Des Peres was really just a large sewer, a drainage channel, which made it perfect for the task at hand.

A few feet away, a plump rat scurried up the bank. Floyd called to his dog, "Nikki! Rat. Go get it, Nikki!"

Nikki's head swiveled around until her eyes locked onto the rodent, then off she went. She bounded after it and pounced. The boys cheered as her jaws clamped around it. The rat thrashed and squeaked, but Nikki held firm until the rodent went limp.

"Good girl." Floyd raced up to her and patted her head.

"Is it dead?" Danny asked.

Floyd hunched over to get a closer look. No movement. Limp as a wet noodle. "Yep." He rubbed behind the dog's ears. "Drop it, Nikki."

The dog complied, wagging her tail at the attention.

"I've got this one." Danny pulled out his pocketknife and cut off the rat's tail. "That makes five for me. How many you got today?"

Floyd dug into his pocket to double-check. "Four."

"Ha!" Mark held up a fistful of rat tails. "I got the most today. Seven."

"That's not fair," Jimmy, one of the neighbors, grumbled. "You never let us collect the tails."

Mark stuffed the tails back into his pocket. "That's 'cause it's our dog doing the work."

Floyd rolled his eyes. "You ready to head down to city hall and turn them in, or do you want to keep hunting?"

They got a dime for every rat tail they turned into the city—St. Louis's way of eradicating, or at least lessening, the rat infestation. The rest of the boys seemed only to care about money for a soda or candy bar. For Floyd, though, the purpose of making the city a cleaner, safer place to live motivated him. He was working for the greater good, a part of something bigger than himself. He might only be ready to turn thirteen, but he could make a difference.

The spending money didn't hurt.

Mark spit in the dirt. "Let's turn 'em in."

He led the way toward city hall, and the rest of the boys followed, kicking up dust as they walked next to the busy street.

Nikki trotted by Floyd's left side. Jimmy jogged up to Floyd's right. "Is it true you're going to seminary next year?"

"Yep. Just got accepted."

"I didn't know they accepted kids."

Floyd shrugged. "It's like high school. You go there from age thirteen until you graduate. It prepares you to be a priest." He'd been warned only a few made it that far, but he wouldn't let that bother him. He could be one of those few. He had to be.

"Why do ya wanna do that anyway?"

Danny looped an arm around his neck and mussed his hair. "'Cause he's a mama's boy."

Mark laughed. "Ain't that the truth? Always sucking up to Mom. Wants to be her favorite."

Floyd shook Danny off. "Do not."

"Do too." Danny shoved him, and he stumbled into the street.

He barely stepped back in time before a streetcar rushed past. "Watch it!"

Why did brothers have to be so annoying? He should punch Danny in the gut. See who cried like a mama's boy then. His fist clenched at his side.

Jimmy, who'd fallen a few steps behind, jogged to catch up. "So, why a priest, then?"

A priest. Floyd exhaled, flexing his fingers. It wouldn't do to have a future priest pummel someone on the side of the road. He studied Jimmy's face. Not a trace of tease there, only curiosity. His friend really wanted to know. Only how could Floyd explain something he didn't fully understand himself?

He squinted over at his friend, who was framed by the sun's glare. "I want my life to count for something, you know?"

Jimmy frowned. "You don't have to be a priest for that."

"I know, but ..." See? He couldn't explain it. Maybe it did have something to do with his mom. So much in life disappointed her, and he could think of nothing that would make her prouder than having a son as a priest. He wanted that for her.

"You could do a hundred different things to have an important life." Jimmy checked possibilities off on his fingers. "You could be an inventor. An astronaut. A doctor, an important one like a ... a brain surgeon!"

Danny snorted a laugh, and Mark nearly doubled over in hysterics at that pronouncement. Floyd narrowed his eyes, but a twitch of his lips betrayed him. He wasn't dumb. As an avid reader, he always soaked up information, mostly from the paper. He got decent marks in school when the subject kept his attention. But a brain surgeon? Floyd nearly laughed himself.

Jimmy stopped walking and put a hand on Floyd's shoulder to halt him. "I don't get it. Why a priest?"

Floyd shrugged. "Why not?"

It didn't take any special talent, it would bust his mom's buttons, and it was a profession he could feel good about. He'd know he was doing something to make the world a better place. And no one would mistake him for being like his father.

They resumed their walk, speaking nothing more about the priesthood. After turning in their rat tails and collecting their coins, they began the long trek home, discussing what they'd buy at the store on their way.

Floyd would get a Coke, no question about it. His hands itched for the cold glass bottle, and he picked up his pace, eager to reach the store around the corner.

"Danny, what are you getting?" Floyd cast a glance beside him, but his brother wasn't there. He spun around. "Where's Danny?" He didn't see him anywhere.

The chatter around him quieted. Mark stopped and turned as well, scanning the horizon. "He was just here."

The two of them jogged back the way they'd come, shouting Danny's name. As they rounded the corner, Floyd spotted a blue ball cap. "Danny!"

His older brother slouched against a building, face pale and contorted in a grimace.

Floyd knelt at his side. "What's wrong?"

Danny's voice came out weak and slurred. "I don't feel so good."

Floyd placed the back of his hand to Danny's forehead. Scorching. "You're burning up. What hurts?"

"My throat. My stomach." He dropped his head into his hands. "My head."

"Sure came on fast," Mark mused.

"I was feeling funny earlier but didn't want to let on." His face twisted in pain. "Wanted to get my money."

Floyd stood, mentally calculating how far of a walk they had. "Think we can get him home?"

Mark puffed out his cheeks. "We can try."

The brothers looped Danny's arms around their shoulders and, one slow step at a time, plodded home.

The neighborhood boys ran ahead to announce what had happened, and by the time the Douglas boys turned onto their street, their mom was jogging toward them with their sister Karen at her heels. When Mom reached Danny, she felt his forehead and cheeks, then instructed the brothers to bring him into the house and help him to bed. Karen followed, alligator tears and Hail Marys dripping like rain. By the time they got him settled, Mom had the doctor on the phone, one of the few who still made house calls.

Hours later, the physician came, then left with sad eyes and a frown. The rest of the siblings huddled in the living room, waiting to hear what was wrong with their brother.

Mom closed the door behind the doctor, then turned to face them. After a shaky breath, she spoke. "He fears it's polio."

Floyd gulped. His best friend's brother had died from polio just last year. The Evensons' house down the street had been quarantined because of it. Everyone knew how dangerous the virus was. How, if it didn't kill a person, it could paralyze them for life.

"Did he get it from the Evensons?" Floyd asked.

Mom shook her head. "Doc thinks he got it from the river. And the—" Her voice cracked. "Rats."

Floyd turned a wild-eyed gaze to Mark. No, it couldn't be true. They hunted rats to make the city a better, safer place. They were doing their part. Doing good. Helping. How could something they set out to do for good turn out so badly?

"Is he going to be okay?" Floyd wiped his sweaty palms on his jeans. Danny's old jeans, hand-me-downs. "He's going to be okay, right?"

"We'll pray." Mom clutched her crucifix. "You can pray the rosary with me."

Floyd nodded. He would. Of course, he would. But then another thought hit him. "It's contagious. Could we catch it?"

"We'll pray," Mom said again, "and then you boys will take a bath."

And pray they did. Floyd went to confession every day and wore his rosary out. In the end, all the Douglas children caught polio. But for everyone except Danny, it passed quickly without more than a few days of discomfort. Danny, however, would walk with a limp for the rest of his life.

And Floyd would enter seminary with a niggling worry that his efforts to change the world for the better would end up bringing pain and destruction instead.

Five Years Later

Floyd shushed his two friends as they tiptoed over tree roots, then stumbled into the creek bank. Marty tripped and collided with Floyd's back, causing Floyd to lose his footing and slip into the shallow, cool water. He grimaced as his socks soaked up the moisture. Not that it didn't feel good on a hot summer day, but how was he supposed to sneak back into class now?

He frowned at Marty, who had spread his arms out to catch his balance. "I told you to be careful."

"Sorry." Marty scanned the clear creek. "Where is it?"

Floyd scratched the back of his head. Good question. "It's around here somewhere."

He could have sworn he'd hidden it right here, in the shady spot behind the giant oak. Maybe he'd gotten mixed up. There had to be more than one large oak. They probably looked similar.

A few inches of water gurgled over rocks and moss. The creek itself wasn't more than five feet wide. Not much to boast of. It wound behind the seminary, shadowed in several spots by groves of trees. A good place to hide if one had the mind to do so. And the crisp, cool water provided the perfect place to hide a six-pack of beer.

Maybe too perfect. He couldn't seem to find it now, which didn't bode well since he'd promised each of his buddies a can for helping him pass his last exam.

"Come on, Floyd. We've only got a few minutes before we have to get back," Rodney grumbled at him from higher ground and stuffed his hands in his pockets.

"Oh, shush." Which direction could that beer be? It was anybody's guess. Floyd sloshed out of the water and started walking to his left. "We'll find it." At least while they looked for the beer, he could enjoy a cigarette. He pulled a Lucky and a lighter from his pocket.

Marty put out his hand. "You owe me."

"Fine." Floyd passed one along and lit it for his friend before lighting his own. "You want one?" he asked Rodney.

"Nah. I don't want to go back to class smelling like smoke. Mother Pricilla always notices."

So did his next teacher, Mother Evangeline. So far, she'd been satisfied with the excuse that his parents smoked. It wasn't a lie. Everyone he knew smoked. Why did they expect their future priests to never enjoy a cigarette? They served wine during communion. Why couldn't Floyd indulge in a beer? The strict rules gave him the heebie-jeebies. Why did everyone expect priests to be perfect? Weren't they human too?

Perfection was like a pair of jeans that just didn't fit. The expectations stifled him. Couldn't he be a good person without being ... well, *that* good? Couldn't he make a difference in the world without having to fit into such narrow parameters? He enjoyed his classes. Kind of. He wasn't half bad at them, at least. He'd made it this far in seminary without quitting like many others had. That had to say something about him. His father wouldn't have made it a week.

Something glinted in the sunlight a few yards away. "I think that's it." He pointed and picked up his pace. "The beer's down there."

As they neared the spot, a dark form stepped out from behind a nearby tree. Father Peabody stared at the three of them, stone-faced, with the six-pack of beer in his hands. "Looking for this?"

Floyd gulped. He dropped the cigarette and tried to snuff it out with his shoe. He squinted at the spot where he thought he'd seen a glinting can. There *was* a can. A soda can. Drat.

Marty had discarded his cigarette as well, and both he and Rodney looked to Floyd as if he could get them out of this mess. He'd better think quick!

"Looking for what?" Ignorance was his best defense, right? Maybe he hadn't heard them.

Father Peabody raised his eyebrows.

"We were just going for a little walk. We needed some fresh air."

"Yeah, fresh air," Marty echoed.

Father Peabody's eyes narrowed. "You're not going to get much of that while puffing on cigarettes now, are you?"

Perhaps the priest hadn't seen them smoking, hadn't seen them ditch the evidence. "Cigarettes?" Floyd's cough betrayed him.

Father Peabody sighed and shook his head. Condescension rained down from him, drenching Floyd to the bone. The priest angled toward Floyd's friends. "Marty and Rodney, this is your first infraction. You'll be written up and issued demerits. Report to the office immediately."

They bowed their heads, shoulders sagging. "Yes, Father," they replied in unison.

"Floyd, you are a different matter." He lifted his heels, then sank, his determined gaze fixed on Floyd. "This is far from your first infraction. We have concluded that you must be expelled."

His throat constricted. "Expelled?" He choked on the word. They were kicking him out?

"Your parents have already been informed. Your mother is waiting for you in my office."

Mom? Here? His breaths became quick and shallow as he pictured disappointment shadowing her features. He'd let her down, just like Pop. Nausea rose, and he grimaced.

"Come with me." Father Peabody walked toward the building.

An urge to run the other way overwhelmed him, but he forced his feet to follow the priest. No use making a bad situation worse.

Still, his feet dragged. "How'd you find out?"

"Another student tipped us off when he saw you hide the alcohol yesterday. Once we validated his story by finding the contraband, we contacted your parents. I'm thankful there are some here who are upright and don't wish to be soiled by worldly influences."

Floyd scoffed. Which Goody Two-shoes ratted him out? The school was full of them. Pictures of perfect piety. His gut twisted. Whoever it was, they were right. He didn't belong. Did he even want to? Church life didn't quite sit well with him. He didn't like pretending to be someone he wasn't. But that person—the upstanding citizen full of goodness and overflowing with charity—if only he could be that. If only he *could* be cut out for the priesthood.

War raged within him. That boy who'd looked his father in the eye and declared he'd do better rose, only to be trampled by an itch for a good time. Had he inherited more of his upstanding mother or his deadbeat father? Which side would win out in the end? He scrubbed his neck, dread over seeing his mother nearly suffocating him.

She would ask him what he planned to do now, and he was at a loss for what to tell her. He could no longer envision his future.

He needed a smoke.

Floyd kicked a tin can as he and Johnny walked toward the water tower a few days later.

Johnny swooped in with a kick and sent the can clinking down the sidewalk. "You gonna come to Mercy High now?"

"I guess so. I'll have more time to work at A&P." His hours at the grocery store had been severely limited due to the long commute to the seminary. Five different buses and a half-mile walk through a cemetery. With all his new free time, he could finish saving up money for a car. Yeah, best to look at the bright side and not focus on the shame that coated him like a thick layer of Vaseline. Maybe he was a failure, but he could at least be a failure with a car. Besides, now he didn't have to try so hard to be perfect.

"I thought you were a carhop at Hamburger Heaven?"

"That too."

The Grand Avenue Water Tower loomed ahead with its spiral staircase and fancy molding. Across the street, teenagers hung around outside of Velvet Freeze, smoking and laughing. The sun beat down on sweaty asphalt. He could go for a beer about now.

A group of girls exited the ice cream shop and sashayed in their direction. Floyd's gaze zeroed in on one brunette with silky hair. She had a scarf wrapped around her face, tucked under her nose, and cigarettes rolled up in her shirt. For someone other than Floyd, the odd placement of the scarf might be a turnoff. For him, it was a magnet. Like

Bonnie to his Clyde. Plus, she wore her Levis well. What a woman!

Johnny elbowed him. "Who are you staring at?"

"Who? Me?" Floyd couldn't take his eyes off her.

"Oh no. Not the one with the scarf. Tell me it's not her."

"It's her, all right."

"That's Susan Sonjak. I've heard about her. She's bad news."

No way. Not someone so beautiful. Sure, half her face was covered, but light radiated from her eyes. A spark of adventure. He crossed his arms, not even bothering to rein in his dopey grin. "I don't believe it."

"She just got thrown out of Beaumont High School." Johnny clasped Floyd on both shoulders and gave him a hardy shake. "For a knife fight."

Floyd shrugged. "She's got spunk."

"And probably a temper."

"She must have had a good reason." He shook off his friend.

"She's got a knife, and she's not afraid to use it."

"I could handle her."

"You'd better watch it, or she'll be handling you."

Floyd stepped toward the enrapturing angel. Forget seminary. This woman was his calling. She had to be. And their grand love story would start right now.

He met her with a swagger. "Hey."

She stopped and studied him with mirthful eyes. "Hey."

The next words out of his mouth could determine his destiny. He'd better make them good. He hesitated for a few fateful seconds as his mind scrambled for the perfect thing to say. How could he impress this woman?

She arched a brow.

He scrubbed the back of his neck. "Could I bum a smoke?"

She pulled her scarf down to reveal a wide smile.

He was in.

Chapter Three

1990

Emira straightened in the spinning chair and fixed her gaze on the customer leaving Papa's booth. She smiled her biggest, brightest smile.

"That will be eight dollars, please." She used her professional voice and held her hand out. Her toes wiggled inside her sneakers as the older man pulled out his wallet. She inwardly chanted for Alexander Hamilton. Papa had taught her he was the one on the front of the ten-dollar bill.

Papa chuckled. "This is my granddaughter, Emira. She's my secretary."

She held her head higher at his words. Only eight years old and she already had a job. None of her friends had ever had a job before, and they were all jealous.

"She looks to be doing great." The customer slid Alexander Hamilton into her hand, and she nearly bounced with glee.

She pressed the key that opened the cash register and slid the bill into its slot, then took out two one-dollar bills and offered them to him. Waiting. Hoping.

He stuffed his wallet back into his pocket. "Keep the change."

Yes, yes, yes! Another two-dollar tip, hers for the keeping.

"Thank you," she and Papa said at the same time.

As soon as the customer walked out the door, she spun the chair in a circle three times.

"You're making a killing today, Princess."

"Yep." She'd have lots of money for garage saling with Nana.

He shook his head as if it bothered him that she was taking all his tips, but of course, it didn't. He teased her all the time, but he loved having her here. Everyone must, with as nice as they all were to her here.

"Now, get in there and sweep. I think I see someone else coming."

She hopped off the chair and scurried into his booth, snatching the broom from the corner. She'd gotten good at sweeping the hair into the standing dustpan. She was also pretty good at dusting shelves, organizing magazines, and cleaning curlers for Nana. But her favorite part of the day was still to come.

While in Papa's booth, she overheard Nana murmuring to her old lady customer in the booth next door. Extra careful not to clank the dustpan, she strained to listen. Why were they talking so quietly?

"It's sad. They'll probably get divorced, but I guess we'll see."

Were they talking about her parents? Emira felt like she was a balloon someone had let air out of. The excitement she'd felt moments before evaporated.

The old lady's voice crackled back. "Has Emira said anything about it?"

They *were* talking about her parents. Suddenly, she itched all over. She brushed her hands over her arms to get rid of any stray hairs, but it made it worse.

"No. She doesn't talk about it much. They've been separated for nearly six months now."

Why would she talk about the worst thing to happen in her life? And they shouldn't be talking about it either. She banged the dustpan first against the floor and then the booth wall to shut them up. It worked. She swiped at some hair on the top of her socks and sulked out of the booth, leaving the dustpan behind.

"When are Mary and Martha getting here?" she asked as she entered Nana's booth and leaned against the side, keeping her gaze on the black rubber mat.

"Any minute."

At least that was something. The two white-haired sisters came every Saturday for a wash and set, and they never failed to bring Emira a Tootsie Roll or mint or one of those hard strawberry candies. They adored her as if she was their granddaughter, and she rewarded them with a star performance.

"I'm going to change shoes." With a sudden burst of energy, she jetted to the back and dug through her purple overnight bag. Her hands clasped the cool metal bottoms of her tap shoes. She'd been practicing "Let Me Entertain You" all week, and this time, she wouldn't forget the words. Too bad she didn't have her recital outfit. The sequins and tulle skirt would really impress the Bible ladies, as Nana called them.

Her arms and legs jittered with excitement as she put them on and laced the shiny black shoes. She *lived* to perform. That's what she'd told her third-grade class during her future career presentation. She even wore big black sunglasses to look like a star. One day, she'd light up the stage. Or the screen. It didn't matter which. Just give her a chance to sing, dance, and act. To be in the spotlight.

Gracie Sotherton called her hungry for attention. She said it with her little freckled nose in the air, huddling with all the other mean girls on the playground. As if Emira was pathetic for always being the first to volunteer to read in class or play the main part in a skit. Whatever. No one thought movie stars were pathetic. No, everyone loved them.

Emira didn't need everyone to love her. She didn't need everyone to look at her. If only she could catch the attention of two people. Just two people. If only she could draw them together.

"Where's our girl?" Mary's gravelly voice boomed through the shop.

"Mary! Martha!" Emira jumped up and clacked to the old ladies, throwing her arms around their thin frames. "I missed you."

Martha stroked her cheek with cotton-soft fingers. "Aren't you the sweetest thing?" She dug in her ginormous purse and pulled out a Tootsie Roll. "A sweet for the sweetie."

Emira grinned up at her as she snatched the treat. Nana's cough behind her reminded her of her manners. "Thank you."

"You're welcome."

Nana waved the Bible ladies to the back. "Come on, ladies. Let's get you taken care of."

Emira followed at their heels. "I've been practicing my routine. I know all the words now. I can almost do the splits too. Do you want to see?"

"Of course, we do, darling, but you better wait until we're under the dryers." Kindness shone from Martha, and Emira spent the next half hour sitting at her and Mary's feet while Nana worked. No matter that she missed getting tips from two of Papa's customers. She didn't want to leave the Bible ladies, even for good money.

As soon as they were settled, hair drying, Emira tap-danced her heart out. She sang and shuffled, twirling with abandon. While they enjoyed her performance of "Put On a Happy Face" and "I'm Going to Wash That Man Right Outa My Hair," they clapped the loudest for "Let Me Entertain You." She'd have to do that one again next time.

Heart racing and spirit soaring, she bowed for her captive audience.

"Bravo."

Applause behind her made her turn. Her mother leaned against Nana's booth, a slight smile lifting her lips. "Great job, Emira."

Emira's heart swelled, and she ran to wrap her mother in a hug. "Were you watching the whole thing?"

"Most of it. I can't wait for your recital next month."

Neither could she. "Dad's coming right?"

Mom's smile dimmed. "I'm sure he will."

"You can watch me together."

Both Dad and Mom sitting so close their knees would touch. They'd cheer and look at each other and say, *That's our girl*. They'd remember that they loved each other and that they wanted to stay a family.

If her dad came, there was a chance, right? A chance Emira could be the glue that brought the two of them back together.

The math lesson had just begun the next Monday when the school secretary's voice came over the intercom. "Please send Emira Krump to the office. Her grandfather is here to pick her up."

Emira smirked at Gracie. "Told you," she whispered.

Gracie stuck out her tongue.

Oh, how she loved ruffling Gracie's feathers. Almost as much as she loved spending time with Papa. Once a month, he rescued her from boring school and took her out for lunch and ice cream. Sometimes, they'd feed the ducks at the park. Sometimes, they'd go to the playground. Always, they visited Aunt Maxie at the nursing home first. The old folks' home, as Papa called it, smelled funny and bored her. But as soon as they got through that part, they could do the fun stuff.

"Hey, Princess." Papa met her in the office and rumpled her hair.

She smiled up at him. "You got here just in time for math."

He chuckled. "Great timing, huh?"

She bounded out the door singing, "I hate math," to the same tune as Oscar the Grouch sang, "I Love Trash."

She slid into the back of Papa's Cadillac and ran her fingers over the soft seats. He rolled the windows down, and the wind whipped her hair around as he drove. If only they could skip the old folks' home this time. As the car slowed and pulled into the parking lot, she rolled up her window so he could hear her.

"Why do we have to visit Aunt Maxie?"

Even though she couldn't see his face, she heard the frown in his voice. "She's family, Princess."

Family how? Emira had never known her as anyone except the old lady who lay in bed at this nursing home. Family ate dinner together and played games and went to your recitals. This old lady hadn't done any of that with her.

"This place is boring." Mom always told her not to grumble, but it was true. She could think of little else worse than visiting this stinky building full of old people. Well, maybe math class.

Papa switched the car off and turned to her, his face serious. "I know this isn't your favorite thing, but Aunt Maxie was there for me when I needed her. Now she's all alone. One of the most important things you can learn in life is that people are important. They're important to God, and they should be the most important thing to us too. More important than anything else but God Himself."

A squirmy feeling wormed around in her belly, and she looked down at her fingernails. Fine. She'd keep herself from whining the whole time they were inside. She opened her door. Might as well get it over with.

They entered, and Papa signed in at the desk. This part was the worst. It was as if she were a magnet. Every eye in the lobby locked onto her and people started shuffling and wheeling their wheelchairs toward her. Hadn't they ever seen a kid before?

"How are you today, sweetie?"

"Aren't you precious."

"How old are you, darlin'?"

Old ladies touched her cheeks. Old men patted her back. She tried to smile and remember her manners, but it creeped her out. See, Gracie? She wasn't attention hungry. Not at all. She'd rather be invisible when she visited the nursing home. They talked about how they had grandchildren her age or how they could remember when their children were eight years old, ages ago.

She widened her eyes at Papa, who chatted with them as if he had all the time in the world and didn't need to grab lunch at Dairy Queen. When she grabbed his hand and tugged, he finally wrapped up the conversation.

"You're in a hurry to get to Maxie, huh?" he said as they trekked down the hall.

No, she only wanted to get away from the mob, but she didn't say so. She just squeezed his hand. They entered Aunt Maxie's room, and Papa took his place in the chair next to her bed. Emira sat in the chair near her feet.

Aunt Maxie lay still, staring up at the ceiling as if she didn't even know they were there. Her white, puffy hair filled her pillow. Her skin was so thin. Purple veins showed on her hand as Papa took it in his. He sat there, holding her hand, and talked to her as if she could hear him. As if they were having a normal conversation. Only it wasn't normal because she didn't answer.

He asked her questions like how she was doing, and when she didn't respond, he went on to tell her how he'd gotten a hole in one and how business at the shop was going well.

"Emira's been practicing hard for her recital next month." He turned his attention to her. "Tell Maxie what songs you'll be doing."

Emira frowned. "Why? She can't hear me."

"Sure she can."

"How do you know?"

"I know. She can hear you. She understands. Tell her about your recital."

Emira sighed. What was the point? It's not like Aunt Maxie would be excited for her, even if she *could* understand. But she did as Papa asked. The old lady's face didn't change. How could Papa tell anything they said made a difference?

They stayed for what felt like forever before Papa leaned forward and kissed his aunt's forehead. "I love you." His voice sounded funny, as if he might cry. Had she ever seen Papa cry before? Not that she remembered.

That squirmy feeling returned. As much as she hated these visits, they were important to Papa. And, if she understood correctly, he felt they were important to God. It didn't make sense to her, but there was something about the kind way Papa looked at Aunt Maxie that made her heart warm.

Chapter Four

2010

Floyd Douglas swept gray clippings into the dustpan. His last haircut. The last time he'd stand behind this brown leather chair and listen to a man share about his job, his marriage, his heartache. He'd never again snip scissors while a customer confessed his woes or his sins or complained about his mother-in-law. Those who'd sat in his chair throughout the years had lost more weight in worries than they ever had in hair.

A jingle at the door stole his attention from his task. Someone else? It was a mere five minutes until six o'clock, closing time. He peeked around the partition to see a stooped gentleman shuffle inside, leaning heavily on his cane. His moth-brown sweater hung so limply on his frame that it swayed with each movement. The hair on Floyd's arms prickled to attention as he zeroed in on the customer's profile.

"Can I help you?" Floyd asked. Who was this man? No one he knew, and he knew everyone. But then, why the odd sense of familiarity?

"I'd like a cut if I'm not too late." The man's voice sounded like tires crunching over gravel.

Floyd consulted his watch. Four minutes 'til six. A hot dinner waited at home. Steak and fried potatoes, his favorite. But what was one last *last* cut? "Sure thing. Have a seat."

He motioned to his booth and waited while the old man shuffled inside. The man sat, and Floyd spread a blue checkered apron over him.

He studied his customer in the mirror. "You look familiar. Do I know you?"

The man lifted a ghost of a smile. "One inch off the top, three quarters for the sides."

He wasn't going to answer the question? Odd. "You got it."

Floyd grabbed his clippers and went to work. He had to know this man. Something so familiar in the light gray shade of his eyes, in the square set of his jaw. Had they played softball together long ago? Golf? Had the man worked at the grocery store or pharmacy? He couldn't place him.

"What's your name?"

"Most people call me Father Larry."

Floyd nearly nicked the man's ear. "Father? You're a priest?"

"Sure am."

If Floyd knew him, it'd have to be from way back. Back before everything changed. Before his life took a different path.

Larry. Floyd scoured the recesses of his memory for a Larry, but all that surfaced was cobwebs and fog.

"What parish do you practice at? St. Rita's?" The children had gone to school there when they were young. Maybe that was it.

"No."

When he offered no further information, Floyd opted for a different tactic. He'd encountered enough untalkative customers to know how to disarm them by leading the conversation. "You're actually my final customer, Father Larry. After fifty years, I'm closing this shop and retiring."

"Is that so?" The drawn-out way Larry said this told Floyd the priest had already known as much.

Who was this man? There were dozens of other salons where he could get a haircut. Why had he come *here*? Best to keep talking if Floyd wanted to find out. "Opened this place back in '64. I was just a kid. Didn't know nothing. Want to guess how many people came through that door?" He pointed with the clippers.

Larry flexed his fingers before resting them on the armrest. Arthritis? "How many?"

"No idea. Hundreds. Thousands. Maybe a million," Floyd said.

Father Larry chuckled at the exaggeration.

"Fifty years is a long time." Floyd shook his head. "It's bittersweet. Retiring." Some days, he hadn't been able to wait to close and lock that door forever. Other days, he couldn't imagine doing anything else.

"What will you do now?"

He was seventy years old. His body complained like a cantankerous nag. What would retirement look like for him? "I think I'll take it easy."

Though the priest said, "Good for you," his expression indicated he believed Floyd about as much as the wife did.

He had never learned to sit still. But how did this man know that? How did he know anything at all?

When Floyd didn't reply, Father Larry met his narrowed gaze in the mirror. "You'll think of something."

"I could swear I know you from somewhere." Floyd paused with clippers buzzing in midair.

The priest held a blank expression. "Many people know me."

"But how do *you* know *me*?"

"Ah. There's a question." He lifted a finger as if he'd been waiting for Floyd to ask that very thing. The gesture, also, reeked of a familiarity thicker than cigarette smoke. Still, he couldn't place it. "Fifty years, huh? A little over fifty years ago, I was an eager, young seminary student."

Him too, actually. But he didn't need to recount *that* history with this man. Instead, he said, "It's a high calling." The words leaked out, almost of their own accord, from a place long dormant. He shook them off. They were from a different time, a different life. "What seminary did you go to?" Maybe that was why he seemed familiar. A fellow student from his seminary days.

"Kenrick."

That *was* it. Mystery solved. "You were one of those who made it, huh? What did they used to say? 'Only the best. Weed out the rest.'" He couldn't help but chuckle at the memory. "I was a weed. They plucked me up and tossed me out of there."

Was it his imagination, or did the priest's shoulders sag at his remark? "I was one of the few that made it through, yes, but I'm confident you are no weed."

A chill rose up his spine at the conviction in those words. It still didn't make sense. They must have gone to seminary together. From the looks of it, Larry must have been a few years ahead of him in school. But Floyd didn't remember the man. Ages had passed and fog veiled some memories, so that didn't mean much. Still, Father Larry spoke as if they were old chums. No, that wasn't quite right. He spoke as if he *currently* knew Floyd. And that most certainly wasn't the case.

Floyd cleared his throat to dislodge the confusion. "I wasn't cut out to be a priest." Should he mention that he was no longer Catholic? Better not.

Larry nodded thoughtfully. "Could be true. Regardless, you've made more impact here than you ever could have in a vestment."

Impact here? He absentmindedly set the clippers down and leaned against the counter, eyeing the man. "What do you mean?"

Larry's brows bunched slightly, and his mouth parted as if to leak an answer, but then he blew out a breath and slid his gaze to the mirror. "A little more off the top, please."

Picking up the clippers, Floyd resumed the cut. As the two spoke of those seminary days, flashes of memories flickered to life. But the memories that shone the brightest were the ones that came afterward. The ones that changed his life's trajectory.

Floyd finished the cut, brushed off the man's neck, then spun him around to face the mirror. "How's that?"

"Excellent work." The priest's smile spread wide.

He unbuttoned the apron, and the man stood. Floyd led the old man to the antique cash register at the front desk. His fingers hit the heavy metal keys with numbers long worn from use. Their clank resounded in the space.

"That'll be ten dollars." The drawer slid open, revealing short stacks of bills. Far less than in the early days.

"A steal." The old man took out his wallet and handed Floyd a wrinkled twenty. "Keep the change."

"Mighty kind of you. Thanks." Floyd set the bill in the cash register and smiled to himself. If only Princess was here, working for his tips. She'd think she hit the motherload. Was that really twenty years ago? He could picture her sitting behind that desk, rolling chair squeaking and ponytail swishing as she twisted the chair back and forth, waiting for the next customer to finish so she could collect her bounty.

Then the man dipped his head and opened the door, jingling the bell for the final time. "Bye now. Good luck to you."

"Goodbye." The door thudded with a finality that echoed throughout the space. Done. His grand finale.

He sagged into the desk chair, expelling air from the cracked, leather cushion. He spun the chair around and trailed his finger on the dusty glass shelving that held bottles of hair products—a shelf Emira hadn't gotten to— then swiveled back and surveyed the place where he'd spent five days a week for the last fifty years. The old box television sat on a wooden end table in the corner, volume low, flanked by rows of cracked faux leather chairs.

Outdated magazines sagged forward on the rack, proclaiming the best recipes and most breathtaking sites. *People* and *Time* spoke of another generation of people from another time.

He sighed, stood on creaky knees, and went to sweep up hair for the last *last* time. After discarding the hair clippings into the trash, he set the broom and dustpan aside and brushed his hands together as if shaking off a lifetime of work. He ensured the clippers, scissors, and talcum powder in his booth were neatly arranged, and then he peeked into his wife's booth. Pink curlers filled the sink. Combs and brushes littered the counter. He chuckled to himself. They'd pack it all up later. Maybe the kids would help. The grandkids could pitch in too. Make it a family affair.

His drooping recliner sat behind the partition, leaning slightly to one side. He grabbed his cigarettes and keys from the table beside it, glanced into the fridge to make sure there was nothing that needed to go home—nope, empty—and took one last look at the open space with hair dryers and wall-to-wall mirrors.

"The end of an era," he whispered to the silence before exiting his shop on his last day of work.

After securing the dead bolt, he turned and nearly plowed into Father Larry, who stood on the sidewalk, peering up at the hand-painted sign on top of the shop.

Before he could ask the priest why he was still there, the man spoke. "New Creations, huh? Such a fitting name for all that happened here throughout the years."

Again, with the cryptic familiarity. Floyd jiggled the keys in his pocket. "You talk as if you know this place. As if you know me. Why?"

Father Larry reached into his pocket and pulled out a torn piece of notebook paper about the size of a note card. "Come to dinner next Saturday?" He held out the paper.

An address was scrawled on the paper in cursive. "You'll tell me then?"

He nodded.

"What are you serving? Fish?" He cracked a smile at the memory of dozens of Catholic fish fries.

"For you? Only the best. T-bone steak."

"I'll be there." And not just for the meal. He'd go to find out what this father knew, or thought he knew. What he saw in the sagging, old shop behind him and the creaky, old man in front of him.

Father Larry nodded and shuffled toward an older but meticulously clean station wagon. Just before he ducked inside, he called, "Bring the wife. I hear she's a fireball."

Floyd chuckled. Maybe the man did know a thing or two.

Floyd stepped into the house to the scent of fried onions and steak seasoning. His stomach grumbled to life. He made a beeline for the kitchen and snatched a plate from the cupboard before Susan appeared from the other room.

"How was your last day?" she asked.

He plopped a fat steak onto his plate. "Fine. Just fine." A scoop of fried potatoes followed. "I had an interesting last customer, though." He took a cob of corn and shuffled to his recliner in the living room.

She brought him a can of Diet Coke and settled onto the couch beside him. "What kind of interesting customer?"

"A priest. We went to seminary together."

"Seminary?" She sat back. "You remember him from seminary?"

He forked a bite of potatoes and nearly gagged. A layer of salt coated his mouth. "You trying to kill me, woman?"

Her forehead scrunched as if he'd lost his mind.

He pointed at the plate with his fork. "The salt."

Her expression clouded. "Did I use too much?"

"I'll say. Are there any potatoes under all this salt?"

She waved him off and gave an airy laugh. "Don't be so dramatic."

Perhaps his last day at the shop had distracted her. He hadn't thought through the emotional implications for his wife, but it wasn't only him retiring. Her life would be different from here on out as well. He'd give her grace for oversalted potatoes.

She stared into space for a minute while he attempted to scrape the potatoes clean. Another tentative bite proved it useless.

"Anyway, no, I don't remember the priest. Not exactly. I knew he looked familiar but couldn't place him. I don't exactly remember him, but he remembers me. He acted like he knows me. *Knows* me, Susan. It was strange. He invited us both over for dinner next Saturday."

Susan frowned. "Strange. We're not Catholic."

"Yeah, I neglected to mention that fact. I doubt he knows." He shook his head, cutting into his steak. He studied the cut of meat. All appeared normal.

"You're not going, are you?" She popped up and headed for the kitchen.

"Well, yeah, I considered it." He took the smallest bite of steak and released a contented sigh when nothing but flavorful juices zinged his taste buds.

Susan appeared a minute later with a dust rag and went to work wiping down the coffee table. "Why?"

He pondered her question as he chewed. Why indeed? What would they possibly have to talk about? It *was* eons ago. Before the life he lived now. Back then, he'd been all about having a good time. Well, not *all* about that, but enough to get booted from the place. Did Father Larry know he'd been kicked out of the seminary? The man seemed to think highly of him for some reason. If he knew Floyd's departure hadn't been voluntary, would he still hold to that opinion?

But the man had been so mysterious, as if he knew something Floyd didn't. As if he couldn't wait to let Floyd in on the secret.

"I don't know. I'm curious. You'll come with me, won't you?"

Susan guffawed as she moved to dust the side table next to him. "Are you crazy, Floyd? No, I don't want to go. You're on your own."

Suddenly, the entire idea seemed ludicrous. Why had he even considered it? Father Larry didn't know him. He hadn't set foot in the shop. They hadn't seen each other in fifty years. What could the man reveal to him about himself that he didn't already know? And if the topic of conversation ventured into theology, it could get awkward. He had a lot of respect for the Catholics he knew, but he didn't hold onto many of their religious beliefs any longer.

"You're right." He scraped the last bite of steak from his plate. "I don't know what I was thinking. There's no reason for me to entertain the man." It was probably just a gust of nostalgia blowing through. Nothing to dwell on.

A clank and thump emitted from the hall closet, and then Susan emerged with the vacuum. Except vacuum lines were clearly visible on the carpeting, proving she'd recently performed the task. The woman was a bit too obsessed with cleanliness.

"What are your plans for tomorrow?" she asked while plugging the machine in.

"Nothing." He grinned. "Absolutely no plans." He laced his fingers behind his head and filled his lungs with air. Finally, he could enjoy retirement. When he headed to bed hours later, he pulled the priest's address from his pocket and crumpled it, then threw it in the trash can.

Chapter Five

1959

All summer, after meeting Susan, Floyd gravitated to the Grand Water Tower like a moth to light. That was where he could find the object of his affection most days. They didn't plan on where and when to meet up again, but Floyd could think of little else other than seeking her out.

Every weekend, there was one party or another going on in the neighborhood. Susan would always be there, and, invited or not, so would Floyd. When he finally earned enough money to buy a gray '54 Ford-O-Matic, he was broke, but people invited him everywhere.

When he could no longer drive his car due to a suspended license, getting down to the water towers became a game of chance. If he missed the last bus of the night, it was a long, miserable walk home. Or he'd have to deal with the guilt coating him from taking a cab to a neighbor's house and then running to their backyard when it was time to pay. That walk home may have been much shorter, but it stunk of shame. Still, there wasn't much he wouldn't do for five more minutes in Susan's presence.

Finally, he worked up enough courage to ask her out. He pulled into her empty driveway and revved his engine, far too much of a gentleman to honk at a lady. He drummed his fingers on the steering wheel and willed his nerves to settle. Tonight was a special night. He needed everything to go off without a hitch. At least her parents weren't home. He wouldn't have to face them until the end of the night. Right now, the only one he needed to impress was Susan.

She ran out of her front door wearing a white dress like an angel, her purse bumping against her hip. Her sister, Jean, followed and stood on the front porch, a worried look creasing her brow. Yikes. He'd forgotten about the older sister. She looked less than impressed.

"Don't worry about her. She's just protective of me." Susan waved goodbye to her sister and turned up the radio. "I thought you weren't supposed to drive anymore. Eight speeding tickets in two months. This ringing a bell?"

He shrugged. This date was special enough to risk driving with a suspended license.

"You got a ticket on the way to the courthouse to pay a ticket, then another one on the way back."

"I'll be careful." As long as he had a car and the ability to drive, he wouldn't allow something as minor as legality to ruin this chance.

His promise must have satisfied her because she settled back into her seat. "So, the Admiral, huh? I've never been."

"Nah, really? You'll love it. Music. Dancing. Good food." He tilted his head. Best not to lie on a first date. "Mediocre food."

She quirked a brow. "Booze?"

He guffawed. "Oh yeah. It's like East St. Louis. No one cares if you're underage."

She rubbed her hands together. "Perfect."

Score one for Floyd. He'd picked the perfect destination for a first date.

When they arrived, excitement pulsed in the air. Electric. What could be more perfect than being here with her? Live music emanated from the ballroom of the second deck's bandstand. They wove around tables and booths, headed straight for the bar. Floyd placed a hand on the small of Susan's back and guided her through the crowd. With this small touch, he anchored himself to her.

At the bar, he ordered beers for both of them. The smile she gave him when he handed hers over did more for him than alcohol ever would. Oh man, he was a goner. How could such a small woman contain such a feisty spirit? Her entire face lit up with that smile, and her bright blue eyes shone. A firework, Susan was, and he wanted her all to himself.

"Let's go to the top lido deck." Away from the crowd.

She preceded him up the stairs—a view he didn't mind in the least. Once at the top, the warm breeze licked their faces and tossed Susan's hair around her shoulders. Magical. Enrapturing.

Floyd inserted a coin into a telescope and watched as Susan viewed the Veterans Memorial and Jefferson Barracks Bridges. A whistle blew and startled her. Her hand flew to cover her heart as she let out a nervous laugh. Moonlight glistened on her smile.

He was going to marry her. No doubt in his mind.

She downed the last of her beer and tossed the cup into a nearby trash can.

"Want another?" he asked.

She looped her arms around his neck. "Yes, Floyd Douglas. I'd like another beer."

She tilted her head up, her mouth but inches away. Could he … Did she want him to kiss her? Her wide eyes searched his. Heart pounding, he lowered his mouth to hers and drank her in. She melted against him, her eyes closing. He'd been hoping for a sweet peck at the end of the night, but this? Far more than he could have dreamed. His hands moved from her back to tangle in her soft hair. Oh, heavens. He could die tonight a happy man.

She pulled back and tapped his chest with her palms. "Now." She pulled her bottom lip between her teeth. "My beer?"

"Of course." He'd get her anything she wanted.

"And then we'll dance." She winked.

Yep. Whatever she wanted.

They drank and danced for hours. The tipsier Susan got, the more she leaned into him. He relished the feel of her in his arms. If only they could stay all night, but she had a curfew, and he'd best get her back in time. It wouldn't do to make a bad first impression on his future in-laws. Good thing he'd only had a couple of beers.

"Time to go." He kissed her temple.

"Already?" Her laugh lilted.

"'Fraid so."

She finished her beer and moved to follow him to the entrance, only she stumbled into a dancing couple. She giggled, then apologized as she backed into another girl. Golly, she was farther gone than tipsy. More like sloppy drunk.

He took her hand and led her off the boat, guiding her clear of obstacles. Coming off the dock, she slipped and fell. Mud caked her white dress, her shoes, even the tips of her hair.

When he bent to help her up, he nearly went down with her but held his footing. She leaned into his strength as they stumbled to his car, and she spilled inside. When he stood at her open car door, she beamed up at him. Even covered in mud, she was the most beautiful woman he'd ever seen.

He leaned over to give her a feather-light kiss. "Did you have a good time?"

She tilted her head back and laughed. "The best."

"Good." He checked his watch and swiped a hand through his hair, leaving residue of mud. "It's almost your curfew. I'd better get you home." And quick. If he could win over her parents, he'd have a much easier time getting her to the altar. He rushed over to the driver's side and revved the engine.

Susan stuck her arm out the window, toying with the breeze. "Waitin' in School" blasted from the radio as he sped down the highway. He couldn't help but sing along, tapping the beat on the steering wheel.

Flashing lights shone in his rearview, sending his pulse into overdrive. He glanced at his speedometer. Shoot. He'd been speeding. Again. They'd put him in the slammer if they caught him. He pressed on the accelerator and swerved into the right lane. The police followed, hot on his tail.

Susan hooted and leaned forward, a glint of adventure in her eyes. Was she loving this? Truly? He couldn't let her down.

Sirens blared. How to evade those cops? He made a sharp right, then a left. Another right. Thinking quickly, he backed into an empty driveway and turned off his lights.

"Shh!" He put his finger to Susan's mouth and motioned for her to duck.

The sound of their heavy, fast breathing filled the car. Outside, crickets chirped. Car tires crunched and squealed. The police passed by. He'd tricked them. He should go. Now, while he had the chance, before the cop circled back around.

But Susan turned to him with a lazy smile. He leaned toward her and kissed her. She tasted of alcohol and cigarettes and his future. He pressed his forehead against hers. What he wouldn't give for a lifetime of adventure with this firecracker. She made everyone else look as dull as dirt. "You are my forever."

"Yeah?" The streetlight made her eyes twinkle.

"Yeah."

When Floyd dropped an intoxicated and mud-crusted Susan off at her parents' house, Mrs. Sonjak screwed her face up tighter than a wound clock. A vein bulged in Mr. Sonjak's forehead as he stared Floyd down, arms crossed, legs spread in a wide stance on their front porch.

"Hello, sir. I'm Floyd. Nice to meet you." He extended a dirty hand, hesitated, wiped it on his slacks, then tried again.

Mr. Sonjak didn't make a move to reciprocate.

Nerves quaking, he managed a trembling smile at Susan's mom. "Mrs. Sonjak." He bowed slightly rather than attempt another handshake.

A wide-eyed Jean peeked out the front window.

He scrambled for his voice. When he pushed words out, they cracked. "I apologize, Mr. and Mrs. Sonjak." What could he say? What excuse could he give? "She slipped."

Laughter bubbled out from Susan as she doubled over, nearly falling to the ground again.

Floyd gestured to her with a shrug. "But as you can see, she had a great time."

Mr. Sonjak's scowl indicated that was the wrong thing to say. He needed to get out of there while he still had all his teeth. This might have been a bad first impression, but he could win the parents over later. Tonight, at least, he was confident he'd secured Susan's affection.

Mission accomplished.

1960

Months later, Mr. and Mrs. Sonjak still didn't like Floyd, but he wasn't about to let such a minor thing stand in his way. Not when everything in him told him this woman was his destiny. At least Mr. and Mrs. Sonjak hadn't forbidden the two lovebirds from dating. Perhaps they knew that placing anything off limits only made it more tempting for their daughter.

As for Floyd's mother, she might have approved if she'd known Susan existed. He'd never mentioned he'd been seeing a girl, much less that he'd fallen in love. She might faint dead away if he told her he planned on marrying a girl she'd never met, so they kept their plans a secret from both families.

Married.

He knew from the beginning that they would wed.

After their date on the Admiral, Floyd borrowed a ring from his buddy Fred and used it as a going steady ring until Fred needed it back for his own girl. It only made sense to replace that one with an engagement ring. It'd taken months of saving from his two jobs to buy a nice ring. He planned to ask her properly at dinner, but it came out while they were walking down the street.

He jiggled the ring in his pocket. "I want to marry you." He rubbed her thumb with his.

She grinned up at him, eyes alight. "Okay."

He removed the ring from his pocket and slid it on her finger. Her quiet smile sent a wave of elation cresting over him. Then they kept walking, easy as a summer breeze.

They'd marry in a courthouse and announce it later. Far easier to ask for forgiveness than permission. Only one slight problem. By law, a woman had to be eighteen to get married—no issue there—but the man had to be twenty-one. Floyd was barely eighteen. Which meant they needed parental permission or a sneaky plan.

Their first attempt to get married at a Missouri courthouse resulted in them being turned away when they'd barely made it through the door. Perhaps they'd have better luck in Illinois. Everything was more lenient across the river.

When they made it before the judge, Floyd breathed a sigh of relief. He squeezed Susan's hand, and she gave him a wobbly smile.

The judge smiled down at them, looking over his spectacles. "As a precaution, I make it a practice of calling the parents of anyone who is underage to ensure consent. What's your mother's number, Mr. Douglas?"

Floyd's throat went dry. No. This couldn't be happening. They'd come this far. They couldn't fail now. He coughed. A number. What number could he give? The only one that came to him was his co-worker Carol's number. She'd play along, wouldn't she? She was a kind gal with a good sense of humor, and she knew what they were up to. She called it romantic. Surely, she'd take the hint and go along with their ruse.

Floyd strained to hear as the judge picked up the phone and dialed.

"Hello?"

"Hello, Mrs. Douglas, I have your son here, and he'd like permission to get married."

"This is Mrs. Ramsey. Perhaps you have the wrong number."

The judge's brows scrunched. "Do you know a Floyd Douglas?"

Floyd held his breath, dread coating his lungs. *Please say yes. Please say yes.*

A hesitant pause. "Yes, I do."

"And he's your son?"

"Son? What are you talking about? I don't have a son! He works with me at A&P. He's not my son."

Heat climbed Floyd's neck and face. His feet itched to run. Susan sent him a panicked look before glancing to the door.

The judge thanked Carol and hung up the phone as if pounding a gavel. Floyd swallowed.

"Get out of my courtroom."

"Yes, sir." He reached out, took Susan's hand, and ran.

Floyd wrapped his sweater tighter around him as he turned the block to Susan's house. Of all the rotten luck. He'd found the woman of his dreams, yet he'd been unable to marry her. Maybe his luck would have been better if he'd called Aunt Maxie. She was the one who got him out of jail when he'd been caught driving with a suspended license last month. He'd used his one phone call to dial Aunt Maxie—not Carol—and she bailed him out, with no questions. She didn't have the two hundred dollars needed, but she knew someone who did. Good ole Aunt Maxie. Why hadn't he thought of her?

Too late now. Not only were their marriage plans foiled, but it was streetcars and buses for them for the foreseeable future. No way was he risking jail time again.

Spring teased the air, beckoning flowers to bloom and birds to sing, but winter didn't want to give up easily. That was something he had in common with the dreary season. Persistence. Susan would be his bride. He only had to figure out how.

He snuck around the back of Susan's house and tapped on her window. The curtain rustled, and she stared back at him with a determined glint in her eye. She slid open the window. "Come inside. Mom's at the grocery store."

He checked his watch. Her father wouldn't be back from work for at least an hour. He grinned and dashed to the back door, greeting her with a kiss.

She placed her hands squarely on his chest. "Give me your draft card."

"My draft card? Why?"

"I have an idea. I'm going to be Mrs. Douglas before the week is through."

What did the fireball have in mind now? He nudged her playfully. "Are you?"

"Sure am."

He pulled his draft card out of his wallet and handed it over. She snatched it and was off down the hallway to the bathroom where a shallow Tupperware container of water stood on the edge of the sink. She dunked his card under the water.

"What are you doing?" He moved to snatch it back.

"I'm doctoring your card." She took a washrag and lightly scrubbed at the spot that stated his birthdate. The ink smudged. "See?"

"Well, I'll be."

After a few more strokes, it had smeared to where the year was unrecognizable. "There." She stared at the card with a satisfied smirk, then spun and grabbed a hair dryer. After only a minute, the card had dried. Susan sashayed into her father's office and slid it into the typewriter. She clinked a couple of keys. "Now you're twenty-one." She grinned at him as she handed back his card.

He hated to dash the hopeful gleam in her eye, but ... "I don't know if this will work. It looks like it's been put through the wringer." The card was as wrinkled as if someone had crumpled it into a ball and tried to flatten it back out.

Her countenance drooped only slightly. "Don't worry. I'll iron it." She snatched it back and scampered down the steps into the laundry room. She extended the ironing board, plugged in the iron, and tapped her foot as she waited. "Come on," she grumbled.

Floyd checked his watch. Her mother would likely be back any minute.

She pressed the iron to the draft card and cast a look over her shoulder. A rumble sounded outside. A car turned into the driveway. An engine shut off. Car door. Footsteps.

Her eyes widened. "Here." She thrust his card into his hand. "Go out the utility room door." She shoved him in that direction. "Quick."

He scrambled with the latch, then swung around to plant a swift kiss on her temple before ducking out the door and behind a bush. The door clicked behind him just as he heard Mrs. Sonjak's voice call out to her daughter.

With holly bush branches scratching his arms, Floyd stared at his new birthdate on the draft card. Would you look at that? She'd done it. His spitfire had fast-forwarded time and paved the way for their marriage.

What a woman.

Today was the day. The day he would finally make Susan Sonjak his wife. Well, hopefully. Susan wasn't quite sure they could pull it off, but his nerves tingled with anticipation. He was the luckiest man alive. The two of them rode the streetcar hand in hand to St. Louis Avenue to get their marriage license. Then it would be off to the courthouse. Fat rain droplets pelted the windows, but nothing could dampen Floyd's mood. Not on his wedding day.

When they got to the office of the Recorder of Deeds, they pooled their money together to come up with the seven dollars required. With only fifty cents left to spare, they didn't have the money to take a streetcar to the courthouse.

They stood hand in hand under the awning looking out onto the wet street.

"How far is it?"

Floyd grimaced. "Maybe thirty blocks." He should have thought of bringing an umbrella.

"Then that's thirty blocks we'll walk together."

It turned out to be forty-nine blocks.

They arrived drenched. Susan shivered, and Floyd rubbed her arms to banish the goosebumps. "We're here.

We made it." They ascended the cement steps, opened the heavy door, and shuffled into line.

"We're here to get married," Floyd said after greeting the clerk. He produced the marriage license from the interior pocket of his jacket. Water dripped from their clothes, forming small puddles at their feet.

"That'll be twelve dollars." The clerk popped her gum and gave them a bored look.

"Twelve dollars?" A nervous chuckle leaked out. "But we have the license right here." He slid the document closer.

Another pop. "Twelve dollars for court fees."

His stomach sank to his toes. They couldn't have come this far only to turn back now.

Susan pressed her lips into a firm line. She twirled her engagement ring around on her finger. Once. Twice. She slid it off and placed it in his palm. "I saw a pawn shop across the street. Hawk this and get the money for court."

He shuffled from one foot to another. Not her ring. "I couldn't."

She closed his hand around it. "You'd better."

The clerk blew her bangs out of her face with an exasperated breath. "Will you please step aside so I can assist the next customer?"

Susan threaded her hand through his and pulled him toward the door. Once again, they emerged into sheets of rain. She led him to the street corner, one hand shielding her eyes from the downpour, the other safely tucked in his. They dashed across the street and spilled into the near-empty pawn shop.

Floyd's shoes squeaked as he walked to the counter and settled the ring on the glass casing. "How much will you give me for this?"

A half inch of the worker's hairy stomach stuck out underneath his plaid button-up shirt as he raised the ring to the light, inspecting it. The man squinted and angled the ring this way and that, his greasy black hair limp around his face.

"I'll give you twenty bucks."

Twenty bucks? He'd paid over a hundred for it not three weeks ago.

Susan clapped her hands together. "We'll take it."

He shot her a glance. What was she thinking? It was a rip-off.

She mouthed, *It's enough,* and his pulse slowed. It was enough to get them married. Enough to even get a ride home after the wedding.

He frowned at the man behind the counter. "We'll take it."

The slimeball handed him a crisp twenty-dollar bill, which he slid into his wallet before giving his girl's hand a squeeze. "Ready?"

She beamed up at him. "Ready."

Twenty minutes later, a judge proclaimed them man and wife. He swept his bride into an embrace and kissed her soundly.

His wife.

Susan Sonjak was his wife! He was the happiest man on earth.

They walked hand in hand out of the courthouse and stood under the dripping overhang. The sun was beginning to set. Time was short. "So ..." He toed the pavement. "See you tomorrow?"

She stood on her tiptoes and kissed his clean-shaven cheek. "See you tomorrow."

Then he got into a streetcar going in one direction while she got into one going in another. Their secret dating relationship had officially become a secret marriage.

Chapter Six

1990

Emira peeked out the window of Nana and Papa's house just in time to spy headlights turning into the driveway. "They're here, everybody!"

She ducked behind the couch. Voices quieted. Her stomach pinged with excitement as car doors shut and footsteps came closer. Closer. So close now. The door handle rattled.

Papa's voice burst through the door. "Really, Susan, you didn't have to demand to talk to the manager."

"I'm not going to sit by and put up with horrible service."

Ugh. Had they spent their whole anniversary dinner bickering? Hopefully not.

They made it three steps before Emira couldn't contain herself any longer. She popped out from behind the couch. "Surprise!"

She set off a chain reaction, and the rest of the friends and family emerged shouting, "Congratulations," "Happy anniversary," and "Surprise!"

Nana clutched her chest.

Papa's mouth dropped open. "What's this?"

"Your surprise anniversary party." Emira bounced on her toes, gliding a balloon toward them by the ribbon.

Mom looped an arm around Emira's shoulder. "Thirty years is something to celebrate."

Everyone backed up and allowed the couple to enter. Nana and Papa hugged each of the guests and gave pecks on their cheeks. Emira excused herself to grab a cupcake and soda now that Mom wasn't guarding the stash. Everyone was here, all her grandparents' friends. Uncle Joseph and Aunt Ruthie. Her cousins and great-aunts and great-uncles. Everyone but her dad.

She stood on the edge of the crowd, the swirl of conversation drawing her in and repelling her at the same time. Because her dad should be here. He was always here at these family things. Nana and Papa loved him like he was their son. He loved them. Why wasn't he here wishing them a happy anniversary? Nana and Papa always griped at each other, but they had stayed married for thirty years. Why couldn't her parents stick it out? Why couldn't they make it work?

"Is this your courthouse anniversary or your church anniversary?" one of their friends asked.

What did that mean? They had two anniversaries? They loved each other so much they'd married *twice*. Her parents couldn't even stay married once.

"Our courthouse one."

"How romantic."

Papa launched into the story of how he and Nana had met and married without their parents knowing. Maybe she should cover her ears. Did they really want her to know how they'd disobeyed their parents and broken the law by writing a different date on his draft card? How strange to think of the two of them as young and in love like people in the movies. They didn't act all lovey-dovey anymore.

Did they still love each other?

Everyone in the room was laughing by the time Papa finished his story.

"Emira, honey," Mom called above the chatter. "Are you ready to do your song and dance?"

She'd almost forgotten. "Yes." Of course, she was. She'd been practicing this supersecret performance alone at home, away from prying eyes. Never at the shop, and never here.

Mom made her way to Nana's record player and found the right record and song. She used her loud whistle to quiet everyone, then announced Emira's performance.

"Stand by Me" began playing, and Emira danced in fluid movements. Aunt Karen snapped a couple of pictures as she twirled. Halfway through the ballet performance, tears clawed up her throat and along the backs of her eyes. Papa and Nana had stood by each other all these years, but her parents couldn't do the same. And they couldn't stand by her. Not both of them at the same time. She had to have one or the other, never both at once. Not anymore. Except for at her recitals and concerts or if she became a star and made them take notice. Made them come together for her.

She had to do that. She would keep practicing until she wasn't just good, but excellent. Amazing. One of a kind.

The song finished, and she bowed, then rushed off to the bathroom before her tears leaked out, and she made a fool of herself in front of everyone.

Emira awoke to Mom ushering the last party guest out the door. Sometime during the festivities, she'd fallen asleep on the couch. A crocheted blanket covered her. Likely Nana's doing. She rubbed her blurry eyes and sat up.

She yawned and then asked, "Did I miss the cake?"

Nana and Papa sat next to each other on the sofa opposite her, looking about as tired as she felt. Emira blinked, staring at their joined hands. They were holding hands. Had she ever seen them do so? Her chest squeezed.

"I saved you a piece." Her mom's steps dragged to the kitchen. She emerged a minute later with a paper plate laden with a thick slice of chocolate cake. A cursive *Fl* was written in blue icing.

"I get to eat the beginning of Papa's name." Emira giggled. "I'm going to eat you, Papa."

"Hey." He faked a gasp, and she dissolved into laughter.

"Your present." Papa patted Nana's knee. "I almost forgot."

Nana waved a hand in front of her face. "You didn't have to get me anything."

"Nonsense. It's our anniversary."

A present? What was it? Suddenly awake, Emira flung the blanket off and jumped up.

Papa creaked and groaned as he stood. "Oh, my back," he said, as always. He settled a hand on his lower back and stretched to one side, then the other. The familiarity of it comforted her. Some things in her life might be weebly-wobbly, but other things stayed the same. This place that smelled like cigarette smoke and Diet Coke with its scratchy sofas and open windows, long curtains flowing in the breeze. Nana with her cleaning and Papa with his stories and sayings. And the shop. She'd always have the barbershop. She sank into that truth like a warm bubble bath.

Papa shuffled into the kitchen. Emira bounded after him. As Papa reached up on top of the refrigerator, she bounced on her toes. What a good hiding spot! Nana was much shorter than he was. She'd never find a present up there. But confusion flooded her when he pulled out a plain brown box instead of a pretty gift bag. That wasn't very present-like. Not much like a romantic anniversary gift. Maybe the present was inside the box.

He carried the box back into the living room to where Nana still sat. Emira followed, far more tentatively now.

"Happy anniversary." He didn't even smile as he set the box on the couch and sat on the other side of it.

Nana's face didn't show a hint of disappointment over the ugly brown cardboard box. Was she even excited?

Emira tilted her head to the side as she watched. What did her grandma think of it? She'd seen that look on her face before. Maybe … Yes, that was it. She looked as if she were opening the mail.

The boring old mail.

Nana peeled off a strip of packing tape and pried open the flaps. "Lightbulbs." She said this not in the same way she'd say "bills" and not how she'd announce a letter from Aunt Jean, but in the way she'd say, "coupons." Like she was pleased but not enough to get all worked up over it. She pulled out a pack of bulbs and held them up for Mom and Emira to see.

"I got them at Sam's Club. There's forty-two of them. That'll last you ten years!"

"Aw. Thank you, Floyd. How thoughtful."

Mom smiled and nodded as if it were the sweetest thing in the world to get someone lightbulbs for their anniversary. Emira looked back and forth from Nana to Papa, waiting for someone to laugh. To say it was a joke and that the real present was in the other room. But after inspecting the box and remarking on how many lightbulbs were inside, Nana thanked Papa again and then changed the subject to what a surprise the party was.

"Hold on." Emira stood, hands planted on her hips. "You really got lightbulbs for your anniversary? That's the *boringest* present ever."

"Emira," Mom chided.

Papa absentmindedly rubbed his belly. "When you've been married as long as we have, you don't much mind practical gifts." He glanced at Nana as if to make sure he was saying the right thing. She nodded a teensy bit. "She's always asking me to buy lightbulbs, saying the house is too dark, and I kept forgetting. Now she'll have plenty."

Nana gave his arm a little shove. "You listened for once."

"But you're supposed to get her flowers and chocolate. You could write her a poem."

Mom and Papa chuckled.

Nana snorted a laugh. "A poem. That's a good one."

Why were they making fun of her? Didn't they see how this made no sense? Emira stomped her foot and pinned Papa with a stare. "But don't you love her?"

Papa's mouth opened. He looked as if her words had slapped him on the cheek. His face reddened. His eyes narrowed. "Of course, I love her." His words hissed out.

Emira dropped her arms and took a step back. She hated when Papa got cross with her.

He continued, his fiery eyes scorching her. "She's my wife. Where'd you get the idea that love looks like flowers and chocolate and fancy words? From the shows you watch? That's nonsense. Love looks like being faithful in the little things and saying yes every day for decades. Like choosing someone every day, day in and day out, for thirty, forty, fifty years." He huffed as he stood. "Anyone can buy a cheap bouquet from the grocery store." He marched to the kitchen, leaving Emira frozen in place.

Anyone could buy cheap flowers, but not everyone could buy lightbulbs? She didn't understand. Nana and Papa didn't kiss and make moony eyes in front of her. They didn't gush about how they loved each other. In fact, that might have been the first time she'd ever heard Papa say he loved Nana, and he'd only done it because of her question. Was this really what love looked like?

How was she to know? Her parents were getting divorced. They couldn't say yes for decades. Couldn't keep saying yes even for her. If love didn't look like what she saw in the movies, why did that make her sigh and feel all fluttery inside? She wanted Ariel to get legs so she could be with Prince Eric. She wanted happily ever afters with a kiss at the end. No one in the movies gave lightbulbs as a present.

She must not know anything about love at all.

Chapter Seven

2010

Floyd folded the newspaper and slammed it onto the side table. Devastation continued to reign after January's earthquake and now an 8.8 magnitude earthquake had just rocked Chile. So many lives lost, so many people in need. And what was he doing? Sitting on his keister watching golf. The world hemorrhaged around him with desperate needs while he chomped on peanuts and snoozed.

Darn it, Susan had been right. She'd told him he'd get bored with retirement within a week. He'd thought such an idea ludicrous. He'd gotten his first job at thirteen and had worked since then.

He hit the lever on his recliner and propelled himself forward. He had to get out of the house before he went batty. Susan was at Kmart. He should go shopping too. They were about out of ice cream. If the great-grandkids visited, he needed to have some to offer. Plus, the grocery store had a sale on blackberries. Susan always liked those.

He made it out the door in no time, opting for sandals instead of shoes so he wouldn't have to bend down to tie the darn things. The cold air nipped at his toes, and he hastened his steps. Ah, yes. This is what he needed. Fresh air and sunshine. A frosty, biting wind to invigorate his senses and remind him it was good to be alive.

The store wasn't nearly as crowded on a weekday as when he usually visited on Sunday. He grabbed a cart and headed straight for the fresh fruit. Finding the sale on blackberries, he added two boxes to his cart and stocked up on bananas, strawberries, and apples. The peaches were pricey, but they looked so good that he added them too. While he'd only meant to purchase two items, he meandered up and down every aisle, boredom and hunger working in tandem to fill his cart nearly to overflowing.

He nodded to a young woman pushing a cart filled with canned vegetables. Yuck. That was one aisle he could safely skip.

"Ugh. What's that black goo on the floor?" She cringed and pointed downward.

Sure enough, a black gooey liquid oozed in a trail down the aisle.

Floyd stared wide-eyed. "I don't know."

A voice boomed over the loudspeaker. "Cleanup in aisle one."

He checked the sign. They were in aisle fourteen. Should he tell someone their aisle needed cleanup as well?

The woman beat him to it. "I'll alert a worker."

She bustled off, but before she turned the corner, the loudspeaker broke through again. "Cleanup in aisle two."

Well, that was closer, at any rate.

"Cleanup in aisle three."

Goodness, what was going on in this store? He walked forward into the refrigerated section where a group huddled, pointing down the aisles he'd already passed through.

"What is it?"

"Do you think it's toxic?"

Was that black goo everywhere? Hopefully, it wasn't hazardous. Just looking at it gave him the heebie-jeebies. He hastened to the next aisle. He'd grab ice cream and then get out of there in case the goo was some sort of contaminant.

An exasperated voice came over the loudspeaker. "Clean up in … all the aisles."

All the aisles? Uh-oh, that was bad. But there was no sign of the black goo on the clean tiled floor in front of him. He cast a glance over his shoulder and startled. There it was! Directly behind him. It was following *him.*

He rushed forward a dozen steps, then looked behind him again. Still there. His head spun, and he gripped the cart with whitened knuckles. What was happening? Out of the corner of his eye, he saw a small, dark dot fall from his cart. Wait. Was that a … blackberry?

Digging under the pile of groceries, he unearthed a near-empty carton of blackberries. Open and on its side. Understanding dawned. The blackberries had been falling this entire time, and he'd run over them with the cart's wheels, creating the oozing black trail throughout the store.

"More assistance is needed in cleanup. Assistance needed in cleanup."

Floyd's neck heated. If he were a turtle, he'd retreat into his shell about now. A flurry of worried voices from the next aisle reached his ears. He needed to get out of there before he melted from embarrassment. He could get ice cream, and blackberries, another time.

Keeping his head down, he abandoned his cart and skedaddled toward the door, making a show of looking at his watch as if he were in a hurry. He breathed a sigh of relief when he made it past the first set of sliding doors without a janitor accosting him. He'd almost exited the breezeway through the second set of sliding doors when a flyer posted on the bulletin board caught his eye.

Make A Difference Now.

A picture of a wide-eyed child, dirty and sitting amongst debris stared back at him. He stilled, then gravitated toward the single sheet of paper as if it were magnetic.

Join Christ's Way on a mission trip to Haiti and make your life count.

Underneath was a website and phone number to call for more information.

Make a difference. That was what he'd always wanted to do, but life had derailed him along the way. He'd never gotten around to his grand plans of making his life count. What had he done with the years he'd been given? He'd cut hair. That was it. He came home exhausted each evening and relaxed in front of the television, then did it all again the next day. Those dreams of being a priest had stemmed from a desire to do something great with his life.

He hadn't.

And now it was too late.

Or was it?

What if he still had time to make his life count for something? What if he could still make a difference? He wasn't dead yet. Sure, it was harder to get around than it used to be, but he could do it. And a chance to travel? Hadn't he always wanted to see the world beyond his barbershop?

Hope lit within him. A purpose for his retirement days. He could do this. Go on a mission trip. Live out his long-postponed dream.

He snatched the tab of paper with a phone number attached. He'd call them as soon as he got home. No matter when, no matter how much, he'd make this happen.

Emira smiled to herself as Papa's picture flashed across her phone screen. She hit accept and settled Kade's fries into the center console so he could eat while he drove home. Then she grudgingly passed the Happy Meal to three-year-old Teddy in the back seat. Ugh. She hated feeding him junk food, but this time, it couldn't be helped. She swallowed down the mom guilt. At least the event that had kept them out past dinner and the children's bedtimes was an educational one at the library. That had to count for something on the good parenting scale. Maybe even balance out Mickey D's.

"Hey, Papa. What's up?" Her pulse ratcheted up a notch. Maybe something fell through with the shop. She hadn't heard from him in over a week. He could be calling to tell her he'd changed his mind and decided not to sell.

"Hi, Princess. Say, do you have a good suitcase? The zipper broke off mine. Your mom's is falling apart, and Joseph has that cruise planned, so he'll need his."

Reagan screamed, reaching for her brother's fry. Emira handed her a sippy cup as her mind raced to keep up with Papa's question. "A suitcase? Why? Are you going somewhere?"

"Yes. Yes. To Haiti. Didn't your mom tell you?"

"Wait, what?" Emira bolted forward with her question.

"What's wrong? What's going on?" Kade whispered.

She shook her head and held up a finger in his direction. "You're going *where*?"

"On a mission trip to Haiti." Something clattered in the background. "Do you have a suitcase I can borrow, or should I go buy one? They're rather expensive."

"So is international travel," she mumbled to herself, then cleared her throat and spoke louder. "What brought this about? Is Nana going too?"

"Not Nana. Just me. I saw a flyer. Figured it'd be a great opportunity."

"Saw a flyer where? When?"

"What's going on?" Kade whispered again.

She angled away from him. How could she answer that question when she didn't understand herself?

"Last week. At the grocery store."

"Fwy! Fwy!" Reagan screeched and kicked the back of Emira's seat.

Emira plugged her other ear with her finger. "You saw a random flyer and decided, hey, what the heck, I'll go to Haiti?" What was with him and these spur-of-the-moment decisions?

"Fwy! Fwy!"

Kade reached an arm back and attempted to soothe the baby. Shoot. They should have fed her jarred baby food at the library. That bottle wasn't holding her over. "Reagan, honey, drink your water."

"I can't hear you very well, Princess. There's a lot of noise in the background."

Emira spun around, snatched a fry from Teddy, and handed it to Reagan. "There."

Teddy's mouth fell open. Kade's did too. Okay, so they didn't normally feed the baby greasy, salty fries. But seventy-year-old men didn't go sporadically joining mission trips to other countries either.

She puffed out her cheeks. Papa was running off the rails. This wasn't safe. Someone needed to do something. "We're dropping by. Be there in twenty."

She hung up before he could ask questions.

"So, I take it I'm making a left at the light?" Kade raised a brow.

She folded her arms around herself. Holding herself together when nothing made sense. Everything was spinning fast, flinging apart. "Yeah."

"You do realize we're bringing the kids to your grandparents' place past their bedtime. Reagan's hungry. They're both tired. Let's just say, not ideal."

"I have to figure out what's going on."

She chipped away at her purple nail polish as he drove. She'd mentioned her concerns about Nana's memory to her mom, but not to Papa. No need to upset him during such a tumultuous time of transition. And what if that was what upset Nana? Perhaps she had been thrown off that day by the talk of the shop closing. If her memory was failing, wouldn't Papa be the first to notice? He hadn't said anything, and Mom said she hadn't detected anything unusual. Way to make Emira feel like she was going crazy.

When they rolled into the driveway, the skin at the back of her neck prickled. What had happened to this home wrapping her in its warm haven? She blinked at the illuminated window, imagining the familiar behind the gauzy curtain. But her dry throat attested to the fact that she'd find the scene inside far different from what she'd grown up knowing.

She heaved a breath. "Come on, Doodlebug." She smoothed Reagan's hair from her face before hoisting her car seat from the car. "Let's go see if Nana and Papa have something for you to eat."

"Papapapa." Reagan waved her chubby fists.

"Yes. Papa. We love Papa." Even if he had gone off the deep end.

Kade and Teddy led the way, bursting through the door without a knock or word of warning.

"Come in. Come in." Nana's gaze lit on her great-grandchildren, even as she admonished Teddy to take off his shoes. He ran to her and wrapped his arms around her knees. Her laughter bounced off the walls. "What a great surprise. I'd forgotten you were coming over for dinner tonight."

Emira gave Kade a pointed look. See. Just what she was talking about. Now he could reassure her she wasn't crazy. Kade merely shrugged. Some help he was.

"No dinner plans, Nana. Just stopped by for a minute."

"Emira," Papa bustled down the hallway, wearing pajama pants and a too-small T-shirt that exposed his protruding belly. His hair stood on end. "Did you bring a suitcase?"

"No, we were out and came straight here."

His mouth twisted into a deep frown. "Drat."

Nana held her arms out for Reagan. Kade unbuckled the baby and handed her over. Nana made exaggerated bright facial expressions, much to Reagan's delight. "I don't know why you need to pack right now anyway. The trip isn't for over a month."

"How am I supposed to see what I already have and what I need to buy if I don't have a suitcase to put things in, Susan?"

Nana rolled her eyes. "Why are you frazzled about this? I'm the one you're leaving for six weeks. Six weeks on my lonesome." She leaned toward Emira. A twinkle in her eye showed the idea wasn't entirely unwelcome. "Can you imagine?"

"Six weeks!" Emira's head swiveled back and forth between the two of them. "You're leaving the country for six weeks?"

"Naturally." Papa ran his hand through his hair. No wonder it looked like that.

"Papa, play ball." Teddy lobbed a tennis ball right at Papa's gut.

He grimaced and hunched forward.

Emira swept her son up in her arms and plunked him on the couch. "Teddy, no throwing balls at Papa. Watch TV." The Home Shopping Network played on the screen. "Look at that blender. Pretty cool, huh?"

Reagan started to fuss. Nana's bouncing attempts only made the cries increase in volume. Frustrating since Kade and Papa were having a conversation Emira couldn't hear.

"Do want me to feed her?" Nana asked.

She gave an apologetic shrug, then grabbed the diaper bag and handed it to Nana. "She *is* hungry. There should be a few different jars in there."

Nana stood before balancing the bag on her shoulder. "Well then, little one. Let's get you something to eat." The two of them disappeared into the kitchen.

"Veggies before fruits, please," Emira called after them.

As the fussing baby left the room, Emira caught the tail end of whatever Papa had been saying. "… nonrefundable deposit."

Kade let out a low whistle. "How'd you manage to pay for that?"

"From the proceeds from selling the shop. Couldn't have come at a better time."

Emira's stomach clenched. Was he saying he'd squandered the proceeds on this trip? He needed that money for his retirement, to live comfortably. No. He was a rational man. Not one to waste his livelihood on some spontaneous trip. Her mouth moved around trying to find words and form them, but no sound came out.

Kade caught her gaze, and his brows dipped. He came close and put a hand on her shoulder. "You okay?"

No. Definitely not. Her head bobbled around. "Just trying to understand what's going on."

He kneaded the tight knot in between her neck and shoulder blade with gentle pressure, grounding her. "I asked your grandpa if he'd already committed to this trip, and it turns out he has. He's filled out his initial application and sent in a nonrefundable deposit."

Papa waved his hand in front of him. "I went ahead and sent in the entire amount. Easier doing it that way rather than bit by bit."

Emira swallowed hard. "How much?"

"Fifteen thousand and some change."

Her mouth dropped open. "Fifteen *thousand*?"

"And some change."

She sputtered. "Can you get it back? If you change your mind, I mean."

He shrugged.

"Papa, you've got to stop payment on that check." How was he completely unbothered by this massive amount of money?

"Too late for that. Besides, it says no refunds. If someone backs out, they can gift their funds to another missionary on the trip, but they can't get them back. It doesn't matter. I'm committed."

"Why?" Okay, probably not the most sensitive thing to blurt out, judging by the way Kade's eyes widened at her question.

"I've waited my whole life to do something like this, Princess. Something that matters."

She thrust a hand to her hip. "What's that supposed to mean? You don't think you've done anything that matters in your whole life? Helping to raise me didn't matter?"

He huffed out a breath. "That's not what I mean."

"What *do* you mean? I'm all for helping people, but Papa, you're seventy years old. You retired three minutes ago. You gave up the only life you've ever known. Then you saw a grocery store flyer, and you made a split-second decision to spend fifteen thousand dollars on a six-week trip? Does none of this shout midlife crisis to you?"

He was past the midlife stage, but she couldn't bring herself to say end-of-life crisis. Surely, he had many good years left.

His scowl scalded her. "It's really none of your business what I do with my life and my money, Emira."

Her mouth parted. Tears burned the backs of her eyes. She was only trying to help. To keep him from making a colossal mistake he'd surely regret. But it he didn't want to hear it ... "Fine."

She pressed her lips together and ran her tongue over her teeth.

"Papa, they need your cwedit card." Teddy held out the phone. "For da blender."

Emira looked from her boy to where giant numbers flashed across the screen. "Did you push those numbers?"

He grinned and nodded. "I know all my numbers."

Kade rushed to the phone, apologized to the representative, and hung up.

"I think that's our cue to leave." Emira patted Kade's arm as she passed by him. "I'll get the baby."

She entered the kitchen to find Reagan in a high chair and Nana holding a bowl of something brown.

Emira froze. "Please tell me that's not ice cream."

"She's tickled pink."

Emira dropped her face into her hands. Out of everything that had happened, something as predictable as Nana dishing out ice cream would be her undoing.

Chapter Eight

1960

Susan fiddled with her purse strap as she entered the hotel room one Saturday evening two months after their courthouse marriage.

Floyd set down his newspaper and eyed her suspiciously. "What's wrong?"

"Wrong? Nothing." She attempted a smile, but it didn't hold.

"You're all fidgety. Something is wrong."

She expelled a breath and plopped onto the bed. "The rabbit died."

His mouth fell open as he ran a hand through his hair. "You're pregnant? You sure?"

"Pretty sure."

"Oh, boy."

She slapped his arm. "Is that a thing to say or what?"

He moved to wrap his arm around her. "I'm sorry. I'm happy, baby. Thrilled. But … we're going to have to tell our parents." He jumped up and paced. "I should probably ask your father for permission to marry you." He shoved his hands into his pockets. "I'll get your ring from the hawk. Put it in a nice box. I'll … I'll wear a tie."

She rubbed her temples. "Oh, Floyd. He's going to kill you."

"No." He sat next to her again. Taking her hands in his, he kissed her knuckles. "He's going to be thrilled to have me as a son-in-law. And to have a grandbaby. Think of it. He'll be tickled pink."

She chewed her lip. "I don't know."

"Trust me." He grinned for effect, but truth was, Mr. Sonjak might very well kill him, tie or not.

Floyd's knee shook as he ate his last bite of mashed potatoes and glanced next to him to where Mr. Sonjak dabbed his face with a napkin. Did the man ever smile? Not even a hint of one throughout the dinner, even when Floyd told of his clever trick to make money by turning in glass bottles from the back of the Tomboy shop.

His antics of finding the bottles near the shop's rear dumpster, then wheeling them inside to receive two cents per bottle, only to do it again an hour later when they put the bottles out back and the workers changed shifts earned a smirk from Susan but nothing of the kind from the parents. Tough crowd.

Even tougher when Mr. Sonjak casually asked him why he got fired from A&P. He expelled a nervous chuckle and forked a bite of corn into his mouth as a stalling tactic. Should he shoot straight with the man? Admit he'd been caught drinking wine on the job? Share that he used some mighty colorful language when a customer asked him where the bathrooms were? Better not. He had a feeling this man would not be amused.

He licked his lips. "I decided that wasn't the best ... career path for me."

Mr. Sonjak lifted an eyebrow. "And what, pray tell, *is* the best career path for you, Floyd?"

Floyd pointed his fork at the man. "I'm not quite sure, but when I find it, I'll let you know." Hopefully, he sounded confident. And competent. Like a man Mr. Sonjak would want as a son-in-law. He ate his last bite of corn, then angled his head toward Susan's mother. "Thank you for dinner, Mrs. Sonjak. It was delicious." Despite all efforts to stay calm, his voice squeaked. He wiped his sweaty palms on his dress slacks. "Mr. Sonjak, if I could have a word with you."

The man's frown deepened. He folded his hands on the table in front of him.

Floyd adjusted his tie to let more air into his tight throat.

Susan and her mother stood and took their empty plates from the table, disappearing into the kitchen.

Floyd sucked in a breath and leaned forward. "I'm sure you know how I feel about your daughter."

A low sound rumbled in Mr. Sonjak's throat.

Sweat beaded in between Floyd's shoulder blades. "I'm in love with her, sir. I want to ask for your permission to marry her."

Mr. Sonjak reared back, revulsion coating his expression. "Marry her? Are you crazy? You're too young. How would you intend on supporting her?"

The trembling spread to Floyd's arms and hands. Crazy. He thought them crazy. What would he think when he found out they were already wed? How *would* Floyd support not only Susan but a child? He stumbled for an answer. What would satisfy this man? "I get seventeen dollars a week in unemployment insurance."

Mr. Sonjak expelled a humorless laugh.

This was not going well.

"I love her, sir." Shouldn't that be enough? Wasn't love enough to overcome any obstacle?

Mr. Sonjak tossed his napkin on the table and stood. "Love doesn't pay the bills. Heck, you don't even know what love is. You're just a kid. My answer is no. My *final* answer." And with that, he trudged out of the room.

What now?

A week later, Floyd knocked on the Sonjaks' door, flowers in hand. Susan answered, face pale and shadows hanging under her eyes like half-moons. She must not have slept either. She stepped onto the front porch and wrung her hands. "Are you sure you want to do this?"

He pushed a weak smile to the surface. "We have to tell them. Got no other choice. Besides, how could it possibly go worse than last week?"

"I sure hope he doesn't kill you with his bare hands." She studied him fondly as if memorizing every detail of a loved one she might never see again. Then she stood on her tiptoes and kissed his cheek. Gesturing to the petunias he held, she asked, "Are those for me?"

He pulled them back slightly. "For your mom."

She nodded. "Good idea." As she turned to enter the house, she mumbled, "Doubt it will work, but good idea."

The stilted conversation around meatloaf and mashed potatoes did nothing to ease Floyd's nerves. They ricocheted around like a pinball in his favorite machine. He had to force down every bite. Finally, when he could stand it no longer, he blurted out the truth.

"Susan and I married at the courthouse two months ago."

The clinking of silverware ceased. Mr. Sonjak's wide eyes turned toward him and narrowed. "What did you say?"

He cleared his throat. "We're already married, sir." He nodded to Susan's mother, who had tears forming in her eyes. "Ma'am."

Mr. Sonjak clenched his fist. Better get the rest out quickly.

"And you're going to be grandparents. Isn't that great?" He tried for a smile. It wobbled.

Mr. Sonjak pounded the table, then reached for the bowl of mashed potatoes and flung a spoonful of them at Floyd. The white mushy goo landed across the buttons of his shirt and sank into his shirt pocket.

Mrs. Sonjak fled from the table in tears. The sound of the back door sliding open and shut indicated she'd taken her grief outside. Susan ran after her, leaving Floyd alone with her father.

Mr. Sonjak pinned Floyd with his glare. "How are you going to support a family? And don't give me anything about unemployment insurance. What are your plans? What career are you going into?"

Floyd's chest tightened. Career? He'd worked all his life. Caddying, setting up bowling pins at the lane, mowing lawns, carhopping, and then working at A&P until he got canned. But a career? At one time, he'd wanted to be a professional boxer. That dream had long died, leaving a bitter film in his mouth. After that, he had set his sights on becoming a priest. But he obviously couldn't cut it there.

Mr. Sonjak's eyes pulsed with fury as he waited for an answer.

What to say? What to do with his life? He needed to decide. Anything but a machinist like his dad. What about something run-of-the-mill? The man who cut his hair was a decent guy. Respected. Well-liked. A man Mr. Sonjak would approve of as a son-in-law.

"I'm going to become a barber." The words were out before Floyd had time to think through all the implications. A barber. Was that really what he wanted to do for the rest of his life?

"A barber, huh?" Mr. Sonjak sat back and scrubbed his jaw. "That's a decent profession." His thoughtful nod held approval. It was like a bright beam of sunshine warming the ground after days of drenching rain. Floyd basked in it.

"Yeah. I'm going to be a barber." Just like that, he'd charted his future course.

Mr. Sonjak shifted in his seat. "Barber school is difficult to get into."

It was? Worry slithered up Floyd's spine. He could not lose the favor he'd only now gained from this man. "I'll get in." He'd find a way. He had to.

"You get in and make your way as a barber, and you just might find yourself worthy of my daughter someday." He took a swig of lemonade and strode from the table, leaving Floyd alone with the backdrop of Mrs. Sonjak's sobs.

The debacle at Susan's house lasted longer than expected. When Mrs. Sonjak finally calmed down, the last bus had already run, leaving Floyd stranded. He had no choice but to call his folks to bum a ride home.

A mixed cocktail of emotions pulsed through his veins at the sight of his pop pulling up in the driveway. He wanted nothing to do with the man, yet everything in him grappled for a scrap of his affection. Of his respect. That was all his old man had ever given him: scraps. He was tired of begging. Gave up on that long ago. So why did old longings rise within him at seeing his dad's silhouette puffing on a cigarette?

He pecked his wife on the cheek, bidding her goodbye as her mother looked on, handkerchief at the ready. Then he ducked out the door and slid into the passenger's seat.

His dad eyed him for a minute before shifting into reverse. "Let's get a beer." Alcohol was the last thing his father needed, but Floyd could use a drink after tonight.

"Sure."

After the bartender slid beers onto the sticky counter, Pop turned to Floyd. "What's going on with you? You've been all secretive, sneaking around. Your mother can't get a thing out of you. She doesn't know where you've been going or what you've been doing. You've got her tied up in knots, praying the rosary a dozen times a day. What gives?"

In a dimly lit pub that smelled of stale cigarettes and cheap whisky, Floyd confessed his secret marriage to the father he'd never quite gotten to know. "Now she's pregnant. We just told her folks tonight. Didn't go well."

Pop whistled on an exhale. "You got yourself into a pickle." He took another gulp, then wiped his mouth with the back of his hand. "But don't worry about it. I can take care of it."

Take care of it? Did he mean … "No. I don't want you to take care of it. I love her. I want to be married to her, to spend the rest of my life with her."

Pop groaned and shook his head.

Floyd gripped his father's arm. "I love Susan. She's my wife. This is our child. I'm happy to be a father."

His voice tripped on the word *father*, betraying him. What did he know about being a father? The man next to him wasn't exactly the best role model.

Pop sighed and shook his head. "Okay, then. It's going to be hard, being as young as you are."

Floyd swallowed. "I know."

He'd have to stop wasting all his money on pinball and start saving it for diapers. He'd have to grow up, and quick. He could do that for Susan.

"Your mother's going to want you to have a church wedding. You know that, don't you? She's not going to put up with any of that courthouse nonsense."

"That's fine."

Maybe a proper wedding would mean a proper honeymoon as well. At least with their secret out in the open, they'd finally get to live under the same roof. Though who knew where that would be? His unemployment insurance wasn't enough to pay for rent. He turned his empty glass around on the bar. Things sure got complicated quickly.

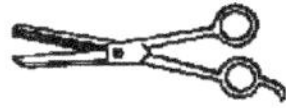

Floyd and Susan got married for the second time at Holy Trinity on July 1, his mother's birthday. It was a toss-up as to who cried harder, his mother or Susan's. Sobs and sniffles peppered the sanctuary. He chose to think it was because everyone was exceedingly happy for them. Best to go with that.

At least one person was thrilled. His sister Karen stood off to the side, snapping one picture after another. Her little scrapbooking hobby had gotten out of hand if you asked him, but since they had her support, he wouldn't complain. She'd gushed about gaining a new sister. Fine by him, as long as he got to live with his wife.

Susan's beauty took his breath away; her flowered tiara framed her forehead as if she were an angel flown straight from heaven. Her trim stomach proclaimed to the world that she was, in fact, not pregnant. The doctor had turned out to be a kook. The misdiagnosis had created a heap of drama, but this was the end result. Floyd's bride stood radiant before him in front of God, friends, and family. No need to hide anymore. He could kiss the doc.

After he kissed his wife.

They were finally going to get a real honeymoon. After the reception, they'd be off to Lake of the Ozarks for a weekend all to themselves. He twirled his finger, gesturing for the priest to get on with the ceremony already.

When they were finally proclaimed man and wife—again—he placed a smacker on his bride that made his sisters giggle and his mother blush. The weight of sneaking around for months sloughed off his shoulders. They were free to be man and wife without judgment, nothing holding them back. He couldn't wait to start their new life together under the same roof, in Susan's parents' house.

He dug a finger under his collar and sucked in a sharp breath. It'd be fine. Great, even. Why, Mr. Sonjak might even be starting to like him. Almost. And so what if Mrs. Sonjak insisted on taking his entire seventeen dollars a week of unemployment for *upkeep*? As soon as he started barber school in a couple of weeks, he'd be making tips. Plus, she was an excellent cook. He'd at least eat well under their roof. As long as no one threw the food *at* him again, it'd be a grand life.

His parents hosted the reception in their yard. Nostalgia overcame Floyd as friends and family fellowshipped not too far from where he'd participated in those legendary boxing matches. He glanced up at the room he'd always shared with his brother Rich. The house held good memories of the six siblings. A mighty fine childhood full of sparks of imagination and ingenuity. Now, he was starting down a new path, the one that would take him into his adult life. What would it hold?

When the festivities wound down, Floyd hopped into his gray Ford-O-Matic and honked the horn. Susan hugged her mother and sister, then slipped into the passenger's seat.

"Ready for our honeymoon?" Floyd waggled his eyebrows.

"Am I ever." She beamed at him.

Mr. Sonjak caught Floyd's eye from his spot on the lawn, his expression serious. Floyd rolled down his window. "Have a good evening, Mr. Sonjak."

"Take good care of her." His voice hung heavy with authority.

"I will, sir." Why couldn't he keep his voice from shaking around this man? His hand trembled as he rolled up the window, and then he nearly ran into the mailbox.

Susan put her hand over his. "Don't worry. He loves you."

Sure, he did. But Floyd shrugged off his nerves and focused on the glorious weekend ahead. "I know."

They'd barely made it onto the highway when a clanking sound erupted from the engine. Smoke billowed out of the hood. Floyd pulled over, waving a hand in front of his face and coughing.

"Oh, great." Susan folded her arms around herself and huffed. She sliced a glare his way.

"Well, it's not my fault."

"It's your car."

"I didn't mean for it to break down."

Erupting into more coughs, he pounded his chest.

She let out a dramatic sigh. "I guess you're going to have to call my dad."

Oh, no. There was no way he'd call Mr. Sonjak. Not when he'd just promised to take care of Susan. Within twenty minutes of being handed the reins, they were stranded on the side of the highway. He'd get more than mashed potatoes thrown at him this time.

"I'll call my dad." His stomach sank at the pronouncement, but it was better than the alternative. His pop hadn't been there for him as a father should, but the man knew a thing or two about cars. He could handle this. Something practical and emotionless. Something he could diagnose and fix.

Vehicles whooshed past them, blowing at Susan's wedding dress, leaving a layer of dust on the gown. Cars honked and people leaned out of their windows to see the spectacle of the newlyweds trudging down the highway. Sizzling heat pushed down on them, and he offered Susan his handkerchief to dab her sweaty brow. After about a mile, they reached a filling station with a pay phone.

When he hung up with his pop, he turned to her, scrubbing the back of his neck. "Looks like we won't be going to the lake." His shoulders sagged in time with hers. He attempted to brighten his tone. "But Pop said he'd drop us off at a hotel. We can stay three whole days."

Her frown didn't waver. "All right."

No one said much as Pop drove them to the hotel.

"I'll have your car towed," Pop mumbled, cigarette in his mouth. "And I'll pick you up in three days."

How embarrassing to need his parent to pick him up from his honeymoon. Floyd's neck heated as he pulled their bags from the trunk. "Thanks, Pop."

"Yeah." The old man nodded and drove off.

"Some start to our new life together." Susan huffed and hefted a bag onto her shoulder.

"Let me get that for you." Floyd reached to take it from her, and she reared back, evading his grasp. "I can carry my own things. I'm not incompetent." She stomped toward their room.

"I never said ..." He tripped over his own foot as he tried to catch up. "I didn't mean ..."

He was only trying to be a gentleman. Wasn't that what every woman wanted?

As they neared the room, he pulled out the key but hesitated. Should he open the door for her? Or would she yell at him for it? She'd left her knife at home, right?

Her mouth twisted as she eyed him. "What are you waiting for?"

He gulped and looked at the door, then at her, then back at the door. "Should I open it?"

"Of course, you doofus. Would you rather stand here all day?"

Good point. He nestled the key into the lock and swung open the door for his bride. Wait, shouldn't he carry her over the threshold? But she was already barreling through the door. Maybe next time.

The next day, Floyd called his father from the hotel lobby. "Hey, Pop, can you come pick me up?"

Pop snorted. The sound of machinery filtered through the background. "You want me to pick you'se up? Something wrong with the hotel?"

Floyd turned away from the front counter, tugging at the phone cord to give him some leeway. "I don't need you to pick up both of us. Just me. We got into a squabble."

"Already?"

Floyd scuffed his shoe on the burgundy carpet. "Yeah. She kicked me out of the room. Said she'd finish her honeymoon alone."

"What'd you do?" Pop's voice held accusation. As if Floyd was the one in the wrong and not his crazy wife.

His cheeks heated. "Nothing. I was just watching Miss America is all."

A groan came across the phone line as the concierge behind the hotel counter gasped, then looked quickly away.

"There's no need for Susan to be jealous. She knows I think she's the prettiest girl in all the States. Even better looking than Miss Mississippi."

The concierge mumbled under her breath.

Floyd covered the phone receiver. "What'd you say?"

She hesitated but a moment before squaring her shoulders. "Then why were you looking at Miss Mississippi in a swimsuit instead of paying attention to your new wife?"

Floyd's mouth parted. "None of your business." He turned his back to the nosey lady and uncovered the phone. "Anyway, Pop, will you pick me up? And can I stay at home until she cools off?"

"I'll be there in an hour." As Floyd went to hang up the phone, his father muttered, "Been married less than twenty-four hours."

He dropped into a chair in the lobby and ran his hand through his hair. "Been married for four months." Four months and this was only their first big fight. That wasn't bad, was it? Not as bad as it seemed. Thank God she'd left her knife at home.

Chapter Nine

1990

Emira's stomach squeezed tight as Mom hung up the phone with tears in her eyes. Mom didn't cry in front of her. Not hardly ever.

"What's wrong?"

Mom's voice shook. "Nana's in the hospital." She swiped at her cheeks. "They need to run some tests. But she's fine. I'm sure she'll be fine." Her smile didn't fool Emira. It wobbled all over the place.

"What kind of tests?" Images of scantron sheets with bubbles to fill in and number two pencils filled her mind, which was silly, of course. They didn't do those kinds of tests in hospitals. But what kind *did* they do?

"They found—" Mom cleared her throat, then tried again. "They found something wrong in her blood. It looked like it could be leukemia, which is a kind of cancer. But they don't know that for sure. They don't know anything for sure yet." She took a deep breath and pushed back her shoulders. "Grab a book or something. We're going to the hospital, and we might be there awhile."

Questions tumbled about in Emira's brain. What was cancer? Leukemi-what? She couldn't imagine reading with her insides all topsy-turvy, but she grabbed a Berenstain Bears book and a Baby-Sitters Club one too. Maybe Mom's words were more right than her face was. Maybe it was nothing. The doctors would do tests and find out Nana was fine. They'd all go home, and Nana would serve them ice cream. They'd laugh about how they'd gotten all worked up over nothing.

When they entered the hospital, Emira wrinkled her nose at the funny smell. It reminded her of the old folks' home, only it stung her nose even worse. They passed a gift shop with brightly colored balloons glimmering in the window. She tugged on Mom's hand. "Can we get Nana one?"

"Maybe later. We don't even know if she's sick. She might not stay."

So, Emira should hope Nana never got one of the pretty balloons. That made sense. She hurried to keep up with Mom's big steps. Once they had gone up the elevator, down a long hallway, and asked about Nana at a desk, they finally found her room. Emira hesitated outside. What if Nana was hooked up to tubes? What if she looked pale and old like some of her customers? What if she smelled funny like the hospital?

Mom nudged her from behind. "Go ahead. It's okay."

She stepped into the room to find the bed empty. Papa sat in a chair next to the bed, the lines on his forehead deep enough to drive a toy car through. She scanned the tidy room. Where was Nana?

As if Papa could read her mind, he grumbled, "She's in the bathroom." He rubbed the back of his neck. "She's cleaning the bathroom."

Mom spit out a laugh. Even Emira couldn't help but smile at that. Cleaning the hospital bathroom? Didn't Nana know that wasn't her job?

"Maybe you can get her to sit down, Marie. She won't listen to me. Been fluttering around here like she's the cleaning lady, scrubbing 'til it sparkles. Had some antibacterial wipes in her purse."

Emira scooted another chair next to Papa and sat, taking his large hand in hers. He squeezed it and tossed her a small smile before focusing on the bathroom door.

"Mom, come sit," Emira's mom called into the bathroom while she smoothed the blanket on the hospital bed.

Papa shifted in his chair. "Yeah, Susan, would you quit that and come out here?"

Nana came out with a wipe in her hand. "Just freshening up the place. You never know who had this room before me."

"I'm sure they clean it in between patients." Mom gave the bed a big pat.

Nana tsked. "I don't trust them."

Nana wore navy slacks and a silky blouse. Her hair and makeup made her look perfectly fine. As if it was just any other day.

"They didn't make you wear hospital clothes?" Emira asked.

Papa crossed his arms. "She refused."

Nana punched a hand on her hip. "I'm not going to wear one of those ugly gowns."

"Oh, Mom."

"She wouldn't keep an IV in either."

"I don't need one of those stupid things. I'm fine."

Mom leaned forward and patted the bed as if begging Nana to sit. "You have to let them put in an IV. What if you need fluids or intravenous medication?"

Nana shook her head. "Oh, there's no way in Hades they're touching my veins again."

"Susan!" Papa looked like a volcano about to explode. "You have to cooperate. You might have cancer."

She waved her wipe around. "When it's my time to go, the Good Lord will take me, and that's that. I'm going to go on my terms, and no nurse is going to tell me I can't have a smoke while I do it."

"She about pushed one of them to the ground when they tried to take her cigarettes." Papa rubbed his forehead.

"They best keep their hands to themselves." Nana whipped the wipe in the air as if it were a sword. This was who Emira had wanted to buy a Get Well balloon for?

Papa pointed at Nana. "What am I going to do with her?"

"Do with me? You don't have to do a thing with me except get me out of here." She scanned the room. "There's nothing left to clean."

Yep. The whole room sparkled like in a commercial.

"Knock, knock." A nurse entered the room and headed straight for the blood-pressure cuff attached to the wall. "Time to recheck vitals."

Nana rolled her eyes.

"Mrs. Douglas, I need you to return to the bed."

Nana's eyes turned into slits. "I keep telling you I'm fine. There's no need to squeeze my arm half to death."

The nurse stared her down. "Are you going to cooperate, or do I need to get a couple more nurses to help again?"

"That won't be necessary." A doctor in a white coat stepped into the room. He looked as if he was straight from TV with his shiny white teeth and dimple. "This beautiful young lady was right about to lay down for me, weren't you, Mrs. Douglas?"

Emira giggled. What a silly doctor. But Nana gave a single nod and scooted into bed, leaning back onto her pillow.

"I'll take it from here," the doctor told the nurse, who didn't look sad to leave.

"Now Mrs. Douglas," the doctor said as he slid the cuff around her arm, "I have some good news and some bad news. I was only mildly concerned at the results of one of the tests. The other, however ... let's just say I don't like the look of those numbers. We're going to need to keep you here a couple of days and run some more tests."

Nana frowned but didn't complain. She wiggled her fingers around, though, which meant she wanted a cigarette. Would they let her go outside to smoke at least?

The doctor talked on and on about blood count and wanting numbers to go up or down. What did it all mean? It couldn't be good. Nana was like a turtle ducking back into her shell. Both Mom's and Papa's foreheads bunched up as they listened. Their nods didn't wipe away their frowns.

When the doctor left, Nana looked small and breakable, and Papa looked heavy. His shoulders rose and sagged slowly with his breaths.

"Maybe you could take Emira to get a candy bar." He had to have been saying this to Mom, but he didn't take his eyes off Nana.

"Yeah, okay." Mom stood and took Emira's hand. "We'll be back in a bit."

Mom's steps dragged as if she was tired, but she was probably just sad. Both her and Papa's eyes looked sad. Emira swirled her tongue around in her mouth, trying to gather the courage to push her questions out. What did the doctor's words mean? What were blood counts? What was wrong with Nana's blood? How were they going to fix it? But when Mom didn't say any words, Emira kept hers behind her teeth. Maybe it was better not to know the answers.

In the hallway, they passed a few people in wheelchairs and a lady carrying a balloon and flowers. Then they went down an elevator and another hallway to a snack machine.

"What do you want?" Mom asked.

Emira pointed to M&M'S.

It only took a minute for the machine to spit out her candy and for them to head back the way they'd come. Her shoes squeaked loudly on the floor, or maybe it only seemed loud because there was no talking to cover it up. How weird to be so quiet when her brain kept yelling questions. Nana wouldn't *die*, would she? No. She couldn't. She'd said she was fine, and Nana didn't lie.

A nurse waited outside Nana's open door. She peeked through the doorway but didn't enter. Mom and Emira slowed as they came near.

The nurse startled, then whispered, "Oh, sorry. I need to start an IV, but I wanted to give them a minute." She peeked back in before giving Mom a sad smile. "You know what, I'll just come back in a few."

Give them a minute? A minute to what? Mom didn't move but Emira tiptoed toward the doorway. What she saw made her chest burn. Papa still sat next to Nana's bed holding her hand. He was hunched over, and his shoulders shook with sobs.

Papa was crying? How could it be possible for her giant of a grandfather to cry like that? Like he was a broken little boy in need of a hug. Oh, Papa. She might break along with him. She could not bear to see him like this. An itchy feeling wriggled inside her. This was so unlike the grandpa she knew.

"Susan, I love you so much." His words dripped out of him, each one like a tear itself. "I don't know what I'd do without you."

Emira gasped as she saw something for the first time. He loved Nana. Papa *loved* Nana. He didn't just put up with her. He didn't just not leave. Though she'd never seen the two of them kiss or make moony eyes at each other, here and now, it was clear that Papa's heart was breaking because Nana's body might be. Nana was his heart.

She understood now why the nurse let them be, why she, too, should join Mom in the hallway and let Papa cry without anyone watching. Only she couldn't make herself look away. It was so different, so beautiful, and it was as if the ground was wobbling underneath her, and yet she was as steady as she'd ever been. Because Papa had told her the truth when he'd given Nana the lightbulbs.

Real love looked like lightbulbs, at least sometimes.

Maybe Papa knew a lot more than just how to cut hair. Maybe he knew about love too. About how to love someone so they'd stay. She gulped in a breath at the realization. She needed to know that too. Needed it now before Dad left her for good.

She could follow Papa around and take notes. Find out his secret. She nodded to herself as he wiped his eyes with his sleeve. She'd make it her mission to figure out what Papa knew about love.

Papa held Nana's hand as the nurse poked an IV into her arm. Nana winced but didn't fight the lady. Maybe all her fight had fizzled out for the day. Emira hadn't even read a whole chapter in her book before Nana fell asleep.

Papa's sigh sounded long and tired. "I'm going to head down to the cafeteria and get something to eat."

Emira popped up from her seat. "I'll come too." She moved her bookmark to the right page and set it on her chair. "Let's go." She didn't have a journal to take notes, but she could remember whatever she learned from him today and write it down later.

"I'll stay with her," Mom said with a nod to Nana. "Can you bring me back a salad?"

"Sure." With an oomph, Papa stood and shuffled to the door.

Emira followed at his heels.

Papa paused at the doorway and looked at Nana. His shoulders sagged. His face bunched as if he was in pain. But then he walked on and seemed to sigh out that sadness because he offered her a soft smile. "Hungry, Princess?"

"Sure." She wasn't really, but she could eat if she needed to, and she needed to be with him.

They made their way through the line at the cafeteria. "Don't let me forget to get your mom a salad before we leave." Papa grabbed a hamburger and fries, and she did the same, only Papa loaded his with onions, pickles, and mushrooms. Yuck. They settled at a table. Papa dug into his burger while Emira twirled a fry in ketchup.

"She's going to be okay. She's a fighter." Was Papa talking to her or himself?

Emira nodded anyway, just in case. "She's funny. Cleaning the hospital."

He chuckled. "Yeah. She's got spunk. You've got to give her that."

Papa's gaze roamed to something over Emira's head. She turned around to see what he was looking at. There was nothing there. Just a man eating at another table. Not even a TV on the wall to watch. "What are you looking at?"

"That man's eating alone." Papa frowned.

So what? Papa would be eating alone if she hadn't insisted on joining him. Papa's chair scraped the floor as he scooted it back and stood.

"Where are you going?" They'd just gotten there. Emira hadn't even taken a bite of her burger.

He held up a finger. "Hold on just a minute."

Emira slowly chomped another fry as Papa approached the man at the table. Their voices were low and muffled, so she couldn't make out what they said. This didn't make sense. Why was her grandpa talking with a stranger? A minute later, Papa returned. Good. Now she could get back to investigating him.

But he didn't sit down. Instead, he took his tray. "Come on, Princess. We're going to move over there."

She scrambled to her feet but didn't move to follow. "You want to eat with that stranger?"

"Yes, I do. Hate to see him eating alone."

Making her eyes big and pleading, she dropped her voice. "We don't even know him."

"That's about to change."

He left her staring with her mouth open and sat down at the man's table. Part of her wanted to plop back down in her spot and eat by herself until Papa changed his mind and came back. But what if he didn't? He might choose that man over her. And that would make her a terrible investigator. If she wanted to take notes on what Papa knew that she didn't, she had to stick by him. With a groan, she dragged her feet to the seat next to him and slouched into it.

Papa smiled at her as if pleased she'd come over. "Princess, this is Vince. Vince, this is my granddaughter, Emira."

Vince's eyes widened. "That's a pretty name." Though he said pretty, he looked like he meant strange.

"My mom's name is Marie. It's her name all mixed up. It means Princess. That's why Papa calls me that all the time."

"Ah." He nodded, his smile finally sparkling in his eyes. "Very pretty." This time, he probably meant it.

Papa turned his attention fully to Vince and asked about some lady named Norma. It took a while, but Emira finally put the pieces together. Norma was Vince's wife, and she had some kind of cancer. She was in the hospital for surgery, but the doctors didn't know if that would fix her or not. Vince fiddled with the chips on his plate but never popped one into his mouth. Papa didn't say much. He asked a few questions but mostly listened. Emira nearly jumped in and said Papa's wife was upstairs sick too, but the way Papa nodded along with Vince's story made her pause. Was there a reason Papa didn't want to talk about Nana?

Vince pushed his full plate away from him. "I'd better get back up there. See if there's an update."

"Of course."

The men stood and shook hands.

Vince picked up his plate and took a step toward the trash can. "Thanks for keeping me company."

Papa waved before sitting back down. "I'll be praying for you."

Vince nodded the tiniest bit, and then he was gone.

Emira eyed Papa as he dug into his burger. "Are you really going to pray for him?"

Papa wiped his mouth with a napkin. "Of course. I wouldn't say it if I didn't mean it."

Interesting. But all people weren't like Papa, were they? People said things they didn't mean all the time. Like Dad telling Mom he'd always be married to her on the video Emira often watched of their wedding day. You couldn't trust what people said. Still, the thought that maybe sometimes you *could* wrapped around her like a blanket.

Something else bothered her, though. She'd sat by herself in the school cafeteria plenty of times, waiting for someone to join her. To make her feel wanted. To *see* her. And yet ... "I didn't even see that man. How did you see him?"

Papa shrugged and pointed to the man's empty seat. "He was right there."

That didn't help. There were lots of things that were "right there" that she couldn't seem to see. The ketchup in the refrigerator. Her shoes when they were in a hurry. Her overdue library books.

Her face must have told him his answer wasn't good enough. He tried again. "Maybe God gives me eyes to see what He wants me to see so I can love the people around me."

She bit her lip. God helped Papa see important things— see people—so he could love? "Do you think God would help me to see too?"

Papa smiled the biggest he had all day. "Sure. If you ask Him."

Emira didn't waste a moment before doing just that.

Chapter Ten

2010

Emira pulled into the arrival lane at the airport and texted her father. Hopefully, he was ready and waiting because Reagan did not usually remain asleep when the car idled. A peek in the rearview mirror showed Teddy zonked out with his head slumped to the side, mouth gaping open. So sweet. If only Dad's flight hadn't been scheduled during naptime. This afternoon was sure to be interesting.

Dad emerged from a throng of pedestrians, rolling a single large suitcase. A canvas bag hung from his shoulder. He looked … older than she remembered. His hair had thinned. His already thin frame had lost additional weight. These were probably changes one only noticed when there was a gap in time between seeing a person. Loss sidled up next to her, a familiar companion when it came to her father.

She waved. His eyes lit when he saw her, and he headed in her direction. She pressed the button to open the trunk. She should probably get out and hug him, but opening her door might wake Reagan, whose car seat sat on her side of the van.

Dad loaded his suitcase, then climbed in the passenger's seat, dropping his carry-on at his feet. "Hey, kiddo." His voice boomed overloud in the quiet space.

She fought the urge to cringe. "Hi, Dad," she whispered. Hopefully, he'd get the hint.

He twisted around in his seat. "Teddy, my boy." He seemed oblivious to the fact his grandson was sleeping.

Teddy shifted in his seat, blinking open drowsy eyes. Wonderful.

"And this must be Reagan." Dad pulled back the blanket covering the baby.

"Please don't wake her. She'll be crabby."

"Oh, she'll be so happy to see her grandpa."

Not likely. Reagan was in full stranger danger mode, and Dad was a complete stranger to her. Emira's chest burned. How could that be? Everything about this situation felt wrong, but she forced a smile and merged into traffic.

Dad reached into his canvas bag. "I brought something for you." He pulled out a CD and peeled the plastic wrapping off.

She tried to make out the artist from the corner of her eye but failed. "What is it?"

"Your favorite."

How would Dad know who her favorite singer was? "Kari Jobe?"

"No." He frowned. "Margaret Becker."

"Oh." She'd forgotten about her. That'd been so long ago.

Dad ejected the Hermie and Wormie CD and inserted the one he'd brought. As soulful music played, memories crashed over her. Dad sang along, quietly at first, but with more gusto at the chorus. Emira winced at the rustling behind her. Just as she feared, Reagan whimpered and then let out a soft cry.

"It's okay. It's all right, baby," she cooed. Hopefully, her voice would reassure her daughter. How frightening to be jarred awake by a strange man's voice.

"Aw, sweetie. It's okay. I'm your grandpa." Dad reclined his seat so she could get a better look at him. A bloodcurdling wail ricocheted through the enclosed space.

Emira turned the music down and gently shushed her daughter. How could she get her dad to stop scaring

Reagan without hurting his feelings? "It might take her a while to warm up to you. She's at that stage."

He grunted as he straightened his seat. After a few minutes of reassurance, Reagan calmed back down to a whimper.

Dad angled toward her. "Hey, I didn't get a chance to have lunch. Let's go out. My treat."

She eyed Teddy, who had fallen back asleep. "That's a nice idea, but how about a rain check? I can go through a drive-thru and grab something for you, though."

"Oh, come on. I was thinking we could go to the food court at the mall, then spend some time at the arcade, just like old times." He elbowed her good-naturedly. "I'll beat you at Skee-Ball."

Was he crazy? She wasn't a child anymore but a mother. She couldn't drag a toddler and an infant to an arcade in the middle of nap time. What a disaster that would be. Besides ... "That arcade shut down years ago. Maybe sometime during your visit we could go to Dave and Buster's while Kade stays home with the kids."

He slumped in his seat. "Yeah. Sounds good."

After a minute of awkward silence, Emira was about to jump out of her skin. She asked about his flight, the weather in Wisconsin, and his job. After each question, she waited a beat to see if he would reciprocate, but he didn't. Apparently, he didn't wonder about her. Perhaps he figured he knew all he needed to know.

When she neared an intersection full of restaurants, she asked where he wanted her to stop.

"How about Long John Silver's? That was our place, you and me."

She forced another smile. She hadn't been to the restaurant in over a decade, but yes, if Dad and her hadn't ordered a pizza, they'd dined at Long John Silver's. She pulled through the drive-thru, and he ordered two three-piece fish meals.

She raised a brow. "Hungry?"

"Always."

That much hadn't changed. His appetite had ever been voracious.

When the worker handed her the food, she passed it to Dad. The smell of fish flooded the van. She'd have to breathe through her mouth so she didn't gag.

He set one of the boxes on the center console. "This one's for you."

She blinked at it. "Oh." She opened her mouth to say more, but what? She should thank him, of course. But should she mention she no longer ate fish? That the very thought of consuming any kind of seafood obliterated her appetite? "Thanks, but I already ate." Hours ago, but still.

"You can save it for later. It's your favorite."

She squirmed in her seat. Her favorite. He kept using that word as if people didn't change over the years. As if she was still a little girl. Maybe in his eyes, she was. If she didn't set him straight now, he might spend three weeks dragging her to seafood restaurants and arcades.

She kept her voice gentle. "Actually, Dad, I don't like fish anymore."

He paused midchew, looking stricken. He finished his bite slowly, then wiped his mouth with a napkin. "No fish, huh?" How could such a small confession hurt him so? "What, are you a vegetarian?"

"Hardly." She patted his arm. "We can get meat-lovers pizza tonight if you want."

Was that still his go-to?

"Yeah. Sure." But he slumped in his seat. Wounded. Disappointed.

"I will eat those hushpuppies. I've missed those." She scooped one out and bit into it. Ew. It tasted of fish, or perhaps that was the smell tricking her taste buds as she'd temporarily forgotten her mouth-breathing-only rule. Still, she faked a pleased sound and nodded. "I'll save the other one for later."

He finished off his meal with much less gusto, the silence stretching between them like Silly Putty. This was going to be a long few weeks if something didn't change. She needed to break the silence with conversation, but it seemed as if trigger wires hid everywhere. What could she bring up that wouldn't traverse into painful territory?

Dad spoke first. "I need a haircut. I was going to get one before traveling, but I thought it'd be a good excuse to see Papa. How about stopping by the shop?"

The pang of loss hit her again. "There is no more shop." She forced a swallow down her suddenly tight throat. "Papa retired. Sold it."

"What?" The incredulity lacing his voice gave her a sliver of comfort. She wasn't the only one. "When?"

"Recently." She pressed her lips together and inhaled deeply. She would not cry about this again. "He made a rather sudden decision. Took us by surprise."

Well, at least it took *her* by surprise. Mom and Uncle Joseph seemed nonplussed. Apparently, no one except her had such a connection to the place.

"Well, then." He sighed. "I guess I'll have to settle for Great Clips."

Ugh. She would too. Next time she needed a haircut, she'd have to go to an impersonal chain and make small talk with a stranger. Not her idea of a fun or relaxing time. Maybe she could find another family-owned salon and develop a relationship with her stylist. That was better, at least. Not the same as sitting in Nana's chair, but better.

"What's he going to do with all his free time?" Dad asked.

"At first, he said he'd relax."

Dad chuckled. At least he remembered Papa accurately.

"Then he got this crazy idea to go on a mission trip to Haiti. He spent fifteen thousand dollars already, and he'll be gone for six weeks."

"Wow." Dad nodded as if impressed. "Good for him."

"Good for him? What about this plan is good? It's insane. He's seventy years old. He's leaving Nana alone for a month and a half to go to a dangerous country and spending his retirement money to do it."

"Haiti's not too dangerous. I've been there. It'll be a great opportunity for him. Everyone should get out and see the world."

Her jaw dropped as she cast a glance at him. "You've been to Haiti? When?"

"A couple of years ago. For business." He took his glasses off and wiped them with his shirt. "I've been to lots of places. Norway. Paris. Sweden. Argentina. Nicaragua. Australia once." He replaced his glasses. "Oh, Kenya."

"You're kidding me." Her dad was a world traveler? How could she have not known this?

"I get free tickets to the Summer Olympics since my company creates the paint used for the diving boards. Beijing was something else." He gave her knee an amiable slap. "You should go with me to London in 2012."

Her mind swirled. The man next to her was a stranger. He no longer knew her, and she for sure didn't know him.

Papa called Emira later that afternoon, giving her the perfect excuse to escape the house.

"Hey, Princess, did you find that suitcase?"

"No." From the kitchen, she eyed her dad's attempt to get Teddy to warm up to him with a game of peekaboo. "But let's go to the store tonight and buy you one. I'll pick you up at six thirty."

"Are you sure? Didn't your dad just get into town?"

"Yeah, but it's fine. It'll give him a chance to bond with the kids."

The excuse rang lame in her ears. Teddy and Reagan would be in bed by seven thirty, leaving Kade to entertain Dad. She should run the idea by her husband, at least. But after three hours with her father, she needed a break.

"If you're sure." His voice dripped with skepticism. "I can buy my own suitcase."

"I know you can, but I want to spend time with you before you leave." It wasn't a lie.

"See you at six thirty."

Guilt prickled, but why should it? Dad would stay with them for three weeks. Three weeks. Lord, help her. He'd held Reagan like a China doll while she squalled in his arms. Teddy still wouldn't come within four feet of him. Her children were leery. They seemed to know what she hadn't explicitly said, but what her core still testified to be true. Her father wasn't safe. Not emotionally. He'd never intentionally hurt anyone, and yet he left wounded ones in his wake.

She clamped her arms around her middle. This whole thing had been a bad idea.

Papa leaned over to inspect the tag on the suitcase. "High-quality polycarbonate shell. Virtually unbreakable. What do you think?"

Emira shrugged. "Do you like those hard kind? I prefer the polyester ones myself. Plus, this one's half the price."

Papa grunted. "Price doesn't matter."

Said the man who'd wanted to borrow a suitcase so he wouldn't have to purchase one. "No use spending money if you don't have to." She unzipped the polyester case. Plenty of room. Several compartments. Sturdy.

"How's your dad?"

Way to change the subject. She blew a stray hair from her face. "Fine." He should be the one shopping for suitcases with Papa. With all his travel experience, he'd likely know better than she. "Dad asked to go by the shop to get a haircut. I had to break the news to him. He was shocked."

Papa knocked against the hard shell as if to prove the case was unbreakable. "Bring him by the house. I can cut his hair there. I put a stylist's chair in the basement and have all my tools down there."

She squinted over at him. "Really?"

She'd known he wasn't ready to give up barbering. He'd only moved locations. Perhaps he could still cut hair on the side. Was that legal without a business license?

"Sure. I'd be happy to give him a cut. He's family."

Not truly. Not to her grandpa. Not anymore. But of course, Papa would never cut someone off just because of a pesky technicality like divorce papers. "Sure. Okay." The two of them could chat it up about adventures in world traveling. It would be great. She rolled her eyes.

Papa startled, then reached over and grabbed her hand. "Let's look at something in the next aisle."

"What?"

He dragged her away from the suitcases, and they now stared at irons and ironing boards. His feigned interest in fabric steamers didn't fool her.

She crossed her arms. "What was that about?"

"Hmm?" He trailed a finger along a price tag.

"Why'd you run away from the suitcases?"

He scoffed, then whispered, "I didn't run away."

She leaned close. "Who are you hiding from?"

He glanced over her shoulder. "The priest."

She spit out a laugh. "Priest? What priest?"

He shushed her, then hooked his thumb in the direction they'd come from. She had to get a better look. She moseyed around the corner, lightly touching luggage as she walked. Sure enough, an older-looking man in full vestment studied something on the endcap.

She came back to Papa. "What's the story?"

"He invited me to dinner, but I never showed up. I threw away his number."

"You're not making any sense. Why would a priest invite you to dinner?"

"No idea. He showed up at the shop one day. Talked all cryptic. Strange." He fingered a laundry basket. She fought back a smile at the irony of her grandpa hiding out in the laundry aisle. If Nana could see him now.

"You're not the least bit curious?"

"Sure, I am, but …" He rubbed his belly. "What would we even talk about? Seminary was a lifetime ago."

She pressed her lips together. "I'm going to find answers."

She spun around and made a beeline toward the mysterious man, ignoring Papa's whispered pleas to wait and stop.

The man looked up as she neared.

"Father?" She should have asked Papa the priest's name.

"Yes? Can I help you?"

She also should have formed a game plan before ambushing this man of God. She had to think quickly. "Do you know Floyd Douglas, by chance?"

His face lit up. "Floyd! Why, yes. Yes, I do. Fine man."

"He's my grandpa."

He grinned, causing his wrinkles to bunch together. "You must be Emira."

A shiver prickled her spine. "Yes. How'd you know?"

"Oh, I keep track."

She backed up a step. Could he be a stalker or serial killer posing as a priest? His frail frame proclaimed otherwise. Teddy could probably beat him in a fight.

"How is Floyd? We were going to have dinner together. He must have lost my number."

"Must have." Her face heated with the lie. What was she doing fibbing to a priest?

"Could you give it to him, dear?"

"Oh. Sure." She pulled her phone from her back pocket. "I'll put you in my contacts. That way we won't lose your number."

"Good." He rattled off the digits, and she entered them under *Priest*. Now it would be awkward when Papa didn't call. Not her problem.

"How do you know my grandpa?" Her insides squirmed with the question, though no telling why.

He rocked on his heels, a soft smile teasing his lips. "We go way back."

Strange. If that was true, why didn't Papa say so? And why avoid him? "You met in seminary?"

The priest angled his head to the side. "You could say that."

She peered at him. What kind of answer was that? She'd asked a yes or no question. Papa had said the priest was cryptic. He hadn't lied. No wonder Papa didn't want to spend an evening talking with him. Though the older man seemed harmless, his strange words gave her the creeps. Had she made a mistake?

She backed farther away. "Well, it was nice talking to you. I'd better go."

"Nice talking with you as well, Emira. Give your grandpa my number."

"Will do." But she doubted he'd call. And she didn't blame him.

Chapter Eleven

1960

In the fall, after Floyd's second wedding, Pop proved good for more than rides to and from the honeymoon. The old man also knew a guy who knew a guy who got Floyd into barber school, bypassing the three-year-long waitlist. Suddenly, Floyd had more responsibility than setting up bowling pins, dishing out hamburgers, or checking out customers. For six months—one thousand hours—he learned about his new profession. The instructor handed his nervous fingers a pair of scissors and a clipper.

After hours of training and some practice on mannequins, the instructor let the students loose to try their skills out on low-income customers, many of them homeless. Those customers weren't paying enough to be too picky.

It was just a normal day at barber school when one such man sat in Floyd's chair and asked for a cut. His thick, matted hair crested his shoulders. A dark beard and mustache framed his face. Floyd turned the man away from the mirror and went to work.

The man's hair was so thick the comb got stuck when he tried to brush through it. Eventually, he gave up on that. He'd cut the tangles out. No need to comb it first. Only it took some muscle behind the scissors to get them to cut. Floyd clenched his jaw as he worked through the straggly mess.

Beside him, his buddy Stan whistled as he clipped and trimmed. On his other side, another student chatted politely with his customer. Floyd seemed to be the only one having trouble. Wasn't that always the case? He let out a soft grunt as he finally made headway, and a chunk of dark hair floated to the floor. The next patch proved just as difficult, however. He had to really clamp down on the scissors.

When he did, the man yelped and flinched. A small piece of flesh flipped into the air like a tiddlywink and landed on the floor. Floyd's eyes went wide as dark red blood gurgled from the tip of the man's ear. He looked from the blood to the floor.

He'd cut the man's ear off!

The customer wrestled with the cape, apparently attempting to free his hand. Floyd couldn't let the guy touch his ear and come away with a bloody hand.

Floyd patted the man's arm, reassuringly. "Don't you worry. It seems I've nicked your ear a tiny bit. Just relax and I'll get it taken care of."

The customer sucked air through his teeth while Floyd's head pounded, and his thoughts raced. What to do? What to do? His training hadn't exactly prepared him for this. Only … what had they said about cuts and scrapes? Talcum powder. That was it. He needed to apply talcum powder.

He pulled out his tube and poured the entire thing on the man's ear, which now spouted like a water fountain. The powder did little to contain the flow. He turned to Stan at the next chair. "Can I use your talcum powder? I got a little cut here."

"Sure." Stan didn't even look his way as he handed it over. The buzz of conversation and clippers must have covered the customer's cry.

Floyd dumped it on. He pressed his lips together, waiting. Nope, still not enough. He went down the line, collecting talcum powders from his fellow students.

"What's going on?" his customer asked.

"Oh, nothing." Floyd tried for a tranquil tone. "I'm just applying some talcum powder in case it tries to bleed. No big deal."

As the bleeding slowed, Floyd gained control of his nerves and finished the cut. They'd been trained to not let minor setbacks stop them from finishing the job, and he was determined to show the overseer that the training had stuck. He was dependable and could see things through, despite this minor dilemma.

When he was finished, he rang the bell to call for the inspector and spun the customer around to view his cut. Not bad, all things considered.

The man paled. "You cut my ear off."

Floyd nodded. "Yes, sir, I did." He looked down at his hair-covered shoes but quickly rallied. "But not all of it." He grabbed the piece of ear from where he'd set it on the counter. "I have the rest of your ear right here." He handed it to the man, who stammered incoherently.

The inspector arrived and stopped short, surveying the bloody, powder-filled scene. "What happened here?" He stepped closer. "Why, Floyd! You cut the man's ear off!"

Again, Floyd nodded. "That I did, sir, and no one feels worse about it than me." He dipped his head once more.

"Why didn't you say something?" The inspector's bushy brows nearly met his hairline.

"We were taught to finish the cut and not let any minor inconveniences stop us, sir."

The inspector huffed. "This is hardly a minor inconvenience, Floyd."

He bent over the customer, apologizing profusely and offering his assistance to the hospital. The two of them bustled out in a flurry, leaving Floyd to clean up the mess around his chair amidst the jests of all the other students.

"Wow, Floyd. You really did it now."

"Only you could pull off a stunt like that."

"I bet you get canned."

"Oh, he'll get canned for sure."

Floyd tried to ignore them as he swept and mopped up the area. What if they fired him? How would he take care of his new wife? His insides twisted. Was he destined to be a disappointment to his family, just like Pop? God forbid. He had to do better.

Floyd arrived at the Sonjaks' home after cutting a customer's ear off to find Susan chucking his clothes out the second-story window into the mud below. With one hand clasping the hat to his head, he rushed forward, shoes squelching in the moist earth beneath him.

"What on earth are you doing that for?"

Susan's pinched face glared down at him. "I'm furious at you, Floyd Douglas. Get your stuff out of my house and go back home!"

"Home?" He blinked up at her, mouth agape. "This *is* my home." He swiped the hat from his head and dabbed at the sweat beading under his hairline. "Our home." Had the woman gone mad?

"Not anymore. Go back to your parents. I don't want you here." She lobbed a dress shoe toward his head.

He ducked just in time. "What did I do?"

She dumped out an entire dresser drawer of socks and underwear. Warmth climbed his neck as his personal items rained to the ground. He checked over his shoulder to ensure no neighbors were watching the display. Thankfully, the street was quiet.

She leaned forward, nose and cheeks red, eyes narrow. "If you don't know, I'm not telling you."

He palmed his face. She wasn't even going to give him a hint? He'd sworn off Miss America pageants, so that couldn't be it. Had he picked his towel up off the floor after his shower that morning? No telling. But surely *that* wouldn't cause *this*, would it? A white dress shirt fluttered down. Now even his palms were clammy.

"Whatever I did, I'm sorry."

She huffed. "Not going to cut it, Floyd."

"Really sorry?"

"Ha!" There came another pair of slacks.

She had to nearly be out of ammunition. Surely, almost everything he owned was out there. He wasn't getting anywhere standing beneath the window, pleading for answers. He needed to go to her and talk some sense into her.

Resolved, he headed inside and up the stairs. He'd bounded up the last step before realizing he'd left muddy shoe prints in his wake. Uh-oh. He'd better take care of those before Mrs. Sonjak pitched a fit. But first, his wife.

She'd locked the door to their room. With a twist of his fingernail, he unlocked the knob and pushed inside.

She spun to face him, glowering at him with her hands on her hips. "What do you think you're doing?"

He stepped forward and took her hands in his. When she tried to yank them away, he held fast. "I love you, baby. Please tell me what I did."

"Did you really forget what day it is?" The fire in her eyes flickered from rage to hurt.

What day was it? He searched the room for clues. If only he could call Karen. She would know. She kept track of everything. When was his anniversary again? Wait, they had two of them. One in March, the other in July. It was only the end of September. That wasn't it. He scratched behind his ear.

She slapped him across the chest. "It's the anniversary of when you proposed, you dimwit."

Oh. That? The day he'd said, *"I want to marry you,"* and she'd said, *"Okay."* Who could remember the day that happened?

"O-of course," he stammered. "Of course, it is. Only we'd never be able to celebrate it while living here. You know how your parents would feel about that, how they feel about the whole engagement and courthouse marriage. Why, if I even got you flowers, your mother might dump them down the garbage disposal."

Thought lines deepened on Susan's forehead. A glint of hope shone through her eyes. She gave a slight nod. "I guess you're right."

"I still should have wished you a happy engagement anniversary when we first woke up this morning. I'm sorry, baby. Forgive me?"

She wrapped her arms around him. "I forgive you."

He lowered his head and captured her soft lips. He kissed her until she smiled again.

"Floyd?" She fiddled with his collar.

"Yes?"

"We're going to have a baby."

He stepped back and searched her face. Not a hint of tease. Nor dread. "The rabbit died?"

She nodded.

"You didn't go back to that kook of a doctor, did you? If he was wrong before—"

"No. My mom took me to her doctor. He confirmed what I suspected." A smile broke through. "You're going to be a father."

A father. What did that look like? What kind of father would he be?

She squeezed his arm. "Good thing you're doing so well at barber school. You'll have a good career to support our little family. We're going to need to move out of here. Find our own place."

The image of the customer's ear flipping through the air flashed through his mind. He swallowed. "Yeah, good thing."

Susan went to the window and peered out at Floyd's clothes below. "I'm sorry about that. I'll wash and iron them."

He kissed the top of her head, not about to argue.

Mrs. Sonjak's voice sounded from around the corner. "Who left muddy footprints all over my floor?"

Floyd grimaced. He'd just gotten out of trouble with one woman and into trouble with another.

Thankfully, Floyd didn't get thrown out of barber school. Instead, he graduated and got hired on at a three-chair shop not far from their new apartment. Well, it wasn't an *apartment* per se. He and Susan rented out an attic room from a beekeeper, whom everyone knew by his last name, Fischer.

Swarms of bees were the least of their problems there.

But after little Marie made her entrance, they'd needed a place of their own, and they had it. No matter that it was hot as the blazes in there. So hot that Susan couldn't stand staying indoors during the daytime. Marie was safer out with the bees than up in that steaming attic.

At any rate, Floyd was free of Mr. and Mrs. Sonjaks' hovering. He could finally be the man of the house. Er, attic. Mom was proud. So was Karen, who came over on moving day to help Susan put away dishes and to snap a dozen pictures of the place.

One day, he was the only one at the shop, reading a paper in the waiting area, when a ruckus caught his attention. Someone farther down the strip mall hollered. Another voice yelled back. A bang and a crash. Paper forgotten, Floyd hurried toward the door. What in tarnation?

The commotion rushed from the clothing store five doors down. Suddenly, a woman flew out of the doorway, piles of clothes billowing from her arms. She took off down the back alley.

"Help!" An older man with a cane hobbled out after her. "I've been robbed."

Robbed? Floyd sprang into action. Dashing toward where the woman had disappeared, he shouted, "I'll go after her!"

The storeowner's "Thank you, son" met his ears as he rounded the corner, as did a woman's pledge to call the police.

Adrenaline pumping, he came to the end of the alleyway and looked in both directions. Which way did she go? A stocking lay in the gravel to his left. She must have run in that direction. He gave chase.

His pop had avoided conflict, choosing instead to hide in the drink. Not Floyd. He'd be the opposite of his old man, for sure. If only Susan could see him now. Wouldn't she be proud? Think him heroic? Dashing and brave? His mother would likely brag on him too. Her son. The vigilante. So what if he couldn't make it as a priest. He could be a local hero. Akin to Batman or something. He could still make a difference, despite the unforeseen direction his life had taken.

When he came to another intersection, he scanned the dark alleyway. There! The woman was huddled behind a dumpster, clothing of all colors spilling over her arms and shoulders.

He marched closer. "You need to return those items right away."

The woman's eyes flashed. "Why don't you make me?"

Well, why didn't he? He towered at least a foot taller and maybe a hundred pounds heavier than the lady. He could wrestle her arms behind her back. Strongarm her into submission. Or maybe just yank the clothes from her and return them himself. He could use his strength for good. Everyone would applaud his valiant efforts. This was his moment to prove himself, to redeem himself. He was nothing like his father.

Narrowing his gaze, he assumed a wrestler's pose.

The woman dropped the clothes and turned fully toward him, something glinting in her hand. A knife!

He threw up his hands and backed away slowly. Forget being a hero. There was only one knife-wielding woman he'd willingly agree to tussle with.

Chapter Twelve

1990

Nana had been home from the hospital one week, and things had returned to normal. The doctors said the rest of the tests showed she was fine—no leukemia. They called it a false alarm but said she needed to have a checkup in six months. They'd do another test on her blood to make sure everything had gone back to normal. Emira could stomp on the doctor's stupid foot for getting Papa all upset for no reason. Weren't doctors supposed to be smarter than that? But it was good Nana was okay.

Emira nearly pounced to answer the phone when it rang one Saturday morning at the shop. She always felt so professional when she got to take down appointments. To think her grandparents trusted her to do such a grown-up thing. A thrill shot through her every time.

She used her most mature voice. "New Creations, how can I help you?"

"Is that Emira? It's Grammy Douglas."

"Yes, this is Emira. Hi, Grammy." Grammy Douglas was sweet as sugar and loads of fun, but now she sounded tired. Maybe she'd woken up too early. Mom sounded that way when Emira made too much noise in the mornings. "Do you want to talk to Papa?"

"Yes, I'd like to talk to your Papa." At least now it sounded like she was smiling, or trying to.

"Okay. Just a minute." She covered the phone with her hand before shouting so he could hear her over the clippers, "Papa, Grammy Douglas is on the phone!"

The whir of the clippers stopped, and Papa asked his customer to please hold on a minute while he came to the phone wearing a frown. "Mom?"

Emira couldn't make out Grammy's words, just the muffled ups and downs of her voice. She watched Papa's face, and it was like dark rain clouds rolled in. His shoulders drooped. "I'm sorry to hear that," he said. "I'll come by in an hour or so."

An hour? The shop didn't close until six, and it was only nine in the morning. He was going to leave work early? She widened her eyes at him, waiting for an explanation. He never, ever did that. He was the boss, after all. The only person there to cut men's hair. Plus, Saturday was his busiest day. What was so important that he would leave the shop? Worry sloshed in her belly.

Was Grammy sick? That had to be it. Maybe Grammy was sick and in the hospital like Nana had been. Would they find out Grammy's sickness was a false alarm too, or would it be a true alarm? Emira clamped her arms around her middle. When would Papa hang up and tell her what was going on?

"I know I don't have to. I want to. I'll bring Emira." Papa winked at her but still didn't smile. "Let me finish up this cut, and we'll head over. Love you, Mom. Bye."

Papa barely put the phone in the holder before Emira's questions burst out. "Is Grammy sick? Is she in the hospital? Is that why she's tired and you're sad?"

He tilted his head as if confused. "No, Princess. She's not sick. Why do you—"

His customer coughed from behind the booth. Both Papa and Emira startled and shot a look in that direction.

"She's fine. Her friend Beanie just died, and she's sad. We're going to go keep her company."

"Oh." Grammy wasn't sick, only sad. Papa was closing the shop because his mom was sad. Strange.

Papa started toward his booth. "When's Nana's first appointment today?"

She checked the appointment book. "She has a perm at ten o'clock."

"Will you call her and let her know we're leaving?"

"Okay."

Papa turned to four customers in the waiting area. "I'm sorry to have to do this, but something has come up. I need to leave as soon as I finish this cut. I'll give you a dollar off the next time you come in."

Though one man grumbled as he snapped his newspaper closed, the others said things like "No problem" and "I understand."

Papa's clippers started again as they all filed out the door.

Emira called Nana, who said, "All right," like the whole thing was normal and not crazy. After she hung up, Emira twisted back and forth in the desk chair, her thoughts and feelings fluttering around like trapped birds. She opened the desk drawer and pulled out her notebook. Her top-secret spy notebook. It had a lock and key and everything, only she'd lost the key weeks ago. It didn't matter. A hard tug would open the lock without it.

She set it on her lap under the desk where no one would be able to see and yanked it open. Sighing, she trailed her fingers over two lines of notes.

Ask God to help you see so you can love.

Listen.

That was it. After following Papa around for a whole week, that was all she had. Some investigator she was. She bit the end of her pen, hesitating before adding another note.

Take off work.

It was kind of silly for her to write that. She was only a kid and couldn't follow that advice on her own. Maybe it would come in handy someday, though.

Her fingers itched to write more, but her mind was blank. She'd thought that maybe everything would be different when they returned home from the hospital. It only made sense that Papa would keep being sweet to Nana, and she'd be lovey-dovey back to him. But no. Once they'd found out Nana was okay, it was as if the hospital had never happened. She could almost think she'd imagined Papa weeping at Nana's bedside. She hadn't seen them hold hands since, but Emira would never forget the way Papa had looked at her.

The buzz of Papa's clippers slowed, then stopped. Papa spun the chair around to face the mirror. "How does it look?"

Emira straightened and pasted on a bright smile, ready for them to emerge from the booth.

"Fine. Just fine." Only the customer didn't sound happy. More like annoyed, or maybe distracted.

They came out, and she rang up the total on the cash register. "That will be eight dollars." She tried to smile extra wide to make up for the customer's frown.

"There you go." He handed her eight dollars even. No tip. She tried not to sound disappointed as she thanked him. What rotten luck. Was he bothered that Papa had interrupted his haircut to take a phone call? If only she could explain.

After the man walked out the door, Papa took a sheet of blank paper from the drawer. With a fat black marker, he wrote *Barber is Out*. He taped it to the front window, then turned toward the back. "I'll grab my things, and we'll go, Princess."

She had jumped down to follow him and to stick her notebook in her backpack when the phone rang again. She spun around and rushed to answer it.

"New Creations, how can I help you?"

"Emira, it's Dad."

"Oh." At the sound of his voice, her insides lifted high, then slammed down low like a roller coaster. Her notebook slid out of her hands. She scrambled to retrieve it. "Hi, Dad." Her voice shook a little.

"I'm just calling to let you know I'll be by the shop to get you at noon for our weekend together."

Emira bit her lip and looked back in the direction Papa had disappeared. Her throat felt hot and sticky as she tried to choke out a reply. But what did she want to say? Yes or no? How could the idea of spending time with her dad sound wonderful and terrible all at the same time? How come she wanted to both run into his arms and run away and hide? She loved her dad. Wanted him near her, with her, always … but not like this. Not apart from Mom. Not in his tiny little apartment with the too-white walls that smelled like the Chinese restaurant next door. Seeing him that way, in that place, ached like a cavity.

She sucked in a breath. "We won't be here."

"What?"

"We're going to Grammy Douglas's house. We won't be at the shop." She twisted the phone cord around her finger. "Maybe next weekend."

"Emira, honey, we're going to go to the arcade and order pizza for dinner. It'll be fun. I've been looking forward to spending time with you."

Great. Now her eyes felt hot too. She sniffed. "I'm not making it up. We won't be here."

"Let me talk to Papa."

She growled and clunked the phone onto the desk before calling out, "Papa, my dad wants to talk to you."

How could he leave their family and still call Mom's dad Papa? That wasn't fair. Her hands balled into fists. Why should she go with him? She should stay with Papa. To keep investigating and learn from someone who didn't leave their family. Who didn't move out of his home into a sad little apartment with a blow-up mattress.

When Papa came to the front and picked up the phone, she stomped to the back and stuck her notebook in her backpack. She was going with Papa. She loved Grammy Douglas's old home. It had a laundry chute. If she shouted down into it, her voice sounded loud and funny. Grammy Douglas and Beanie also had an attic with all kinds of old clothes packed into trunks. They let her go up and try on their old fancy dresses and hats so she could pose in front of the mirror.

Her chest prickled. Beanie was gone. It was just Grammy Douglas now. That *was* sad. Grammy probably could use some cheering up.

Yes, that was where Emira needed to be. Not in some dark arcade pretending she was okay when her insides were on a roller coaster. She hoisted the backpack onto her shoulders and started for the front, ready to tell Papa she would go with him instead of her dad when she nearly ran into Papa's belly.

"Whoa, there, Princess. You ready?"

"We're going?" It couldn't be that easy. Surely, she'd have to convince him.

"Yep. I'm going to drop you off at your dad's when we're done."

Her shoulders sagged.

"Come on. He's your dad. He loves you. You love him."

"Yeah." That was true. So why couldn't her feelings be simple? If you loved someone, you should want to be with them. If you loved someone, you shouldn't want to hide from the way they made you feel. It didn't make sense.

"Don't you enjoy spending time with your dad?" Papa's face wrinkled with his question.

"I do. But then when it's over, I get sadder. So sad it feels like I'm breaking. So sad I wish the happy wasn't there in the first place."

124

He sighed. "I see." He took her hand and squeezed. "I wonder if that's how Grammy Douglas feels right now."

"About Beanie?"

He nodded.

That was a good question. Beanie was her bestest friend in the whole wide world. They'd been friends since before either of them was old, and when their children had grown up and their husbands had died, they'd moved in together. Emira used to think they were sisters until Papa explained they were just best friends. Maybe Grammy Douglas felt like she was breaking without her friend.

She squeezed Papa's hand back. "Let's go see."

The ride to Grammy's in Papa's Cadillac took Emira's mind off her weekend with Dad. Papa played Elvis songs and sang in a silly way that made her giggle until her sides hurt. When they got to Grammy's house, Emira skipped up the steps and rang the doorbell. Papa followed behind, hands in his pockets. When Grammy opened the door, Emira threw her arms around the older woman, who made an "umph" sound and folded her into a hug.

"Oh, sweet girl. Welcome." Grammy's favorite short-sleeved sweater felt soft against Emira's cheek. Emira had always thought the shirt silly. What was the point of a sweater with short sleeves? But she leaned into it now and smiled at the way it smelled like cinnamon toast.

"Are you sad, Grammy? So sad you feel like you're breaking?"

Papa put a hand on Emira's shoulder. "Give her a minute, will you, Princess?"

Grammy's sad smile spread over them like jelly. "She's fine, Floyd. It's a valid question." She settled her gaze on Emira. "I am sad." She let out a deep sigh.

Papa stepped around Emira to hug Grammy. They hung on to each other tight and long. Who was hugging whom? Who was holding the other up? It seemed they both needed the other to stand.

When they pulled apart, Grammy stepped back and waved them inside. "Come in, come in."

"Actually," Papa said, "I thought we could go feed the ducks."

Emira popped onto her toes. What a great idea! Beanie had loved to feed the ducks. Grammy smiled. "I'll get the bread."

The three of them walked across the street to the park and strolled around the lake, saying little. The warm breeze kept tangling strands of hair into Emira's face and mouth. She pushed them away and kept walking between Papa and his mom, watching intently. Papa wasn't saying hardly anything, and yet, it was obvious he loved Grammy. But how?

Emira's mouth twisted as she concentrated. How was he loving Grammy without words? She hung back, intent on being the best investigator she could be. There. Papa's steps were slow, and he moved … soft. Slow and soft, not hurried and distracted. There was kindness in the way he walked next to her, like he didn't have anywhere better to be. Like nothing in the world was more important right now than her.

That was how Papa made her feel too.

As they neared the dock, Grammy fished into the bread bag and handed Emira a few pieces. Emira ran to the edge and tore her slices into the smallest bits she could to make them last longer. As she tossed them into the water, she watched the ducks flock to the feast and laughed while they fought over lunch.

Grammy came up next to her and tossed a chunk of bread onto the water. "For Beanie," she said.

"Grammy?" Emira peered up at her. "Does the sadness make the happiness hurt?"

"Hmm." Grammy nodded like she was thinking about Emira's question. "Yes, I guess it does a little. But it also makes the happiness bigger."

Emira frowned. "How could it hurt and grow bigger at the same time?"

Grammy shrugged. "Love is funny that way."

Bread eaten, the ducks left, tail feathers wiggling as they swam. Emira bit the inside of her cheek. "My dad doesn't live with us anymore."

Fading quacks sounded in the distance.

Grammy's voice was softer than a feather. "I heard as much."

Emira crunched a piece of gravel under her shoe. "He has to come back. I want to make him come back."

"You can't make anyone do anything, sweetheart."

Her gaze snapped up to meet Grammy's ocean-blue eyes. What? That wasn't true. Mom made her do stuff all the time, like clean her room and eat her vegetables. She was following Papa around taking notes so she could figure out how to make Dad stay. It would work. It had to. She just needed to investigate more.

Grammy smiled at her as if she were a little kid. Ugh. How embarrassing. "I don't know much about what's going on with your parents, but I know enough to be certain it has nothing to do with you. Your father loves you more than a monkey loves bananas."

Emira smiled at that. Silly Grammy. But after a minute of picturing monkeys, her smile faded. If only that were enough. If only Dad loved her enough to stay.

She had to make him love her more.

Chapter Thirteen

2010

Emira sat in a folding chair next to Nana's washing machine as Papa plugged in his clippers. Dad sat in Papa's barber chair, positioned under shelves bulging with old Christmas decorations. A strand of gold garland snaked out of its box and dangled over Papa's head.

"Are you sure the lighting's good enough in here?" Emira's stomach soured at the comparison of this experience with every cut she'd witnessed in the past.

She shouldn't do that. Compare. *Forgetting the past and pressing forward to what lies ahead, right?* But how could she not feel disappointed at the concrete floor and walls of this utility room, stuffed with boxes and bins, with only a small window and hanging bulb for light? It was like when the Israelites rebuilt the temple. Those who hadn't seen the first temple rejoiced, but those who remembered the former glory, wept.

"I can see just fine," Papa grumbled. He went to work, glasses positioned at the end of his nose.

She inhaled slowly. She'd focus on the similarities. The blue cape covering her father. The sound of the clippers, then of snipping. The smell of mousse.

"Thanks for doing this, Floyd." Her dad wore a sheepish grin. Perhaps he knew, as she did, he didn't belong here. Not anymore.

"Think nothing of it. You're family. Always will be."

Emira shifted in her seat. How could Papa do that? Welcome his ex-son-in-law with open arms. Forgive and love so freely?

"I appreciate that." Dad's voice thickened with emotion. He coughed, and it cleared. "So, I hear you're going on an adventure."

Papa's shoulders straightened. "Emira told you? Yeah, a mission trip to Haiti. Never been more thrilled."

She fought the urge to recoil. Never been more thrilled? Apparently, his life with her had bored him. He was off to bigger and better things. Just as she'd never been enough for her father, she wasn't enough for Papa either. After a lifetime of obligation to her, he'd finally freed himself to pursue what he really wanted.

She was being ridiculous. Childish.

But the knife twisted deep. How could she extricate it? These feelings of betrayal seemed to have a mind of their own.

Maybe if she listened to Papa's point of view, she'd understand. She hadn't truly gotten to the heart of why he wanted to go. What about this prospect thrilled him? She clamped her lips together.

Dad spoke as the expert he apparently was. "Haiti's a great place for a mission trip. Deep poverty, of course, but the people. Precious. What will you be doing there?"

Papa's brow furrowed. "I don't know exactly."

"Building houses? That's what many missionaries do."

"Perhaps."

How could he be ready to jump on a plane when he didn't have a clue as to the agenda? And if they were building houses, what would his role be? Not only was he seventy years old, but he also had no handyman skills whatsoever. Those poor Haitians didn't need another house falling on their heads.

"Where in Haiti will you be working, do you know? Port-au-Prince? Petit Goave? Or are you going to rough it in Marchasse?"

She stared at her show-off father. Who was this man who spat out names of foreign cities like they were brands of snack cakes?

Papa shifted his weight. "Oh, you know. All around."

Code for *I have no idea*. Did he know anything about this fifteen-thousand-dollar trip he'd purchased? Tension built in her temples.

Nana bustled in, laundry basket balanced on her hip. She set the load on top of the dryer and lifted the washer lid. "How's it going in here?"

"Fine. Fine," Papa said, but he loomed much closer to Dad's head than normal. Must be the poor lighting. So much for the idea of a side business in this basement. Though maybe if they moved operations to his office …

"Teddy's show ended, thank goodness. Only so much of that Dora girl I can take." Nana poured a hearty cupful of heavily scented blue goo into the washing machine.

Emira chuckled. "Yeah, it can get annoying." One of the reasons she limited his screen time to one episode a day. The other being the American Academy of Pediatrics's recommendations. At Nana and Papa's, however, rules sprouted wings. "Reagan's still sleeping, right? What's Teddy doing now?"

She strained to listen, but no footsteps or shouts found their way to her ears. She hadn't made a mistake in leaving the two of them upstairs with Nana, had she? Even if her grandma's memory *was* declining, surely, she wasn't dangerous to be around. Besides, Emira was close enough to hear if something went awry.

"Reagan's still asleep in her pumpkin seat. Teddy's watching *I Love Lucy*."

She gaped. "You serious? What episode?"

"Candy factory. Got you hooked when you weren't much older than him." A nostalgic smile lit her face.

Emira had to see this. She snuck upstairs and peeked into the living room. Sure enough, Teddy stared at the screen, enamored as Lucy and Ethel stuffed chocolates into their mouths. Interesting. A peek at Reagan showed her fast asleep in her car seat.

She tiptoed back downstairs to find Nana leaning against the washer, talking with Dad. "I had no idea you'd been to Haiti."

Join the club.

"There's a lot of networking involved with my job. We source raw materials from various places. I'm required to schmooze."

Nana barked a laugh. "Bet you love that."

"Hate it, but"—he stuck out his bottom lip—"they make it worth my while. And I like traveling."

"You should go with Floyd. The two of you would have fun together."

Emira's heart snagged on Nana's suggestion. The two of them together? It would bring a large dose of relief to know Papa wasn't alone. He'd be safer that way, surely. She'd worry less. But the two of them having a bonding experience without her? Bile rose in her throat.

"Sounds like a great experience." Genuineness rang in Dad's voice. "Unfortunately, this three-week break I'm taking now is the accumulation of years of personal days. No way work could spare me for that long."

Emira's neck muscles relaxed, and with them, her tongue. "Papa doesn't seem to know what he's going to be doing over there or even where in Haiti he'll be ministering." She raised a brow to Nana.

"I guess not. He hasn't gone to the intro meeting yet. When is it, Floyd? Tomorrow evening?"

"Wednesday." Papa huffed. "But I know all I need to know."

"Wait, wait, wait." Emira planted her hands on her hips. "They're having an intro meeting to explain the trip?"

"Yes." Papa didn't meet her eye.

"Papa! You did this all backward. You're supposed to go to the meeting first and learn about the trip, *then* decide if you want to go. After you hear what's involved, if you decide you're ready to commit, you put down a *deposit*. Not the whole amount." She shook her head. "What are you going to do if you go there Wednesday and find out you're in over your head?"

He cast her a scowl and exchanged his clippers for scissors. "Stop worrying about me, Emira."

She threw up her arms. "Nana? A little help here?"

Nana turned to the dryer and opened the barrel. "He's always had his own way of doing things." She fished out towels and placed them in the basket.

Was it unreasonable for her to worry about her elderly grandpa spending an obscene amount of money to travel to a dangerous country on a whim? Apparently, *she* was the crazy one for being concerned.

"Mama?"

Emira turned at Teddy's whimpering voice. His cheeks bulged like a chipmunk's and brown streaked his face.

"Buddy, what's wrong?"

He clutched his tummy. "I don't feel so good."

Nana moved toward him. "What's in your mouth?"

"What's all over your face?" Emira felt his forehead with the back of her hand—no fever—then trailed a finger over his smudgy cheek.

"Did you get into my chocolates?" Nana asked, sticking a finger into his mouth, then pulling it out with a suspicious glint in her eyes.

"I Lucy." He patted his tummy.

Why was his shirt lumpy? Uh-oh. Emira untucked his shirt from his shorts. A dozen chocolates fell to the floor. She closed her eyes and inhaled deeply.

Dad stifled a chuckle. He might not think it so funny if Teddy vomited in the car on the way home.

"Come on. Let's get you cleaned up." Nana took Teddy's grimy hand and led him upstairs.

Huh. Teddy was a mess. Papa had gone off the deep end. Her dad was a stranger to her. But Nana seemed perfectly fine. Perhaps she'd worried about her grandma for nothing.

Floyd shuffled into the sanctuary of Christ Community Church, welcome packet in hand, headed for the third row. It wouldn't serve well to sit directly in front and be singled out for any examples. Nor would it be in his best interest to lounge in the back and appear unengaged. Third row. Invested, yet not overeager. Not the insanity that Emira had basically accused him of. The third row screamed respectable. Sober-minded. Intelligent, even.

He shifted in his seat to get comfortable, then squinted down at the papers in his hand. He should have brought his glasses. Of course, he'd forget something, and wouldn't that be just the thing? He lifted the packet closer to his face and made out the table of contents. Mission and Values. Itinerary. Packing List. Miscellaneous Costs Not Covered by Mission Fee. He harumphed. More money? He'd have to spend more money? How much? He tried to flip to that page, but everything blurred. Drat.

The rumble of voices around him siphoned his attention. These were the people he'd be spending six weeks with. A dozen men who looked like they'd just walked off a construction site, muscles boasting they could build a house or lift a fallen one off a person as easily as Floyd could trim a beard. Four women wearing long skirts and colorful woven headbands spoke to each other in another language. Spanish? Creole? Tongues?

Two nuns in habits sat silently next to the charismatic foursome. *Nuns.* He flexed his fingers, remembering the burn on his knuckles where Sister Evangeline struck them with a ruler five times in one day. Silly for an old man to still tremble at women in habits, but the intimidation they'd drilled into him as a boy had stuck.

Floyd's gaze shifted to what appeared to be a father and his teenage son. Now *that's* what he should have done, the kind of father he should have been. The kind who taught his children—by example, not words only—how to live generously.

"Well, hello, Floyd."

Floyd yelped and nearly pulled a muscle in his neck turning to the source of the greeting. Father Larry stood to his right, bright smile in place. Floyd pressed a hand to his hammering heart. "What are you doing here?" Instinctively, he made the sign of the cross, then winced. Where had that come from?

"I'm one of the sponsors." The corners of his eyes crinkled as he settled into the chair next to Floyd.

"Of course, you are." It would be just his luck. He straightened in his seat.

Larry shifted his cane in front of him. "Well, not me, of course. My parish. I'm the representative."

"Those two dynamic ladies with you?" Floyd pointed to the nuns.

"They are." Larry's bony finger darted to the group of construction workers. "As are they."

"Oh. Nice." He'd be on this trip with a bunch of Catholics. He pulled at his collar. Not that he minded Catholics. His mom had been one until the day she died. His sister Karen remained a devout one still. It was a surprise, though, as he'd assumed all the trip's attendees to be Protestant. What other surprises might be in store?

Both men spoke at the same time: "Will you be going on this trip?" Floyd asked as Father Larry said, "I had to feed your T-bone to my rottweiler."

They took a breath, then spoke over each other again: "No," Father Larry said as Floyd asked, "You have a rottweiler?"

They both laughed, and Floyd motioned for Father Larry to continue.

"I'm here only as a parish representative. I'm not attending the trip to Haiti."

Thank God. He didn't know if he could take six weeks of the edginess he felt in this man's presence.

"And, yes, I have a rottweiler. His name's Vicious."

Floyd sputtered, "Y-you're joking."

"I'm as serious as hellfire and brimstone."

He looked it, too. Straight-faced and sober. Who was this man?

Father Larry faced the front but gave Floyd the side-eye. "I assume Emira gave you my number."

Floyd squirmed. "She did." He fumbled for an excuse. He was busy … doing what, exactly? Watching golf? Packing for this trip? His scalp tingled. This guy was a priest. He could likely scope out a convincing lie, much less a pathetic one. It'd be better to just tell the truth. Out with it before Father Larry could call his bluff.

"Look." He angled toward Father Larry and swallowed hard. For an old, frail man, he sure could intimidate. "I don't know you. I'm not in the habit of having dinner with strangers, however kind they may be. Plus, now that I know you have a vicious, T-bone-eating rottweiler, I'm not exactly eager to make his acquaintance." He forced a chuckle.

"Oh, Vicious is a teddy bear. Don't worry about him." Larry winked. "Ironic name."

"Okay, but I still don't know you."

"You know me well enough to share a meal."

Why wouldn't he leave this matter alone? What a stubborn old codger. He opened his mouth to ask why this was so important when a man up front called the meeting to order.

He shifted his attention to the stage and attempted to absorb the flood of information. Names of cities he would never be able to pronounce drifted over his head, and frustration mounted as the leader referenced pages of the packet Floyd couldn't read without his glasses. But at least now, he'd have something to tell Emira. He'd be passing out food and Bibles. Hopefully, that would be the group they'd put him in. The other group would perform manual labor.

"Before you leave," the mission trip leader said, "make sure you pick up your application from the back table and pay your deposit if you're ready to do so. Deposits are due in one week and are necessary to secure your spot."

Floyd stood, the sharp pain piercing his back and the creaking of his knees reminding him that, besides the priest next to him, he was easily the oldest person in attendance. He'd have to prove himself among all these young people. Show them that he had what it took.

He glanced to his right. Father Larry used his cane to stand. How could he extricate himself from further conversation gracefully? He patted the man's hand on his cane. "It was nice seeing you again. Thanks for the company."

Father Larry's eyes narrowed. "Give me a call, Floyd. We have things to discuss."

Floyd shuddered and had to stop himself from doing the sign of the cross again. Unbidden, prayers from long ago churned to life in his mind. *Hail Mary, full of grace.* He pressed his lips together to keep from voicing them and instead gave a single nod to Father Larry before scurrying toward the exit.

He shook his head at himself. What was that about? How could the sight of a priest turn him into a blubbering schoolboy? Ridiculous.

He'd just stepped past a table when someone called to him.

"Excuse me, sir."

He turned and faced the woman. "Yes?"

She sat at the table, clipboard in hand. A line was beginning to form across from her. "You're forgetting your application."

"Oh," He hiked his pants higher on his hips. "I filled it out already." He'd mailed it in with his deposit.

Her forehead scrunched. "I don't think so. What's your name?"

He stepped closer, casting a glance into the sanctuary to ensure Father Larry wasn't hovering close. The strange father had disappeared. "The name's Floyd Douglas."

Her eyes skimmed the papers in front of her. "It says here you already paid in full."

"That's right."

"And that you filled out the interest form."

"Okay." If that's what they wanted to call it.

"But not the application."

He huffed. "I filled out something. Wrote down all my information. My address, phone number …"

The woman smiled at him as if he were a child. "That was merely the interest form. This"—she handed him a packet nearly the size of a dictionary—"is the application."

He gaped at it, speechless. The thing might have weighed as much as Father Larry's rottweiler. It would take him six weeks to fill all of it out.

"If you'd rather, you can complete the application online." She rattled off a web address and instructions. He didn't bother mentioning he'd only figured out how to check his email a couple of weeks ago, and if anything popped up on his screen, he had to have Kade come and fix whatever he managed to break. He'd stick to pen and paper.

He took the application and scampered to his car. As he exited the parking lot, the car behind him gave a little honk. His gaze jolted to the rearview mirror and locked onto Father Larry's. The priest waved.

Floyd expelled a breath and did likewise. "Hail, holy Queen, mother of Mercy …"

Chapter Fourteen

1964

Floyd stayed on at the three-chair shop, narrowing his focus to cutting hair only instead of also attempting to fight crime. When his boss, Buck, retired, he sold his shop to Floyd for two thousand dollars. Look at him now—a proud business owner. Floyd was liable to bust out of his britches. He even let Karen take a picture of him in front of the place for her scrapbook. As silly as her hobby was, it felt good to have someone proud of him. And Mr. Sonjak thought he'd never amount to anything. He'd shown his father-in-law. It'd been years since he'd even come close to cutting anyone's ear off.

Of course, the neighborhood was going downhill, but that didn't mean he couldn't make a decent living. As long as he remembered to lock the door before starting on a haircut, he wasn't liable to get robbed. Although, one time, someone stole his air conditioner while he took his lunch break.

But he wouldn't let it get him down. No, siree. With little Marie at home and another baby on the way, he had to keep pride in his work. He had a respectable job. Not only that, but he owned a respectable establishment. Good for him.

A knock on the door alerted him to another customer. He perked up. Maybe this one would even pay up front. He stood and set his newspaper on the table.

When he cracked the door open, though, it was Drinks Tonic Water again. He was pretty sure the bum lived in the park across the street. He never had as much as two nickels to pay, surely not the $1.75 for a cut. Floyd had asked his name once, but the man mumbled, and he couldn't make it out. Since the shaggy-haired blonde always had tonic water in hand, Floyd knew him by the drink.

"Hey there." Floyd tried not to let his disappointment show.

Drinks Tonic Water shuffled inside. "Can I get a cut? On the cuff. I can pay you next week."

Sure he could. After locking the door behind them, Floyd flipped open his leather-bound recordkeeping book and found the column labeled Drinks Tonic Water. It was right under Leg Up in Face While Cutting Hair. He added another $1.75 to the man's mounting tally. "Let's get you taken care of."

He motioned the man toward his chair. As he cut, the man murmured about his life. His experiences. Floyd leaned forward to understand as much of the muffled speech as he could. Apparently, Drinks Tonic Water used to be a CEO of a steelworks company. Either that or he used to keep seals and birds for company. Floyd squinted and concentrated harder. It had to be steel. When his wife left him for the boss—or was it Ross?—he turned to the bottle and ended up losing everything.

"I'm sorry to hear that." Floyd fell silent as he shaved the man's neck. He finished and turned the man around to face the mirror and spoke again. "You know, I could tell from the moment I saw you that you were intelligent. Full of potential."

The man's brows slanted in a puppy dog expression. "Really?"

"Why, of course! You walked in here, and I thought to myself, that's one clever man. He's bright. He has potential." Floyd dusted the man's neck with the brush.

"I've wasted it all." His breath leaked out like a deflating balloon.

"No." Standing over his shoulder, he peered at the man's solemn eyes. "It's never too late. As long as you're breathing, there's hope."

The man blinked rapidly as if fending off tears and nodded. "Thank you, Floyd."

Floyd removed the apron and shook the man's hand. "You're welcome, friend. Have a good one."

Floyd arrived home to find Susan crying in the front yard. Marie sat on a blanket in the grass, playing with blocks. Sweat dampened Susan's brow and collar as the sun beat down.

Floyd parked the car and rushed over to his wife. "What's the matter, baby?"

Her shoulders shook as he held her soft frame, her slightly rounded belly pushing against him. "The bird died."

The bird died? But she was already pregnant. No, wait. She'd said bird, not rabbit. Bird. Bird. He shifted his jaw from side to side, trying to put the pieces together. Their cockatoo? "Fred?"

She nodded, sniffling. "Fred died."

A pinprick of relief oozed from him. It was only that silly bird. Nothing more serious. She was fine. Marie. The baby. The people he loved were safe and sound. He ran his thumbs along her wet cheeks. How could such a fierce woman get so attached to animals? He'd never understand it. She had a remarkable capacity for love.

He weighed a dozen possibilities of what to say. Each one could make things worse. *It was just a bird* wouldn't win him any favors. Neither would a joke about Ethel from her favorite show. He opted for "I'm sorry, hon. How did he die?"

She fisted her hands. "It's too dang hot up there. I took Marie outside, but I didn't take Fred. I killed him. I killed Fred." She pounded his chest, tears flowing down her face. "All because you made us live in that stupid attic." The blame and anger were far more familiar than the tears, and oddly comforting. Those pregnancy hormones were throwing him for a loop.

"Shh." He stroked her hair. "We can get a new bird."

She pounded harder. "I don't want another bird. I want out of the jaws of hell."

A bee buzzed past their ears, and he ducked. "Okay, okay. We'll get a new place. A place all our own." Though, how would he be able to afford it with a ledger full of on-the-cuff customers?

"Floyd Douglas, that's the first decent thing you've said in months." She relaxed into him and sighed.

Instead of reading the paper at the shop the next day, Floyd went over his finances. If only everyone who owed him money would pay up. The cops dashed past for the second time in one day. Did he need to find a new business space in addition to a new home? Maybe if he could edge his way into a safer part of town, he could find customers who had the money for a cut. He'd ask Karen what she thought during their weekly phone chat on Sunday. His sister usually had good advice.

Someone knocked. Thoughts consumed with numbers, he answered the door. A scruffy Pekingese rushed in, sniffing each chair leg. Oh, great. It was Man with Dog. The guy had to owe him at least twenty bucks by now.

The copper-haired rascal lifted his leg near the table.

"Nope!" Floyd called out in a stern voice. Scruffy put his leg down and scuttled next to his owner.

"I need a trim." Man with Dog rocked back on his heels, ignoring his small companion.

Floyd eyed the man. "You gonna pay this time?" He was done with charity. He had a house to buy.

The man had the audacity to look offended. "What kind of question is that? Of course, I'll pay."

Floyd put up his hands. "All right. All right. Have a seat."

He did, and the dog jumped into his lap, not seeming to mind when Floyd covered him with the apron.

Floyd's mind wandered as Man with Dog jabbered on. Floyd nodded and replied with an "Oh, sure" and "Naturally" on occasion, but future plans consumed his thoughts. Where should he look for a place to live? Pagedale? U City? How much might he get for this shop? Would it be enough to purchase a new place?

Soon, he finished and spun the man around to face the mirror.

Man with Dog beamed. "Great work, as always." Scruffy hopped off his lap and nipped at his ankles.

Floyd meandered to his desk and pressed the keys of the cash register. A bell dinged and the drawer opened. "That will be $1.75."

The man stuffed his hands in his pockets. "I don't quite have the money right now, but I'm good for it. Next week, most likely."

Floyd's neck heated. "You said you could pay."

"I can. And I will. Just not today." He looked over Floyd's shoulder, down at the floor, then out the window. Anywhere but in his eyes. "Write me down in that book of yours. I'm good for it."

Floyd's breath came out like a hiss of steam. "You need to pay me today."

Man with Dog shrugged. "I can't. What are you going to do about it?"

Floyd clenched his jaw. What *was* he going to do about it? How could he make this man pay? He scanned the man's person. No watch. No rings. Not even a nice belt.

Scruffy barked at someone walking outside.

Floyd straightened and raised his chin. "I'm taking your dog."

The man tilted his head. "My dog?"

Floyd nodded. "Yes, your dog." That would show him.

He nodded. "Yeah. All right." He turned and sauntered off, giving Scruffy a little rub on the head as he left.

Well, that was odd. Why wasn't he upset? Wasn't that dog his close companion? A best friend of sorts? He should have been outraged at the suggestion. Instead, he seemed almost … relieved. A niggle of unease sliced through Floyd, but he shook it off. Best not to think too much about it. He might not have gotten money for that cut, but he'd gotten a pet for Marie. Susan would be thrilled.

Scruffy yapped the entire ride home, racing back and forth from the front seat to the back. Floyd rolled the window all the way down at the stoplight, halfway hoping the dog would jump out and find someone else to pester. He didn't.

"Honey, I'm home," Floyd said, opening the door of their apartment. "And I brought a surprise."

Susan turned to him, eyes wide with anticipation. When she saw the dog, her brows furrowed. "I told you I didn't want a bird, so you got me a dog?"

What? "N-no. Not exactly. I took the dog."

"Took him?" She placed a hand on her hip. "You stole him?"

"No, I didn't steal him. I … demanded him from a customer."

"Extortion?" Her eyes narrowed.

"No. The man—"

A scream interrupted his explanation. The dog stood over Marie as she lay on the ground covering her face. Susan's hands flew to her cheeks, then she ran to their daughter. "Marie! What happened?" She scooped the toddler into her arms. "The dog bit her in the face!" She turned a hard glare to Floyd. "How could you?"

"Me? I didn't bite her in the face."

"You brought that monster into our house."

"I ... uh ..." Gee whiz. He'd gotten into a big pickle this time. "He wasn't a monster in the shop." Not that he'd noticed.

"Oh, yeah. I'm sure it's all Marie's fault, then, huh, Floyd?"

He ran his hand through his hair. "I didn't say that." He took Marie from Susan's arms, bouncing her.

Susan chased the dog. "Come here, you brute." She grabbed him by the frayed collar. "He doesn't have any tags on his collar. Does that mean he hasn't had rabies shots?"

Floyd winced. "Probably not. I think his owner is homeless."

Susan stomped her foot. "Floyd! Marie's going to have to get rabies shots."

Rabies shots? That sounded painful and expensive. So much for trying to solve his financial problems.

Susan's glare sliced through him. "Get rid of the mutt or else."

Yikes. Maybe he should run before she caught *him* by the collar.

Chapter Fifteen

1990

Emira had just finished tap-dancing for the Bible ladies when Papa's greeting drew her to the front of the shop. Papa was friendly to everyone, always. "The customer is always right," he said. But the way he welcomed this customer was special. He sounded excited, and Emira's shoes clacked as she raced to see who the mystery guest could be. Maybe it was a movie star or a famous sports player. She ducked to the left to see past Papa. Hmm. Interesting. He didn't *look* special. Just a regular-looking man in a gray suit and red tie. Maybe he was rich. That was probably it.

"Well, what do you know? It's wonderful to see you, Ronald. My, don't you look great!" Papa stepped forward and pumped the man's hand.

Emira ducked behind the desk and smiled at the customer. If he were rich, he'd probably give a good tip. She should stay up front until he left. She'd already performed all her dance routines anyway.

"What have you been up to, my friend?" Papa asked.

The man rocked back on his heels. "I'm a real estate agent now. Got my license. Business is going well."

Papa's grin spread wide. "You don't say? That's wonderful. Just wonderful."

Wonderful? A real estate agent sounded boring. Not rich *or* famous. Maybe she should go back to Mary and Martha. She scooted to the edge of the chair, debating whether or not to slide off.

"Me and the wife got back together."

Emira froze. Got back together? Had they been divorced, and now they were … not divorced? She planted her elbows on the desk and leaned forward. Maybe he wasn't rich or famous, but suddenly, the conversation didn't bore her.

"Oh, excellent news." Papa looked over at her. "Say, Ronald, have you ever met my granddaughter, Emira?"

"Can't say that I have." Ronald smiled and nodded at her. "Nice to meet you."

"Nice to meet you too," she said.

"I used to call Ronald Drinks Tonic Water," Papa said, and both men laughed.

Emira frowned at their joke. It wasn't funny. It didn't make any sense. "Why?"

"Because he drank tonic water." Still chuckling, Papa clapped him on the shoulder and invited him into the booth.

She still didn't get it, and it was no fun being on the outside of a joke. She left the goofy guys to their nonsense and clacked back to the Bible ladies. She danced and sang "I Feel Pretty" once more before their dryers dinged.

"Time's up," Nana clucked, gently shooing Emira back before lowering her voice. "Why don't you go wait for Papa to finish cutting the homeless man's hair so you can work the cash register."

Emira scrunched up her nose. "Homeless man? What homeless man?"

Nana tilted her head toward Papa's booth. "Drinks Tonic Water."

"He's not homeless. He's a real estate agent." Emira puffed out her chest, feeling important.

"Is that so?" Nana stuck her hand on her hip. "Well, he used to be homeless. One of the many your Papa gave free haircuts to." She rolled her eyes.

Emira's mouth nearly fell open. Mr. Suit-and-Tie-Real-Estate-Man used to be homeless? Is that why he and his wife got divorced? She needed to get a good look at him.

Time to investigate. She shuffled up front, snatched her journal from the desk drawer, and then peeked into Papa's booth. The two of them were talking like best friends. She hadn't seen Papa look that happy in a long time. Not even when his favorite golfer won the championship.

What should she write in her journal? She didn't have any answers. Nothing about Ronald gave any hint that he used to be homeless. Where had he lived? She saw a commercial once about poor children who didn't have homes or food. They slept right out in the open, in the dirt, but they lived in Africa, not America. Veronica Snowbridge from school said homeless people lived under bridges, but that sounded too much like the story about the trolls. It couldn't be true. Ronald didn't sleep in the dirt or under a bridge, did he? How did he go from being homeless to being a man with a job, dressed all fancy?

Papa met her eye and winked. She giggled and dashed off, jumping into the spinning chair and kicking her feet against the desk as she waited for him to finish. When they finally came out of the booth, Ronald didn't seem in a hurry to pay and leave.

He leaned against the outside of the booth. "Do you still have that old ledger book? I have a feeling I still owe you a pretty penny."

Papa chuckled. "It's around here somewhere, but that's water long under the bridge."

"Still." Ronald straightened and pulled out his wallet. Emira was about to tell him his total when he handed Papa a bill she didn't recognize. "I owe you. Here's for a great many cuts back in the day."

Papa pushed away Ronald's offer. "You don't have to do that. It's nothing."

"No. It was everything. Truly." Ronald looked Papa straight in the eye, and for a minute, it seemed like they were talking without words. What was going on? It was no fun being left out, and here it was happening again twice in one day.

Papa nodded and slipped the bill into his pocket. His pocket! "I appreciate it."

Emira frowned. What was that about? The money was supposed to go into the drawer, and *she* was supposed to get the tip. Her breath huffed out her nostrils.

After Ronald left, questions scrambled from Emira's mouth. "How much did he pay you? He used to be homeless? What happened?"

"Whoa there, Princess." Papa inched behind her, opened the drawer, and took out two dollar bills. He handed them to her, and even though he didn't tell her how much the water guy paid him, her frustration melted away.

Papa dropped into a chair in front, facing the windows. He watched Ronald get into a shiny red car. "As for the rest, that was so long ago." He rubbed the wooden chair arm. "He's an intelligent man. I always knew that. A smart one, for sure." He sounded like he was drifting far away.

"But what happened?"

Papa stuck out his lip. "I don't know. Maybe he changed. Or maybe he started being who he always truly was."

Emira tilted her head to the side. "Huh?"

"Sometimes, people just need a reminder of who they are, Princess."

It didn't make much sense, but something told her his words were important. She opened her notebook and scrawled a line.

Be who you are.

Then she recapped her pen. It wasn't enough. She tapped her pen against her chin a few times before adding one more.

Remind other people who they are.

On Sunday morning, Emira awoke on Nana and Papa's couch. She jumped up, sending the blankets tumbling, and checked the time. Eight o'clock. Good. Still early enough to roll Papa out of bed. She giggled as she tiptoed to his room.

Last weekend, she'd woken up on a blow-up mattress in Dad's boring apartment with the white walls and Chinese smells. This was so much better. Warm and familiar and comfy, like hot cocoa and her favorite blanket. Not like a roller coaster. Here, she knew what came next.

She opened Papa's door as softly as she could, but it still creaked. She winced, pausing to make sure he didn't stir. Papa's snores filled the room. Good. She crept onto the bed, then burst into laughter as she pushed his back. "Good morning, Papa!"

He awoke with a start. "What? Huh?"

She pushed harder, huffing as he slowly angled to the side. "Time to get up."

"Are you rolling me out of bed?"

"Yep."

From his side to his belly onto his back again, Papa rolled. When he reached the edge of the bed, he cried out, "No! No!"

She dissolved into giggles so hard she had to fight to breathe. Finally, with a final shove and a kerplunk, Papa fell onto the floor.

"You did it again, Princess."

Nana peeked through the door. "You got him up, I see."

"I did." She grinned as she stood and extended her hand to help him stand. He placed one arm on the bed and lifted the other to her. She hoisted him up. Her nose perked as the scent of pancakes wafted. "Come on, Nana's making breakfast."

Nana made the best pancakes with blueberries and whipped cream on top. Much better than Cheerios at Dad's apartment, even if he did sprinkle sugar on them. Her steps slowed as she approached the kitchen. The arcade with Dad had been fun. They'd played Skee-Ball until her arms overflowed with tickets. It'd been enough to get the stuffed elephant from the second shelf from the top. She peeked over at Fant, the elephant, where he lay on the couch half covered by the blanket. He was nearly big enough to use as a pillow. He smelled like Dad. Like fresh paint and stale chips and a little like the Chinese restaurant next door, but not too much. More like how Dad always smelled and not the new smells. She could sleep with Fant and almost not remember how everything had changed.

"You ready for your recital next weekend?" Nana asked while squirting whipped cream onto Emira's stack of pancakes.

"Yep." She forked a bite and closed her eyes as the sweet goodness pirouetted in her mouth. No one cooked better than Nana. Each meal made Emira battle between wanting to scarf down the food as fast as possible and wanting to let each bite sit on her tongue for hours. But as she had to eat this one before the whipped cream got too melty from the warm pancakes, she allowed herself only three deep breaths before swallowing. "I've practiced every number a bajillion times. I'm going to do great."

Other girls talked of stage fright, but Emira could barely imagine what that would feel like. Only she had the confidence that came with knowing she was born for the stage, made to perform. Nothing could shake her.

"Do you have a solo this time?" Nana sat across from her, the single pancake on her plate loaded with butter and syrup instead of whipped cream.

She shook her head, mouth full.

"But no one does, right, Princess?" Papa loaded his plate with pancakes to take and eat at his chair in the living room.

Emira swallowed. "Right. No solos this concert." She still didn't understand why, but at least it didn't mean Ms. Mulberry picked someone else over her. That would have been humiliating. There'd been a lot of talk about teamwork this quarter and "moving as one." Emira kept her mouth shut and did what she was told. Hopefully, if she got on Ms. Mulberry's good side, she'd get a solo next recital.

"Well, we can't wait." Nana popped up from the table and scurried to the sink to rinse a few dishes.

"We're so proud of you," Papa said before disappearing into the living room.

He grunted as he settled into his recliner, and the television flicked on. The soft voice of the golf announcers filled the background.

Last weekend, she'd cuddled up next to Dad while they watched the Muppets together. When he'd tucked his arm around her, she'd lost herself in the comfort of his closeness. She'd forgotten the strangeness of where she was, forgotten that she hadn't wanted to be there. When she got hungry, Dad popped popcorn. They ate some and threw the rest at each other, making a gigantic mess that he didn't make her clean up. It was … fun. But it still wasn't right. Nothing would be right until he was back home with Mom and her. Until they were all together again.

She had to make him come home.

When she finished her last bite, she set her plate in the sink and found Nana folding towels in the laundry room. "Can I call my dad?"

Nana smiled at her, but it was a sad smile. "Sure, honey. You miss him?"

Yes, but that wasn't why she needed to call him. Still, she nodded. It was too hard to explain.

"Go ahead. You know his number?"

"No." Dad had a new number, and she wasn't about to learn it.

"It's in my address book. I'll get it for you."

Nana fetched her address book and left Emira alone in Papa's office, giving her privacy to make the call. The phone rang and rang until it seemed like no one would pick up, but then a groggy voice answered. Had Dad still been asleep? What did he do all by himself anyway?

"Dad? It's me."

"Hey, kiddo. What's up?"

"My recital's next weekend. You have to come."

"Of course, I'll come, sweetheart. I have it on my calendar."

"Don't forget."

"I won't."

A long pause dropped between them while Emira blinked back the moisture gathering in her eyes.

Dad yawned. "Is that it? Is that why you called?"

Her voice squeaked out like a small, scared mouse. "Yes."

"Okay, then. I love you."

She loved him too. Why couldn't she say those words? She tried to push them out, but the only thing that came up her throat was "Don't forget."

She hung up the phone and let a single tear fall.

Chapter Sixteen

2010

Floyd stared numbly ahead from his spot on the second pew as the murmur of voices rose around him. He blinked at the shiny black coffin that held his sister. His throat tightened.

"I'm sorry for your loss."

He nodded and mumbled, "Thank you," without even looking to see who offered the condolences. He couldn't seem to take his eyes from the coffin. As if daring it to spit out his sister. His friend.

"Papa?" Emira's voice snapped him from the haze. He stood and engulfed her in an embrace. "Can I sit with you? Kade wanted to come, but the babysitter canceled last minute, and with Reagan's ear infection ..."

"Of course." Why would she ask that? "Did your dad come with you?"

"No."

"Then couldn't he watch the kids?"

She grimaced. "Not sure I'm comfortable with that."

He studied her. The simple black dress she wore brought out the bags under her eyes. Maybe it wasn't the time to point out that it wasn't like Jay had never been around children before. Instead, he scooted over. "Have you seen your mom?"

"She texted she was running late. Uncle Joseph's deep in conversation with Uncle Danny."

"And Nana?"

"When I entered, she was shuffling the floral arrangements around in the foyer."

He chuckled. "She'll probably sit in back. If she came up here, she'd make a disturbance every time she stood up to leave." No way would she be able to sit through the entire service.

"And my mom will likely sit with her. Looks like it's just you and me." She slung an arm around his shoulder and nestled close. The scent of coconuts wafted from her hair. "It's crowded. Hard to find a parking spot. Aunt Karen must have impacted a lot of lives."

He glanced over his shoulder. She wasn't kidding. Nearly every pew was filled except for a couple of rows in the back. He took inventory of the sea of people. Brother. Brother. Sister. Cousin. Cousin. Aunt. Niece. Nephew. Was that Karen's neighbor? Stranger. Stranger. Stranger. Who were all these people?

"You're speaking?" Emira asked while reading the order of service.

"Yeah. Going to say a few words." He checked his pocket for the folded piece of notebook paper. Good. Still there.

"That'll be nice." She patted his hand, and then her gaze traveled to the packet of papers sitting on his other side. "What's that?"

"Oh, just the application for the mission trip. I got here so early I thought I might work on it." He shook his head. "Don't know what I was thinking." Silly to imagine he'd have the brain power for such things today.

Her mouth twisted as she continued to eye the application, curiosity seeping from her pores. He slid the packet an inch farther from her. She didn't need to read about his failure. Best to distract her with something else.

He took hold of her fingers and squeezed. "It's no fun getting old. Watching the people you love die." Her gaze unglued from the packet and landed on Karen's casket. A successful distraction, the statement was one hundred percent true. The past year alone, he'd gone to a dozen funerals. Each one reminded him that he could be next. Every morning, he awoke, it could be his last day on earth. What a morbid thought. What he wouldn't give to be young and invincible again.

She nudged his side. "You've still got some good years left in you."

That was probably what Karen had thought too. Of course, she was happier now than she'd ever been on earth. In heaven with her Savior, she lived—truly lived—pain-free and full of joy. Knowing she was far better off gave him peace, of course. As did the assurance that he'd join her when he left this world. But what about his life on earth? How much of it would be proven wood, hay, and stubble? How much would stand the test and come forth as gold?

A priest began the service. He just couldn't get away from them.

"I've never been to a Catholic funeral before," Emira whispered.

Floyd winked at her. "You're in for a treat. Follow my lead."

He suppressed chuckles as Emira fumbled through the service. Standing, kneeling, making the sign of the cross, reciting prayers. The poor girl's pale face had beads of sweat dabbing the sides.

"I should have sat in back," she whispered.

"You're doing fine."

One of Karen's daughters sang "How Great Thou Art," then Karen's son spoke of what a wonderful mother she'd been.

The priest returned to the podium. "Now we'll hear a few words from Karen's brother, Floyd Douglas."

Floyd used the back of the pew in front of him to hoist himself up. His nerves skittered like a rabbit as he moved to the front. When was the last time he spoke publicly?

That sermon he gave in church? Best not to think about that memory.

When he turned to face the audience, emotion choked him. Not only was every seat filled, but a handful of people stood in back. How many lives could one person touch? Karen hadn't been a celebrity. She had never held a ministry position. Had never been in the paper or on television. She hadn't gone on mission trips. And yet, her funeral was standing room only?

How many people would attend his funeral? He pictured an empty room with only Marie, Joseph, Emira, and the great-grands. He swallowed. He had to do better. He would. It wasn't too late for him to make a change.

After a deep inhale, he pulled the paper from his pocket, unfolded it, and forced himself to speak. "If it wasn't for my sister, I might never have come to know Jesus as my Savior." Maybe God would have gotten hold of his heart some other way. Still. "Karen prayed for me, and prayed, and prayed. If you knew her, you know she was as stubborn as it gets." Laughter percolated through the audience. "She wouldn't give up on me."

From somewhere near the middle, a female voice called out, "Wouldn't give up on me neither."

He pressed his lips together, holding his emotions in check. He'd cry later. Right now, he had an idea. "Raise your hand if you became a Christian because of Karen's influence."

Hands popped up. Dozens and dozens of them. Thirty, forty, fifty … more? He couldn't keep count. So much for his resolve not to cry. He lifted his glasses and pinched the bridge of his nose. Moisture clung to his fingers. He sniffed and gathered his resolve. He could do this. Make it through without sniveling.

"Karen had an encounter with the Lord that changed her forever, and she never stopped talking about it. Only, she wasn't the kind of person to force her religion down anyone's throat. Though"—he tilted his head—"maybe she was a bit more forceful with her brothers."

More chuckles arose.

"But it was the way she lived that made a difference, not just what she said. The way she cared about each and every person she came across. The way she'd talk to a stranger as if they were the most important person in the world. When you were with her, you felt like you were the only other person in the room." He broke into a smile. "That was her way." Heads bobbed their assent. "So, I'm thankful to my sis for loving so well. For loving me so well. And all of you."

That was it. He couldn't say more. With a few quick nods, he left the platform and stumbled toward his pew.

With a damp tissue clutched in her fist, Emira maneuvered through pockets of mourners until she reached Nana. Her grandma stood at the back of the sanctuary, staring blankly at the stained glass window depicting the empty tomb. Without a word, Emira wrapped her arms around Nana, who startled at the touch.

"Oh, Princess." Nana pulled back and beamed at her with glassy eyes. "That was simply lovely."

The radiant smile seemed out of place among the sea of black surrounding them, but it had been a beautiful service. Emira nodded. "Very touching."

Nana took Emira's hands in her own. "Congratulations. I know you and Kade will be happy together."

What? Emira's stomach plummeted. Oh no.

Nana's brows pinched. "What happened to your veil?"

"Nana." Emira's voice trembled. "It was a touching *funeral*, wasn't it? For Aunt Karen."

She blinked a few times, then sucked in a quick breath. "Oh, yes. A touching funeral. Floyd did a good job."

Oh, thank goodness. She remembered where they were. Had she temporarily been transported to Emira's wedding six years prior? This was more serious than forgetting a minor detail. Nana had lost all sense of reality for a time. How often did this happen? Did Papa have any idea? Apparently, Mom and Uncle Joseph didn't. Emira loathed the weight of having another conversation with them about it.

Uncle Danny hobbled up to them and gave each a gentle hug. "Floyd's speech moved me. Couldn't have said it better."

He likely could have said plenty. He'd been radically saved around the same time as Papa. No doubt Karen's prayers had proven instrumental in his encounter as well. He had his own stories to tell. He began to tell one of them, but Emira's phone buzzed in her purse.

Kade asking how high of a fever was too high. Oh, dear. She needed to get home.

"I'm so sorry to interrupt, but I have to get going." She pointed to her phone as if that would explain everything.

"You aren't coming to the burial, then?" Nana's frown of disapproval likely had the opposite of its intended effect. It proved her fully back in the present, thank the Lord.

Emira felt no shame in ducking out of one family obligation for another. "Reagan's sick." She needn't explain further.

Nana hugged her again and wished her well. She found her mom, Papa, and Uncle Joseph and said her goodbyes, shot a text to Kade letting him know she was on her way, then hustled home.

Half an hour later, she burst through the door, arms aching to hold her little girl. She'd expected to find Kade pacing the living room, shushing a cranky baby. Instead, her dad sat on the couch next to Teddy, bowl of popcorn between them as they watched television.

She stopped so abruptly her purse fell off her shoulder and clunked to the floor. "What's going on? Where's Kade? Where's Reagan?"

"Gone. He took her for a drive. Said it helps her sleep."

Okay, but … "He left you in charge?" She cringed at how those words came out. Far ruder than intended.

He raised a brow. In question? In challenge? How frustrating that she could no longer read him. "Of Teddy? Yes, he asked me to keep an eye on the little guy while he was gone."

She schooled her expression. Kade had missed the funeral precisely because she hadn't wanted her dad to be alone with their children, and yet, here they were. Her chest burned, but she kept her voice even. "What are you watching?"

"*The Three Stooges.* I thought since he enjoyed *I Love Lucy*, he'd love the Stooges. You did at his age."

And now he'd tell the story of how she'd snuck into her mom and dad's bed late at night to watch the show as a young child. They'd awoken to her laughter. He loved that story.

"You remember when—"

"Yes." She couldn't stand to hear it again.

"You woke us up, doubled over in a fit of giggles."

"I know." Couldn't he take a hint? That picture of her mom and dad together in the same house, sharing the same bed … it pained her. Which made no sense. Shouldn't those be the best memories? The ones she'd long to cling to? But no. They were the ones that pierced her through. A reminder of all that she'd lost.

Ridiculous. These feelings that warred within her weren't rational. She couldn't reason with them. She'd tried explaining to those pesky emotions how well she had it, how things had turned out better this way. How she didn't need her dad anyway. Or how she knew her father loved her even if he'd left. They wouldn't listen. They only pulsed. Ached. Screamed to protect her children from this man who wasn't safe. She needed to be a buffer between her precious little ones and her father. His love scratched and rubbed raw, and they had baby skin.

"I'm going to call Kade." She ducked into the kitchen, hiding herself behind a cabinet. How little shelter there was with her father in her home. She couldn't hide from the feelings she'd avoided for years. They stared at her, unblinking, daring her to confront them.

She'd think about that later.

The phone rang, and Kade picked up. "Hey, baby."

"How's Reagan?"

"Better, I think. Asleep, finally. I'm afraid to stop driving. Mind if I end up in New Mexico?"

She chuckled. "Whatever it takes. But can you swing by and take me with you?"

"Sure. Be there in two hours."

A snort escaped before she sobered. "What about her fever?"

"The nurses' line said it's nothing to worry about. I gave her Tylenol, and it's already gone down." He sighed. "Sorry to worry you. I feel horrible you left early."

"Don't."

"How's your dad doing with Teddy?"

She groaned. "Why, Kade?"

"I don't understand what the big deal is. He's not a monster, and he's not incompetent. He's your *dad*. He loves you. He loves his grandkids."

"I know."

"But?"

"I can't explain it." She pulled at a loose thread on her dress sleeve.

"Maybe the Lord brought him back into your life at just the right time. So He could heal some things between the two of you."

She peeked around the corner at a scene that resembled one from her childhood. The flicker of the television illuminated Teddy's innocent face as he popped a piece of buttered popcorn into his mouth. A laugh reel played in the background. Teddy broke into a grin. Dad did too, but his gaze wasn't on the screen. It remained fixed on his grandson, as if he was soaking the moment in to treasure forever.

"Maybe."

She said goodbye and hung up the phone. With measured steps, she entered the living room and picked up the popcorn bowl from between the two of them, then sat down and settled it on her lap. Wedged between the past and the future, she crunched a piece of popcorn. This felt familiar. This felt safe. One of so many good memories with her dad. What if Kade was right? What if the Lord wanted to heal the rift between them, but her stubbornness stood in the way. Maybe she could offer a truce. She held a piece of buttery popcorn between her fingers. Then she let go, throwing it at her father.

He lobbed one back at her with a mischievous glint in his eye.

"Popcorn war!" This was one memory she'd happily recreate for her son.

Chapter Seventeen

1967

Floyd closed and locked the door to his new shop, then stood back to admire the sparkling, clean windows and gleaming barber pole. He paused and listened. Ah, how refreshing. No police sirens. What an improvement.

It had taken a few years, but this new shop in a better neighborhood was worth every minute of waiting. He now had the luxury of working with the front door unlocked … when he worked, that is.

The population of Maryland Heights couldn't quite support his new business. Not enough people for a nine-to-five, six-days-a-week job. Instead, he worked three days a week and spent the rest of his time parking cars and selling insurance. He even worked as a professional pallbearer from time to time. Anything to make ends meet.

But the town was bound to grow. It was just a matter of time before things would pick up, and he'd be able to work his profession full-time. Until then, he'd do what he had to do. He'd never been afraid of hard work.

And they had a new home, one where Marie and Joseph enjoyed their own rooms. One that he was eager to get home to now. But when he pulled into the driveway, Pop's car was parked on the street in front of their house.

A slimy feeling oozed down his spine. What was the old man doing here? He better not have given Susan and the children any trouble.

Shoulders rigid, Floyd exited his car and walked toward the front door porch. Pop sat on the concrete step, hat in hand. Floyd's gaze swept the perimeter in search of a beer can or bottle. He found none. "Hiya, Pop." He withheld welcome from his voice. He'd made a new life for himself, and this man wasn't invited into it. "Where are Susan and the kids?"

"The store."

Figured. His spitfire had enough sense to hightail it out of there at the first whiff of a rat.

He wiped his sweaty brow. That was too harsh. His father wasn't a bad man. Troubled, for sure. Plagued with addiction. But good underneath. Somewhere underneath all the alcohol and broken promises.

"I'm sober." Pop crunched his hat in his hands, squinting in Floyd's direction but never fully making eye contact. "Working through AA."

So that was it. He was working through the steps again and had finally come to make amends. Wasn't that step eight of nine? He'd hung on longer this time than most. Floyd pressed his lips together, trying to keep all sarcastic and biting words inside. They rolled around his mouth like pinballs in a machine.

Pop shifted on the step, his expression pained. "I know what all my kids think about me except for you. You've never said a word."

Floyd shook his head. Mom had always told him if you didn't have anything nice to say, don't say anything at all. Not that he'd followed that advice religiously. But in front of this man? Every vulnerability lay exposed.

"Tell me, son." Pop's eyes pleaded with him.

Floyd scrubbed the back of his neck. Here went nothing. "I spent my whole life feeling sorry for you. I never had a relationship with you, never knew you. You never knew me. You were never there for me like a father should be."

His chest burned at a memory. "Instead, I was the one carrying you inside when you passed out drunk in the front yard."

Mom hadn't been able to lift him. She'd called for the boys to help. How humiliating. How degrading.

Heat burst through Floyd's veins. "Maybe I can forgive you for all of that. But what I can never forgive you for"—his voice hitched—"is that I think I'm just like you."

Pop nodded, face crumpled, eyes watery. Had he broken his old man? A wave of remorse followed on the tail of his anger. He shouldn't have said those things. They were too harsh. Too bitter. Too true.

Floyd watched helplessly as Pop slunk back to his car and drove away.

Floyd felt like scum after his encounter with Pop until Danny called him the next day from their father's shop.

Saws and machinery whirred in the background as Danny spoke. "Did Pop swing by your place last night?"

Floyd slumped in his recliner at the back of his shop. "Yeah. He came by to make amends. I feel terrible. I was so rough on him. Wish I could take back what I said." He rubbed his neck as if he could scrub off the shame that coated him.

"You're kidding. He came into work today happy as a lark. I've never seen him so upbeat. He's whistling, Floyd. Whistling! Listen."

Sure enough, a merry tune filtered through the phone line. What in the world?

Danny chuckled. "Must have done him good to get that off his chest. Or maybe to know you got it off yours."

"Well, I'll be." Of all the oddities. His pop in a delightful mood.

Something twisted inside him. It didn't seem fair. Here his father was free and easy, but Floyd was not. Memories of his father in a drunken rage flashed through his mind. The way the crazed monster would yell so loud, it'd terrify everyone in the house. The time he'd been arrested for driving the wrong way on the highway. The time he'd hobbled through the front door and slurred that he'd lost his car. He was so drunk, he had no idea that it was stuck in a snow drift miles away.

He ground his teeth together. No. He couldn't whistle about those experiences, couldn't skip through the day as if Pop had made everything okay. How many times had the old man started AA? And how many times had he stuck with it? Zero. Because he couldn't be counted on for anything. Not a blasted thing.

Floyd mumbled a goodbye and slammed the phone onto the receiver.

One Saturday, he had just flipped the lights off in the shop when the phone rang on the front desk. He picked up. "Barbershop."

He'd yet to name the place. Every time he'd tried, he came up blank. Surely, something would hit him at the right time.

"Floyd? It's Karen."

His sister. He scooched onto the desk, letting his feet dangle and thump against the front. They'd had phone chats for years every Sunday afternoon, but it was rare to talk to her outside of that routine. Of course, Karen had recently suffered a mental breakdown that landed her in the hospital, disrupting the norm. Depression was a nasty beast. "Hey, sis. How are you?"

"Fantastic." She rushed ahead, her words gushing forth as if from a fountain. "I have to tell you about what happened to me."

He pulled the phone away from his ear and eyed it. Was this the same woman he'd spoken to last week? The one who'd said she wished the Lord would just take her home. "Are you out of the hospital?"

"Yes. I'm out. And I'm telling you, I'll never be the same."

"What did they do to you?" This was odd. Too strange. Anxiety snaked its tentacles around him.

She laughed, pure and free. "Not them. Jesus! Jesus met me there."

"Jesus." The Savior's name felt foreign on his tongue, which was ridiculous. He'd spent all his life saying that name, as any good Catholic would. He had studied to be a priest, for crying out loud. But something in the way Karen had said it was different.

"Yes, Jesus. He flooded me with His love, Floyd. It overwhelmed me. He is so much more than we've ever known. He loves us so much more than we ever could have believed. I will live the rest of my life telling people of His love."

Floyd shifted his jaw. Maybe they'd given her too much medication in the hospital. They'd flipped the switch from depressed to delusional. What could he say to that? He needed to respond, but he couldn't encourage this radical nonsense. "That's nice." Ugh. Did that sound like he agreed? He palmed his forehead.

"Nice?" Another giggle. "It's extraordinary. Oh, Floyd, I want you to experience this too. I want you to know Jesus."

He huffed. "I believe in Jesus, sis. The whole family does."

"No. The whole family goes through the motions of a religion that means nothing to them. I'm talking about so much more. I'm talking about having Jesus as a best friend."

"I don't know about that," he grumbled.

"I'll keep praying for you and Susan."

"Which prayer?" He'd memorized them all. He could recite Hail, Holy Queen and Anima Christi in his sleep.

"A prayer from my heart."

Her answer swelled in the air around him, pushing at the chip on his shoulder, at his pride.

"Don't worry, Floyd. God will make it clear to you. He'll show you He's real and personal in a way you won't be able to deny. I'll talk to you soon. Bye now."

The phone felt heavy in his palm, as if the conversation they'd just had held enormous weight. But that was ridiculous. Obviously, Karen wasn't in her right mind. She'd been in the hospital for mental problems, after all. This conversation proved it. If he gave her some time, allowed the medication they'd doused her with to flush out of her system, she'd mellow out.

Time to leave, yet he was too ruffled by the conversation with his sister to go home just then. He grabbed his jacket and headed over to the bar where a few of the regulars would no doubt be engrossed in a game of poker. Maybe he could double what he'd made in tips after a few lucky hands.

He opened the front door as quietly as he could. If Susan was asleep, he didn't want to wake her. She wouldn't be happy with him for skipping out on dinner and family time in favor of gambling with his buddies at the bar. He couldn't blame her. Why'd he let Karen's remarks needle him? He'd only proved her point that he wasn't as upright as he claimed. His stomach roiled at the stench of alcohol wafting from him. He even smelled like his father. A good night's sleep and perhaps he could forget any of this ever happened. He only needed to slip in undetected.

He ascended the stairs to the dimly lit living room. Empty. He exhaled deeply, relieved. He hadn't quite figured out an excuse that was likely to satisfy his wife. Now, he didn't need to. At least, not tonight.

But as he stepped into the kitchen to rustle up a snack, he stumbled. Susan sat at the kitchen table in her nightgown, hands folded serenely in her lap. She turned her head to face him and smiled. "Come have a seat."

He swallowed. Oh boy. Here it was. He was in for a dressing-down. He shuffled over and sat, scrambling for an excuse. But when he met her gaze, he found not a hint of accusation there. Peace exuded from her. Peace and something like … light? That uneasy feeling that came over him when things were out of order wrapped around his middle for the second time that day.

She smiled again, and it was bigger, brighter, freer than he'd ever seen. "I've got to tell you what happened to me."

Floyd glanced around. Déjà vu hummed in the back of his brain. Was Karen here? Was this all a setup? But they were alone. He braced his hands on the table and spoke cautiously. "Go on."

"I was lying in bed, and God spoke to me."

"Spoke to you?"

"Yes." She nodded. "He spoke to me and told me to look in the mirror. So, I got up and stood in front of the mirror and looked at myself. Then God said—" Tears pricked the corners of her eyes as her voice cracked. "He said, 'I love you.'"

"God spoke to you and told you He loved you?" The familiarity sent a shiver up his spine.

She flicked tears away from the corners of her eyes. "Yes. Me! Can you believe it? Lord knows what a mess I am, but He loves *me*."

Floyd stood so fast he banged his thigh on the table. Wincing, he rubbed the spot as he paced.

"You believe me, don't you?" Susan asked.

"I don't know what to believe." He ran a hand through his hair.

God will make it clear to you. He'll show you He's real and personal in a way you won't be able to deny.

One look at his wife told him she was different. Something had happened to her. But was it real? Was it God? He'd grown up going to church all his life, and this kind of thing did not happen. His religion was rational and practical. It was full of order. Regular people did not have crazy experiences with God. Everything went through a priest.

"Jesus loves me, Floyd. And He loves you too."

Floyd pulled at his collar. The room had suddenly grown stifling hot. He couldn't stay here, couldn't stand to be in this place another minute. "I've got to get out of here." He rushed to his bedroom.

Susan followed. "Where are you going?"

He grabbed a canvas bag from the top shelf of the closet and rummaged through his drawers, tossing things in. "To the cabin."

Hopefully, the hour-long drive to his parents' cabin at Lake Tishomingo would give him time to clear his mind. They wouldn't be there this weekend, and the time alone would give him some distance from this insanity.

Susan put her hand on his bicep. "I'll be waiting."

"Yeah," he mumbled, stuffing socks and underwear in the bag. "You and Jesus."

His time at the lake did nothing to settle his soul. A few beers by the water's edge and his gut churned more than ever. *Jesus.* How could two women he cared the world about talk about Jesus as if He were more than an archaic deity in a recited prayer? God, talking to people. God, encountering people. Absurd. He dug the toe of his boot into the mud.

But how could he account for the peace that radiated from his wife? He couldn't describe it. Susan had looked the same—same hair, same dress, same face—and yet, she'd been entirely different, as if lit from within. What else could have done that? Who else? She was one way when he'd left in the morning and completely different when he'd returned at night. He shivered. He couldn't come up with an alternative explanation. Unless … had Karen called her? Gotten into her head? But Susan wasn't likely to be swayed by anyone. She was her own woman with an iron will. Good luck bending it.

Blast it. Why couldn't he get the whole mess out of his mind? It had followed him. He tossed his empty beer into the nearby trash can. Might as well head home. There was nothing for him here.

He grabbed his things and piled into the Volkswagen. What had happened to his wife? Was it real? Was it God? The questions nipped at his heels. He pressed hard on the accelerator in an attempt to outrun them. Still, they persisted.

Flying down the highway, he let out a guttural howl. His eyes filled with tears. Truth was, he was miserable trying to make his life work by himself. He only served to make a mess of everything. God as a best friend? It sounded good. Too good? Maybe. But if not …

"God!" His shout reverberated around the interior of his speeding car. "If You're real, You've got to show me. Now."

Immediately, it was as if the sun invaded his Volkswagen. Brilliance overtook the peripheral of his vision, and he swerved to the side of the road and jammed the gear into park. Warmth enveloped him as he heaved in sweet-smelling air that oozed like honey into the deepest parts of him. The skin on his arms tingled. His pulse slowed. His shoulders relaxed. A soothing presence drenched him, washing away all worry, all fear.

"God, is this you?" Even as he asked the question, the answer was clear. This was the God Karen had talked about, the God Susan had encountered in front of the mirror.

Something was written in graffiti on the wall of an overpass in front of him. He rubbed his eyes. His vision cleared to see *Thank you, Karen.*

A laugh bubbled from him. *Karen.* He'd thought her crazy, yet she'd been right about everything.

This was the Jesus who was more than a routine mention in a scripted prayer. This Jesus was alive. Personal. Willing to wade into Floyd's mess and offer what no ritual ever could: life.

A sob caught in Floyd's throat. He didn't need anyone to tell him how underserving he was of this kind of love. His faults glared menacingly at him. He couldn't seem to take a step without landing in one pile of dung or the other. He didn't know how to be a good husband, even less how to be a good father. He'd never seen those roles modeled.

Tears coursed down his cheeks. How could God choose him? Love *him*? It was unfathomable, yet the presence filling the car told him there was nothing so true. If this amazing love was real—and he had no doubt now that it was—how could he not give his whole heart and life to *this* Jesus?

As soon as Floyd arrived home and told Susan what had happened to him, the course in front of him was clear. He had to forgive his father, truly forgive him. And he needed to do it to his face. They made arrangements to have Pop over for dinner the following weekend.

He couldn't tell who was more thrilled about his encounter with the Lord on the road: Susan or Karen. When he called his sister to tell her, he had to hold the phone away from his ear so she didn't burst his eardrum with all her hooting and hollering.

"I've been praying for you."

Full of awe, he whispered the graffiti words that had been scrawled on the wall, "Thank you, Karen."

As for Susan, he'd never seen anything quite like her transformation. She was as joyful as a little kid. She nearly danced from place to place instead of walked, her smile stretching wide. The next-door neighbors asked if she was on drugs. Even they knew something had changed.

The night before Pop came for dinner, a knock on the door at two in the morning awakened Floyd. He stumbled out of bed and to the door, hiking up his pajama pants as he went. Who on earth would be at the door at this hour? He scratched his head, then cracked the door open to reveal his brother Danny.

Danny's hair stood on end as if he'd run his hands through it one too many times, but his eyes were bright and alert. "It's true," he said with a smile.

Though his statement could have referred to a lot of things, the way Floyd's heart leapt at the pronouncement told him Danny spoke about this radical love of God. Karen must have been praying for all her siblings to encounter this Jesus because Danny's countenance revealed the same change Floyd saw in himself when he looked in the mirror.

"I know."

Danny shook his head as if he could hardly believe this good news and walked back to his car without another word. Floyd watched him drive away, then shut the door. There was another man who would never be the same.

The next evening, both of Floyd's parents arrived for dinner. Pop's gaze shifted around as he stuffed his hands into his pockets, took them out, and shoved them in again. He was clearly uncomfortable. After their last chat, Floyd couldn't blame him. It was time to set the man at ease.

As they sat around the table, Floyd began by telling what had happened to him on the way home from their cabin. Floyd's mother clapped her hands. "Oh, that's wonderful. You know what you ought to do? You should get involved with the Life in the Spirit seminars. They have one—"

"Mom, I need to talk to my father."

His mother sat back, frowning slightly. "All right, but I can give you the number to register. I have it at home. Karen is going. I think you'd—"

"Mom!" He'd spoken louder than he'd intended. "I want to talk to my father."

Her eyes grew solemn as she nodded.

Floyd turned his full attention to Pop, who shifted in his seat, eyes focused on the checkered tablecloth. "I was tough on you last time you came out. I said some really harsh things."

"It's all right, son. I deserved it."

Floyd shook his head. Maybe so, but … "Pop, I love you, and I forgive you. I know—" His throat burned, and tears spilled from his eyes. "I know you're a good man."

These heightened emotions were new. He wasn't prone to crying at all, least of all in public. And in front of his father?

But Pop's wet face matched his own. A sign and a wonder. Pop opened his mouth to speak, but only strangled tearful sounds leaked out. The old man's shoulders shook. Floyd stood and placed a hand on his shoulder.

Finally, he managed to speak. "Thank you, son."

In a flash, Susan rounded the table and wrapped her arms around Pop. "We love you." She held his face in her hands and dried his tears with her fingertips. "We love you."

Floyd's mouth unhinged. Who was this woman? She'd never liked Pop. She tolerated his mother but certainly hadn't been gushing with love for his parents. Mr. and Mrs. Sonjak had never liked either of them, so perhaps that had rubbed off on their daughter.

But now, as Susan told Floyd's father of their love for him repeatedly, she exuded authenticity. Anyone with working eyes would be able to see that she meant it. Love poured from her, puddling over Pop. His breathing slowed, and the pained lines on his face relaxed. When he smiled, it had the effect of a rainbow after a long, hard rain.

A few minutes later, Susan returned to her place at the table next to Floyd's mother, who sat in stunned silence. He'd forgotten she was there she'd been so quiet.

"Here, Susan, I've got something for you." Pop reached into his back pocket and pulled out his wallet. Inside the fold was a small card. He took it out and studied it while putting his wallet away. "I want you to have this." He slid it across the table to her.

Floyd leaned over to see but couldn't make out the words printed on it. "What does it say?"

Susan trailed a finger underneath the words as she read. "Success is getting what you want. Happiness is wanting what you have."

Floyd nodded. "That's wise."

Did his father live with such contentment now? He certainly hadn't when Floyd was growing up. But the man sitting in front of him wasn't the same man. He was changed. Had love changed him like it had changed the rest of them?

"I'm going to keep this forever." Susan grinned up at Pop. "Thank you. I'll treasure it."

The next weekend, Floyd would hold that card in trembling hands, racked with equal parts grief and gratitude as he processed the tragic events of the day. Because a week after Floyd forgave his father, Pop died in a car crash.

"You did what?" The awe in Karen's voice made him smile. He shifted the receiver to his other ear and crossed his ankle over his knee, leaning back in the leather chair. The only light in the shop came from sunset glimmering through the front windows. He'd already turned off the lights, about to close up for the night, when he had the impulse to call Karen.

"I forgave the old man. Invited him over for dinner and told him myself."

"Just like that? After years of despising our father, you were able to offer forgiveness?"

"It wasn't ..." How could he explain it? His mouth twisted as he scrambled for words. "It wasn't of myself. It was the Lord through me."

Before Jesus had changed his heart, he might have been able to force out the words, but he never could have meant them. This was an act of God.

"Well, I'll be, Floyd. Jesus really got ahold of you, didn't He?"

"He sure did. His love is like nothing I've ever experienced before. I'll never be the same."

"The Bible says if anyone is in Christ, he is a new creation. The old is gone. The new has come. Sounds like what you're experiencing, huh?"

A new creation. Yeah. It was as if he had new eyes to see the world, new ears to hear things he'd never heard before. His new heart beat fresh blood throughout his body. "Exactly."

"Hey, do you still need a name for your shop?"

He cast a glance at the sign on the window proclaiming a generic *Barbershop.* "Yes."

"What about New Creations? It'll forever remind you of what the Lord did in your heart."

As if he could ever forget. But yeah. It fit well with a place where people came in looking one way and left looking another. "I like it."

"Me too. Make yourself a sign and hang it up so you'll always remember who you are."

Why did she keep talking to him as if he had dementia? That encounter with the Lord was forever branded in his heart and mind. He didn't need a sign to remind him. But customers would need one to identify his shop.

"Okay, sis."

"Let me know when it's up, and I'll come take a picture for my scrapbook."

He chuckled. Of course, she would. Some things didn't change.

Chapter Eighteen

1990

The house lights dimmed. Emira's dance teacher ushered the students onto the stage, sparkly tutus ruffling with each movement. Emira found her place just off-center stage left and posed, arms down at her sides, hands fanned outward. Their class would perform numbers of ballet, tap, and jazz. Jazz first. Probably because Ms. Limerill wanted to get the most boring part out of the way.

In the dark, it was impossible to see the audience clearly, but Emira still squinted, trying to pick out her parents and Nana and Papa. All she could make out were shadows. Then the music started, and the spotlights nearly blinded her. She had to focus to remember all the steps—no way would she embarrass herself in front of all those people—so she couldn't spend time looking for her family.

When the number finished, however, her mom's loud whistle sounded above all other cheers. Emira's head turned in the direction of the noise, and she found her mom grinning at her. She started to wave but dropped her hand. Waving from stage was unprofessional. If she wanted to be a famous performer, she had to act like one. Papa stood next to Mom, tall and proud. Nana beamed shoulder to shoulder with him. But where was Dad?

The rest of the dancers shuffled around into their positions for the next number, but Emira rose on tiptoes searching for her father's face. He wasn't there. Her shoulders slumped. He hadn't come. No matter that she'd practiced every day. No matter that she knew each number perfectly. He wouldn't be there to see it. All her hard work wasn't enough.

"Come on, Emira," the girl next to her whispered.

Emira settled into her spot. But why? Why should she even do these stupid dances anyway? This was useless. It wasn't bringing her dad back to their family. What was the point?

As the new song began, Emira's body moved to the steps and motions from memory. With each spin, she sought out her family's row, hungry for a glimpse of her father. Maybe he was only running late. He might have just arrived. She concentrated on her next plié. It had to be perfect, just in case he *was* out there.

But disappointment rose with each glance. No Dad. No Dad. No Dad. She stumbled and nearly took a nosedive onto the stage but caught herself just in time. She bit her lip, holding back the sting of tears.

She wouldn't look for Dad anymore. Doing so only made her mess up. If he even remembered to ask about her recital, it would be embarrassing if Mom said, "She did so well until she fell on her face." No. She would make him sorry he missed it.

When the time came for the ballet numbers and her series of pirouettes, she was supposed to pick a focal point in the audience so she wouldn't get dizzy. She concentrated on the middle of Papa's left eyebrow. It didn't matter that her dad hadn't come. Papa was there. He was always there for her, someone she could count on. Someone she could trust. Her heart warmed as her focal point rose in appreciation.

When she curtsied, Papa's applause thundered above the rest of the crowd. Those giant hands that had lifted her in the air when she was a baby slammed together for her now. Surely, this was enough. His love was big enough to fill her when Dad's leaving made her feel empty. He was the best man in the whole world, and he was hers. All hers. She could do anything if he believed in her.

As the recital ended, the girls rushed down the steps and into the audience to find their families. Emira raced and leapt into Papa's arms.

"Did you like it?" she asked as he squeezed her tight. She rested her head on his shoulder.

"Like it? I loved it. You were amazing!"

While Mom and Nana rubbed her back and told her what a good job she'd done, she clung to Papa, breathing in the scent of his smoky shirt and Irish Spring. She'd done well, performed like a star, and she smiled to herself. It felt good.

Something caught her eye over Papa's shoulder. A familiar figure with slightly stooped shoulders and sandy blonde hair.

"Dad?" He'd come? He must have had the wrong time because he was very late.

Everyone turned to see her father weaving through the crowd toward them. Emira pulled back from Papa's arms.

Dad beamed at them as he neared. "There you guys are! I was looking all over for you. I sat over there." He pointed to the other side of the auditorium. "You were wonderful, sweetheart."

He'd been there the whole time? He'd seen it all? A strange feeling tugged at her chest. He held his arms out to her. She hesitated, not ready to leave the warmth of Papa's embrace entirely. Papa tapped her back lightly, a little nudge, as if telling her to go where she belonged—in her dad's arms.

She leaned toward Dad but didn't wrap her arms around him. He nestled his arms around her, though, and kissed the top of her head.

"Wasn't she great?" Papa asked again, although they'd all said she was.

"I'm so impressed," Dad said, kissing her head again.

Slowly, an idea formed in her dazed mind. She snaked one hand up to grab her dad's, and with the other hand, she took her mom's. With a parent in each hand, she smiled her brightest. "We should go out for ice cream to celebrate."

Mom looked at Dad. "Want to?"

"Sure."

Yes! Emira swung her hands high, making her parents' knuckles touch. Maybe her plan wasn't silly after all. She *could* be the glue that stuck her parents back together, one performance at a time.

Emira sat around a sticky table at Baskin-Robbins, banana split oozing deliciousness in front of her. She only picked at it. On the left side of their square table sat Dad and Mom, close but not close enough to touch. Dad ate a chocolate cone. Mom, of course, ate nothing. She didn't like ice cream. Across from her, Nana and Papa dove into hot fudge sundaes. Emira should have been thrilled her plan had worked, except for one thing—Rachel sat on the right side of their square table. With her triple-scoop strawberry sundae and her black hair in a topknot, she was the center of all the attention. *Rachel.*

They'd been so close to walking out those doors, just the five of them, when Papa turned and studied the stage with a frown. It was empty except for one girl who sat dangling her legs over the edge, a far-off look in her eyes.

"Who's that?" he'd asked.

Emira cast a glance backward to see what Papa was talking about. "Oh, that's Rachel." She dropped Mom's hand long enough to take Papa's and tug him forward.

He didn't budge. "Does she not have family? Didn't anyone come to see her perform?"

Emira shrugged. She didn't know Rachel well. Hadn't given the girl much thought. Rachel kept to herself. She didn't seek out the spotlight or audition for solos like Emira did. She seemed to prefer to stay hidden in the background, but what was the point of being on stage if you didn't want to be seen? It didn't make sense.

Papa tugged back, a surprise that loosened Emira's grasp on Dad's hand and sent her stumbling straight into Papa's belly. "Why don't you go invite her to come with us?"

She blinked up at him. "Her? You want her to come with us?"

"Sure. Why not?"

Why not? Because this was her special time with Dad and Mom together. And *she* was the glue. Because she didn't even really know Rachel, and the little mouse might ruin everything.

But the soft look on Papa's face reminded her of the way he'd looked at the stranger in the hospital. Of how he'd sat and listened as a man he didn't know shared his sadness. That man had left a little lighter because Papa's listening had taken some of the heaviness away. Hadn't she prayed with him that day and asked God to help her to see people? Yet here Papa was again seeing what Emira didn't.

"Okay," she mumbled. She would do it, but she didn't have to like it. Still, she couldn't invite Rachel with a frown. She forced the sides of her mouth to turn up a little, for Papa.

Rachel agreed with a shy smile and asked Papa to call her mom, who was stuck at work, and let her know. They left all together as if they were one big happy family.

Now Emira's ice cream melted as her stomach twisted.

"How long have you been in dance?" Mom asked Rachel.

Rachel swallowed a humongous bite before answering. "Four years."

Mom's eyes widened. "Four years? Wow. You started young."

"Emira didn't start until she was what, six?" Nana asked.

Papa nodded. "Six."

So what? Rachel started dancing when she was four. Emira didn't start until she was six. Why did it matter? It didn't mean Rachel was a better dancer. She poked at the banana with her spoon.

"What do your parents do?" Mom asked.

Rachel's shoulders fell. "It's just my mom."

"Oh. I see. What's her job? You said she had to work today?"

She let out a deep sigh. "She's a social worker."

"What's a social worker?" Emira asked. From the look of Rachel's frown, it had to be horrible, like working in a funeral parlor.

"She helps children whose parents aren't taking good care of them. She comes home sad and quiet a lot."

Emira wanted to ask Rachel more questions, like what happened to her dad and why her mom couldn't take off work to see her, but Rachel looked like a turtle that had stuck its head back into its shell. It was clear she didn't want to answer more questions. She seemed to only want to eat her ice cream and pretend like there was nothing sad in the world.

Emira understood that. She made eye contact with her dance friend and offered a small smile. Then she scooped a bite of melty ice cream and stuffed it into her mouth.

Chapter Nineteen

2010

Floyd ran a hand through his hair and tugged at the ends. This application was a thousand pages long. Why'd they need to know all this information anyway? The busybodies. Why didn't they just hire a personal investigator for each missionary volunteer while they were at it? For the love of all that was holy. If he hadn't already paid, the application alone might make him reconsider.

He flipped the page, having completed detailed information about his church.

Please describe your salvation experience.

His salvation experience. He remembered it as if it was yesterday. The look on Susan's face, the peace radiating from her. Her outrageous claims. His drive to Lake Tishomingo. The way he'd challenged the Lord in the car, and then … how God had met him there. He could close his eyes and recount each moment of it. But how could he put it into words?

He picked up his pen and scrawled, "Back in 1967, I cried out to God to show me if He was real, and He did."

There. He'd answered that question. But as he peered at the question again through his glasses, he groaned at the next sentence.

Please use at least 200 words.

Two hundred words? Who did they think he was? A novelist? How in the world was he supposed to write two hundred words about something he couldn't explain? It was as if he were a schoolboy with an English assignment.

He wouldn't do it. Couldn't. What would they do if he was a little short on the word count? Kick him out of the trip? He scoffed. If something came to him later, he'd add to his answer. For now, he'd move on.

How has your salvation impacted your life?

He stared at the question. Everything had changed that day, right? That's what he'd always claimed. Jesus had changed him from the inside out. He was a new creation. But what did that mean *really*? He pictured the crowded pews at Karen's funeral. Now, *there* was someone whose salvation had impacted her life. The ripples of her conversion reached far and wide. They touched life after life after life. Far more than he could comprehend. While she lived on earth, she probably had no idea how far her impact reached.

Could he pretend to be her when answering this question? The corner of his mouth twitched. It was just like him to want to cheat on a mission trip application. See, this was what he was talking about. The Bible said he was a new creation, but he remained as Floydish as the boy who had gotten kicked out of the seminary. His salvation certainly hadn't transformed his handyman skills. It hadn't changed the trajectory of his career. Before he was saved, he raised a family, cut hair, and golfed when he got a chance. After he was saved, he did the same. Shouldn't he have something important to fill out in this blank?

Forget it. He'd skip to the next question. Circle back to this one later.

List past mission trips/volunteer experiences.

His palms grew sweaty. The pen slipped in his grasp. Past mission trips? None. He'd never even gone into the city for a service project. Volunteer experiences? Susan had served at the food pantry a few times, but him? There was that one time he was going to fill in as an usher, but he'd gotten sick and hadn't been able to. Was it the thought that counted?

Of course, he'd led that teen small group. Did he have to mention how long ago that was? *I served once forty years ago* seemed almost more "pathetic than simply leaving the question blank.

His breath came in hot bursts. How could his salvation experience have been so powerful, and yet he had nothing to show for it? The blank space stared up at him. Nothing.

His entire life. A waste.

He had to change that. Now.

"Susan!" He stood quickly, and pain knifed his back, causing him to pause and catch his breath. "Susan." Her name came out like a strangled cry.

She rushed into the dining room, blue feather duster in hand. "Floyd, what's wrong?"

He grimaced and forced his question past the ache along his spine. "When are you going to the food pantry next? I need to come along."

She blinked back at him as if he'd taken leave of his senses.

"When?" he repeated.

"Tuesday, but—"

"I'll join you."

"Right now, you look about to tumble to the floor." She grabbed his elbow.

He shook her off. "I'm fine."

Her eyebrow arched.

"Just a teeny back spasm."

"Why'd you call me in here with all the urgency of an alien invasion if you were fine?"

He worked to relax his facial muscles. No way she'd be convinced with his face contorted in pain. "I have nothing to list on the application for service projects." She opened her mouth, but he cut her off. "Nothing recent, at least."

She rested a hand on her hip. "And you think they'll kick you off the trip unless you rush down to the food panty?" Her mouth quirked at the edges.

"No." He huffed. "But I need to do this. For me."

She rolled her eyes and set to dusting the china cabinet. "Sure, Floyd."

Oh, it rankled him when she responded that way. She had to know it too. That must be why she did it. But he plopped back into the chair as if her dismissiveness didn't bother him in the least. That'd show her.

He'd leave that question blank as well and come back to it. He flipped to the next page, pen poised to knock out some questions. Instead, a physical form glared back at him. His blood chilled. He had to get a physical? From an actual doctor? No one had mentioned this. He scanned the myriad of questions. Which one might disqualify him? Blood pressure? List of current medications? He shivered.

"What's the matter now?"

He glanced up to find Susan eyeing him.

"Nothing," he nearly growled.

She stared him down.

"I have to get a physical."

She barked out a laugh. "It's about time."

Like she was one to talk. She was more likely to get into a fistfight at Kmart than go to a doctor.

"Have Emira go with you. She'd love that." Susan winked, then resumed dusting.

No way he'd let Princess take her poor, elderly grandpa to the doctor. She'd probably take notes and call and remind him to take his medicine each day. Or worse, come and hover over him until he did. He did not need to remind her why he should not go on this trip. "I can go myself."

And whatever the results, he'd keep them away from his granddaughter's eyes.

Hopefully, the doctor would agree he was healthy enough. He did not want to have to falsify a document for a mission trip. And he wouldn't. Of course, he wouldn't. If it came to it, he'd have Susan do it. She had experience in forgery.

Emira had put this off for long enough. She'd given Papa a couple of days to grieve after Karen's funeral, but if she didn't take action now, she might lose her courage. Straightening her spine, she marched up to Nana and Papa's front door and walked right in. "Hello. It's me."

"Emira? What are you doing here?" Papa set the newspaper on his lap and grinned over at her. "You just missed Nana. She went shopping with your mom."

"I know. Mom took the kids too."

Papa's smile dimmed. Did he sense the setup? She'd had to do some wrangling to make it all come together. Nana hadn't needed anything from the store. She had to manufacture a sale on bed linens. Guilt prickled the back of her neck at the thought of Mom having to deal with the backlash when Nana found out queen sheet sets were indeed full price. But desperate times …

"Where's your dad?" Papa pulled the lever to incline his chair. With a *thunk*, it thrust him forward.

"At the hardware store. He's going to help Kade install a ceiling fan."

"You mean he's going to install the fan while Kade watches?"

She lifted a shoulder. "And hand him the needed tools."

"I knew I liked your husband."

She chuckled. Yep. Those nonhandymen had to stick together. Just like she and Papa needed to do. She could not have their relationship fracture from this conversation. She'd rehearsed what she would say the entire ride here. Now, though, cotton seemed to fill her mouth and her brain. What was the game plan?

She tiptoed over to the couch and perched on the edge as if stepping too heavily might disrupt the peace between them. "So," she said, attempting a casual tone, "how's Nana been?"

"Fine. Just fine."

Pretty much what she'd expected him to say. Her tongue swept her teeth. She had to broach the subject carefully. "Have you noticed anything ... different with her lately?"

"Different?" His brow furrowed.

"Unusual."

He shook his head, a frown marring his face. "No. Not at all."

Okay, maybe she could go about it from a different angle. "When's the last time you guys went to the doctor?"

A scowl overtook his features. She scooted back an inch. Definitely not the reaction she'd anticipated.

"She told you?" His voice rose an octave.

"Told me what?"

"About the physical. I told her not to say anything."

"Papa." She put out a hand. "No one said a thing to me about any physical. I was only making conversation." Not exactly a lie. Or not entirely one.

The lines on his forehead smoothed. "Nana didn't mention anything?"

"No, but now I'm curious."

He folded his arms across his belly. "It's no big deal. The trip requires me to have a physical. That's all."

He'd sure had made it seem like a big deal. Why? She closed her eyes for a moment to block out the distraction. She hadn't come to talk about Papa's health. If she didn't discuss the pressing matter at hand now, disaster might strike before she had the chance. She choked out strangled words. "I came to talk about Nana."

His chin dimpled with another frown. "What about her?"

Enough beating around the bush. She had to be direct, come what may. "I'm concerned she may be having lapses in her memory."

He waved her off. "It's called getting old."

She firmed her jaw. "No. I think it's more than that."

"What are you saying?" His eyes narrowed.

"Dementia." She whispered the word. There. It was out there. That horrible word.

"You mean like Oldtimers?"

"Alzheimer's. Possibly." She clutched her hands in her lap.

"Nah." He snorted, then laughed, but it fell flat. "She's fine. Her mind's as sharp as a skewer. Trust me."

"She thought Karen's funeral was my wedding."

He froze for a second before shivering slightly. "She had to be joking with you."

"She wasn't joking."

His voice hardened. "Emira, she's fine."

"A few weeks ago, when I was here—"

"I said, she's fine!"

The roar of Papa's words hit her like a slap. Fine, huh? If she was fine, he wouldn't be so defensive. If she was fine, he wouldn't be in such denial.

Face hot, she snatched her purse and marched toward the door. "I hope you come to your senses." Before something terrible happened. She stopped at the front door, clenching and unclenching her hands. "I love you, but you are so stubborn."

His voice quieted, but his gaze contained every ounce of that same steely determination. "Runs in the family."

The sides of her lips twitched upward. How infuriating. She couldn't stay mad at him. "Love you, Papa."

"Love you too, Princess."

Lord, help them both.

Chapter Twenty

1968

Business started to pick up at New Creations, allowing Floyd to quit his part-time job parking cars and scale back on his insurance sales. He wasn't too good at that anyway. Finally, he could cut hair four days a week in his very own shop with the front door not only unlocked but wide open to let in the fresh air.

He was living the dream.

Not his dream, exactly. At least, not his original dream. He could close his eyes and still taste the orange mouth guard as his fist flew through the air. *That* dream of acclaim had been replaced by a softer, quieter one. One where Marie and Joseph had shoes without holes as grade-schoolers and more than an orange and a tube of deodorant in their stockings at Christmas when they got to be teenagers. Not that he blamed his parents for being poor. They'd worked hard, and the Lord knew his mom had raised him well with what she had. Now he had the opportunity to do a smidgen more, and not just materially.

He could be there every night for dinner. He could go to Joseph's games and Marie's recitals. He could take them out for ice cream or play catch in the yard. He could do any number of things because he resolved to be *there*. He would be present as a husband and a father. He would be everything his father wasn't, Lord bless him. This love God had poured into Floyd's heart ... he would pour it onto his family.

And if he got to play a little baseball and golf as well, and if he got to breathe in fresh air and soak in sunshine, well, that was a darn good life if you asked him.

But no one was asking him. Instead, new clients filed in each day. Paying clients, mostly. He made a point to learn their names.

Ferris was in desperate need of a cut when he shuffled in. Floyd pegged him as the nervous sort from the beginning from the way he wiped his Coke-bottle glasses on his shirt every two minutes.

Ferris shifted in the chair in the middle of a cut. Though his movements were slight, he threw off Floyd's equilibrium and thinned his patience.

Floyd turned off the clippers and spun the man around to face him. "Do you need to get a load off, Ferris? Because if you move again, you'll either end up with a lopsided cut or with half an ear."

Ferris shuddered. He must have heard the story from someone and probably couldn't tell if Floyd was joking or not. "Sorry, Floyd. I'll hold still."

Floyd shook his head and put a foot on the lever at the bottom of the chair, lowering the customer until Floyd towered over him. "Nothing doing. Talk first. I'll cut after."

"Oh, golly." Ferris fidgeted under the apron. "I just don't know what to do."

"What to do about what?"

"There's this neighbor. A friend." Ferris expelled a giant sigh. "At least I thought he was a friend. Now I think he's only been using me the whole time."

"Using you how?"

Ferris leaned forward and dropped his voice to a whisper. "He's in the Mafia."

Floyd took a step back. "No kidding?"

"Sure is. Found out when a guy came looking for him." He cringed. "It's a long story. What I'm meaning to say is we've done everything with this fellow and his wife. We go to church with them, had them over for birthday parties. We go out to eat with him quite frequently."

Ferris knotted the apron in his lap. "I always thought it was strange. He never had to pay a dime. The most highfalutin restaurants cater to him like he's royalty. 'Hello, Mr. Girardi. Is there anything we can do for you, Mr. Girardi? Would you like more champagne, Mr. Girardi? It's on the house.' Peculiar, you know? But I thought it was because he owns the meat packing company, and perhaps the restaurants love his cuts." Ferris turned wide eyes to Floyd. "No. It's because he's a consigliere."

"A crime boss's advisor? You sure?"

Ferris nodded.

Floyd pressed his knuckles to his lips. A real-life crime story, playing out in front of him. What were the odds? "What are you going to do?"

"I don't know. The thing is, I'm hurt as the dickens. I thought the Girardis were our friends. In reality, I think they're only using us as a front to project themselves as a typical, upstanding American family." His eyes darkened. "They're using us."

"Are you sure?" Didn't Mafia men need friends too? Ones of the less dangerous variety.

"It's obvious to me now. I feel like such a fool."

Floyd shook his head. "Don't beat yourself up over it. It could happen to anybody. I bet you're the man's favorite fake friend."

Ferris's shoulders lifted with his chuckle.

"Are you going to turn him in?"

His answer came swift and sure. "No. Too dangerous." He fiddled with the ashtray on the chair's arm. "The question is whether I should play dumb or refuse to be friends with him any longer."

"Great question." One he had no answer for. But he knew a guy. "Have you tried praying about it?"

"Praying?"

"Yeah, you know, asking God what to do."

Ferris had mentioned he went to church. But that didn't mean much when it came to whether someone had a personal relationship with the Creator. Heck, he'd planned on becoming a priest when he'd never even encountered the God he wanted to represent. But now, everything had changed.

"Huh." Ferris tilted his head as if just now considering this option. "I might try that."

"Great. Now, you think you can hold still while I finish your cut?"

Ferris threw his head back and laughed. "You might want to pray about that one."

A couple of days later, during some downtime, Floyd had just tossed a few slices of ham onto some rye bread at his little table in back when a booming voice startled him so much that he dropped a dollop of mustard on his shirt.

"Is this Floyd's place?" The Italian voice sounded from inches away, right on the other side of the divider. It rang with authority. Finality. A voice that was used to cause people to listen.

Floyd grabbed a paper towel and dabbed at his shirt, wincing as he managed to enlarge the yellow stain instead of erasing it. "Y-yes. I'll be right with you."

Why were his knees shaking? This was his shop, for crying out loud. He was the king of this domain. The big man. Besides, it wasn't Mr. Sonjak's voice.

Giving up on the stain, he puffed his chest out and prepared to step around the partition. His stomach growled a protest at the abandoned sandwich. He ignored it and nearly plowed into a stocky man at least three inches shorter than he was. The man wore a black suit and crisp tie. He swiped the fedora from his head and pointed with it.

"You Floyd?"

"Th-that's me." Something about the man put him on edge. Maybe it was the liver spots dotting his face. Or the way the guy marched into Floyd's shop like he owned the place. Whatever it was, Floyd needed to pull himself together.

"I want a haircut, and I want a good one. I got an important meeting tonight. I hear you're just the guy for it."

"Where'd you hear that from?" Floyd itched at his ear like a dog with fleas.

"My buddy, Ferris. He said you're the best. Are you gonna prove him right or wrong?"

Floyd swallowed. Ferris? Was this …?

"And w-what's your name, sir?"

"Giano. Giano Girardi." His smile revealed a gold tooth on the top left, slightly off-center.

"G-Girardi?" Floyd nearly hiccupped the word.

"Ya heard of me?"

As if the fleas had spread, Floyd scratched the middle of his forehead. What to say? If Floyd said Ferris mentioned him, would he get wise to his neighbor's reservations? *Think, Floyd. Think!* "Aren't you the one with that big meat packing company?"

Giano straightened and hiked his britches up an inch or so. "That's me. Best meat in town."

Floyd forced a smile. "Let's get you taken care of, Mr. Girardi." He gestured toward his booth. "Right this way."

Floyd worked to keep his hands from trembling as he spread his best apron over the man. Giano was used to only the best, and if he didn't deliver … He bit the inside of his cheek. He was *not* in the mood to end up on the nightly news. At least, not as a victim.

Floyd listened intently as Giano described, in exact detail, what type of cut he wanted. He filled his lungs with air that swirled with the scent of his last cigarette and a mix of cigar and expensive cologne emanating from the Mafia man in front of him. Straightening his shoulders, he gave a confident nod. He could do this and do it well.

Now, to make conversation. How to start? Probably not by mentioning the news article about the dead body that washed up on the riverbank, though it kept coming to mind. No. He had to keep it casual and avoid touchy topics.

"So," he said over the clippers' gentle buzz, "what's this big meeting tonight about?" Did he just ask that? He'd palm his forehead if that wouldn't mean disfiguring his face.

If Giano was miffed at Floyd's question, he didn't let on. "Business. I'm always trying to bring in new clientele, you know."

"Aren't we all?" Floyd's chuckle morphed into a croak. He cleared his throat.

"But it's not tonight. Tomorrow evening. My schedule is booked solid tomorrow, so I had to sneak in today."

Floyd murmured his understanding. "This meeting gonna be at a fancy restaurant?" Ferris said the guy liked to wine and dine.

"No." From where Floyd stood working on the man's left side, his profile was clear. What did it mean when his eyes narrowed and his lower lip protruded like that? Surely, nothing good. Floyd could nearly see him piecing together a sinister plan. "It's at a warehouse by the old water tower."

A genuine smile overtook Floyd's face. "The Grand Water Tower? That's where I met my wife."

"You don't say?"

"Best day of my life. Besides the day she married me. And the other day she married me."

"That sounds like a story."

"It is." And he told it, leaving out the parts about Susan carrying a knife. He wouldn't want Giano to draft his wife into the Mafia.

By the time he finished the cut, both men were laughing like old chums. Floyd turned Giano around to face the mirror. "What do you think? Acceptable?"

"Well, I'll be. Ferris was right. You do a mighty fine job."

Floyd dusted him off and removed the apron. "Thank you. Happy for your business." He strolled over to his cash register and pressed a button but then hesitated. Ferris said Giano never had to pay for a thing when they went out. People catered to him. Most likely because they didn't want to end up a dead body in the river. Should he even charge the man? Perhaps it was safer not to. Before he could make up his mind, Giano handed him a fifty-dollar bill.

"Oh." He stared at the large sum. So that's what a fifty looked like. "Let me get your change." Was he even able to make change for that amount?

Giano waved him off. "Keep it. I like to support local businesses. Plus, any friend of Ferris's is a friend of mine." He winked. "Thanks for making me look sharp."

Floyd's jaw dropped. By the time he recovered, the bell was jingling, and Giano had one foot out the door. "Th-th-thank you."

But then, it was as if the bill heated in his hand. He'd just accepted money from a consigliere. Was it a bribe? An exorbitant amount to ensure his cooperation and silence? No, it couldn't be. Floyd had played his part of an ignorant barber well, hadn't he? Giano had no idea Floyd knew he was in the Mafia. Or did he?

It took everything within him not to race outside and yell, "I don't want your blood money!" Somehow, Giano had roped him in, just like he had done with Ferris. He'd worked his magic to ensure Floyd was squarely an ally. He acted charming, friendly, even interested in little old Floyd. Except what if it wasn't all an act? What if, deep down, he was a good guy? Ugh. See how the guy had twisted Floyd's thoughts?

He punched the last button, and the cash register slid open. Floyd thrust the dirty money into the register and slammed it closed. Blast it. He'd told Ferris to pray about the situation, and what did the doofus do? Sent the Mafia man straight to Floyd's door.

The next day was Saturday. Men sat in the faux leather chairs with newspapers and magazines open wide as they waited for their turn. Smoke hazed the air and ashtrays filled to the brim as each puffed on their Luckys or Pall Malls. The television hummed about the Vietnam War in the background. Once in a while, someone would get up and meander through the crowded shop to adjust the antenna.

Floyd knew each man by name as well as exactly what type of cut each preferred. He chatted with them about their jobs, children, and hobbies as he worked. Occasionally, a woman would pop her head through the door and ask if the shop did ladies' hair. Each looked sorely disappointed as he told them no, and they walked away. He really should hire some stylists for female clientele.

Floyd didn't even notice a new customer come through the front door, as engrossed as he was with Mark Manhattan's tale of hitting a hole in one. But halfway through Mark's cut, Floyd checked over the divider to survey how many customers waited and spotted an officer in full uniform reading *Times* magazine.

His palms instantly began to sweat. What if the cop was there to question Floyd about the bribe he'd accepted? No.

That was ridiculous. He'd done nothing wrong. He'd cut a man's hair and accepted payment. It wasn't his fault Giano had overcompensated him. He knew nothing—nothing—about anything other than hair.

After he accepted the typical twenty-five cent tip from Mark, he waved the cop back. Sure, Lenny and Ralph had been there first, but with their animated discussion, they had nowhere better to be. Experience told him that after their cuts, they'd still stick around, avoiding their wives and responsibilities at home for a chance to relax and read in peace. And he wanted to get this cop's cut over with.

"Good morning, Officer. What can I do for you?" Floyd started to spread the apron, realized there was hair on it from the last customer, and stopped to shake it off in the corner first before spreading it over the policeman.

"Go ahead and give me a clean shave. I'm sick of the whole thing." His face twisted in disgust.

"Sick of your hair?"

"My hair, my job, my life. Only one of those things is in my power to change, so let's make the noggin' shiny."

"If you're sure." Floyd turned the clippers on but hesitated, ogling the man's thick brown curls. "There are many men who'd trade heads with you if they had the chance."

Spittle shot from the cop's mouth as he snickered. "Sorry." He wiped his mouth with the back of his hand. "Let 'em. Maybe another brain could figure this mystery out."

"What mystery?" He still hadn't moved the clippers any closer to the man's head.

Good thing because the cop turned abruptly in his chair to catch Floyd's eye. "I can't nab him. My boss is looking to me to lock the guy up, and he's like an itch I can't scratch."

"What guy?" He was lost.

"The Glinting Ghost."

"Who's that?" Might as well turn the clippers off and settle in for the conversation. Floyd leaned his hip against the counter.

"A Mafia guy. A consigliere to the head honcho himself. This guy is rumored to be responsible for over thirty deaths in the area. I've got to nab him before we find another body washed up on the riverbank or in an abandoned warehouse."

Floyd's knees knocked together, causing his hip to slip on the counter. He nearly lost his balance and almost tumbled into the man's lap. "A Mafia guy? Oh boy."

The cop nodded solemnly. "Rumor has it, there's some big meeting tonight. I just have to find out where."

"Try the Grand Water Tower," Floyd blurted out. "Any warehouses in that area?"

The cop's brow bunched. "I think so. Why?"

He tried for a nonchalant shrug but probably looked like he was having a seizure. "I've got a hunch. A strong one."

He pictured Giano sitting in that same chair, laughing at Floyd's stories as if they were the best of friends. A sliver of remorse cracked through for betraying the guy, but he refocused his imagination on a picture of a dead body sinking into the Muddy Missouri.

The cop snorted. "I can't run all over the city sniffing out hunches."

"You got any other leads?"

"No."

"Then what's the harm of checking out mine?"

The cop frowned for a beat but then nodded. "I guess you've got a point."

"If you nab this guy, what will it mean for your career?"

Finally, a smile. "A whole lot."

"Then I wish you the best." Floyd reached out his hand. A gesture of goodwill. A promise that he wouldn't lead this officer astray.

The cop snaked his hand out from under the apron and shook on it.

"Now." Floyd returned to the back of the chair. "How about a trim instead of a shave? You'll want to look sharp if your picture ends up in the paper."

One corner of his mouth ticked upward. "I guess so."

"I know so." Floyd picked up the shears instead. "Besides, your cut is paid for." By Giano.

Chapter Twenty-One

1990

Emira awoke in a cold sweat to police sirens blaring outside Dad's apartment. She trembled so hard her teeth chattered. Wrapping the scratchy blanket around her, she crept from her blow-up mattress in the corner to Dad's bed and shook it. When that didn't work, she climbed up and shook him. He jostled awake, gasping in a breath that sounded like a hiccup.

"What is it? What's wrong?"

"There are bad guys outside," Emira whispered, just in case they'd already found their way into Dad's apartment. Maybe they were lurking right outside the door.

"Bad guys?" Dad sat up, forehead wrinkled.

"Don't you hear it? The police sirens?"

His shoulders relaxed. "You think bad guys are outside because you heard sirens?"

She nodded. "Really loud. Right outside."

He patted the spot next to him. "There are a lot of reasons for sirens. It could be a medical emergency. Someone might have had a heart attack."

She raised a brow at him. Could those have been ambulance sirens instead of police car ones? Maybe. Still, she couldn't stop trembling, couldn't help but imagine a huge man in a black mask leaping out from behind the door. "I'm scared. I want to go home."

His frown deepened. "You're safe with me. Come here." He tucked her underneath his arm, but the fear didn't go away. It was silly, of course. Dad was big and strong. If a bad man came to get her, he would protect her. There was no doubt about that. Even so, it was as if every cell in her body shouted out this wasn't a safe place. She'd learned about cells in school. Each cell had a brain, a nucleus. All those brains yelled at her now to get out, to run away to where peace would wrap around her again.

"I want to go home," she said again, then bit her lip.

Dad looked as if she'd pricked him with a needle, but he was trying to be brave. "Okay, sweetheart. Call your mom."

That wouldn't work. It was crazy how quickly Dad seemed to have forgotten all about Mom. She needed three blaring alarm clocks to wake up in the morning, and half of the time, she'd sleep through them if Emira didn't give her a little shove. But Emira was too tired to argue. She scooched over to the phone at the side of Dad's bed and dialed home. Only rings. Time to call Papa.

Without explaining, she pressed the button to hang up and dialed Nana and Papa's house. Papa answered on the third ring. "Hello?"

"Papa, it's me. I'm scared at my dad's, and I want to come home."

"I'll be there in twenty minutes."

She didn't have to explain why, didn't have to prove bad guys were out to get her. She didn't even have to apologize for being so silly. He was coming. She knew he would. He always came. Papa never let her down.

Papa arrived eighteen minutes later wearing sweats and sandals, hair sticking out all over the place. He'd never looked more like a prince in a fairy tale, rescuing her from an evil dragon. Dad hugged her goodbye and watched as they left. She turned for one last look before they drove away. He held his middle like he had a stomachache. Had she done that? Hurt him? She hadn't meant to. Maybe he hadn't meant to hurt her either when he'd moved out. This hurt between them was a big ball of tangled yarn, and she hadn't a clue where to start yanking to unravel it.

Once in the car, Emira spilled the whole story, even though Papa never pressed her for details. She hunkered in her seat and double-checked to make sure the car doors were locked. "Is this a dangerous neighborhood?"

"Not particularly," Papa said. "But I understand why you were afraid. Did I ever tell you about the time I tried to hunt down a robber only to run away scared?"

"What?" Emira leaned forward, seat belt stretching against her chest. "No. Tell me."

While Papa told the story of going after the lady who'd stolen clothes only to run away from her knife, Emira giggled, picturing the scene. Papa had tried to be a superhero, like Batman, but then realized he was only Papa.

"I used to have a different shop, in a different part of town. There was a lot of crime down there. I had to cut hair with the doors locked."

As Papa kept telling stories of the olden days, her eyes widened. Papa had been brave. Way braver than she'd ever thought. Emira would have moved away the first time that a nearby store was robbed. He stayed there for years. He stayed.

Of course, he did.

"Then when I moved into the shop I have now, I had a run-in with the head of the Mafia."

"What's the Mafia?"

He paused. Emira pulled on her seat belt, willing it to loosen another inch so she could get closer and hear him better. Finally, he answered, "It was a group of people, men mostly, who committed crimes together."

"So, it's gone. There's no more Mafia?"

He tilted his head to the side. "Not like there was. Not here at least."

Thank goodness. Whatever it was, she didn't have to worry about it. Suddenly tired, she yawned and laid her head against the cool windowpane. Streetlights bounced off the pavement, and she relaxed into the familiar rhythm of the turns into Papa's neighborhood. He wasn't taking her home. He was taking her to his house. She closed her eyes and smiled as a blanket of safety draped around her shoulders.

She barely registered Papa shutting the car off, opening her car door, and carrying her into the house. She stirred and placed a kiss on his cheek as he set her on the couch and covered her with her favorite quilt. She snuggled into her pillow. Wait, that wasn't a pillow. It was Fant. She burrowed her nose into it and inhaled Dad's scent, then drifted off to sleep.

She awoke to sunlight and bacon, eggs, and toast with so much jelly on it she could barely see the bread. Nana bustled about in the kitchen. Papa was nowhere to be seen.

Emira finished off one piece of toast and licked jelly from her fingers. "Is it true Papa went after a robber, only to run away scared?"

Nana chuckled while drying her hands on a dish towel. "He told you that story, didn't he?" She sat across from Emira. "I wasn't there, but it's probably mostly true. Papa's stories usually are." Her smile spread. "He's not one to lie, just maybe embellish a little."

"Embellish?"

"Exaggerate. You know the story where he cut off the guy's ear?"

Emira nodded. It was his most famous story.

"When he first told it to me, he said the piece of ear he cut off was the size of a dime. By the time we'd been married five years, it had grown to a nickel."

She gasped. "He said it was the size of a half-dollar." She'd never seen a half-dollar, but he always showed the size by making the shape with his fingers.

Nana pointed. "Exactly."

So, Papa didn't lie. He only made the truth bigger. Did that mean she could trust what he said? Her mouth twisted as she considered. "He said he had a run-in with a Mafia guy."

Nana laughed again. "Did he tell you he single-handedly shut down the Mafia in St. Louis?"

"No." They hadn't gotten that far. She'd fallen asleep.

Nana dusted some crumbs off the table. "I still don't know what to believe about that one." Shaking her head, she stood and threw the crumbs away. "Come to think of it, though, we don't have a problem with the Mafia anymore." She shrugged. "Maybe it *is* because of Floyd."

Chapter Twenty-Two

2010

Emira flew through the automatic doors and down the white-tiled hallway to the elevators, pushing a double stroller. On the hospital's intercom, an urgent voice called for Dr. Malcom in triage. She stepped onto the elevator alongside a few other frazzled-looking occupants and pressed the button for the fourth floor. Teddy dropped his board book an inch from a woman's high-heeled foot. Emira swiped it up and deposited it back into his lap, checking to make sure Reagan was still asleep. Yep. A deep inhale filled Emira's nostrils with the scent of astringent. She scrunched her nose to prevent a sneeze.

She couldn't rush in there like a hornet whose nest had been disturbed. Papa needed her to exude calm. She'd be the first of the family to arrive—she'd been just down the road when she got the call—which made her demeanor especially important. Her stress would only transfer to him. Nana should be there soon, along with the rest of the family. Maybe she'd have enough time to figure out what was really going on with him before mass chaos ensued.

With a long, slow exhale, she stepped off the elevator and forced herself not to race to room 411. Calm. She must remain calm. She pasted on what would, hopefully, come off as a serene smile and entered the room.

Papa, lying in the hospital bed with wires strapped to his chest, startled at the sight of her. "Emira, what are you doing here?"

"Nana called. I came right away."

He frowned. "You didn't have to do that."

"Of course, I did." She set her purse on the windowsill, parked the stroller, and perched in the chair next to his bed. "Do you think I wouldn't come when you're admitted to the hospital?"

"I'm fine. It's all a misunderstanding." He pulled at one of the wires that had gotten tangled in his unflattering gown.

Judge Judy's voice filtered in on the television above her, merging with the gentle hum of machines. An IV dripped saline into his left arm.

"You blacked out at a doctor's appointment, and it was only a misunderstanding?" She raised her brows.

"Ah." He flicked his hand. "They made me fast for bloodwork. Plenty of people pass out when they don't eat."

She might buy that if he didn't donate blood on a regular basis. Needles were not his nemesis. "Nana said something about A-fib?"

He fiddled with the wires again, tangling them more in the process. "That woman and her rumors." He shifted his attention to Teddy. "Hi, Teddy Bear. How are you?"

Teddy dipped his head and offered a shy smile. Was this the first time he'd been in a hospital? The scene probably intimidated him. She'd forgotten how overwhelming it could be to a child.

She came to Papa's bedside and righted the mess of wires. He appeared to be plugged into a heart monitor. A blood pressure cuff inflated. Papa winced as it squeezed. When it finished, the monitor dinged repeatedly. Emira bit her lip. "Your blood pressure's high."

"I'm fine."

She rolled her eyes. "Would you stop saying that? If you were fine, you wouldn't be here."

Behind her, Reagan squirmed, then fussed. Emira fished her out of the stroller and hoisted her on one hip.

"Doodlebug," Papa said, "it's all right. Everything's okay." Was he saying it for Reagan's benefit or his own?

A doctor breezed in. His distinguished gray beard and hair were perfectly in place. Every inch of him spoke authority and wisdom. Emira straightened.

Papa propped himself up on his elbows. "Doc, good to see you. When am I breaking out of here?"

The doctor flashed a half smile, but his eyes remained serious. "Not anytime soon." He turned to Emira and extended a hand. "I'm Doctor Emerson."

She shook it. "I'm his granddaughter, Emira."

He rolled out the stool from under the computer and sat, clipboard on his lap. "It looks like we're dealing with several issues here. High blood pressure, for one." His gaze flicked from Papa to Emira. "High cholesterol. Those we can treat with medication. The A-fib, however—"

Nana burst through the doorway, Mom and Uncle Joseph on her heels. Teddy bounced in his seat, crying out for Grandma, who swept him up and planted kisses on his cheeks.

The doctor introduced himself and shook hands with everyone, then repeated the information before continuing. "As I was saying, I believe the best course of action is to do a catheter ablation to correct the A-fib." He directed his gaze to Papa. "I'll put a thin tube into a blood vessel in your neck, guide it to your heart, and use it to scar the cells causing the arrhythmia. It's less invasive than surgery and has a high success rate."

Papa shook his head. "What about medication? Isn't there a pill you can give me?"

Dr. Emerson frowned. "There is medication we can use, but considering the severity of your condition, I'd highly recommend—"

"I'll try the medication."

Uncle Joseph crossed his arms. "Now, hold on, Dad. If—"

Papa scowled at his son. "I've made my decision."

"But—"

"It's decided."

Emira gaped at Papa. He wasn't even going to consider the option of ablation? Worry lined Mom's face even as Teddy patted her cheeks.

Dr. Emerson stood. "I'll leave you to discuss your options. Please let the nurses know if you have any questions for me."

Nana pulled a cigarette from her purse.

The doctor stopped midstride. "Mrs. Douglas, you can't smoke in here."

Nana feigned innocence. "Oh?"

"There are designated smoking areas outside."

"Okay, thanks."

Emira bit her lip to hold back a smile at the way Nana pretended to put her cigarette away while truly fishing out her lighter. That man did not know whom he was dealing with. As soon as Dr. Emerson crossed the threshold, she lit up.

Mom rolled her eyes. "Seriously?"

Nana shrugged. "Just a few puffs."

"Let me have a drag," Papa whispered.

Nana passed him the cigarette. He got one good puff in before Emira snatched the cigarette and put it out on his bedside tray. "Enough of that." She plunked it into the trash can and threw a napkin on top. As if that would cover the indiscretion. Anyone with nostrils would be able to tell the smell didn't come from someone's clothing. "Let's talk about the treatment options."

"Nothing to talk about." Papa folded his arms across his belly. "I'll pop another pill and be as good as new."

Why did he have to be so stubborn? Reagan wiggled in her arms and fussed. She shifted her to the other hip. "Papa, let's just talk about all the possibilities."

"Yeah, Dad." Mom stepped closer. "It doesn't hurt to consider them. You don't have to do anything you don't want to."

Nana snorted. "He's not going to do anything that would jeopardize his trip."

Emira's gaze snapped to Nana and then back to Papa. "You're not thinking of still going to Haiti, are you, Papa?"

His brows bunched as if *she* had lost her mind. "Of course, I'm going."

"But you're in the hospital with A-fib. You blacked out. There's no way you could travel to another country right now."

Reagan's whimpers intensified. Emira bounced her on her hip.

Papa's voice sounded over the baby's protests. "You can't tell me what to do."

"You sound like a child." Emira clamped her mouth shut. She shouldn't have said that, no matter how true it was.

Reagan thrashed and let out an ear-piercing wail. Emira cringed. Experience told her no amount of bouncing or rocking could calm her now. Reagan needed to nurse, but she wouldn't do it here with all the distractions. "I have to go."

Mom strapped Teddy in the stroller while Emira did the same for a screaming Reagan. Before slipping out of the room, she kissed Papa goodbye and told him to take care of himself. Yeah, right. The man had a death wish. He wanted to deny lifesaving treatment and travel with a serious condition. Why? What made him so irresponsible? It didn't make sense.

Mom and Uncle Joseph weren't going to be able to get through to him. Nana didn't seem like she'd even try. Hopefully, the missions board would take one look at his medical records and decline to accept him. But what if he omitted that information? For whatever reason, he seemed desperate enough to lie.

A light mist greeted her when she stepped into the parking lot. It did little to douse the fire within. She shouldn't get so worked up, but how could she not? No one loved her like Papa, and she loved him like no one else. As she ducked into the van to nurse Reagan, she racked her brain for someone who could talk some sense into him. If only Karen was still alive.

Teddy watched Dora on the iPad in the back seat while Emira thumbed through the contacts on her phone. Who might have influence? She didn't have his pastor's number. She could call the church office, but that seemed like an overreach. His church wasn't connected to the trip. She wasn't connected to his church. The whole idea made her squirm.

What was this? *Priest.* Father Larry. Her finger hovered over the number. Was that an overreach as well? He'd told her to have Papa call him. He was connected in some way to the trip. Wouldn't he want to know that Papa was in the hospital? She had relevant information to pass on. Not overreach at all. The responsible thing to do. The right thing to do at this moment. She dialed the number.

Floyd pulled the thin blanket up over his chest and fumbled with the remote. Didn't they have any decent channels in this stupid hospital? He pressed a button, but instead of a change on the television, the head of his bed lifted an inch. What in tarnation? Wrong remote. Which one of these buttons did he need to press to watch the news? A push of another button and the intercom dinged.

A voice filtered through. "Did you need something, Mr. Douglas?"

Hmm. The nurses' call button. "Just trying to switch the darn TV."

"Push the green up and down switch by your bed." A laugh tinged the edge of her voice. As if she found his predicament humorous. Figured.

What green up and down switch? He searched for it but only succeeded in dropping the call button down the crack between his bed and side table. And now he'd gotten his wires and IV twisted again.

"Knock, knock."

The voice was familiar, but he couldn't place it. He leaned forward but couldn't decipher who stood outside the door. The family had finally left, thank goodness. As if being in the hospital wasn't bad enough, he'd had to deal with their nagging. When they'd finally filed out the door, he'd figured he could relax the rest of the evening. Apparently, he'd been wrong. But who visited now?

When no one entered of their own accord, he called, "Come in."

Father Larry strolled in. Floyd cursed under his breath. Hail Mary. Had he just used foul words in front of a priest? *Lord, what is wrong with me?*

"Good evening, Floyd." Larry settled onto the chair as if he had every right to be there.

Floyd cleared his throat. "Father Larry, I didn't expect to see you." Understatement of the century. This priest had to be a stalker. There was no other reasonable explanation.

"Emira called me."

His neck heated. Okay, so there was *that* explanation. A meddling granddaughter. Why had she done it? He shifted in his hospital bed.

After a beat of awkward silence, Larry leaned forward and plucked the container of Jello and spoon from the bedside tray. He slid a green glob into his mouth, closing his eyes as if savoring the flavor.

Larry's eyes popped open. "Sorry, did you want this? I can ask the nurse to bring you another."

Floyd scoffed. "No, I don't want Jello. I want out of here."

"She's concerned about you. Emira." Larry nodded his head in a knowing way. "Apparently, you're concerned about the mission trip."

"I want to still go. I'll be able to, right? The doctor said medication would make me good as new." Not his exact words, but close enough.

"As long as a doctor signs a medical clearance, you should be fine."

A doctor. Any doctor? Susan's brother-in-law practiced internal medicine in Arizona. He'd sign off on a form if Floyd asked. Begged. Surely, he would. Floyd breathed deep for the first time in hours. Everything would be all right.

Father Larry's eyes narrowed. "My question, and Emira's too, I believe, is *why* this trip means so much to you. Why is it more important than your health?"

"My health is fine." As if in protest, the IV machine issued a series of loud beeps.

"C'mon, Floyd. I'm too old to play games."

Who was this guy to think he could march in here and demand answers? Floyd clamped his jaw shut and stared the priest down. The monitor continued to blare every two seconds. If a nurse didn't come in soon, he'd yank the plug out of the wall. It wasn't like he needed the saline anyway. He didn't need to be here at all.

Father Larry laced his fingers together and leaned forward, the lines on his face gentling with his voice. "Why?"

Floyd's scalp tingled with the question. Why, indeed? Why did this trip mean so much to him? Why was he grasping for it like a drowning man for a life raft? Desperation bubbled on his tongue. "I'm not like you. I didn't live a meaningful life. Seventy years on this earth and what do I have to show for it?" On the monitor, bold red numbers flashed his blood pressure. His chest burned. "I'm running out of time."

"Oh, Floyd." The lines around Larry's eyes dipped. "Let me show you how wrong you are."

The nerve of the guy. "You're a stranger. Where do you get off telling me I'm wrong? You don't know the first thing about me." Derision laced his voice, guilt slipping in behind it. That was no way to talk to a priest. His ears went hot.

Father Larry stood, the chair and his knees creaking in protest. "Apparently, you're not ready for what I have to say. I'll leave you be for now and pray the Lord works on your heart. I hope to see you soon." With a soft smile and nod, he turned and shuffled out, the dull clunk of his cane accentuating his exit.

Chapter Twenty-Three

1968

Floyd relaxed in his recliner in the back of the shop a couple of days after cutting the cop's hair. He flipped the page of his morning paper, and his eyes zeroed in on a headline. As he read the article, he chuckled. "Would you look at that?"

"Look at what?" Susan bustled over to him, broom in hand. It was good having her at the shop. He was halfway to convincing her to quit her job at the shoe store and work as his secretary. At least, it seemed like she might cave. With Susan, it had to be her idea. No one could tell her what to do.

He pointed to the article.

She leaned over his shoulder and read. "Two nights ago, police took down the biggest Mafia ring in town thanks to a tip from a local businessman." She gave him a withering look. "So what?"

"So, I'm the businessman." He splayed his hand on his chest. "The one who gave the cop the tip."

She guffawed and returned to sweeping.

"No, really." He pulled the lever and set his chair upright. "An officer came in here, and I told him where to look for the consigliere."

"How would *you* know where the Mafia was hiding?" Suddenly, she stilled and laid a hand over her heart. "Floyd, have you been keeping something from me?"

He smirked. Maybe he'd play along. Convince her he'd been part of an undercover crime ring. The longer the silence stretched, the more her eyes widened. No, he couldn't do that to her. He shook his head. "A customer told me."

Her shoulders relaxed. "I don't know. It could have been anybody."

But he'd done it. Without a doubt. As soon as his chest puffed out in satisfaction, a thread of guilt snaked in. Giano had trusted him, but he'd betrayed that trust. A Mafia man didn't deserve loyalty, did he? Especially not if the guy had attempted to bribe him. Plus, what if the crime boss had a boss? Perhaps this was a victory he ought not to claim.

When the bell jingled, Susan abandoned the broom and sashayed up front. "New Creations, how may we help you?"

It sure was nice to hear Susan's feminine voice in the shop. He needed more ladies. Beauticians would boost business. It could be a salon for both men and women. He made a mental note to put an ad in the paper.

Standing, he brushed scattered peanut fragments from his pants and followed Susan. He could barely make out the customer's reply, the voice was so soft.

"Sure thing." In contrast, Susan nearly shouted. "Floyd will get you into tip-top shape."

He approached from behind her. A wiry but good-looking man with thick, curly dark hair shifted his weight from foot to foot.

"He said he'd like about an inch off." Susan put a hand on Floyd's arm. "And if you don't need anything else right now, I'll head to the store before my shift at Shoe City."

"That's fine. Thanks." He gave her a peck on the temple before waving the customer to his booth.

"Hello, sir. Come on in and have a seat." Floyd flashed a reassuring smile that seemed to do little to set the man at ease judging from the way the man fidgeted with his hands. "What's your name?"

"Fred. Fred Walnut."

"Why, you're named after one of my favorite foods."

Fred's nervous chuckle fell flat.

"You've got a good name and a great head of hair. Looks like you've been handed the world on a platter, my friend."

Fred rubbed his fingertips together. "I wouldn't say that."

"Nah. None of us has an easy ride, do we?" Floyd pumped the chair up to height. "But a fine man like you must have a good future ahead of you." He could see it, could picture Fred's happy destiny in his mind. A festive wedding with a glowing bride, followed by half a dozen kids. A plaque on his desk and his name on the door. Why'd the guy look scared half to death?

"What do you do for a living, Fred?" Floyd spread the apron over him and took a comb to his thick hair.

"I'm an administrative assistant at an accounting firm." He spoke softly, as if ashamed.

Floyd frowned. Not what he'd expected. "Just an assistant? Why aren't you a partner?"

Fred's eyes widened. "E-excuse me?" he stammered.

"A man like you with a head of hair like yours? You ought to be a partner with a plaque on your desk and your name on the door." Floyd retrieved the scissors.

Fred squirmed underneath the apron. "I do have the education. Maybe someday. If they ever notice me." His gaze lowered to his shiny shoes.

"If they ever—" Floyd huffed. "Maybe they don't notice you because you don't give the impression that you deserve it." He spun the chair around and dipped to meet Fred's eyes. "You're quite intelligent, aren't you?"

Fred tilted his head, a clear indication he was but didn't want to brag.

"I knew it. I saw you and said to myself, 'There's an intelligent young man.'"

Pink tinged Fred's cheeks.

What else? Who had God created the man before him to be? What was God's opinion about Fred? It had to differ from Fred's lousy thoughts about himself. Floyd ignored the awkwardness of the moment and simply looked at his customer, asking God to help him see Fred through the Lord's eyes.

"Know what else?" Floyd crossed his arms. "You have integrity. Other people have cut corners to get ahead, but not you. You keep your hands clean. Am I right?"

The wisp of a smile emerged. "It's true."

Floyd patted the man on the back. "Good job. Continue to work with integrity, and you'll receive your reward. But go in there with your head held high. You're a respectable, intelligent, good-looking man. I bet the ladies are crazy about you."

His cheeks turned from light pink to blazing red. "I doubt it."

"What do you mean? No girlfriend?"

He shook his head. "There's a gal I'd like to ask out, but I can never find the courage. She's the sweetest gal in the bunch. I doubt she'd go for a doofus like me."

"Now there. What did I say? You're no doofus, that's for sure. You think God would grant any old fellow hair like this?" He ran a hand through it as if to demonstrate. "No. This is the hair of someone important. Someone with both brains and gumption. The hair of a winner."

Fred chuckled again. "You probably say that to everyone."

"Not a chance. You should see the hair I cut in here. Fine. Brittle. Greasy. Nothing like this. Want to run you hand through the clippings in the trash bin?"

"No, thank you." He threw his hands up.

"Then trust me. Go ask the girl. Look up at the world instead of down at your shoes. God made you for a purpose, and it isn't to hang your head and wallow through life."

Fred's mouth firmed into a fine line, but his eyes sparked to life. "You know, you're right." He straightened his shoulders. "I *do* have something to offer."

"Without a doubt." Floyd beamed. "But first, let's quit yapping and finish this haircut."

Six women answered Floyd's ad in the paper, and he hired them all. It only took two hours for him to realize he'd made a mistake. Six hairstylists plus one secretary stacked the female-to-male ratio heavily against him, even when he had a few customers waiting.

"Oh, boy," he mumbled to himself as he exited the restroom into what sounded like a den of squawking hens. "What have you gotten yourself into, Douglas?"

He dug a finger into his ear to drown out the shrill pitch of Shelby's voice.

"Have you watched the new soap opera *One Life to Live*?" Almira paused in wrapping Mrs. Humphrey's hair in curlers to place her hand over her heart. "Simply fascinating. I couldn't take my eyes off the screen for the entire episode."

Shelby snapped a curler into place in Mrs. Young's hair. "Nah. I stick to comedies. *Rowan and Martin's Laugh-In* and *The Beverly Hillbillies* are the shows I like."

"Oh, but honey, that Dr. Larry Wolek is a dream!"

Gretta chimed in, "I'd rather watch *Speedway* again. I can't get enough of Elvis."

The women squealed and did a little tap dance. The clack of their heels grated.

Floyd shot a pleading glance to Susan and widened his eyes in an exaggerated fashion. She smirked. His gal never did put much stock into popular culture. She never could sit still long enough to watch a movie all the way through, much less swoon over Hollywood's leading men.

"Ladies." Susan paused from dusting the shelves and pointed to Mrs. Mizrat under the dryer. The old lady's pronounced scowl screamed disapproval. "It looks like Mrs. Mizrat would like to take her afternoon nap. Would you mind keeping it down? For the customers, of course."

How did she do that? She smoothed those hens' feathers like nothing he had ever seen. He still couldn't get over how different she was since meeting Jesus. Remarkable. The chatter quieted, and the women returned to their tasks while making friendly conversation with the customers. The rotten egg perm smell permeated the air, punctuated by occasional puffs of hair spray. The smells would take some getting used to as well.

The phone rang, and Susan hurried to answer with, "New Creations. How can I help you?" It had been swell having her help at the shop. She took a load off him in more ways than one.

The bell jingled as a broad-shouldered man with red hair sauntered through the front door. The corner of the man's mouth tipped in a half smile. "Good afternoon. You got time for a cut?"

He looked so familiar, but Floyd couldn't place him. Had he been to the shop before? "Certainly." Floyd extended his hand. "The name's Floyd."

"Jackie." The customer's cheeks reddened slightly.

Floyd sucked in a breath as realization hit him. "Jackie Smith?" *The* Jackie Smith? Tight end for the St. Louis Cardinals?

Jackie shrugged. "That's me."

Behind them, the women quieted. Floyd glanced over his shoulder to find them gaping at the football player. He doubted any of those ladies had ever watched a football game in person or on television, but perhaps they recognized the name of the local legend from the news or from hearing their husbands talk. He tried to ignore the whispers and girlish giggles.

"Come right this way." He motioned to his booth, sending a seething glare in the hens' direction. "What can I do you for?"

As Jackie explained his preferred haircut, Floyd kept looking over the partition, attempting to shush the women with his eyes. They continued to gossip about their guest in loud whispers. Ridiculous. Embarrassing. How could he get them to stop?

He spread the cape over Jackie's muscular frame and pumped up his chair. The clang of the receiver told him Susan had finished her phone call. Maybe she could get the hairstylists to act civilized.

Instead, she huffed. "Who tracked mud into my shop?"

Her shop? Since when was this her shop? She started working as a secretary, and already, she ran the place. Figured.

Jackie leaned over, inspected the bottom of his mud-encrusted shoes, and grimaced. Poor guy. Floyd motioned as if he were zipping his lips, then winked. He wouldn't rat the star player out. Jesus might have redeemed Susan, but his wife had inherited the cleanliness gene from her mother. If there was one thing that could still get her riled up, it was a dirty mess.

Jackie tossed him a sheepish smile before Floyd grabbed his comb and scissors and went to work.

Susan popped through the entryway and pointed to the floor, a tight frown pulling her face taught. "There's mud all over the floor."

Heat flushed his neck. Why'd she have to embarrass him in front of a local celebrity? He forced a friendly tone through gritted teeth. "Jackie didn't mean anything by it."

"Jackie?" And now she was looking at him as if he'd grown a second head. "Why do you have a girl's name?"

One of the stylists gasped behind them. Floyd sputtered for a second before he tried to fill the awkwardness with a strained laugh. He couldn't see Jackie's face, but the man sat unmoving and silent. Likely horrified. Goodness gracious. Floyd needed to say or do something to smooth this situation out quickly.

If he sweetened his tone, would Susan take the hint? He tried it. "Honey, this is Jackie Smith." He emphasized the name.

No recognition lit her eyes. Instead, she jammed her hands onto her hips. "I don't care if he's Santa Claus. I just mopped the floor not an hour ago, and now it's muddy again."

Pressure built at his temples. He'd massage them if his hands were free. Soft tittering filtered to his ears. He cleared his throat to shush the women again. They would only make a bad situation worse.

"I apologize, ma'am." Jackie continued facing the partition wall as Floyd snipped, but his gaze sought Susan out. "That was my mistake. I'd be more than willing to mop the floor after he's finished with my haircut."

Susan nodded. "That's kind of you. Thanks."

"But not necessary." Floyd widened his eyes at Susan. She couldn't be serious.

Now she was looking at *him* as if *he* were crazy. "He offered."

"Yes, but ..." Since when did they make customers clean the shop? People tracked dirt inside all the time. Not once had any grabbed a mop and played the part of janitor. He'd never even made Drinks Tonic Water or Man with Dog clean up after themselves, and they weren't paying customers. This was a *celebrity*. "It's Jackie Smith."

Again, with the whispers and giggles from the back. Those women were going to be the death of him if he didn't die of embarrassment first.

"You keep saying that like it's supposed to mean something to me."

Jackie put up a hand. "I really don't mind cleaning up after myself."

Floyd chuckled, but it fell flat. "It's not necessary."

He peeked at Shelby over the partition and motioned to Susan. He mouthed *Tell her*.

Her brow scrunched in confusion as he repeated his plea a few times and then understanding dawned in her features. She scurried over to Susan and whispered in her ear.

Susan had never known how to whisper, and her reply sounded overloud in the space. "All this hoopla over a stupid football player?"

Silence fell. Oh, if he could sink into the floor. He cringed. Maybe Jackie hadn't heard her? But slowly, a rumble sounded from deep in Jackie's throat. A moment later, he erupted into a full, gut-busted laugh. Floyd had to abandon the haircut for the moment as Jackie's shoulders shook. "I take it she's not a football fan?"

Floyd released a breathy chuckle. "Not at all. Not even a sports fan, I'm afraid."

Jackie inhaled deeply and puffed the air out with a grin. "My wife, Gerri, would like her."

Floyd resumed the cut, engaging the quiet man in conversation around the *stupid* sport. Thankfully, Susan said nothing more about the mud, and the stylists stopped their chatter. Or maybe he just couldn't hear them anymore over his friendly banter with Jackie.

When Floyd finished, he spun Jackie around to look in the mirror. "How does it look?"

"Excellent. Thanks."

Floyd dusted off Jackie's neck and removed the cape. "Tell all your friends. About the cut, not about the ..." He gestured outside the booth. "You know."

Jackie chuckled. "Want me to take care of that muddy floor now?"

"Please, no. I'll do it. Don't report the incident to any papers or newscasters."

"Don't worry. The only one who will hear about what your wife said is Gerri. She'll get a kick out of it."

Floyd walked him to the cash register. No way was he taking a chance with Susan taking Jackie's money. Who knew what would come out of her mouth next? He sighed in relief to see she was in back and not behind the desk anyway. And despite her protests, she must have mopped the floor herself. All traces of mud were gone.

He rung the tight end up and accepted payment, then shook the man's hand again. "It was a pleasure meeting you."

"You as well." With a wave, Jackie turned to leave.

"Hey," Floyd called.

Jackie looked over his shoulder, eyebrow raised.

"Is it true what they say? That you never get tired or run out of breath? That someone would have to shoot you to stop you?"

Jackie shrugged, his smile turning sheepish again. "They exaggerate."

"Still." Floyd pointed a finger at him. "Mark my words, you'll be in the Hall of Fame one day."

"We'll see."

"Don't you give up until you get there."

"Thanks, Floyd." He gave a solemn nod before leaving.

As soon as he was gone, the stylists erupted into a frenzy of chatter.

"Isn't he dreamy?"

"He's even more muscular in person."

"I should have asked for his autograph."

Floyd stomped his foot. "Ladies."

Mrs. Mizrat awoke with a start.

"This is a professional establishment. You need to act ... professional."

Did Gretta roll her eyes at him? He ground his teeth. This was ridiculous. He couldn't work in such a chaotic environment. What was he thinking bringing on all these women? Clearly, he wasn't thinking. He couldn't stand their pecking another day.

"You're all fired."

Seven pairs of eyes stared back at him. Susan's were the only ones that didn't hold a hint of betrayal.

Shelby put a hand on her hip. "What did you say?"

"You heard me." Blood boiling, he stomped out the back door into the alley. He needed fresh air. A minute later, Susan followed. Before she could lay into him about what a foolish business decision he'd just impulsively made, he spoke first. "I know, I know. I'll figure something else out." He paced, running a hand through his hair.

She tilted her head to the side. "I've been thinking. What if I went to beauty school? I could work with you. Just you and me. A team."

He stilled. "Beauty school?"

"Why not?"

She'd never finished high school. Never had further vocational training. However, she'd succeeded at every job she'd ever had, and wildly so. Within months, she was basically running the shoe store she'd worked at. She'd worked for a beauty supply shop and done well there too. While she had a few ... rough edges ... no one worked as hard as his wife. His woman had a drive that rivaled Jackie Smith. In fact, when she put her mind to something, it might take a bullet to stop her as well. He bit back a smile, lest she think he was mocking her. But yes, she had something in common with that *stupid* football player.

"Okay."

Her face brightened. "Partners?"

He squinted back at her. "You can't insult my customers."

"*Our* customers."

He'd give her that. "Our customers. They make any messes, you've got to deal with them. Not another word about it."

"It wouldn't hurt you to pick up a mop, *partner*."

He harumphed. But when she grinned at him, he smiled back. "Partners."

Chapter Twenty-Four

1990

It had been a month since Emira's concert, and Mary and Martha still hadn't tired of those same dance numbers. They clapped as loud as they ever had. How amazing to have such big fans.

Moments after Emira hugged the Bible ladies goodbye, a family strolled into the shop. The man and wife had a teenage son and a daughter maybe a little older than her. The husband and wife's joined hands swung between them a little. Sweet. Emira smiled at the girl, and she smiled back. Maybe if the girl wasn't there for a cut herself, the two of them could play in the back.

Papa rushed to the front, voice booming with excitement. "Fred! Fred Walnut. Wonderful to see you." Papa grasped the man's hand, and the two grinned at each other with dopey smiles on their faces.

Was this another homeless person turned real estate agent? Or someone else who started out poor and now was important? Emira eyed the intact family, jealousy swirling in her gut. That girl had a mom and dad who still loved each other. Fred Walnut stood not an inch away from his well-dressed wife. He wore dress pants and a button-down shirt and matched Mrs. Walnut except she had on a skirt instead of pants. They looked like they fit perfectly together. Emira frowned. Never mind. She didn't want to play with the girl anymore. What would they have in common?

"It is so good to see you," Papa said again.

Emira looked behind her and rolled her eyes. He was repeating himself. Why was this man so exciting anyway?

Fred stuffed his hands into his pockets. "I'm surprised you recognized me. It's been forever."

"I could never forget a head of hair like yours. Is this your wife?"

"Sure is." He wrapped an arm around her shoulders, drawing her close. "This is Gracie. She's the one I told you about all those years ago. We've been married eighteen years now."

Gracie poked his side. "It'll be nineteen next month."

"True. True."

Eighteen years? A long time to stay together, and the two of them looked all starry-eyed and lovey-dovey. She narrowed her gaze at the girl. How unfair. Some people had all the luck.

"This is our son, Cody." He ushered the teen forward. "And our daughter, Cornelia."

Emira covered her mouth to hide the funny noise that bubbled up from her throat. Cornelia? Never mind. That girl did *not* have a perfect life.

"Nelly," the girl said with a look that showed she was trying to be annoyed but loved her parents too much to truly be grumpy with them.

"Whoa, Nelly." Papa laughed as if he hadn't made everything worse by joking like Nelly was a horse. "Did you come in for a cut?"

"Yeah, yeah. Cody and I both need a trim."

"No problem. Come on back."

Papa ushered Fred into his booth while the rest of the family sat and paged through magazines. Emira leaned against the wall where she could see into Papa's booth and the waiting area at the same time. Happy chatter drifted from the two men.

"Is your name on the door yet?" Papa asked Fred. Whatever that meant.

Nelly kept glancing at Emira's tap shoes and opening her mouth a little like she wanted to say something but was too shy. When Emira caught her gaze, Nelly's cheeks turned bright pink. Was she embarrassed or scared like the girls who got stage fright? Emira inched closer. Nelly's plaid skirt looked itchy, and her polo shirt was buttoned all the way up. Didn't she feel like she was choking, wearing it like that? Plus, she wore tights. *Tights.* Those were fine during a performance but horrible to wear any other time. At least her forest-green headband had a pretty daisy attached.

Emira smiled at her no longer enemy. "I like your headband."

Nelly bit her bottom lip. "Thanks."

"Want to go in the back and play with Barbies?"

Nelly gave her mom a puppy dog face. "Can I, Mom? Please?"

"All right."

In back, they sat on a black rubber mat, and Emira dumped out the contents of her backpack. Along with six Barbies, her notebook tumbled out and landed in Nelly's lap. Shoot. She must have forgotten to put it in the desk.

"What's this?"

Nelly reached for it, but Emira snatched it away. "It's top secret."

Nelly recoiled, her face reddening again. "Then why'd you give it to me?"

"I didn't mean to." Emira shifted to her knees and leaned close. "I'm kind of spying on my grandpa to find out his secrets." Yeah, it sounded super interesting when she put it that way.

"Oh." Nelly's eyes widened. "Can I help?"

"How?" This was the first time Emira had seen this family, and it seemed like Papa hadn't seen them in forever. How did Nelly know they'd be around again?

Nelly shrugged. "My parents said your grandpa was to thank for their marriage and that if it wasn't for him, Cody and I would have never been born."

Emira's mouth dropped open. "How?" Now *she* was repeating herself, but seriously, how could Papa be responsible for this picture-perfect family? The three of them had watched *Fiddler on the Roof* last week, and now Emira pictured Papa with a scarf on his head playing the part of matchmaker. She almost started singing the song.

"I don't know. Maybe he set them up on a blind date."

The girls erupted into giggles.

An idea hit her. She dropped her voice to the tiniest whisper. "Let's sneak up to the booth and snoop on what they're talking about. Maybe we'll find out what happened."

Nelly covered a chuckle with her hand. "Better take off your shoes."

Oh yeah. Emira still wore her tap shoes. She unlaced them and led the way to the back wall of Nana's booth, the closest they could get to Papa and Fred without being seen. She put her finger to her mouth.

She could only make out snippets. *Drunk driving* and *award from the mayor* and *local hero*.

Nelly rolled her eyes. "They're not talking about how my parents got together. They're talking about my brother."

"Cody?" From the looks of it, Nelly was not a fan.

She padded back to their spot on the mat and plopped down, shoulders sagging. "Yeah. Cody." She waggled her head around. "Mr. Perfect. He's getting some kind of award from the mayor at this fancy ceremony tonight. He put together a play at his high school about how dangerous drunk driving is, and everyone thinks he's the most amazing person who ever lived. He was even in the paper."

"Oh, I see." Emira smirked. Nelly was jealous. Who could blame her? It must be hard having an older brother everyone loved. Still … "It *is* kind of cool. The play, I mean."

Mom had talked to her about drinking and driving when they passed a horrible accident one night. She shivered as she remembered that car crunched up like a soda can.

"Yeah, yeah, I know. If someone watched that play and decided not to drink and drive, it's kind of like Cody saved their life."

Emira sat quietly processing until it hit her. She gasped and grabbed Nelly's arm. "Wait. Cody wouldn't even be here if not for Papa. Your parents said so themselves. So, the real hero is …"

"Your grandpa."

The girls gaped at each other.

"Papa should be getting an award from the mayor."

"He totally should."

Her excitement melted. "But that isn't going to happen." She had no idea how to let the mayor know how important her grandpa was.

Nelly fiddled with a Barbie's hair, twirling it around her finger. "Maybe you could make him an award yourself. A trophy. I could help."

Emira brightened. "Great idea. What can we use?"

The girls jumped up and scurried around the shop, searching for odds and ends.

Nana peeked her head out of her booth. "What are you two doing?"

Emira smiled innocently. "Nothing."

"Don't make a mess, you hear?"

"We won't."

But they did, a little. They needed an empty bottle, but the only one they found still had a little shampoo in it. They dumped it out in a sink and tried to clean it. The whole area filled with bubbles. They found skinny black tape in Papa's dusty toolbox on the shelf and used it to tape combs all around the top of the bottle, making a teepee. Emira fished out paper from the extra register roll, and Nelly helped her color it. They taped it around the bottom. There, a beautiful trophy for Papa, and just in time. A minute after they finished, Mrs. Walnut called out for Nelly, saying they had to go.

Emira held the trophy behind her back as the girls ran up front. "Will you all come back?" Emira asked Mrs. Walnut.

"We ought to," Fred said, shaking Papa's hand again.

What did that mean? It wasn't a yes or a no. Definitely not a promise. Not that promises meant much anyway.

Mrs. Walnut nestled her arm around Nelly's shoulder. "We just might."

Papa walked with them all the way to the door like he couldn't bear to see them leave. "Please do come back. It was wonderful meeting your family."

When the door swung closed behind them, Papa stuffed his hands into his pockets and smiled to himself. "Would you look at that?" He stared out the windows into the parking lot with a far-off look on his face.

"Papa?"

"Hmm?" He startled, as if awakened from a daydream.

"I have something for you." She bounded to him and thrust the homemade trophy into his hands.

"What's this?" He turned it around so that the #1 Hero sign faced him. She leaned forward, waiting for his grin to break forth. Instead, his lip trembled, and his mouth twisted into a frown. "Oh, Princess," he whispered.

Uh-oh. He wasn't supposed to cry. This was supposed to make him happy, not sad. But he sniffed and stared at her with watery eyes.

She flung herself at him in a bear hug. "You deserve a hero trophy more than Cody." Her words were muffled against his belly.

He ruffled her hair. "I'll have to figure out the perfect place to put this."

She took it from his grasp and set it on the desk. "How about here?"

"No." He shook his head. "This is too special to place on the desk. Maybe I'll put it in my office at home."

She frowned. If it was special, wouldn't he want to put it where everyone could see it? Special things were meant to be the center of attention. Why would he hide the trophy away? Maybe he was embarrassed of it. It probably wasn't good enough for him. It didn't look like a real trophy. Nothing like the award Cody would receive.

"Okay," she mumbled.

He opened his arms to her. "Can I have another squeeze?"

She sulked over and let him hug her, but her arms hung like wet noodles at her sides.

"This is the best gift anyone has ever given me."

Did he mean that? Maybe he wasn't embarrassed of her.

When she looked up at him, he tweaked her nose. "Sometimes, the most precious things deserve to be hidden." She gasped. It was like he had read her mind. "Jesus called it not throwing your pearls to the pigs."

She giggled at that, imagining a pig wearing a pearl necklace. Jesus was silly. It still didn't make sense, hiding the trophy away *because* it was special, but it couldn't be because Papa didn't love it. It couldn't be because he didn't love *her*. She felt his love all the way to her bones. He would never be embarrassed of her. When he said she was his pride and joy, he meant it.

Wrapped in Papa's warmth, Emira barely registered the bell's jingle over the door. It wasn't until Papa pulled back that it was obvious someone was there.

"Jay. What a nice surprise."

"Dad?" What was he doing here? Her heart yanked in two directions as she shifted her weight from one foot to the other. She peeled herself from Papa's warmth and went to her father's waiting arms.

"Hey, kiddo." Dad rubbed her back and nodded at Papa. "Floyd. Sorry to drop in like this, but I have some news I need to tell Emira."

"News?" Papa's brow lifted. "Does Marie know?"

"Just got off the phone with her. She said"—he puffed out his cheeks—"I needed to tell Emira in person." He squeezed her shoulder. "What do you say? Pizza?"

But Emira wasn't hungry. Last time Dad had news, it was that he was moving out.

Emira nibbled on a breadstick only because Dad kept bugging her to eat something. Her tummy was all jumbled, and anything she put into it might not stay there. Dad, though, scarfed down four pieces of stuffed crust before the waitress had time to refill his soda. Emira wiggled in her seat. He always ate fast when he was nervous. What was he afraid to tell her?

She couldn't bear to ask. It might be bad news. Maybe even worse than the last bad news. Maybe if she kept taking little bites, he'd never say it. It'd never happen. Whatever it was.

"So, kiddo …"

She winced. No such luck.

"Do you remember that new paint I invented? The one that prevents mildew?"

She nodded. He'd gone on and on about the boring paint last time she'd spent the night.

He leaned forward, propping his elbows on the table, and his smile jumped to life. "There's a company in Milwaukee that heard of it and was so impressed that they want to hire me on."

She scrunched her nose and tasted the foreign word on her tongue. "Milwaukee?" That was in Hawaii, right? Near a beach.

He nodded. "Milwaukee. They made me an offer I can't pass up. Head chemist. The pay increase will mean I can pay your mom decent child support. Consistently. And I'll be doing what I love."

Her heart crashed against her ribs. No. That didn't mean … couldn't mean … "You're not moving."

His smile faded. "I have to move for this job, kiddo."

It hurt to breathe. She squeezed her eyes shut. "Is Milwaukee far away?"

"Only a five-and-a-half-hour drive. Not bad. I'll visit."

When she opened her eyes, his hand lay open to her, inviting her to take hold. She wanted to slap it away. How could he leave her? How could a job be more important than her? She narrowed her eyes and crossed her arms.

"Oh, come on, Emira. We'll still see each other. I'll come back every month. It'll be so much fun to stay in a hotel room together for the weekend. Think about it. We'll go swimming and have a huge breakfast."

She bit her lip. That *did* sound fun. Much better than a blow-up mattress that smelled like Chinese food. But only once a month? Hawaii was a different country. How was she supposed to make her parents get back together if he lived in a different country?

It wasn't going to happen. Her hope shattered like glass. Her parents wouldn't get back together. Forever, she would live with Mom, who worked all the time. She'd only see Dad every once in a while. Even if she was the best dancer in the world, it wouldn't be enough. *She'd* never be enough.

She clenched her teeth and balled her fists. "I'm mad at you." It was the only thing she could say. The rest of her feelings were too big.

His shoulders drooped. "I'm sorry. I hope you'll forgive me."

Nope. She wouldn't. Not ever.

Chapter Twenty-Five

2010

Floyd scanned the hospital bill and groaned. He could have roomed at a Ritz penthouse for a week at that price. And that was after insurance. Someone was making a killing off thin blankets and saltwater drips. What a waste of money. His stomach sank. Where would the finances come from? His savings, for sure. But he still had those miscellaneous costs for the trip to consider.

This was all starting to seem a bit … rash. If he would have known he'd end up spending three days in the hospital, he might have thought twice about dishing out fifteen grand up front for the Haiti trip. Would they refund his money if the doctor didn't give medical clearance? They'd have to, right?

From the kitchen doorway, Susan peeked her head into the living room. "The garbage disposal broke again."

"Great." All he needed was another thing to go wrong.

"And don't you say you'll try to fix it. Last time, you nearly chopped your finger off. Call someone."

He scowled at her. That woman and her exaggerations. He hadn't come close to … *that*. He'd merely lost half of his fingernail. "We don't need a garbage disposal anyway. Throwing food down the drain is disgusting. We never did that back in the good old days."

Susan crossed her arms over her chest. "If we don't fix it, the kitchen will stink to high heaven."

"Pour baking soda down the drain." That stuff cost far less than a repairman.

She quirked a brow. "Seriously, Floyd?"

He tossed the hospital bill on the side table and snapped open the newspaper. He'd read about how volcanic ash from Iceland was disrupting travel plans across Europe. Better than viewing Susan's sassy look. Except he read the first sentence four times and still couldn't make sense of it.

Was Emira getting to him? Did he need to rethink his trip? At the thought of not going, a pebble of loss clunked in the hollow of his chest, sending ripples outward. He imagined hovering over his own funeral one day. He pictured the pastor saying, "He almost made a difference," and everyone shaking their heads, disappointment dripping from them in place of tears. He couldn't come this close and not go all the way. He'd bought a suitcase, for heaven's sake. If he didn't go, he'd regret it for the rest of his life. He'd always wonder *what if*.

He had to go.

A low humming sound emitted from the kitchen. It paused, started again, then ceased. He set the paper in his lap. What was his wife doing in there?

"Floyd?" Susan called.

"Yeah?"

"The garbage disposal isn't working."

Trepidation slithered up his spine. "What?" Maybe he'd misheard.

Susan emerged in the archway, wiping her hands on a dishrag. "Disposal's broken. You need to call someone to fix it."

Emira's warning echoed in his ears. *Dementia.* He shook it off. No. She was probably just nagging. He was notoriously slow to call repair people. He wet his dry lips. Only it'd been minutes, not days, since she'd told him to call. But even if she'd forgotten that they'd had the conversation, it didn't mean she had dementia, did it? Old age bested all of them now and then. A slip here and there didn't constitute a diagnosis. No need to worry. Still ...

"We just talked about this." He kept his voice measured and calm. Best not to give her a reason to snap at him. "I told you to pour baking soda down the sink."

She snickered. "Baking soda? Seriously?"

He pointed at her. "That's what you just said. Don't you remember?"

Her brows bunched. "I remember when you nearly cut your finger off trying to fix the thing yourself. Don't do that again. We have the yellow pages around here somewhere." She disappeared down the hallway.

Saints alive, what should he do about this? She might need to see a doctor, but getting her to go to one would be a feat beyond his ability. Why'd he have to marry such a stubborn woman? Maybe he could trick her. Tell her they were going shopping, then show up at the doctor's office. A dozen reasons why that wouldn't work filed through his brain. Okay, then. He'd sedate her and drag her to an appointment.

She reemerged with the yellow pages in hand and plunked it into his lap. His newspaper crinkled under the weight. Perhaps he was worrying over nothing. "What were we just talking about?"

Her eyebrows nearly touched her hairline. "You're about to call a repairman for the garbage disposal. Gee, Floyd. You really are getting old." As she scuttled back into the kitchen, she mumbled, "He's losing his mind."

Oh, man. He *had* gotten himself worked up for no reason. Emira had gotten into his head. Susan had merely not wanted him to wait to call a repairman, and she wasn't going to settle for baking soda as a solution. She wasn't losing her memory; she was losing her patience. He chuckled to himself. If his wife had Oldtimers, he'd be the first one to know, not Emira. Susan was as feisty as she'd ever been. Sharp as a tack.

He flipped open the yellow pages and made a call.

Chapter Twenty-Six

1969

Cigarette dangling from his mouth, Floyd maneuvered the ladder until it rested solidly against the front of the house, then stood back to survey the position. No, he needed it to be slightly higher if he was going to reach the fascia board along the lower edge of the roof. A gallon of bright blue paint waited for him, as did his wife's expectations. She'd been wanting him to paint that fascia board for over a year. Well, he'd do it today even if it killed him.

He dropped his Lucky onto the concrete porch and snuffed it out with his shoe. Time to get to work. With a grunt, he grabbed hold of the ladder again and angled it upward and to the right. At least, he tried to. A sickening crash resounded, and the weight dropped from his hand. Uh-oh.

"Dad?" Joseph called from inside.

Susan flew out the front door. "Floyd?"

He cringed as glass continued to crackle.

"You put the ladder through Joseph's window?" Her hands flew to her head.

He scratched his chin. "Looks like I did."

"My goodness, Floyd. We should have just paid someone to paint."

He huffed and stretched his shoulder muscles before hoisting the ladder out of Joseph's bedroom with a moan. "No need for that. I can do it."

"The blazes you can." Susan's mouth twisted.

Joseph peeked out from behind her, brown hair tousled. "Dad, am I going to sleep with no window? It'd kind of be like camping."

"No, honey." Susan patted his head. "You can sleep on the sofa bed tonight."

He jumped up and down at that new adventure, then spun around and raced back inside.

"Floyd? Are you sure about this?"

"Trust me, will you?" He'd scooted the ladder down a foot or so and had it balanced sturdy and secure. So what if he'd never been much of a handyman. He could paint a little fascia board, for crying out loud.

"Okay." Her tone proved her unconvinced, but she closed the door behind her as she disappeared inside. He hoisted up the ladder, blue paint and paint brush in hand.

Moments later, he leaned back to survey his work. Not bad! Susan was going to be tickled pink at their home's new look. They'd have the spiffiest place on the block. He brushed more on, but he couldn't reach far. When he leaned even slightly to the right, the ladder wobbled. This was going to take a while if he had to climb up and down to move over every few minutes. But anything for the wife.

He climbed down, dripping a few drops of blue paint onto the porch in the process. Darn it. He'd have to squirt that off with the hose before it dried. But first things first. With a manly growl, he lifted the ladder and moved it down a little. Only the bulky thing was a bear to maneuver. He tumbled forward as another crash rang out, followed by a cascade of crunching sounds. The porch looked to be littered with diamond fragments as glass shards twinkled up at him.

"Floyd!" Susan burst out of the front door. "What in the world?" Mouth agape, she surveyed the scene. "Did you just put the ladder through Marie's window?"

He itched underneath his collar. "I guess so."

"How?"

He shrugged. "It could happen to anybody."

She shook her head, mumbling under her breath. "No, I think this could only happen to you."

Joseph tugged on the hem of Susan's shirt. "Does this mean Marie gets to sleep on the sofa bed with me?"

"Yes, bud. Now let's go eat a cookie while I try to figure out how to pay for this expensive paint job." She rolled her eyes at Floyd. "Ready to call a professional yet?"

A professional? Did she think he couldn't paint his own house? "No." He stood back and studied the task before him. "I have an idea."

"Oh boy." Once again, she slipped inside.

He moved the ladder to the end of the house—no windows there—and climbed onto the roof, bucket of paint in tow. The fascia board was so close he could lie on his belly and paint it with no problem. Call him a genius. Susan would have to admit she'd been wrong to doubt him.

He got a few inches coated before he couldn't stand the roof shingles poking into his abdomen any longer. Talk about uncomfortable. He lifted his shirt to find marks from where they'd dug into his flesh. Okay, no problem. He'd kneel, lean over, and paint.

Except that bit into his knees. He lifted into a crouch, and his balance shifted. "No!"

He clamored for something to grab onto so he didn't plummet. His hand grasped the paint bucket. Next to him, a waterfall of blue paint toppled from the roof to the porch below.

Then, his breath left his lungs as he tumbled downward into the bushes. He hit with a thud. The pain pounded his backside and prickled his limbs.

"Floyd?"

"Over here." He raised a hand.

"What are you doing in the bushes?"

"I fell."

"Fell?" She looked to the sky as if it was raining goofy men.

"From the roof," he said.

"From the—" Puffing out a breath, she waved her hands in front of her. "I don't want to know." Then her gaze dropped. "Our porch!"

Head aching, he creaked to kneel and then stand. His vision hazed around the edges, but the bright blue splotch covering a good four or five feet of the concrete was clear enough. Shoot. His back cracked as he straightened, and he winced. "No one will notice."

The bushes hid the view from the street, right? He squinted. Why'd she have to pick out such a bright color? A pastel would have been far less obvious.

She pressed her lips together and stared at him as if he were mad.

"Give me a break, will you? I'm trying."

Her hand hoisted to her hip. "Are you going to stop *trying* and call someone? Betty Rambert hired a nice young man to paint her deck. I could get his number."

His neck heated. "Betty Rambert is a ninety-two-year-old widow. *I* am a nice young man." He thrust a thumb to his chest. "Me. I can do this."

Why didn't she believe in him? Didn't the Bible say he could do all things through Christ who strengthened him?

She blinked back at him, then retreated inside, leaving him to form a new plan.

Okay, no ladder this time. He didn't need one anyway. The house wasn't tall enough to need much to reach the fascia. Just a boost. He only needed a little boost. He stood on the porch chair and reached as far as he could, but it wasn't quite enough. What could he stand on that was a little higher than the chair? He scanned the area, and his gaze snagged on his car. That was the ticket! He could pull his car up to the house and stand on the hood. Brilliant! Good thing he'd purchased extra paint, just in case.

An hour later, he'd gotten half of the fascia painted. Sometimes, he surprised himself with his intelligence. Every few minutes, he needed to step off the hood and move the car over a trifle so he could paint the next section, but each inch down the row oozed with the satisfaction of a job well done. It became tougher when he got to the bushes. He couldn't get quite as close to the house, which meant he had to lean over farther. But no worries. He could manage.

In the middle of patting himself on the back, he stepped backward. The space under his foot gave way. The windshield splintered and scraped his ankle as his shoe hit the dashboard. He winced as glass shards poked into his foot, but he dared not move or utter a sound. He stood frozen, gaze glued on the doorway. Surely, Susan would come out at any moment. But when an agonizing minute passed with no sight of her, he breathed easier. She must not have heard the windshield break. Maybe he could get it fixed before she noticed.

Pulling his foot free proved more difficult than he'd anticipated. He jiggled it, only to end up in more pain. Then he yanked it, and the glass crackled and shattered into the car like the pelting of a hailstorm.

The door swung open. "Floyd?"

Floyd might not have had much success in the home improvement arena, but Susan had successfully graduated from beauty school. He was so proud of her that his buttons might pop.

Susan handed Mrs. Nash the bottle of shampoo, then rang up the purchase. The cash register dinged, and polite chatter continued as money exchanged hands. Floyd couldn't help but smile as he returned to his booth to sweep up hair from the last customer.

"Thanks again. Have a wonderful rest of your day." Susan's sugar-sweet voice swelled throughout the space.

The front door clicked shut. Susan hummed as she returned to her sink and turned the water on. Washing curlers, no doubt. He didn't need to ask if she was enjoying her new role as stylist. He'd never seen her so content. And boy, was it nice to not have to contend with those bickering hens any longer. He could deal with his wife's … er, leadership qualities. He'd had years to grow accustomed to them.

The bell jingled, and he peeked over the divider, eager for a customer. Two ladies sauntered in. "Susan," he called.

It wasn't quite fair that she'd had more business than he did on her first day on the job. Still, business was business. He wouldn't complain.

Susan greeted the ladies with a delighted grin. "Hi, can I help you?"

She hadn't treated him with such endearment in years. He stalked to the back, dumped the hair in the trash can, then retreated to his recliner. He'd console himself with peanuts and his paper.

"I'm Mary. This is my sister, Martha. We want to look just like Jackie O. Can you manage that?"

He held back a snort as he sank into his chair. How many women sported Jackie's flip bob nowadays? But if these sisters weren't twins, they might as well be. To match haircuts and styles was comical.

The one who must have been Martha spoke up. "*You* want to look like Jackie. *I* want to look like Mary Tyler Moore."

He rolled his eyes. What was the difference? They both wore the same hairstyle.

"I'll do my best." Susan's voice conveyed more confidence than her words. No one would be able to tell it was her first day on the job.

The phone rang. Floyd reached to answer it from his comfy spot in the recliner. "Hello?"

"Hi, Mr. Douglas?"

He humphed an acknowledgment.

"This is Little Fish Preschool. Marie has a fever and needs to be picked up."

"Yeah. Sure. Okay." He hung up and stood. After making his way to Susan's booth, he repeated what he was told.

Susan had the apron draped around one of the Bible ladies. Her foot was poised to pump the chair higher, about to bring the customer to the right height to recline into the sink for a shampoo. She looked at him like a deer in headlights. He likely mirrored the expression.

She always picked up the kids when they were sick. But now? Could the Bible ladies come back later? Ms. Jackie O Wannabe arched an eyebrow at him. Or not. Clearly, the dynamics had shifted. If he and Susan were going to be partners in work, they had to be partners in parenting as well.

"I'll get her." He swiped his keys from the counter and headed out the front door.

Chapter Twenty-Seven

1997

Emira held the ladder as her mom ascended the middle rungs to the roof of New Creations, a gallon of paint and bag of supplies in hand. Billowy white clouds shaded them from the summer sun, yet humidity still glued their clothes to their bodies.

"Yeah, this isn't too bad. Just don't look down," Mom called.

Emira grimaced. "I still think I should have gone first. Then you could have caught me if I fell."

"I wanted to check things out." Mom reached the top and swung her leg onto the roof. "It's sturdy. Come up."

"Here goes nothing." This was crazy. What mom brought her fifteen-year-old to the roof of a building to paint a sign? They could have paid someone to do it. Surely, saving a few bucks wasn't worth risking their lives.

Her knees shook as she took one tenuous step after another, but she managed not to look down. Instead, she peered through the shop window as she rose. Ugh. Someone had messed up the magazines again. She'd have to reorganize them tomorrow.

Soon, she'd turn sixteen and get a real job, one that paid an hourly wage instead of Papa's tips. The prospect elicited dual twinges of excitement and regret. Maybe she could still work here a few hours a week, at least in the summer.

"You're almost there."

Mom's encouragement bolstered Emira's speed, and soon, she climbed over the gutters onto warm black shingles. She'd made it. She scooted on her bottom, away from the ledge, and took in the bird's-eye view. So, this is what it felt like to be on top of the world.

Mom stood and walked over to survey the sign. Images of her mother tumbling to her death on the concrete below flooded her mind.

Emira sucked in a breath. "Mom, be careful."

"I'm fine." She bent over the monstrosity.

It had to be over six feet wide and maybe four feet tall. Much larger than it seemed from below. How were they going to paint it?

"Just figuring out a strategy."

Emira gauged how far it stood from the ledge. A good five feet. They probably wouldn't fall off the roof. Still … "What about calling a professional?"

"Ha ha." Mom's voice dripped with sarcasm. "We've made it this far. Might as well finish the job." She knelt by the can of paint and worked the lid open. Her voice softened. "It's the least I can do for them after all the ways they've helped me over the years."

True, they owed Nana and Papa the world. Emira's grandparents had helped to raise her when the demands of single parenting meant long hours at the office for Mom. How could she not repay them?

As Mom peeled off the lid, the scent of paint wafted and, with it, a pang of longing. Her throat tightened.

Mom's brows furrowed. "What's wrong?"

She shook her head. "Nothing. The smell of paint just reminds me of Dad."

"Oh." Mom handed her a brush. "It's been several years since you've seen him, hasn't it? I've lost track."

A muscle in her cheek twitched. "Five."

Five long years. So much for his promises of visiting every month. They'd had one night in a hotel. One. And it had been glorious.

"I'm sorry."

"Not your fault." Emira stood and stretched. Not now. She had to put thoughts of her father far from her mind and focus on the task at hand. Good thing she'd had plenty of practice. "So, what's our strategy?"

Mom stood on her tiptoes and bent over the sign. "Like this for the top. Then one of us can scooch underneath and paint the bottom. Like a mechanic with a car."

Only the top person would have to lean far over, and the bottom person would need to nearly do sit-ups to reach high enough. "I didn't know I was signing up to contort my body into all these weird positions. This is a strange way to paint."

"Do you want top or bottom?"

Neither, but … "Top."

Mom slithered under the sign and started on the *s* at the end while Emira began on the large *N*.

"Emira, be careful. You're dripping paint all over the place, and I'm going to have to lie in it in a minute."

Oops. She'd always been a sloppy painter. "Sorry."

Mom chuckled, then erupted into all-out laughter.

"What is it?" Nothing about this was funny, unless … okay, the whole thing was ridiculous.

"Have I ever told you about the time Papa painted the fascia board?"

"No." She hadn't heard anything about Papa painting. Something about caulk, but not paint.

Mom told the story, and by the time she finished, Emira was laughing so hard her paint lines were wiggly. "Good thing Papa never tried to paint this sign himself." She snorted at the thought.

"Good thing the house is one story."

When they met in the center, they discovered a gap in the middle of the letters, which neither paint brush had reached. Emira strained, stretching her arms as far as she could. She pulled on the old dance training locked away in the recesses of her memory for the needed flexibility. Mom grunted as she reached upward. Just an inch more. Emira lifted higher onto her toes. There. The two brushes met, briefly mingling, before both women relaxed with panting breaths. They'd made it work, the two of them, without needing anyone else.

It felt like a picture of their life together. Always straining to cover the bare spot Dad had left.

No. That wasn't fair. Papa had been there. His love covered so much. When she was tempted to think about all she'd missed out on when Dad had packed up and left, she'd think about everything she had in Papa. The goofy man who'd fallen off the roof into the bushes and spilled blue paint all over the porch. She chuckled again.

After more stretching and straining, they finished the sign just as the day began to wane. A rooftop spot next to Mom proved a perfect view of the sunset. She'd never felt especially close to her mother, not like she had to Nana and Papa. Mom had been at work too much to get to know her well. But this moment of companionable silence was a sweet end to what would certainly become a happy memory.

Emira bumped Mom's shoulder with her own. "They're going to be so surprised. I can't wait to see their faces."

"You should take a video. What time does Papa get here in the morning?"

"Eight thirty on the dot."

"I'll set my alarm."

Emira scoffed. Like that would do anything. "I'll wake you up."

Mom let out a long, contented sigh. "We'd better go. It would be hard to get down the ladder in the dark."

Yikes. She hadn't prepared to go *down* the ladder.

They gathered the supplies and crept to the ledge. The ground loomed far below.

"You go first," Mom said. "I'll hold the ladder steady."

Emira's eyes widened. "No way. I'm not going first." How did one even do something like this? What if her foot missed a rung? She wrapped her arms around her middle. "I might just stay up here forever. Or until the fire department rescues me."

Mom's voice came out breathy. "Don't be silly. We can do this. We have Floyd Douglas's blood in our veins."

"That does *not* help." It might have been more encouraging before she'd told the painting story.

"Hey, he didn't die. He's always been like a cat, landing on his feet."

"I hate cats."

"Well …" Mom surveyed the scene. "Okay, I'll go first. You steady the ladder."

Oh goodness. She was about to watch her mother plummet to her death. She clenched the top of the ladder with white knuckles. Mom crouched onto her belly, then shimmied backward until her feet found the ladder rung. Emira averted her eyes. If this was going to end badly, she couldn't watch. Eyes averted to the skyline, she cringed with each creak of the ladder.

A few minutes later, Mom called out, "I made it. Your turn."

Okay, she could do this. She had to. When she turned around, the paint can and bag of supplies stared back at her. Panic surged. "I don't know how to carry everything down with me."

"Oh, I forgot about that. Just leave it."

Okay, then. She held her breath as she mimicked the way Mom had climbed down the ladder. With an iron grip, she clung to the ladder. She could do this. She only needed to pry her grasp free and lower herself to the next rung. There. Two, three, four steps. The world around her swayed, then spun. She should probably breathe before she passed out. She gulped air into her burning lungs, but that only made her vision haze more. Oh no. She *couldn't* do this. She was going to faint.

Her throat burned. Just as she choked back a sob, the shop's waiting room came into focus through the window. There was Papa's desk, and on it, a picture of her as a girl on Papa's lap.

In Papa's lap, she'd always felt safe. Secure. Loved.

I'm your good Father.

What was that? Not an audible voice, but one so distinct in her mind.

Come to Me. Sit on My lap.

Now she trembled for a different reason. Was this … Papa had talked about the still, small voice of the Lord. Could this be it?

She'd heard about God all her life, gone to church, attended Vacation Bible School. Her whole family believed in Jesus, and if pressed, she'd have said she was a Christian. What else would she be? But when people started talking about Father God, she zoned out. One absent father was enough for her.

But what if *Father God* was more like the picture in front of her? More like Papa's lap. What if Papa's love was only a glimpse of something far greater?

Strength entered her. Strength and warmth and light. If that was true, if God cherished her that much, she was far too loved to give up.

God, I'm sorry for pushing You away. Show me who You really are.

A simple prayer, but enough to fill her with hope at the possibilities.

Gaze focused on that picture, she descended rung by rung until her feet planted on the concrete. She stretched her cramped hands. "I did it."

That trek down the ladder may have begun a whole different kind of journey.

Chapter Twenty-Eight

2010

Floyd double-checked to make sure he'd tucked all his medications into his small carry-on duffle bag, then zipped it up. After all his failed schemes over the years, it was crazy to think this one had worked. He'd still have the hospital bill to contend with when he returned, but at least he could go on his trip. It only took a little sweet talk from Susan, and his brother-in-law signed off on the medical release. His wife could turn on the charm when she wanted just as easily as she could crank up the sass. He smiled to himself. He'd miss her during this trip.

Should he triple-check his massive suitcase? He eyed its bulging middle. Considering he had to sit on the thing to get the zipper closed, best to trust his earlier judgment. A glance at the packing list showed everything marked off. That feeling he'd forgotten something likely came from all the times Emira had forced him to watch *Home Alone* when she was younger. He'd be fine. He took one last peek in the mirror and grimaced at his reflection. He must have run his hand through his hair repeatedly for it to stand on end like that. Had he packed a comb? He rustled through the bathroom drawers. He must have packed *all* the combs. Gee whiz. He smoothed down his hair with his fingers. Good enough.

When he wheeled his suitcase into the living room, he found Susan sitting on the sofa massaging her foot. She wore fuzzy blue socks, no matter that it had to be eighty-five degrees in the house, and he felt like stripping to his skivvies.

"All ready?" She smiled in his direction, but it was tight. Forced.

"What's wrong?"

"My foot's hurting. No big deal. I must have stubbed my toe on something."

He sat next to her. "Let's see it. Take the sock off."

"No." She put her leg down. "It's fine."

"If it's fine, let me see it." With an oof he bent over. The tips of his fingers grasped the sock. He yanked.

She winced as he peeled the sock off to reveal a foot the color of a plum.

He recoiled. "What the devil? Your whole foot is purple!"

"I told you, I must have stubbed it on something."

"On what? An elephant?" Not only was it purple, but it had also swollen to double its size. How could it have gotten this bad without him noticing? Oh dear. He checked his watch. His cab would arrive in half an hour. This was bad. "You've got to go to the doctor."

"Naw." She plucked the sock from his limp grasp and gently slid it back onto her foot. "It'll be fine. There's nothing they can do for it anyway. I'll take a warm bath."

What good would a warm bath do? It could spread. By the time he came back from Haiti, he might come home to a purple Muppet. "I'm calling Emira."

She had a way with Susan. Maybe she could talk some sense into her.

He nearly tripped over his suitcase in his haste to get to his phone on the kitchen counter. Emira answered on the first ring.

"Hi, Papa. Calling to say goodbye?"

If only. And here he'd thought things were complicated half an hour ago when he couldn't find a comb. "I need your help. We've encountered a snafu."

Laughter bubbled from her end. "A snafu?"

Wrong word choice if he wanted her to take him seriously. "Nana's got a ... little problem."

Guilt prickled his arms, but he couldn't claim a full-scale emergency. That would make him look horrible, leaving her in such a state. He did feel like pond scum. But this was his trip, his chance. And he'd spent fifteen thousand nonrefundable dollars on it. There was no postponing the thing for a quick doctor's appointment. This is what family was for, right?

Emira sobered. "What problem?"

He hesitated. He should have worked out what to say before he called. "Her foot hurts. She needs to go to urgent care."

"Oh, okay. I can take her. No problem."

Relief swept over him. It would work out. Emira had this. She'd get Susan squared away. *No problem.* He repeated those words to himself like a mantra. There was no problem here. Nothing keeping him from following through with his plan. "When can you get here? I'm leaving in"—he checked his watch—"twenty minutes."

"Oh, she needs to go right away, then?"

"I'd rather her not be alone. At least not for long."

"It'll take me maybe forty minutes to get there."

"That's fine. Thanks." Now to convince Susan not to fight Emira when she showed up.

He'd nearly flipped his phone closed when Emira's soft voice came through. "Papa?"

"Yes, Princess?"

"I'll miss you. I love you."

"Love you too." His chest twinged. Six weeks suddenly seemed like a long time.

Emira pulled into the driveway behind Papa's black Saturn. For a moment, her mind played tricks on her, telling her he was still there. That he'd reconsidered and hadn't gone after all. But of course not. He'd taken a cab, despite her multiple offers to drive him to the airport. His car was here, but he wasn't. And wouldn't be for some time.

At least she could make herself useful by taking Nana to urgent care. As much as Nana hated doctors, it was surprising that she'd allow for Emira to take her to one. Or ... Emira's steps faltered on the front porch, and she stumbled over her own feet, barely catching her balance to prevent plowing into brick. Papa wouldn't have asked her to come if Nana hadn't been willing, right? He wouldn't place her in that position. Surely not.

She cracked open the door. "Nana, it's me."

"Emira?" Nana's voice sounded strained. "What are you doing here?"

Emira headed toward the dining room in the direction of her grandmother's voice. "Didn't Papa tell you I was coming?" Had he hidden the information from Nana so he wouldn't upset her, or had she forgotten a conversation that happened mere minutes earlier?

"No. I had no idea."

Emira rounded the corner to find Nana sitting on one kitchen chair with her foot propped onto a bag of frozen peas on another chair. Warmth filled her chest. Her tough-as-nails grandma likely wouldn't have been caught in such a position if she'd known—or remembered—Emira was coming. She'd have pushed through the pain and offered Emira a snack.

"Papa said your foot is hurting. What happened?"

Nana's cheeks flushed pink. Embarrassment at being caught in need? "I don't remember."

Emira's breath caught at the admission. If Nana knew her memory was failing, maybe they could make strides to get her care for it, even if Papa never came on board. But for now, she needed to focus on Nana's injury.

She knelt by the chair where Nana's foot rested. "Can I see?"

Nana opened her mouth, but Emira plunged forward. She wasn't going to listen to any assurances that everything was fine. Papa wouldn't have called her for no reason. She gently tugged the sock down and exposed Nana's foot. Her grandma whimpered.

Emira's mouth dropped wide. What was Papa thinking, not warning her ahead of time? He'd said Nana's foot was bothering her. That was like saying someone who'd suffered a gunshot wound had a scratch. "Oh my." She winced at the purple, splotchy flesh.

"You think it's bad? Floyd said I need to see a doctor."

Emira kept her voice calm but firm. "Nana, you need to go to the emergency room."

Nana's face paled. "No. That can't be necessary."

"If you don't get this taken care of, they might have to amputate."

She hated to scare Nana, but it might be the only way to get her in the car. And Nana needed to get in the car. Kade's dad had lost his leg to a severe blockage. She might not be a doctor, but this certainly wasn't a broken toe, and it did require immediate attention.

Nana replaced her sock, determination steeling her features as if she planned on soldiering on as normal. "They make you wait forever at the emergency room. It's a waste of time."

Emira planted her hands on her hips. "If I take you to urgent care, they're only going to send you to the ER."

"I don't need to go anywhere." Nana narrowed her gaze.

Emira slammed her eyes shut. Teddy's tantrums were easier to deal with than this. She needed backup. She removed the sock again, snapped a picture, and texted it to her mom. A few seconds later, her phone rang.

"What was that?"

"Nana's foot. I need your help getting her to the hospital."

A few choice words and then, "I'll be there in fifteen minutes."

Darn traffic. Floyd was going to be late. In the sky ahead, gray clouds hung pregnant with rain. The weather better not slow him down any more.

Floyd tugged at his seat belt. "Can you step on it? My flight leaves in a little over an hour."

"Relax, man." The hippie met his gaze in the rearview mirror. The young man's straight, long hair was bound in a headband at the top and a ponytail in back. He wore a fringed vest and a tie-dyed shirt. Just Floyd's luck to get a hippie cab driver. It was like he'd stepped into the twilight zone. A blast from the past.

"I can't miss my flight." He didn't mean to grumble like a crabby old man but well ... "I'm going on a six-week-long mission trip. It's important."

Hippie's eyes narrowed with determination. "I dig it, man. I'll get you there."

The shaggy lime-green seat covers on the front two seats and hound dog bobble head did little to reassure Floyd that the chill *dude* could make good on his claim. *Please, God. Get me there in time.*

The engine purred as Hippie accelerated. Well, then. Maybe Floyd had misjudged. Or perhaps God would answer his prayer quicker than normal.

Hippie winked at him in the rearview mirror. "Hang on."

A sharp swerve sent Floyd sliding toward the middle seat. A car honked. Hippie threw back his head and laughed. Floyd's nervous chuckle sounded awkward in his ears. Had he gotten in the car with a psychopath? Or just someone especially dedicated to customer satisfaction? The car breezed into the other lane, cutting off the person behind them. Another horn blasted.

Oh well. God worked in mysterious ways. At this rate, he'd arrive with enough time to grab a beer before his flight. He probably wouldn't get many of those on the mission trip.

Floyd's phone buzzed in his pocket. A text from Emira. Taking Nana to the ER.

The ER? That seemed like jumping the gun. He scratched the back of his neck. How'd Emira convince Susan to go to the ER? He'd figured she'd have a tough enough time sweet-talking her into an urgent care visit. He fumbled with his phone. At times like these, one of those smart phones did seem more convenient. Instead, he punched buttons multiple times to send his one-word text—*Why?*—then somehow ended up calling the cable company. He flipped his phone closed, hanging up.

Her response came not a minute later. How did young people text so fast? He squinted and pressed on the button to read it.

She probably has blockage. It's serious.

Blockage? As in a clogged artery? She'd said she stubbed her toe. He held the phone in a trembling hand. Of course, that wasn't the problem. Bumping into something wouldn't lead to such a sight. He should be with Susan right now. Or be there to support whatever poor nurse had the unfortunate task of tending to his wife.

Susan would be okay, right? She was as tough as they came. *Oh, God, what do I do?*

Another text came through.

Don't worry. Mom and I are taking care of her. We've got this. Enjoy your trip.

So, Marie was with her. Good thing. The tension in his neck eased a little. Until the side of a black pickup veered within inches of his window. Floyd's heart leapt into his throat as Hippie swerved to the right to avoid a collision. Brakes squealed. Tires skidded. Multiple horns blared. Floyd squeezed his eyes shut. This was it. He was going to die. Every muscle tensed as he prepared for glass to shatter and shards of metal to sear him.

"You okay, man?" Hippie's voice came on a breathless burst.

Floyd cranked open one eye. He was alive. Unharmed. The car remained in one piece, easing forward back into the flow of traffic. "Yes?" Floyd's fingers traveled over his arms and legs. No blood. Not even a scratch. "Yeah, I'm fine." A glance over his shoulder showed the highway littered with a multicar pileup.

"That was a close one. The dude in the black truck was driving like a maniac. Could have messed us up. I was scared for a second there," Hippie said.

"You and me both." What an understatement.

Hippie flicked a strand of hair from his face before speeding up. "Did your life flash before your eyes?"

"No." The whole life montage might happen to others in near-death moments, but for him, only one image burned on the retina of his mind. He would have thought his greatest fear in that moment would have been missing out on his trip. Dying before getting a chance to make the difference he longed to make. Instead, Susan's face swam in his imagination. His wife's beautiful face as he'd first seen her standing outside Velvet Freeze with the scarf under her nose. His firecracker.

The car slowed. Hippie tossed a grin over his shoulder. "We're here. Told you I'd get you here on time."

A wave of homesickness swept over Floyd. Ridiculous. He hadn't even left the city. Yet he ached for Susan. For family.

The cab pulled to the curb. Hippie announced the total owed. Numb, Floyd pulled out his wallet. He was going through the motions now. Doing what he needed to do to get to where he needed to go. This bout of homesickness was normal and would pass soon enough. He had to push through it to get to his destiny.

But when he opened the billfold, a folded card stared back at him. Gingerly, he took it out and read it.

Success is getting what you want. Happiness is wanting what you have.

His eyelids burned. The card his father had given Susan the day Floyd had forgiven him. She'd kept it all these years. And she'd snuck it into his wallet. His gaze traveled to his wedding ring. The metal pressed heavy against his finger. A promise to have and to hold, in sickness and in health.

"Everything okay?" Hippie's voice interrupted his musing and caused a sharp intake of breath.

Floyd looked around at people bustling to and fro, rolling suitcases, walking with purposeful steps. This was it. "It's now or never," he whispered.

He twirled the ring around on his finger.

What if … Was he okay with never?

If he never went on this trip, then what? Would his life be an utter waste?

"What's it going to be?" Hippie tapped his fingers on the steering wheel. "You getting out, or did you change your mind?"

Floyd's gaze zeroed in on the ring again. "This trip could change everything. It could be the hinge point of my life. My crowning moment." How could he let something so significant slip through his fingers?

A smile edged through Hippie's voice. "In my experience, life isn't made of one big moment, but a thousand little ones. How old are you?"

Floyd snorted. "Old."

"If you think this month-long trip will trump sixty-something years of living day in and day out, you're looking in the wrong place."

How true. He couldn't make up for seventy years of failure with one trip. And if he abandoned his wife in her time of need in order to aid strangers, he'd be breaking a promise he made before God to care for her. The trip would be yet another failure to add to his mounting list.

Is that who he wanted to be? Someone who left his own family to fend for themselves in the ER while he endeavored to save the world? In reality, wasn't this trip truly about boosting his own ego? Assuring himself that he was a good person?

No, he couldn't live with himself if he got on that plane now. For whatever reason, Susan had chosen him all those years ago. He would choose her now.

"Take me back."

Chapter Twenty-Nine

1970

It was another year before Susan brought up anything in the house that needed fixing or tending to. The front porch remained traumatized with blue paint. Floyd took comfort in the slightly lower electric bill due to the new more energy-efficient windows. By the time he retired, the amount saved might nearly make up for the amount spent.

He was washing his hands in the bathroom one day when Susan leaned against the doorjamb and frowned toward the tub. "It could really use a new caulk job." She sighed. "I'll have to ask around. See who can do it for cheap."

Floyd dried his hands, then smoothed the scowl that attempted to creep onto his face. "You don't have to call anyone. I can do it."

She raised a brow. "Really?"

"Of course."

"Have you ever caulked before?"

He guffawed. "No, but how hard could it be?"

"That's what you said about the—"

"I know, I know. But this is simple. Leave it to me." He flashed a reassuring smile that she did not return.

At the local hardware store, he found the caulk no problem. See? He could do this. He handed it to the cashier. "Caulking a tub is easy work, isn't it? You just open this thing and squeeze it on?"

The man in the red apron eyed him warily. "You got a gun?"

"Gun?" Floyd reared back. Why did the man switch subjects to firearms? "I don't got any guns."

"A *caulk* gun. You're going to need one to use this." He waved the caulk. "Here. I'll show you." He led Floyd back to where a few different types of contraptions hung on hooks. "You put the caulk in here like this." He demonstrated. "Cut the tip off. Just the tip, mind you. Then as you squeeze the gun, the caulk will come out nice and even."

Ah. A caulk gun. Seemed simple enough. "Okay, I'll take that too."

When he strutted into the house, supplies in tow, Susan's brow pinched. "Are you sure about this?" She followed him into the bathroom.

"Completely. The man at the hardware store told me exactly what to do. Quit worrying, will you?"

He wasn't incompetent. Surely, an intelligent, well-read man like himself could do something so simple as caulk his own tub.

She huffed a sigh and threw her hands up, exiting the room. Good. Now he could work in peace. He pulled out the caulk and gun. Okay, so first, he needed to cut off the tip. He rummaged through the drawers and found Susan's hair scissors. Clamping them around the tip of the caulk, he squeezed. Nothing.

Fine, he'd find a knife. Caulk in hand, he stomped to the kitchen and searched through drawers there.

"Why are you making such a racket?" Susan swatted him away. "What do you need?"

"A knife. A sharp one."

With furrowed brows, she handed him a butcher knife and nudged him along. "Now get out of my kitchen. And don't injure yourself with that."

He bristled. Did she think him incapable of using a knife? "I won't. I promise."

Back in the bathroom, he took the giant knife and sawed at the tip of the caulk. Grunting, he put more muscle into it, and finally, the plastic gave way. Except in the process of sawing, the knife had slipped from the tip of the caulk to the base of its spout. A thick stream of caulk spewed out.

"Ah!" he shouted as the white molten lava dripped onto his sink and floor. He fumbled to get the caulk into the gun, then rushed to the tub. Making a neat, thin line was impossible with it spewing so thick, but he tried his best. He finished his ring around the tub. How was he supposed to turn the thing off? It just kept coming. He made another caulk ring as he scrambled for what to do. What else needed to be caulked? The sink? Toilet? Baseboards? There was enough in there to do them all and have more left over.

"Susan," he called, trying to keep the tremor from his voice, "I've got it going pretty good. Is there anything else you need caulked?"

He moved to the base of the toilet. Thick drips of caulk dotted the floor and sides of the tub.

"What?" Susan called back.

He raised his voice. "Is there anything else you need caulked?" Moving to the sink, he pushed down the climbing panic.

"Why?" Susan appeared in the doorway. Her hands flew to her cheeks. "Oh no, Floyd. What did you do?"

"What do you mean, what did I do? I caulked."

She pulled at the roots of her hair. "We're going to need a whole new bathroom. Look at this!"

He would, but he couldn't take his eyes off the caulk gun. He moved the still-flowing stream to the backsplash and ran it along the lines between the tile squares. "It's not that bad, is it?"

"Not that bad? Floyd, it's a disaster." She walked away, mumbling to herself.

The flow was finally easing, and he caught a breath. Too bad it was laden with disappointment. How come he couldn't perform the simplest home improvement tasks? He was a man. He should be able to take care of things around the house. He shouldn't have to pay someone to do something so simple. His shoulders slumped. Now he'd be paying for a bathroom remodel.

Maybe he should stick to cutting hair. But was that all he was capable of?

New Creations stood across the street and down a stone's throw from New Beginnings, a growing church whose rumblings Floyd couldn't ignore. Customers talked of overflowing youth services where hippies sat cross-legged and barefooted, swaying to the beat of "Jesus music." Floyd had stuck with the Catholic church after his encounter with the Lord, attending the Life of the Spirit seminars like his mother insisted. Still, it was as if there was an itch he couldn't reach. Might he find what he was looking for in the church across the way?

He walked in one Sunday night, Bible in hand, and stopped in his tracks. The room swarmed with bodies. Where had so many people come from? His gaze zeroed in on a nun in full habit worshipping with upraised hands. He'd heard about the hippies, and they were everywhere. Bell-bottoms and halter tops, shoeless and long hair hanging free, they filled the space. But interspersed among them were others. A man in a three-piece suit. A trio who would most definitely be labeled "squares." Was that his neighbor, Mr. Brown? And a nun.

It seemed impossible *not* to belong here.

He found a spot next to a young lady in a billowing pink skirt and T-shirt sporting a peace sign. In front, a full band played a soft melody. He closed his eyes and inhaled deeply, taking it all in. A mix of cigarette smoke, weed, and incense tinged the air, but heavier than that was a sweet floral smell. Roses maybe? He inhaled again, deeper this time, to get a better whiff of it. No telling where it came from, but one thing was clear: he felt the presence of Jesus in here. Peace and joy gurgled within. He could see why this place was packed.

When he left late that night, he did so with a resolve to bring Susan there as soon as possible and to return himself as often as he could.

As New Beginnings continued to grow, an influx of longer-haired men found their way to his chair, wanting a mere trim for split ends. More and more, Floyd used his scissors and shears instead of his clippers. Their stories fascinated him. Many had given up a life of drugs and seeking earthly pleasures to follow fully after Jesus. Some teared up sharing their testimonies. Some radiated such joy Floyd could nearly feel the warmth emanating from them. He'd never seen anything like it.

One day, a long-haired man of a different kind moseyed in. He wore a fringed vest and bell-bottoms, but instead of peace, the atmosphere around him emitted mostly pot. Even under the mellowing influence, his dilated pupils contained a hard glint to them. A challenge. He appeared to be in his early twenties, but the lines around his eyes spoke of a lot of hardship packed into those few years. The man picked up a magazine and leafed though it but didn't sit. He was obviously restless. Searching.

"What can I do you for?"

When the man made eye contact, it was as if a tunnel had been erected from this customer's heart to Floyd's own, and a freight train shot through. He felt the man's pain as if it were his own. And yet, just as clearly, he knew God had a great purpose for him. This was not the end of this man's story.

"I just need a trim." The customer tilted his chin up slightly, as if to say he didn't really need anything from anyone.

Floyd smiled. "Come on back."

The man shuffled inside the booth, then looked around as if disoriented and confused.

"You're fine." Floyd patted his shoulder. "Take a seat. What's your name?"

"Tom." He sat but kept looking over his shoulder. "Who are you?"

"I'm Floyd, the barber."

"Okay, but who *are* you?" Tom squinted at Floyd. "There's this weird vibe coming off you."

Floyd chuckled. So, Tom could feel the Holy Spirit just as he could. "I assure you, I'm just a barber." Should he say more? No. He needed to wait and engage the man in conversation first. "How much do you want off?"

"An inch." That was about how much Tom's shoulders had creeped up.

"Will do. Just relax. I'll get you taken care of." He pulled out his scissors and started cutting. "Nice weather we're having, isn't it?"

A huff was the only response.

Okay, then. Something else. "You live around here?"

"Not far." Tension emanated from him as if he might jump out of his skin.

Floyd needed to put him at ease. "So, Tom. What do you do for a living?" Hair drifted to the floor as Floyd snipped.

There. Tom visibly relaxed with that question. "I'm a musician. A songwriter. Lead guitarist."

"Impressive. Do you have your own band?"

"Yeah. The Dropout Dudes. Heard of us?"

"I can't say that I have, but that doesn't mean much. I'm not hip to the music scene."

"We're going places. If you haven't heard of us yet, you will soon. Everyone will."

Floyd stilled midsnip. He needed to say this now. He came around the front of the chair and crouched to where he could look Tom in the eye. "I have no doubt you're going places. Great places. You're like a rocket that just needs fuel to blast off. And I know where to find the fuel."

Tom quirked an eyebrow. "Where?"

Floyd pointed to the front window. "Go out there and take a left. About a block down the way, take a right. New Beginnings Church. You can't miss it."

The disgust on Tom's face was palpable. "A church? No way I'm setting foot in a church. I told you, I'm a musician. They think music is from the devil."

"God created music. He loves it, and heaven is filled with music."

"Yeah." Tom snorted. "Harps."

Floyd stood and brushed hair from his trousers. "I think you'll dig the music they play at New Beginnings. They don't play harps there."

"Organs?"

"Not a chance." Floyd returned to the back of the chair to finish the trim. "A full band. Guitars. Drums. Keys."

"Really?"

"No joke. And there are tons of people who look like you. A bunch of hippies. No shoes required."

"Why would I go to some church? I've got everything I need." Tom's hand darted from beneath the blue cape to clench the armrest.

Oh, but there was so much more. How could he express it? "The vibe you felt when you walked in here? That's a Jesus vibe. It's power. It's love. And you can experience it there."

Floyd wasn't always so bold. He didn't push his church on everyone who walked through the door. This young musician, however, was special. It was clear from the moment he walked in that he longed for something more. How could Floyd not offer the solution?

Tom was quiet for a few minutes, and Floyd didn't interrupt the silence. Perhaps God was doing something in the man's heart.

When Floyd finished, he turned Tom around to view the cut. "How does it look?"

"Fine," Tom mumbled.

Floyd's chest deflated. He hadn't gotten through to him at all. Instead, he'd only irritated him and probably ruined any chance of a repeat customer. That's what he got for speaking up.

As Floyd led him to the cash register and took his money, Tom didn't once make eye contact.

"Thanks for coming. Hope to see you again." Floyd forced a smile as he waved goodbye. Tom tossed a small wave over his shoulder. "Remember, turn left, then right," he called out the door. He watched Tom's car turn right out of the parking lot before slumping into a chair facing the front windows.

Some difference maker he was. He thought he'd been saying what God put on his heart to say, but obviously not. He'd made another mess out of things. Wasn't that always his way? One mess after another. He lived to spill blue paint all over the world.

Chapter Thirty

1998

Emira stood in front of her mailbox and ripped open the cushioned envelope from her father. So much had changed between them in the last year. As the Lord began to heal her broken heart, a pocket of space inside of her opened for her dad. It only took her tossing out a tiny breadcrumb of interest for him to rush in with phone calls and gifts. Acts of love. Had she been pushing him away all those years?

Now, as she slid out a cassette tape of Margaret Becker's *Never for Nothing*, she squealed and did a little dance. She'd only just mentioned how she'd fallen in love with these classics last week. Dad must have gone out right away and purchased Becker's first album. Strange how after all this time, after all the silence, they'd bond over the soul-piercing lyrics of Christian music.

Paper peeked out of the envelope. She tugged it loose. A note that simply read *See you Friday*. Friday? What in the world? Wait, there was something else in there. She reached inside and pulled out … two tickets to a Margaret Becker concert this Friday. She squealed again. She was going to get to see her favorite singer in person! And with her dad, no less.

If he showed.

But of course, he'd show. He wouldn't go through all the trouble of mailing her this special surprise and then not come, right? Besides, they talked nearly every week. He rarely forgot phone dates. Her heart twinged at the memories of those few times he *had* forgotten. But why dwell on those? He'd remembered far more. Considering their history, it was a vast improvement.

She jogged inside and headed straight for her boom box player. His thoughtfulness in getting her a cassette instead of a CD proved his consideration. He'd listened when she told him that although her boom box boasted both a CD and cassette player, her older car didn't have a CD player. Such a small gesture, but it meant the world.

She stripped the plastic wrapping off and inserted the tape, forwarding it to track three, *Never for Nothing*. The lyrics and melody lapped over her like waves. Had she loved with no return? For years, it'd sure felt like it. Now, she was beginning to see things differently. Perhaps life and love were far more complicated than she could conceive of as a child. Her dad *did* love her. He always had. Just not in the way she'd wanted.

She was about to see him for the first time in six years. Six years. How would he look now? She could only picture him as she'd seen him last, at the airport during a layover to Denver, when he'd looked as undadlike as she could have imagined. He'd been wearing a suit and tie, and his hair had been styled stiff with some kind of gel. He was on his way to a business meeting, off to impress someone more important than herself. He'd managed to let Mom know that he'd be at their airport for a few hours if she wanted to bring Emira by to see him. They'd eaten lunch. He'd proudly encouraged her to order whatever she wanted as if flaunting that he had money enough to spare now.

She shook her head to dislodge that awkward memory. Everything had changed since then. She didn't have to feel nervous about spending time with him now. Still, every interaction between them seemed to teeter like a seesaw inside of her. Back and forth. Delightful and uncomfortable. Satisfying. Worrisome. Pleasing. Disconcerting. Which held more weight? Which would win out this time?

If he didn't show, it would break her. Any trust they'd built over the past year would crumble under the weight of betrayal. Maybe she should call and remind him. Ensure him she was counting on this. Or maybe she wouldn't need to say as much. She could just mention she'd received the package. That should jog his memory. He'd probably bring up the concert then, and she'd say she was looking forward to it. Enough said.

She turned the volume down on her boom box, picked up the phone from her windowsill, and dialed. Why did making a simple phone call cause her heart to pound? This was her father. Not a cold call to a stranger. Her stomach twisted. This was her *father*. She shouldn't have to remind him to follow through on his word. She shouldn't need to worry that he'd drop her like a hot potato. She slammed the phone into the receiver on the second ring and buried her face in her hands. If she didn't love those songs so much, she'd throw the cassette out the window.

She was a new creation, right? The old was gone, the new had come. So why did interactions with her dad cause her to feel like that same hurt little girl? She must not have come as far as she thought she had in the healing process.

Emotions in a knot, she ejected the tape and headed for her car. She'd visit the shop. Time with Papa always had a way of calming the storm inside her.

Applause erupted as the first song ended. Emira stood on tiptoe and spoke into Papa's ear. "What do you think? You like it?"

She'd invited him to hear a local Christian band play at a concert her youth group was hosting. She still wasn't sure why—it wasn't exactly his scene—but she'd sensed the Lord's leading, and here they were.

Papa squinted toward the stage. "What's the lead singer's name again? He looks familiar."

"Tom Hallt. He's got a song on the radio now. Maybe he's been in the paper or something."

"No. That's not it."

The crowd quieted as Tom's melodic voice filled the auditorium. Emira patted Papa's arm. "This is the one they play on the radio. I love it."

All around them, people sang along. The lyrics about Christ's salvation plucked raw emotion from Emira's soul. Such an authentic song, a prayer of thanksgiving set to music.

Nearly as beautiful, perhaps just as beautiful, as Margret Becker's concert a couple of weeks ago. She'd stood next to her father, singing along with him, their voices blending together. She'd never felt as close to him as she had in those moments. Their love for Jesus wove them together, threads of forgiveness and understanding within. Yet, as her heart still throbbed with childhood memories, those threads seemed thin and tenuous. Would they snap with one more wounding?

She pressed her lips together. She wouldn't think about that now. She was here with Papa, and she'd enjoy this time with him.

Papa sniffled, and his eyes were misty. "I could swear I know him."

She released a watery chuckle. "You know everybody. You sure he hasn't come into the shop?"

"Maybe."

After the concert, Emira was chatting with a group of friends when she turned around to find that Papa wasn't next to her. She scanned the auditorium. There he was, up front with the band. Excellent. Maybe she could get Tom to sign the cassette she'd purchased. She grabbed it from the bag at her feet, excused herself, and jetted down the aisle.

"The Dropout Dudes, right?" Papa asked Tom.

"Yeah." His grin spread wide. "I can't believe you remember."

Emira sidled up next to Papa, holding the CD strategically in front of her.

"I cut your hair once. I'm Floyd, the barber at New Creations."

Tom's mouth parted. "The barber at ..." He tapped the bandmate to his right to get his attention. "This is the man who told me to start coming to church, way back in the day. He's the barber." Tom raked a hand through his hair. "Man, if not for you ..."

"Hey! We've heard about you." The bandmate shook Papa's hand. "He mentions the barber whenever he gives his testimony. Talks about how you never know what kind of difference you might make in someone's life."

Emira's gaze ping-ponged back and forth between the men. What were they talking about?

Papa gave a bashful headshake.

Tom beamed. "No, seriously, man. I gave my life to the Lord a month later."

Papa waved him off. "Coincidence."

"Hardly."

As if just noticing Emira's presence, Papa draped an arm around her shoulders. "Anyway, it was driving me crazy wondering where I knew you from. Mystery solved." He bounced onto his toes and then settled back onto his heels. "I'm proud of you, Tom. You have amazing talent. I'm glad to see how you're using it."

Tom wrapped Papa's hand in his own, leaning close. "Thank you. Truly."

Gratitude burst from Emira. Even without hearing the full story, she sensed the gravity of Papa's part in it. The music that had brought an auditorium of people to tears may not have been possible without his intervention years ago. Had people come to know Jesus through Tom's music? Through his testimony? How far reaching was the impact? And Papa had lived years without a clue.

Tom's gaze flickered to the CD in Emira's hands. "Did you want an autograph?"

Autograph? She blinked, refocusing. "Yes. Yes, please." She handed the CD over.

He grabbed a Sharpie from a music stand and signed his name with a flourish. "Are you related to Floyd?"

"I'm his granddaughter."

He handed the CD back with a smile. "You're blessed, for sure." He angled himself toward Papa. "Hey, would you mind autographing my guitar?"

Papa's eyes widened. "Me?"

"It'd mean a lot."

"If you really want me to."

"I do." Tom handed Papa the Sharpie and grabbed his guitar from the stand. Band members gathered around as Tom braced the instrument on the podium, and Papa adorned it with his signature.

This was incredible. If only Emira had brought her camera. Would Tom Hallt play his next hit song on that guitar? Whatever concerts he held, Papa's name would go with him. How cool was that?

Tom was right. You never knew the difference you might make in someone's life.

Chapter Thirty-One

2010

Emira jumped up from her corner chair and rushed to Nana's bedside. Too late. Nana had already managed to yank off the blood pressure cuff. Again.

She swung her legs over the side of the bed as if she planned to walk right out of the hospital. "Why am I here?"

Emira placed a firm hand on her shoulder, guiding her back down. "Because of your foot, remember? Your foot hurts."

"My foot hurts." She groaned.

Mom had stepped out to call Uncle Joseph. She'd better hurry back. Emira couldn't shoulder this alone. Surely now, everyone would see what had been clear to her for a while. Nana's memory was in a sharp decline. No more avoiding the subject. It glared at them. Time to face it.

Nana pulled at the IV in her arm, nearly ripping it out. Emira covered the taped spot with her hand. "Leave it alone."

"Why's this here? What's going on?"

A nurse's calm voice answered her question from the doorway. "The IV is keeping you hydrated, and we may need it to give you medicine here shortly." A hiss and hand sanitizer dispensed. The nurse scrubbed her hands, serene smile in place.

Thank God for backup.

Mom returned and stood watching in the doorway.

The nurse neared. "I see you've taken off the cuff again." She snuggled it back onto Nana's arm. "Your blood pressure is sky-high. We need to keep this on to monitor it.”

Nana’s frown deepened. “I don’t know why I’m at the dentist anyway. I don’t have any teeth.”

Emira shot Mom a wide-eyed look. See? This is what she’d been talking about. Maybe now they’d believe her.

The nurse replied with practiced nonchalance. “You’re not at the dentist. This is the hospital.”

“Hospital? Why?”

“Your foot hurts. It’s purple.”

“It *does* hurt,” Nana mumbled, as if to herself.

Emira jumped to interrupt the painful conversation. “Any idea when the doctor will see her?”

The nurse turned, sympathy crinkling the edges of her eyes. “Hopefully, within the hour.”

After she took Nana’s vitals and left, Mom stood vigil by the bedside, prohibiting Nana from removing anything. Her sigh sounded weary. Defeated. “Joseph’s on his way.”

“Good.” They could use all the help they could get. “Do you finally believe me?”

Mom’s chin trembled. “Yes.”

Nana turned a suspicious gaze to Mom. “Do you have my teeth?”

Mom gaped.

“I do.” Emira sat forward and caught Nana’s eye. “I have them right here. They’re safe.”

“Oh, good. Thank you.” Nana settled back on her pillow and laced her fingers together.

At Mom’s questioning look, Emira shrugged. She’d had more time to come to grips with the situation. Though how could she ever truly accept it? Her grandma had always been like a firework. Bright. Spunky. Full of life. How could she stand to see that light fade?

Nana’s peace only lasted until the cuff inflated. She catapulted up with panicked eyes as it squeezed her arm. “Get it off! Get it off!”

Mom took her hand. "It's okay."

"It'll be over in a minute." Emira patted her knee.

Nana gulped in air, chest heaving. Puddles formed in her eyes. She looked like a confused child. Emira's heart crumpled. Too much. This was too much to handle.

Suddenly, Nana stilled. Her features smoothed. "Floyd?"

"Susan, it's okay. I'm here."

Emira spun around at the sound of Papa's voice. He stood in the doorway, bedraggled, yes, but tall and strong as a mountain. She rushed to him and fell into his open arms.

Floyd held a trembling Emira in his arms. Was she crying? When Marie hugged him and gave him a kiss on the cheek, her eyes misted as well. Did his presence mean so much to them?

Yes. Yes, it did. They were his world, and he was theirs. They were the family God had knitted together despite their fumbling and their faults. God would forever be at the center of that world, and here, with these people, is where his heart lay. He didn't need to travel clear across the ocean to find his purpose. It was right in front of his eyes.

He squeezed his girls tight. "I'm so sorry—" he began, but they interrupted his apology with questions.

"You came back?"

"You're not going on your trip?"

"Not going at all?"

"What happened?"

He loosened his grasp on his daughter and granddaughter and neared Susan's bedside. His wife's mussed hair and wrinkled face were a world away from the feisty pistol he'd fallen for back in the day, but her eyes shone the same clear blue.

He kissed her temple and took hold of her veined hand. "I'm not going to Haiti. I'm staying right here with you."

A half smile inched up Susan's face. "Can you sneak me a cigarette?"

Emira laughed. "There she is! Oh, thank You, Jesus. Nana's back."

What a curious statement. What had he missed? A doctor stepped into the room before he had a chance to ask. They were admitting Susan and would perform surgery on the blockage the next morning. If it worked, they'd be able to save her foot. If not, amputation would be the only option. Floyd cringed. Susan was the very definition of an independent woman. Her needing assistance to navigate without a limb was unthinkable. The risks of surgery at her age … He couldn't allow his mind to go there. She'd make it through all right. She had to.

The doctor referenced his papers. "The nurses have mentioned a lot of confusion. Do you have concerns about her memory?"

Floyd shook his head. "No."

Both Marie and Emira nodded. "Yes."

Floyd shot them a glance. What? Emira had brought something up with him before, but they'd settled that. And Marie and Joseph had agreed everything was fine.

The doctor looked between them. "Considering the nurses' notes, I feel it's best to have an evaluation by a neurologist. We'll schedule that for you."

He blinked, head swimming. *Oh, Lord, I can't handle this.* Flying across the world to feed the hungry didn't scare him. Watching his wife succumb to dementia? He'd rather die.

In sickness and in health. This is your mission.

His whole being resonated with the certainty of having heard God's voice. If the Lord had called him to this, God would strengthen him for it. It might be too big of a task to do in his own strength, but God's power flowing through him would prove more than sufficient.

If the Lord had called him to this, it wasn't too small of a task to matter.

He didn't need to make a difference for thousands. He only needed to follow the voice of One and love the few in front of him. His wife. His family. It was enough.

Okay, Lord. Help me love well. Till the very end.

Floyd pulled out his buzzing phone on the way to the parking lot. He'd ignored calls and texts from the blasted thing all day. Now, they'd finally gotten Susan settled for the night, and he was headed home for a hot shower and a few hours of sleep. Marie would stay in case Susan woke up disoriented. He'd return in the morning. *Lord, give me strength.*

He only intended to check and make sure it wasn't Marie calling already or Emira in need of something. He had no intention of speaking with anyone else. Yet, curiosity compelled him to answer.

"Father Larry?"

"Floyd, hello. I got word that you missed your flight. Everything okay?"

He let out a deep groan as he dug in his pocket for his keys. "No, actually. Susan's in the hospital. She needs surgery to save her foot."

"Oh no. I hate to hear that." His voice rang with sincerity. "Are you with her now?"

"Just leaving for the night."

"Have you eaten?"

His stomach grumbled a protest. "Not since breakfast."

"Why don't you come by here. I'm just sitting down to a late dinner, and there's plenty. Meatloaf and mashed potatoes."

Floyd's ears perked. Sounded loads better than a microwaved TV dinner. And after what he'd been through today, a listening ear would prove an even better comfort. He'd fought Susan for hours, trying to get her to keep her IV in and blood pressure cuff on. He didn't have any fight left in him. "Sure. What's the address?"

Larry had to repeat it four times for Floyd to get it right, but finally, he'd gotten into his car and written it on the back of a receipt. "I'm on my way." If he could find the place.

"Bring Emira if you can."

Princess was on her way home. Those kids probably needed her. But he said, "I'll see."

He called her as soon as he hung up with the priest. She hadn't left the parking lot yet and agreed to join him. A minute later, she slid into the passenger's seat. "What's the address? I'll put it into my GPS."

He handed her the receipt. At least now he wouldn't get lost. "Don't they need you at home?"

She shook her head. "The kids are asleep already. It's fine." After punching buttons on her phone, she told him to turn left out of the parking lot. "Besides, I'm curious about this priest. He's been trying to get you to come over for dinner for months. I want to know why."

True. His scalp prickled. What was Larry's agenda? He was too tired to worry about it now. At least he was fairly certain the old man didn't intend to murder them and bury their bodies in his backyard. Beyond that, it couldn't get much worse.

He blew out a breath. "What a day."

"For real."

"I never did get to apologize." He reached across the console and took her hand. He was too tired for a meaningful confession, but he needed to offer something. "I should have never left you to take care of Susan."

She shifted in her seat. "Turn right at the light." Her thumb caressed his. "You didn't know it was serious."

Truly, he didn't, but ... "That's no excuse. She's my wife. I made a promise before God to take care of her."

"Left at the next street." A sniff alerted him to the fact she was crying. Or at least trying not to. "You *have* taken care of her. You've taken care of all of us. You're a good man. A good husband, father, and grandfather."

And that was enough? Apparently, it was all God was asking of him now. No adventurous trips. Where had he gotten the idea that he needed to do big things for God? Had he ever stopped and asked God Himself what He wanted of him?

Emira pointed. "Second house on the right after the stop sign."

He pulled up to a humble bungalow surrounded by bushes nearly the size of the house. As soon as they parked, loud barks pierced the air.

He chuckled. "Must be Vicious."

Emira quirked a brow.

"A rottweiler," he explained. "Supposedly, an ironic name. Let's hope."

Larry stepped onto the porch to meet them, wearing khakis and a gray polo. "Oh, good, you brought Emira." The dog snarled at his heels.

She stepped out of the car with a polite smile. "Nice to see you again."

"Come in, come in." He waved them forward. "Dinner's hot."

When they hesitated, looking at the dog, Larry patted Vicious's head. "Don't mind her. I promise she won't bite, though she might lick you to death."

They cautiously approached and were greeted by the rottweiler's warm tongue. Emira giggled.

They entered to find a living room full of overstuffed couches and bookshelves crowded with not books but knickknacks. Floyd stepped closer to peruse the sight. Figurines of farm animals. Chickens, hogs, and cows. Some cartoonish in nature, some bearing realistic features.

Larry sidled up next to him. "I find them at garage sales."

Floyd chuckled. "You and my wife would get along well."

Larry's brow creased. "How is she?"

Suddenly, Larry no longer seemed like a stranger. As the priest led Floyd and Emira to a small, circular kitchen table laden with food, Floyd poured out the day's ordeal. Not only Susan's purple foot but her memory deficit. "How could I have missed it?"

Larry's smile was lined with sympathy. "Easy enough to do. All of us see what we want to see, especially when love is involved."

Over a savory meal of Floyd's favorites, conversation flowed freely as Vicious lay at Floyd's feet. How could he have ever thought that time in this man's presence would be awkward? It was as natural as snipping hair. Emira pitched in here and there but mostly watched the two men with weary contentment on her face. She looked as if she wanted to collapse in bed. He should probably wrap things up and return her to her car. She'd likely be back at the hospital early tomorrow.

He opened his mouth to say they'd better get going when Larry stood.

"I need to show you something. Sit tight." The priest took their plates to the sink, then disappeared down a hallway.

Emira ran a finger along her farmhouse place mat, appearing lost in thought.

"We'll leave soon," Floyd said.

"It's fine. I don't mind." Yet, she yawned.

Larry returned with a large book of some kind—a photo album? He sat down, placing the book on the table in front of him, both hands gently splayed on top of it. What was it? Floyd squinted to make out the print on the cover. If only he hadn't left his glasses in the car. But wait … was that his name? Yes, *Floyd* was printed on the cover. A chill spread through him.

He pointed a shaky finger. "What's this?"

Larry's somber eyes stared back at him. "This is what I've been wanting to show you. I have a confession to make."

Floyd's pulse thrummed in his neck. A confession? That this priest was really a stalker? A murderer? A fiend?

Larry's head dipped with his deep sigh. "I'm the one who got you kicked out of seminary all those years ago."

Wait, what? Floyd leaned forward.

"I'd like to say I had noble intentions. I thought I did back then. 'Only the best. Weed out the rest.' Right? I hid under the excuse that zeal for His house consumed me. In reality, pride consumed me. I was riddled with jealousy. Everyone loved you, yet you seemed to have no regard for the proper order of things." Larry brushed off the book's cover as if dusting off unpleasant memories. "At any rate, I complained about you on multiple occasions. Ratted on you when I saw you smoking outside." He expelled another long breath. "And I found you hiding beer in the creek and promptly told Father Peabody."

Floyd scoured his memory for any recollection that coincided with Larry's confession. Everything blurred in those long-ago memories. The man who sat across from him had once set himself against Floyd as an enemy. He waited for a feeling of betrayal to sweep over him, but it didn't come. Instead, he chuckled.

Larry quirked a curious brow at him.

"I deserved to get kicked out. If you hadn't told on me, someone else would have. I wouldn't have made it regardless."

Larry's stiff headshake showed he didn't accept Floyd's pronouncement. "I've spent the past fifty years steeped in regret over that decision. After I met Karen—"

"You knew Karen?" He propped his elbows on the table.

The ghost of a smile lifted Larry's lips. "A remarkable woman of God. Your speech at her funeral was quite touching."

"You were there?"

A single nod.

How could he not have noticed? Then again, so many people came to Karen's funeral. It would have been easy for someone to get lost in that crowd. "How'd you know Karen? For how long? She never said anything. You never said anything."

Emira's hand wrapped around his. "Let him explain, Papa."

Of course. "Go on."

"Karen attended my parish and took part in our weekly scrapbooking circle."

"You scrapbook?"

"No, not personally. A clergy member is required to attend any event on the premises. I was assigned to the scrapbooking circle." A wistful smile pulled at his lips. "A divine appointment, I would say. When I met Karen there, I recognized her last name and connection to the man whose life I'd ruined—or so I thought. I asked about you. Frequently. Your sister was quite proud of you." He patted the book as if it were a beloved child. "She created this scrapbook with every intention of giving it to you one day, but after I spilled my regrets at her feet, she bequeathed it to me." He shrugged. "Said she wanted me to see that I didn't ruin your life. I know that now." He slid the book to

Floyd. "It's time for you to know the impact your life has had."

Nerves abuzz, Floyd flipped open the cover and sucked in a breath.

Emira stood. "I'll grab your glasses."

When she returned from the car, she sat next to him.

His wedding photo stared back at him. Susan shone like the sun. Radiant. In the photo, they were cutting their wedding cake.

"Karen put this together?"

"Yes, sir."

Of course, she did. She was always taking pictures. He turned the page. Pictures of Marie and Joseph as babies and children. Pictures of his first shop, then of New Creations. Then—how had she gotten ahold of this?—a picture of Floyd's baptism. His face glowed. One of him standing with the group of young people from the Bible study he led. Another of him preaching to the congregation.

"I'd forgotten these pictures existed," he whispered.

Magazine and newspaper articles about the Jesus Movement plastered several of the next pages. Larry nodded toward them. "You were a part of that movement. You and your church welcomed the hippies into the kingdom of God. My parish wasn't so"—his nose scrunched—"inclusive." A pained look crossed his face. "Many came to know Christ in those days thanks to you and those like you."

Floyd shook his head. He hadn't done anything noteworthy. God had radically intercepted his life. Changed its trajectory. All he did was bask in the love God had lavished on him and point other people in that direction. It hadn't been hard. It was an overflow of what God had done in his heart.

On the next page was the newspaper article about a local businessman's tip busting the Mafia ring. Susan hadn't taken him seriously. Karen had? Apparently, Larry had as well.

Another article he'd never seen before proclaimed his township as among the safest places to live in his state. "Well, I'll be." He narrowed his gaze at Larry. "You don't think *this* is because of *me*, do you?"

Larry shrugged, his eyes twinkling. "Who can say?"

Ridiculous. Clearly, Karen had lost her mind.

Emira turned the page. "Oh, there's me."

She pointed to a picture of Floyd holding her as a baby. Other pictures of the two of them, including ones with Susan, graced this page.

Another newspaper article adorned the next page.

Local Student Earns Medal of Honor.

He scanned the article for his name but didn't find it. "Why is this here?"

Emira pointed. "Cody Walnut. Remember him?"

"Fred's son?"

"Yes." She nudged his shoulder. "If not for you, Fred and his wife would never have gotten together. Cody would never have been born. He wouldn't have written this play about drunk driving. No medal of honor. Do you remember the goofy trophy I made you the day they came into the shop?"

He closed his eyes and could see the shampoo bottle covered in black combs. "Of course. It's still in my office."

"I made it because I thought you were the one who truly deserved an award. If not for you, there would be no Cody."

"Huh. I never made the connection." He rubbed the back of his neck. "You told Karen?"

She bumped his shoulder with her own, a smile tugging at her lips. "I told everyone. I was so proud of you."

He warmed under her praise.

The next few pages showed Tom Hallt, formerly of the Dropout Dudes, now a hit Christian music artist. Included were testimonies from people impacted by his concerts and songs. In a small picture of Tom with his guitar, Floyd could just make out his own signature. Unbelievable. He'd officially made it into the paper.

The next page had the family at Emira's wedding and then Floyd holding each grandchild.

Emira turned her attention to Larry. "I have to admit, I found it kind of strange that you knew who I was, and I didn't know who you were."

"Creepy, you mean?" Larry waggled his eyebrows.

"Yeah." Her face bunched in that adorable way of hers.

"I understand. I've watched your family from a distance for decades."

"But why?" Floyd's gaze lingered on the final scrapbook page—a family picture taken soon after Reagan was born. "Why didn't you say something sooner? Why now?"

"Fair enough." His mouth twitched. "Guilt, I reckon. I did a shameful thing in the seminary."

Floyd blew a raspberry. "Water under a very old bridge."

"Contaminated water."

Floyd patted the priest's hand. "Everything turned out just as it should have. I don't regret how my life turned out."

"Don't you? Why, then, did you insist on going to Haiti?"

A twinge in his chest, and truth pushed to the surface. His shoulders hunched forward. "I did have regrets." Did? Do? "But not about never entering the priesthood." Susan's sweet face filled his mind. He wouldn't give her up for anything. "I grew up longing to make a difference in the world. When I retired, I panicked. I thought I'd squandered my chance to do great things for God." He snorted at the mental picture of himself in a vestment. "When I was young, the only model I could conjure of what that looked like was a priest. As I grew, I found that it could look like many things. But it never looked like being a barber and raising a family. It never looked like *me*."

Larry leaned forward. "Oh, but it does." He tapped the scrapbook's cover. "Don't you see how many people you've impacted with your 'little, insignificant life'? Not so little or insignificant, is it?"

Floyd closed his eyes. "I'm beginning to see that."

And it stunned him. How humbling to think he could have such an effect. But what caused him to miss his flight today wasn't a group of hippies or a mayor's award. It wasn't an article in any paper. It was his wife.

Happiness might indeed be found in wanting what he had. A loving family. A God who had snatched him from destruction and given him life. Freedom. Ever-expanding wholeness.

But was success truly getting what he wanted? Or was success simply obeying God in the two greatest commandments set before him? "You shall love the Lord your God with all your heart, with all your soul, and with all your mind" and "You shall love your neighbor as yourself." The book of Matthew had laid it out perfectly. Love God. Love people. If he never got what he thought he wanted, but if he lived out these commandments, wouldn't that be a successful life? Maybe not in the eyes of man, but their opinions weren't the ones that counted. Only His.

Perhaps Floyd had both success and happiness after all.

Chapter Thirty-Two

1970

Floyd walked through the front door after a long day of work, every aching muscle in his body yearning for the comfort of his recliner. He'd gone to the gym to exercise for an hour and a half before work that morning, and he felt every minute of it. The scent of onions and peppers wafted toward him. Susan must be frying up potatoes. His favorite. His stomach rumbled.

"Daddy!" Marie and Joseph echoed in unison before crashing into his legs.

He chuckled and gave them a squeeze. They hustled out back, and he trudged toward his chair and dropped his keys and wallet onto the table next to it. Ah. His haven beckoned him to take a load off. He'd worn an indent in the old thing from hours of sitting there watching TV and reading the paper.

Susan rounded the corner, dishrag in hand. "What do you think you're doing?"

He frowned. "Relaxing before dinner."

"Oh no, you don't. You promised to replace the windshield wipers on my car." She whipped the dish towel in his direction as if he were a work animal. "Get on with you before it gets dark."

His shoulders slumped. He *had* promised that, hadn't he? He cast a longing glance to his recliner and whispered, "So long, old friend."

In the garage, he found the wipers he'd purchased a couple of months prior. The package boasted "Easy installation." Just what he needed. He could snap off the old blades, snap in the new ones, and retreat to his chair for a restful evening.

He backed Susan's car out of the garage and into the driveway so he could reach the wiper blades more easily.

Susan opened the window and called out to him, "Hurry up. Dinner's almost ready." Was that meatloaf he smelled? Yes, it must be. She didn't have to ask him twice. He'd be as quick as possible for a dinner like that.

He leaned over and pulled to get the old blade off the arm, but it didn't budge. He yanked harder. Nothing. Maybe he needed to twist it. Placing his foot on the tire, he leveraged his weight and attempted to wrestle the blade off. Why wasn't it working?

"Read the directions."

He looked up to see Susan peering at him out the window. With a harrumph, he abandoned the wrestling match and picked up the package from the driveway to read the instructions on the back. Oh, there was a tab he needed to press to dislodge the blade. They should have made that clearer.

A glance at the window showed that Susan was no longer watching him. He felt along the wiper and found the tab. He pushed it, but nothing happened. Perhaps he hadn't pushed it hard enough. He reached a bit farther and pushed harder. There. A click. He smiled. He'd done it. See? Simple.

He tried to stand back and remove the old blade, but his finger pinched when he tried to move it from its spot along the blade. Wincing, he pulled harder. It didn't budge.

Uh-oh. Did he … Was he … stuck? With panicked, flustered yanks, he tried repeatedly to free his finger, but the wiper held it fast. He was stuck to his car!

Through the open window, Susan announced that dinner was served. The children squealed, then chattered. What should he do? How could he get out of this mess?

"Floyd?" Susan's face appeared behind the screen. "Come on now. Time to eat."

"I uh …" His face heated. "I'm stuck."

Her brow furrowed. "You're what now?"

"I'm stuck in the wiper."

She tilted her head, then shook it. "How?"

"I don't know! Just help me." He yanked again, but all it got him was the pinch of pain.

She disappeared from the window and came out the front door a moment later. She rushed to him to examine his predicament. She took his finger in her hand and heaved.

"Ouch!" Pain reverberated down his nerve endings.

She winced. "You really are stuck."

She tried prying the blade open to free his finger, but it was no use.

"Maybe butter would help."

Just the mention of his favorite condiment made his stomach growl.

Susan's gaze dropped to his belly. "You want me to bring your plate out to you?"

"I'd appreciate it." The ham sandwich he'd had for lunch seemed like eons ago.

A few minutes later, she emerged with a steaming plate of meatloaf, corn on the cob, and fried potatoes, as well as a stick of butter. She set the plate on the hood. While he forked mouthfuls of the feast with his left hand, awkwardly splattering the hood with remnants he dropped, Susan attempted to butter his finger out of the wiper.

Dusk fell around them as she worked. He finished his meal. Fireflies lit up the sky as cicadas strummed outside, and the children giggled and shrieked inside. Man, he could really use a smoke. Finally, his finger budged. He twisted it around, then slowly slipped it out. He was free!

"Thank you." He smiled at his rescuer. "Let me just pop the new blade on—"

She put her hand on his arm. "Oh no, you don't. I'll have the guys do it when they change my oil."

"Are you sure? I can do it." They charged an arm and a leg to do a simple thing like switching out the wiper blades.

"I'm sure. No use wasting good butter." She took his plate and sauntered inside.

He'd been going to New Beginnings for a little over nine months when one of the leaders approached him after service one Sunday.

Gary's warm smile radiated welcome. Even though the stout man's traditionally short haircut and crisp blue suit contrasted with the hippie style, everyone seemed to feel at home in his presence. He extended his hand. "Floyd. Great to see you again." The handshake was reminiscent of a puppy wagging its tail.

Floyd chuckled. "How many cups of coffee did you have this morning, Gary?"

"Who's counting?" He nearly bounced on his toes. "I have a proposition for you, and I hope you'll say yes."

Floyd slid his hands into his pockets and eyed the man. No one at church had ever asked him to do anything before. What was this about? "Go on."

"You have a way with young people. Teenagers. They listen to you."

Floyd glanced over his shoulder, then back at Gary's earnest face. He pointed a finger to his chest. "Who, me?"

"Yes, you. I've heard your name mentioned by at least a dozen of them over the past month."

What was the crazy guy talking about? Teenagers? Mentioning him? He gaped back at Gary unable to formulate a response.

"You cut their hair, don't you?"

"Why yes, but ..." Quite a few young men had passed through the shop lately. Some of them sixteen, seventeen, eighteen. Did they listen to him? Seemed like they did most of the talking, and he was the one listening. "What are you getting at?"

"We want to start a small group. A home group, as we'll call it. The leadership team met about it last week, and your name came up as a possible host and leader."

A laugh puffed out of him. "Me? A small group leader?"

"Yes!" Gary patted him on the back. "Is that so hard to believe?"

Didn't small group leaders have to be more ... perfect? He nearly confessed that he'd spent last night stuck in a windshield wiper. The teenagers would have to step over the blue-painted porch to enter his home. He was forever making mistakes. Did he have what it took to lead? "What would I be doing?"

"Just reading through the Bible with them. Answering their questions."

"What if I don't have the answers?" He'd spent the past year since his encounter in the car pouring over his Bible, and he'd nearly read it all the way through. That didn't mean he understood everything. Would he ever?

"Then you can study and find them together." Floyd must have looked worried because Gary added, "You can call me anytime with questions."

"You really think they'll come?"

Gary rubbed his hands together as if he couldn't contain his excitement. "Of course. Do you really think they all need haircuts?" He shook his head. "They're going to New Creations to talk to you. Some don't come from a good home life. They're hungry for a mentor who cares about them."

Long ago, the desire to make a difference had burned inside of him, but the daily demands of life had doused that blaze. Now, Gary blew on smoldering embers, awakening to life a flame Floyd had thought long dead. Maybe he could still bring positive change to the world.

Wait, he had Jesus now. Everything was different. Of course, he could. He must. How could he sit back and live only for himself after Jesus sacrificed His life for him?

"I'll do it." Floyd held out his hand for another enthusiastic shake. He would change the world, one teenage heart at a time.

Floyd's family room was full to bursting. Young men and women filled every couch cushion and sat cross-legged on most of the available floor space. It made Susan's job of delivering beverages and snacks to the crew challenging. She tiptoed around, stepping on a few skirts and pant legs here and there, but spilling not a drop or crumb.

What had he been nervous about? The group chatted among themselves and with him, happy to be there and thankful to have a place to study the Word together. When Floyd announced it was time to begin and opened in prayer, the room quieted. They gave him the utmost respect.

He'd prepared some discussion questions. The teenagers took turns reading a chapter of 1 Corinthians, then Floyd led the group in robust discussion that lasted for hours. The food ran out long before the conversation.

When the guests finally filed out, one young man lingered, fiddling with the hem of his lavender polo.

"You okay, Mikey?"

The kid toed the carpeting. "Yeah. Yeah, I—" He audibly swallowed. His eyes skittered around the room like a rabbit. "I just …"

Without warning, he smashed into Floyd with a hug. Where had that come from? Floyd patted his back. He should say something, but what?

Before he could formulate a response, Mikey continued, "My dad is a … He's not a nice guy. I thank God you're in my life. Like a father."

"I-it's a privilege." That much was true. But how could he have impacted this young man's life to such a degree? He didn't even know Mikey's last name or where he lived, yet the kid considered him a father figure? His head spun.

"Thanks, man." Mikey's smile burst forth. "I'd better go. I'm gonna talk to pastor, though. I think you should preach at church. You'd be good at it."

Floyd balked. "Me?" What on earth gave him that idea?

Mikey only laughed as he made his way to the door.

Floyd's nerves tumbled about as he watched the sanctuary fill. Why had he ever agreed to this? He wasn't a preacher. Had never been a public speaker. When he'd once pictured himself as a priest, he'd never imagined himself leading mass. Had there always been so many people at their church? Good gravy, was that his devout Catholic sister Karen sneaking onto the nondenominational back pew? Something bounced against her hip. Oh no. She wouldn't. But she had. She'd brought her camera. He offered a small wave before turning around. Best not watch any more people file in.

Sweat beaded at the back of his neck as he shuffled through his note cards. Maybe it was a good thing there'd be thirty minutes of worship before the pastor cued him to step to the pulpit. Then again, it gave him more time to worry.

By the time the music ended, he was so flustered that he dropped the note cards. A flurry of activity ensued as a few young people scrambled to pick them up.

"And now, Floyd Douglas, leader of our home group for teens, is going to share with us from the Word of God. Please join me in welcoming him."

Polite applause splattered through the room as the Good Samaritans thrust note cards into his hand. Floyd moved forward on shaky legs and ascended the three steps to the stage. He shook the pastor's hand and centered himself behind the podium, squinting out at the audience against the harsh stage light. As if taking his cue, the light dimmed, and his eyes relaxed as they adjusted. There, among the sea containing many familiar faces, he found Susan. Her half smile seemed to say, *Attaboy*. He rolled his shoulders back. He could do this.

"In the tenth chapter of Luke, Jesus had a conversation with an expert in the law. This man asked what he must do to inherit eternal life." Floyd glanced at the top note card and frowned. The bullet points on it were from the middle of the parable of the Good Samaritan. The cards must have gotten out of order when they fell. He flipped through them. No, not that one. Not that one either. His pulse galloped. He flipped a card over. Yep, he'd written on the backs too. Where was the right one? *He went to him and bandaged his wounds.* No, that was further on. *Who is my neighbor?* Closer, but no. It could be his imagination, but he could swear every person in the congregation fidgeted.

Oh, forget the cards. He knew the passage well enough, right?

"Jesus asks him what the Bible says and what his take is on the Scriptures. So, the lawyer guy spouts off the Sunday School answer, right?" Floyd wrinkled his nose. "Lawyers. I've never liked them."

A soft gasp sounded from the congregation.

Floyd threw up his hands. "No offense. I mean, in general. I'm sure there are some good ones out there. If you're listening and you're a lawyer, you might be one of the good ones."

Susan covered her face with her hands. The shake of her shoulders showed her to be laughing, though, instead of dying of mortification. Had he crossed a line? Oh well. He couldn't get distracted now.

"The lawyer said, 'Love the Lord your God with all your heart, with all your soul, with all your strength, and with all your mind,' and 'Love your neighbor as yourself.' Great answer, right? He should have walked away then. He'd have gotten a gold star from Jesus and called it a day. But he wanted to justify himself. It's a lawyer thing, I think. So, he asked Jesus, 'Who is my neighbor?' And that's what I'm asking you today."

Looking out among the crowd, he saw all kinds of neighbors. Young and old. Hippie and square. There sat Mikey, an amused grin spread on his face. Sitting behind his surrogate son was a man whose matted hair reminded Floyd of that infamous incident from barber school. His mind traversed back in time. What had he been talking about again? Never mind. This crowd had to hear this story. "Did I ever tell you about the time I cut a guy's ear off?"

Chapter Thirty-Three

1998

Papa had beaten them to the cemetery. By the time Mom parked the car, his form was but a spot in the distance.

"He couldn't wait for us?" Emira asked. They'd followed him there and would have been directly behind him if not for hitting a red light.

Mom turned off the ignition but didn't move. "Maybe he wanted a few minutes to himself."

That made sense. Every year on Grammy Douglas's birthday, they came to visit her grave. Hers and Grandpa Douglas's. Since Grandpa had died before Emira was born, the latter was an emotionless routine. But Grammy … She fingered the pink roses in her lap, rubbing a soft petal in between her fingers. Grammy was like the sunshine. It'd been six years since she'd passed, and the pang of missing her had hardly waned. How much worse was the ache for Papa?

Her heart leapt toward him. Was Mom going to sit here all day? Emira would join him in his grief. Hadn't he taught her that it wasn't good to be sad alone? He'd taken off work to be with Grammy when Beanie died. She could *be* with him now. Unbuckling her seat belt, she said, "I'm gonna go."

"Mmm hmm," was Mom's only response as she stared into the distance.

If Emira wanted time alone with Papa, she'd need to hurry. Uncle Joseph would be here any minute with Nana. Flowers in hand, she jogged along the immaculately trimmed path to catch up. Papa stood in front of a gravestone, jiggling something in his pocket. As she neared, the name on the headstone became clear, and it wasn't Grammy Douglas's. She silently sidled next to her

301

grandfather, their arms brushing, and waited for him to speak. Or not. Whatever he needed.

He reached into his pocket and pulled out a toy car, an old-fashioned Model T. "My dad owned an autobody shop. Did you know that?"

"No." She knew next to nothing about the man Papa rarely mentioned.

"He was good at what he did. An expert at rebuilding automobiles. The outside of them, at least. The inside, well—" He tilted his head to the side. "He knew more than I ever did. Could change the oil and what not. But he excelled on the outside." He held the car with one hand and spun the wheels with the other.

A breeze tousled his hair and brought with it the scent of flowers from nearby grave sites.

"He was a good man." He shifted his jaw. "I never learned a thing from him. Never wanted to. I couldn't see past my anger … my disappointment."

This was as much as Emira had ever heard him speak about his father. Perhaps as much as she'd heard him speak from the heart at all. She needed to keep him talking.

"Why were you disappointed?"

He shrugged. "Because he wasn't perfect."

"No one is. He was there, wasn't he?" As far as she knew, Papa's parents had never divorced. Anyone who had two present parents was fortunate in her book.

"He was there, all right. Even when we wished he wasn't."

A murmur of voices stole their attention, and she didn't have time to think on his strange statement. She'd file it away for later. Nana, Mom, and Uncle Joseph ambled toward them on the path.

Papa expelled a heavy breath. "Anyway, he was a good man. I wish I would have forgiven him sooner." He placed the toy car on the headstone among a bouquet of daffodils.

Regret pooled. She hadn't even thought of bringing flowers for Grandpa's grave. She sneaked a rose out from the arrangement in her hand and placed it by the car.

The three others gathered round.

"A Model T this year, huh?" Uncle Joseph nodded to the car.

"Yeah. He loved those old cars."

"Didn't he lose his car once? Got so drunk he forgot where he parked?" Uncle Joseph's eyes squinted with his laughter.

Mom nudged him. "Stop it. Not here."

Whoa. Grandpa Douglas was a drunk? There was so much of the story she didn't know. She took in Papa with new eyes. He'd always been larger than life to her. Her hero. Nearly invincible. But he'd been young once, and he'd known disappointment. More than disappointment. Pain. What had he gone through to make him the man he was now? Each line on his weathered face told a story, and she wanted to hear them all.

Wordlessly, the group turned to Grammy Douglas's neighboring grave. Here, everyone had a story to share about the sweet woman's love and generosity throughout the years or about her devout Catholic faith. Emira spoke about the adventurous times she had in Grammy's attic. Mom talked of how Grammy always cooked her favorite meal. Uncle Joseph mentioned his long conversations with her late into the night when he was a teen struggling with life decisions. Nana smiled as she recalled how Grammy welcomed her into the family.

"You know," Papa said, "I was terrified when I got kicked out of the seminary. Father Peabody said my mother waited for me in the office, and my knees were knocking together. I just knew my failure would crush her. I pictured her crumpling, the look of disappointment on her face killing me." He broke into a wistful smile. "But when I walked into the office that day, she sat straight as a light post, purse in her lap, and looked me up and down. 'Well, Floyd,' she said, 'I guess the Good Lord has something else for you.' And that was it. She didn't chew me out. Didn't tell me how I'd embarrassed the family." He shook his head as if baffled. "I still wonder what it was the Good Lord had for me."

Uncle Joseph's brows knit together. "Oh, Dad, you can't mean that. You've led a great life."

"That I have." Papa smiled and nodded, making brief eye contact with each of them, but the shadowed look in his expression proved him less than convinced.

After a beat of awkward silence, Nana handed Uncle Joseph the hydrangeas she carried, and he placed them on the grave. Emira followed suit. Papa pulled a little duck figurine from his pocket and placed it next to the flowers.

"Aw." Emira's hand flew to her heart. "I loved feeding the ducks with Grammy."

Mom chuckled. "She was crazy about those ducks."

"They ate better than she did," Uncle Joseph chimed in.

Papa sniffled and blinked rapidly. "She was the best mother I could have asked for." He turned his face away from their probing gazes. "I only hope I made her proud."

"Of course, you did." Nana patted his arm.

But again, this reassurance seemed to do little to alter his somber mood, leaving Emira to wonder what Papa's parents had thought of him after all.

Worship music blasted from the stage, but Emira couldn't seem to enter in. From her spot in the front row, she kept glancing over her shoulder. The packed sanctuary made it impossible to tell if he'd come or not. It didn't matter. Wasn't that what the Lord had been teaching her over the past few months? Her heavenly Father was never changing, always consistent. He never broke a promise, never let His children down. No matter how her earthly father failed, she could put the full weight of her trust behind Abba.

Yet she couldn't deny her desire to see her dad beaming up at her as she preached her first sermon for youth Sunday. When Pastor Craig had chosen her to bring the Word during the one Sunday a year the youth group took over the weekend service, she'd been honored … and terrified. It was one thing to preach a sermon to her peers. She'd done that a few times in their youth service. But to address the entire congregation? *Lord, help me.*

The music transitioned from upbeat to mellow, and she closed her eyes, swaying to the rhythm. She tried to concentrate on the words. No use. Her mind kept rehearsing what she was going to say. *First Timothy 4:12: Don't let anyone despise your youth.* A sermon on the importance of youth in God's kingdom was sure to convict and inspire, right? Ugh. She'd never been so nervous. The least she could do was pray.

Lord, I'm petrified. I need Your peace. I know You're always with me. Speak through me today. Touch hearts. Change lives. Do what only You can do.

She pictured herself cuddling in her heavenly Father's lap. Slowly, her heart settled, and she was able to lift her voice in song. When the music ended and the pastor invited her up, she breathed deep and ascended the stairs. Standing at the podium, she looked out at the congregation, searching for her father's face.

Nowhere to be seen.

But there, in the third row, Papa smiled back at her, Nana and Mom next to him. Her very own cheering section. Her support system. How fortunate she was to have these three people who had loved her consistently all her life. Her gaze locked onto Papa's, and he winked. All her sermon notes scattered from her brain. So much for preparation.

"Proverbs 13:22 in the CSB says, 'A good man leaves an inheritance to his grandchildren.' I want to talk to you today about spiritual inheritance."

Chapter Thirty-Four

2010

Nana's right arm draped around Emira's shoulder while Papa grasped her left. The two of them guided her through the front door.

Nana's shoulders sagged in relief. "It's good to be home."

"I'll bet." After two weeks in the hospital, Nana must long for her own domain. Emira paused to set down her purse and one of Nana's bags before angling toward the couch.

Papa cleared his throat. "You sit right here. I'll get you something to drink. Diet Coke?"

"Sure."

Emira picked up the remote and turned on a classic movie. Maybe now, unable to get up and around on her own, Nana would finally sit through the whole thing.

Nana's fingers fidgeted in her lap. "Where are my cigarettes?"

Emira fished through Nana's purse and found a pack. She pulled one free, along with a lighter, and held them out to her grandma. She should insist Nana stop smoking before she added lung cancer to her growing list of health issues, but it wasn't worth the breath. When someone smoked for that long, they weren't likely to give it up. Not someone as stubborn as Nana, at least.

Once settled with her cigarette and Diet Coke, Nana seemed content. Papa and Emira stood watching her. Weariness etched deep creases onto the edges of Papa's eyes. How much sleep had he gotten over these past couple of weeks? Couldn't be much. Now, though, they faced the end of one trial and perhaps the beginning of another. They'd set up an appointment with a neurologist. Emira's insides shriveled at the thought of wading through her grandma's dementia and all that entailed. At least she wasn't alone in this.

Papa nudged her shoulder. "I've got something for you. Come with me." When Emira hesitated, he said, "She'll be fine for a few minutes."

True. It wasn't like Nana could run off with her foot still sore. Emira followed him to his office. Her gaze fell on that childish trophy, displayed front and center on Papa's bookshelf. How could she have questioned if he remembered it? Clearly, he treasured the memory.

Papa took a gift box from his desk and held it reverently. "After our visit to Father Larry's, I ordered something for you. Had it engraved. I see it as ... well, kind of my legacy."

"For me? What about my mom? Uncle Joseph?" If anyone should receive a legacy gift from Papa, it should be his children.

"Don't worry about them." His lips twitched into a smile. "I've got plenty for them. But this is for you. You're the one who gave me the trophy." He nodded toward the comb-lined shampoo bottle.

"Okay ..." She took the box from his outstretched hand. Anticipation uncoiled inside of her at the surprise. She lifted the lid. Stared. "Scissors?" A gold pair of scissors. She hadn't seen that coming.

"Open them."

When she did so, an engraved message appeared. *Love God.* On one blade. She turned it over. *Love People* was etched on the other blade.

"This is my life. It's been a good life."

Her throat burned as she nodded, words lost. She ran her fingers over the words. All the law and the prophets summarized by those four words. Papa's life etched onto a pair of scissors. So simple, and yet so profound. Powerful. At one time, she'd craved the spotlight. Fame, glory, prestige. Humans chased after so many things. Her hands clamped around Papa's gift. What would it be like if God's people lived grounded in this simple mandate? Might God's light shining through each of them right where they were change families, cities, and nations?

"Thank you," she eked out. "This is remarkable."

Papa snorted. "I don't know about that. But it's my way of saying thank you." He adjusted his pants on his waist and stepped toward the door. "Now, enough of this. Let's dish up some ice cream."

People swarmed the back porch, wine glasses in hand, filled to the brim with either alcohol or sparkling cider. Many Catholics filled the space. Floyd waved off Emira as she walked by with another tray laden with sandwiches. He'd already stuffed himself full of hors d'oeuvres. Twinkle lights and tiki torches lit the space and created a homey atmosphere among the family and friends. Classic sixties rock played in the background. So odd how they'd been able to move the party outdoors, but that was Missouri weather. In late February, it was anyone's guess whether one would need gloves or shorts.

Danny lifted his glass. "To Floyd, the best man to ever cut someone's ear off." Laughter bubbled around him. "Happy retirement, brother."

Floyd nodded his thanks and sipped his champagne. As he had been all evening, he kept one eye on Susan. Instead of flittering about as her usual hostess self, she sat in a rocker and chatted with his siblings and Kade. The smile she sported seemed genuine. Hopefully, she truly was

309

having a good time despite her inability to get around easily. The familiar faces were likely good for her. She hadn't had an obvious memory lapse since the guests arrived.

Emira's raised voice caused him to turn. "Oh my goodness, Nelly!" His granddaughter wrapped her arms around a young woman. Nelly … Nelly … Who was she again? A familiar face came up behind her.

"Fred Walnut." He'd recognize that head of hair anywhere. He headed to greet his guests. He'd barely shaken Fred's hand when the radio quieted and a live guitar strummed. Tom?

"Any special requests?"

Someone shouted, "What's your favorite song, Floyd?" Wait, that was Mikey's voice. Young, bashful Mikey, all grown up and married with grown kids of his own. Crazy how that happened in the blink of an eye.

He grinned at his surrogate son as he returned to the center of the action. "'Waitin' in School.'"

Tom began to play, and Floyd sang along. That song had been on the radio during his first date with Susan. Did she remember? He caught her sparkling eyes and winked. Each word belted from him clear and jubilant. People clapped, hooted, and hollered. Ha! He still had it.

"Any other requests?" Tom asked when that song ended.

Emira called out, "'Stand by Me.'"

The mood shifted with the new chords. Oh, how he longed to hold his wife in his arms. He walked toward her, met her bright gaze, and held out his hand.

She shook her head. "My leg." Her shrug was laced with apology.

Of course, she wouldn't be able to dance now. She'd recently undergone surgery. Still, the loss gouged him. The disappointment made him feel two inches shorter.

A tap on his shoulder caused him to spin around. Emira.

"Can I have this dance?" She held her hand out to him. His princess.

He took it. "I'd be honored."

Surrounded by pockets of laughter and chatter, they glided together. She'd once danced to this song. When was that? At a birthday party? No, anniversary. Her tap shoes. She'd nearly driven him bonkers with all that clacking. Nearly bankrupted Marie with the dance costumes and classes. But she'd been born to be a star, even if mostly in his eyes.

He studied her face, finding so much of Marie there. So much of Susan. Would Reagan bear the same resemblance? What a privilege to get to protect, serve, and love these feisty women. Sure, raising and relating to the boys came more naturally. But these females, though he might never understand them, were such a delight to his heart.

"Thank you." Emira's voice thickened with emotion.

"For what, Princess?"

"For standing by me." She swiped at her cheek, then rested it on his shoulder.

He kissed her hair. "It's been a joy." He let the silence linger between them for a few minutes before disturbing it. "A great turnout tonight."

"So many people love you."

He guffawed. "A lot of people appreciate a good haircut."

"That too." She let out a contented sigh. "My dad said to tell you congrats again. He wishes he could be here."

"And you? With everything going on, I haven't asked. Are you glad he came? Glad he left?"

"Glad he came. Not devastated when he left." Her soft chuckle mixes with a gentle breeze. "I mean ... We're good."

"Good." He angled so that he could check on Susan again. She munched on a cookie and chuckled at something Drinks Tonic Water's wife said.

Emira followed his gaze. "She seems good."

"Great, really. Too bad we can't bottle up this blast from the past. Her mind remains sharp with all the memories surrounding her."

Emira's mouth twisted into a wry grin. "We could kidnap everyone and hide them in your basement."

With a hearty laugh, he twirled and dipped her. Cheers erupted as the song finished. He gave Emira another squeeze. "Love you, Princess."

"Love you too, Papa."

Floyd gave a small bow to the crowd, then went in search of something to munch on. Dancing had kicked his appetite back into gear. Had he seen meatballs on toothpicks?

"Hey, Floyd," a neighbor called to him from a semicircle of folding chairs. The chatter amongst the group quieted as Floyd neared. "Is it true you fell off the roof into the bushes?"

"Oh, that's not the half of it." He pulled up a chair and regaled them with the full tale. Sidesplitting laughter ensued.

"So that's why the porch used to be blue." Grady from two houses down wiped tears from the corners of his eyes as he sucked in breaths.

"Didn't you also get your finger stuck in a windshield?"

"Tell them the caulking story."

Floyd lifted his hands. "One embarrassing failure at a time, friends. And get comfortable. We'll be here awhile."

People gathered around to listen. Some sat, others stood. All leaned close in rapt attention. Floyd couldn't help but remember those neighborhood kids surrounding him while he boxed as a boy. Then, they'd chanted, "Flo-oyd! Flo-oyd!" Now, a crowd pressed close to hear another story. Not of his grand accomplishments but of his foibles. If he was going to fail, at least he'd done so with humor.

No, this wasn't the life he'd imagined for himself, but it was a good life. Full to the brim with the Lord's blessings. Beauty for ashes. Through the crowd, he sought the gaze of a familiar priest and winked.

The End

Author's Note

Thank you for reading my tribute to one of the biggest influences of my life: my grandpa, Douglas Floyd. This novel is my feeble attempt to say thank you to him for a life well-lived and to honor him.

The names were changed, but many—not all—of the stories within these pages are true (especially regarding the 1960s storyline). And most are *mostly* true. After all, we may never know exactly how much of that man's ear Papa cut off when he was in barber school. Was it the size of a dime, a nickel, a quarter, or a half-dollar? Maybe we'll get the full story in detail in heaven, or maybe Jesus will merely wink and say, "It could happen to anybody."

How my grandparents met, married in secret, and later broke the news to their parents are all legendary family stories. Though my grandpa's home improvement exploits sound like they belong in *National Lampoon's Christmas Vacation*, they're true. And yes, Papa created quite a fuss when he ran over blackberries with his cart at the grocery store. However, he has never booked an expensive trip to Haiti and, to my knowledge, has never been stalked by a priest.

As far as the 1990s storyline, you may have guessed that Emira is based on me. I spent my childhood working at my grandparents' shop, collecting Papa's tips in place of a paycheck. I danced for many older ladies as they sat under dryers. It was a marvelous part of my childhood.

Though things didn't go down exactly as this novel states, my parents divorced when I was young. Transporting back to my childhood self and seeing the very grown-up situation through a child's eyes has been therapeutic for me. I love my dad. He's been an amazing father to me. If, in portraying the complex emotions children of divorce wade through, I left a bad taste in your mouth regarding my father, I apologize. He's truly a gem, and if you met him, I bet you'd enjoy his company.

I hope you enjoyed *New Creations*. Here are a few pictures of the real-life inspiration behind the story. To see more, visit the Behind the Book section of my website at www.sarah-hanks.com.

My grandparents' wedding picture, taken after their second wedding at the church.

My grandma at New Creations doing "Aunt Karen's" hair.

My grandparents, mom, and uncle.

My grandpa in his recliner in the back of the shop.

My grandparents and me at New Creations.

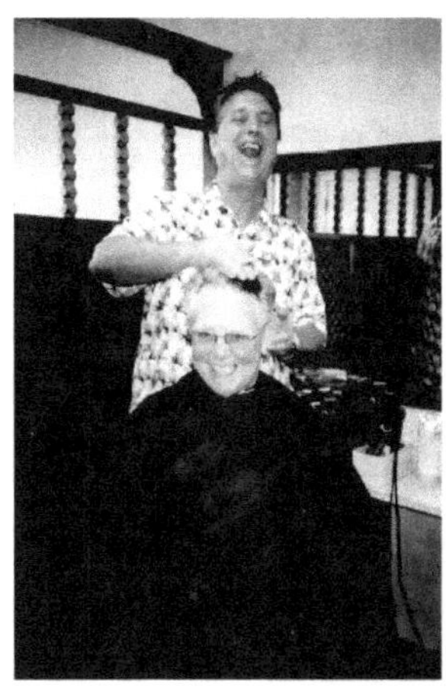

I wonder what story Papa is telling here.

Me in one of my dance outfits.

Other Books by Sarah Hanks:

The Mercy Series
Mercy Will Follow Me
Mercy's Song
Mercy's Legacy

Sisters in Arms Collection
A Battle Worth Fighting
Fall Back and Find Me

Time Sailors Series
Braving Strange Waters

Stand Alone
Awakened to Life